A COLD HEART

Books by JONATHAN KELLERMAN

FICTION

A COLD HEART (2003)
THE MURDER BOOK (2002)
FLESH AND BLOOD (2001)
DR. DEATH (2000)
MONSTER (1999)
BILLY STRAIGHT (1998)
SURVIVAL OF THE FITTEST (1997)
THE CLINIC (1997)
THE WEB (1996)
SELF-DEFENSE (1995)
BAD LOVE (1994)
DEVIL'S WALTZ (1993)
PRIVATE EYES (1992)
TIME BOMB (1990)
SILENT PARTNER (1989)
THE BUTCHER'S THEATER (1988)
OVER THE EDGE (1987)
BLOOD TEST (1986)
WHEN THE BOUGH BREAKS (1985)

NONFICTION

SAVAGE SPAWN: REFLECTIONS ON VIOLENT CHILDREN (1999)
HELPING THE FEARFUL CHILD (1981)
PSYCHOLOGICAL ASPECTS OF CHILDHOOD CANCER (1980)

FOR CHILDREN, WRITTEN AND ILLUSTRATED

JONATHAN KELLERMAN'S ABC OF WEIRD CREATURES (1995)
DADDY, DADDY, CAN YOU TOUCH THE SKY? (1994)

JONATHAN KELLERMAN

A COLD HEART

BALLANTINE BOOKS • NEW YORK

A Ballantine Book
Published by The Random House Ballantine Publishing Group

Copyright © 2003 by Jonathan Kellerman

A Cold Heart is a work of fiction. Names, places, and incidents either are a
product of the author's imagination or are used fictitiously.

All rights reserved under International and Pan-American Copyright Conventions. Published in the United States by The Random House Ballantine Publishing Group, a division of Random House, Inc., New York, and simultaneously in
Canada by Random House of Canada Limited, Toronto.

Ballantine and colophon are registered trademarks of Random House, Inc.

Book design by C. Linda Dingler

ISBN 0-345-45255-0

Manufactured in the United States of America

To the music men:

Larry Brown, Rob Carlson, Ben Elder, Wayne Griffith, George Gruhn, John Monteleone, Gregg Miner, John Silva, Tom Van Hoose, Larry Wexer.

And to the memory of Michael Katz.

A COLD HEART

1 The witness remembers it like this:

Shortly after 2 A.M., Baby Boy Lee exits the Snake Pit through the rear alley fire door. The light fixture above the door is set up for two bulbs, but one is missing, and the illumination that trickles down onto the garbage-flecked asphalt is feeble and oblique, casting a grimy mustard-colored disc, perhaps three feet in diameter. Whether or not the missing bulb is intentional will remain conjecture.

It is Baby Boy's second and final break of the evening. His contract with the club calls for a pair of one-hour sets. Lee and the band have run over their first set by twenty-two minutes, because of Baby Boy's extended guitar and harmonica solos. The audience, a nearly full house of 124, is thrilled. The Pit is a far cry from the venues Baby Boy played in his heyday, but he appears to be happy, too.

It has been a while since Baby Boy has taken the stage anywhere and played coherent blues. Audience members questioned later are unanimous: Never has the big man sounded better.

Baby Boy is said to have finally broken free of a host of addictions, but one habit remains: nicotine. He smokes three packs of Kools a day, taking deep-in-the-lung drags while onstage, and his guitars are notable for the black, lozenge-shaped burn marks that scar their lacquered wood finishes.

Tonight, though, Baby Boy has been uncommonly focused, rarely removing lit cigarettes from where he customarily jams them: just above the nut of his 62 Telecaster, wedged under the three highest strings, smoldering slowly.

So it is probably a tobacco itch that causes the singer to leap off-stage the moment he plays his final note, flinging his bulk out the back door without a word to his band or anyone else. The bolt clicks behind him, but it is doubtful he notices.

The fiftieth Kool of the day is lit before Baby Boy reaches the alley. He is sucking in mentholated smoke as he steps in and out of the disc of dirty light.

The witness, such that he is, is certain that he caught a glimpse of Baby Boy's face in the light and that the big man was sweating. If that's true, perhaps the perspiration had nothing to do with anxiety but re-sulted from Baby Boy's obesity and the calories expended on his music: For 83 minutes he has been jumping and howling and swooning, ca-ressing his guitar, bringing the crowd to a frenzy at set's end with a fiery, throat-ripping rendition of his signature song, a basic blues setup in the key of B-flat that witnesses the progression of Baby Boy's voice from inaudible mumble to an anguished wail.

> *There's women that'll mess you*
> *There's those that treat you nice*
> *But I got me a woman with*
> *A heart as cold as ice.*
>
> *A cold heart,*
> *A cold, cold heart*
> *My baby's hot but she is cold*
> *A cold heart,*
> *A cold, cold heart*
> *My baby's murdering my soul . . .*

At this point, the details are unreliable. The witness is a hepatitis-stricken, homeless man by the name of Linus Leopold Brophy, age thirty-nine but looking sixty, who has no interest in the blues or any other type of music and who happens to be in the alley because he has been drinking Red Phoenix fortified wine all night and the Dumpster five yards east of the Snake Pit's back door provides shelter for him to sleep off his delirium tremens. Later, Brophy will consent to a blood alcohol test and will come up .24, three times the legal limit for driving, but according to Brophy "barely buzzed."

Brophy claims to have been drowsy but awake when the sound of the back door opening rouses him and he sees a big man step out into the light and then fade to darkness. Brophy claims to recall the lit end of the man's cigarette glowing "like Halloween, you know—orange, shiny, real bright, know what I mean?" and admits that he seizes upon the idea of panhandling money from the smoker. ("Because the guy is fat, so I figure he had enough to eat, that's for sure, maybe he'll come across, know what I mean?")

Linus Brophy struggles to his feet and approaches the big man.

Seconds later, someone else approaches the big man, arriving from the opposite direction—the mouth of the alley, at Lodi Place. Linus Brophy stops in his tracks, retreats into darkness, sits down next to the Dumpster.

The new arrival, a man, also good-sized, according to Brophy, though not as tall as Baby Boy Lee and maybe half of Baby Boy's width, walks right up to the singer and says something that sounds "friendly." Questioned about this characterization extensively, Brophy denies hearing any conversation but refuses to budge from his judgment of amiability. ("Like they were friends, you know? Standing there, friendly.")

The orange glow of Baby Boy's cigarette lowers from mouth to waist level as he listens to the new arrival.

The new arrival says something else to Baby Boy, and Baby Boy says something back.

The new arrival moves closer to Baby Boy. Now, the two men appear to be hugging.

The new arrival steps back, looks around, turns heel and leaves the alley the way he came.

Baby Boy Lee stands there alone.

His hand drops. The orange glow of the cigarette hits the ground, setting off sparks.

Baby Boy sways. Falls.

Linus Brophy stares, finally builds up the courage to approach the big man. Kneeling, he says, "Hey, man," receives no answer, reaches out and touches the convexity of Baby Boy's abdomen. He feels moisture on his hand and is repelled.

As a younger man, Brophy had a temper. He has spent half of his life in various county jails and state penitentiaries, saw things, did things. He knows the feel and the smell of fresh blood.

Stumbling to his feet, he lurches to the back door of the Snake Pit and tries to pull it open, but the door is locked. He knocks, no one answers.

The shortest way out of the alley means retracing the steps of the newcomer: walk out to Lodi Place, hook north to Fountain, and find someone who'll listen.

Brophy has already wet his pants twice tonight—first while sleeping drunk and now, upon touching Baby Boy Lee's blood. Fear grips him, and he heads the other way, tripping through the long block that takes him to the other end of the alley. Finding no one on the street at this hour, he makes his way to an all-night liquor store on the corner of Fountain and El Centro.

Once inside the store, Brophy shouts at the Lebanese clerk who sits reading behind a Plexiglas window, the same man who one hour ago sold him three bottles of Red Phoenix. Brophy waves his arms, tries to get across what he has just seen. The clerk regards Brophy as exactly what he is—a babbling wino—and orders him to leave.

When Brophy begins pounding on the Plexiglas, the clerk considers reaching for the nail-studded baseball bat he keeps beneath the counter. Sleepy and weary of confrontation, he dials 911.

Brophy leaves the liquor store and walks agitatedly up and down Fountain Avenue. When a squad car from Hollywood Division arrives,

Officers Keith Montez and Cathy Ruggles assume Brophy is their problem and handcuff him immediately.

Somehow he manages to communicate with the Hollywood Blues and they drive their black and white to the mouth of the alley. High-intensity LAPD-issue flashlights bathe Baby Boy Lee's corpse in a heartless, white glare.

The big man's mouth gapes, and his eyes are rolled back. His banana yellow Stevie Ray Vaughan T-shirt is dyed crimson, and a red pool has seeped beneath his corpse. Later, it will be ascertained that the killer gutted the big man with a classic street fighter's move: long-bladed knife thrust under the sternum followed by a single upward motion that slices through intestine and diaphragm and nicks the right ventricle of Baby Boy's already seriously enlarged heart.

Baby Boy is long past help, and the cops don't even attempt it.

2 Petra Connor, barely out of her no-guys phase, knew the pantsuit had been a stupid idea.

Three-month no-guys phase. The way she saw it, she deserved more self-indulgence than that, but her forgiving nature had taken over, and now she could look at carriers of Y chromosomes without wanting to punch them.

She was the only female detective working nights at Hollywood Division, and pretending to be nice was hurting her facial muscles.

The first month of the phase had been spent convincing herself it wasn't her fault. Even though here she was, barely thirty and a two-time loser in the Serious Relationship Sweepstakes.

Chapter One: the rotten husband. Chapter Two was even worse: the boyfriend who'd gone back to his ex-wife.

She'd stopped hating Ron Banks. Even though he'd been the one to come on to *her*, had pursued her gently but unrelentingly. Weakening her resistance by being courtly and caring and tender in bed, a genuine nice guy.

Like so many nice guys, essentially weak.

Some would say Ron had done the right thing. For himself. For his daughters.

Something else that had attracted Petra to him: terrific father. Ron was raising Alicia and Bea while his ex, a Spanish beauty, trained horses in Majorca. Two-year-old divorce, you'da thought it would stick.

Sweet little girls, six and seven. Petra had allowed herself to become attached to them. Pretending . . .

Petra had endured a hysterectomy at a freakishly young age.

Toward the end, when Ms. Caballera was laying on the pressure big time—calling Ron ten times a day, talking dirty to him, e-mailing him bikini shots, *begging*—he'd been a basket case, crippled by conflict. Finally, Petra shoved him in the right direction, and he took leave from his Sheriff's Homicide job in order to sort things out and flew to Spain with the girls.

To Petra, Spain had always meant art. The Prado, Degas, Velasquez, Goya. She'd never been there. Had never been out of the country.

Now, Spain meant *over*.

Ron called Petra once, breaking into sobs. *So sorry, baby, so, so sorry, but the girls are so happy, I never realized how unhappy they were . . .*

The girls had always looked okay to Petra, but what did she know about kids, barren thirty-year-old spinster that she was.

Ron stayed in Spain for the summer and sent her a consolation gift: stupid little carving of a flamenco dancer. Castanets and all. Petra broke off the limbs and tossed it in the trash.

Stu Bishop, her longtime partner, had bailed on her, too. Resigning a promising career to care for a sick wife. Oh, that spousal obligation.

Soon after, she switched to the night shift because she couldn't sleep anyway, felt in synch with the special poison that scented the air when Hollywood streets turned black.

Comforted by the sorrows of people in a lot worse shape than she.

During the ninety days of the no-guys phase, she caught three 187s, worked them all solo because staffing was thin and she didn't protest when the nightwatch commander raised the possibility. Two were easy-solves that had gone down on Hollywood's east end: a liquor-store clerk shooting and a knifing at a Latino dance club, multiple witnesses all around, both files closed within a week.

The third was a whodunit, an eighty-five-year-old woman named Elsa Brigoon found bludgeoned in her apartment on Los Feliz Boulevard.

That one took up most of the ninety days, a lot of it spent chasing false leads. Elsa had been a drinker with an abrasive personality who quarreled at every opportunity. She'd also taken out a hundred-thousand–dollar term life-insurance policy on herself last year, and the beneficiary was a do-nothing son caught in a stock-market bind.

But none of that panned out, and Petra finally put the case to rest by running meticulous checks on every habitue of the apartment complex. A handyman hired by the landlord turned out to have a record of indecent exposure, sexual assault, and burglary, and his eyes jumped to Mars when Petra interviewed him in his filthy downtown SRO. Subsequent, skillful interviewing by Detective II Connor brought the jerk around.

Three for three. Petra's overall solve-rate was approaching the champ's—Milo Sturgis's over in West L.A.—and she knew she was fast-tracking to DIII, might make it by year's end, was sure to incur lots of envy among her colleagues.

Good. Men were . . .

No, enough of that. Men are our biological partners.

Oh, Lord . . .

Day Ninety, she decided that bitterness was eroding her soul and resolved to be positive. Returning to her easel for the first time in months, she tried painting in oils, found her sense of color wanting, switched to pen-and-ink and filled pages of bristol board with tight, hyperrealistic faces.

Children's faces. Well drawn but tacky. She ripped the drawings to shreds, went shopping.

She needed to go for color, one look in her closet made that painfully obvious.

Her casual clothes consisted of black jeans and black T's and black shoes. Her work duds were dark pantsuits: a dozen black, two navy blues, three chocolate browns, one charcoal. All slim-cut to fit her skinny frame, all designer-labels that she purchased at discount outlets and the Barney's warehouse sale and last-day markdowns wherever she found them.

She drove from her Wilshire District apartment to the big Neiman Marcus in Beverly Hills and splurged on a half-price Vestimenta soft wool number.

Silk-lined lapels, ticket pocket cut on the bias, strong shoulders, pegged trousers.

Powder blue.

She wore it that night and drew shocked looks from the other detectives. One wiseass covered his eyes, as if shielding himself against glare. Another said, "Nice, Petra." A couple of others whistled, and she grinned at the lot of them.

Before anyone else could crack wise, phones began ringing, and the squad room filled with the business of death. Taking her place at her metal desk, in a corner next to the lockers, Petra shuffled paper and touched a powder blue sleeve and figured she knew what was running through the guys' heads.

Morticia changes her style.

Dragon Lady comes up for light.

She came across funereal, but a lot of it was biology. She had sharp features, ivory skin, thick, straight jet hair that she kept in a glossy wedge cut, deep brown eyes that leaned toward piercing.

Kids brought out the softness in her, but now Alicia and Bea were out of her life and Billy Straight—a young boy she met working a case who'd touched her heart—was nearly fourteen, had found himself a girlfriend.

Billy never called her anymore; the last time Petra had phoned him, more silence than conversation had passed between them.

So she supposed she could be forgiven a Dragon Lady persona.

The D.A.'s office had faxed her some questions on the Elsa Brigoon case—stuff the novice ADA could've known from reading the file. But she answered anyway and faxed back her replies.

Then her phone rattled and a patrol officer named Montez went on about a 187 cutting on Fountain near El Centro and Petra was out of the station in a flash.

She arrived at the scene and conferred with the assistant coroner. He informed her that the morgue was backlogged and the autopsy would take a while. But cause of death didn't look to be any great mystery.

Single knife wound, exsanguination, most of the blood pooled beneath the DB, establishing the kill spot. Petra, in powder blue, was glad there wasn't more gore.

Then she read the victim's license and got sad because, for the first time since she'd been a detective, this was a name she recognized. She'd never been into the blues—not musically, anyway—but you didn't have to be to know who Edgar Ray Lee was.

AKA Baby Boy. The driver's license in his pocket just stated the basics: male Caucasian, a DOB that put him at fifty-one. Height: six-two, weight: two-seventy. Petra thought he looked bigger than that.

As she recorded the data in her pad, she overheard someone—one of the morgue drivers—remark that the guy was a guitar god, had jammed with Bloomfield, Mayall, Clapton, Roy Buchanan, Stevie Ray Vaughan.

Petra turned and saw a ponytailed and bearded ex-hippie type in morgue coveralls staring at the body. White ponytail. Wet-eyed.

"Talented," she said.

"Those fingers," said the driver, as he unfolded a black plastic body bag.

"You play?" Petra asked him.

"I noodle. He *played*. He—those fingers were . . . magic." The driver dabbed at his eye, yanked angrily at the bag, virtually ripped it open. *Zzzzzzzip.*

"Ready?" he said.

"In a sec." Petra crouched by the body, took in the details, again. Jotted in her pad.

Yellow T-shirt, blue jeans, shaved head, tiny chin beard. Tattoos blued both arms.

Ponytail walked away looking disgusted. Petra continued studying. Edgar Ray Lee's mouth hung open exposing broken and rotted teeth that made Petra think: *Junkie?* But she spotted no track marks among the tattoos.

Baby Boy hadn't been dead more than an hour, but his face had already taken on that greenish gray pallor. The EMTs had cut the shirt around the stab wound. Three-inch vertical slit up the belly, gaping at the edges.

She sketched the wound and slipped the pad back into her purse. She was stepping away when a photographer behind her announced, "I want to make sure my lighting was okay." He moved in, lost his balance, fell on his ass. Slid feetfirst into the blood pool.

His camera landed on the asphalt and rattled ominously, but that wasn't Petra's concern.

Crimson splotches and speckles decorated her pants. Both trouser legs ruined.

The photographer lay there, stunned. Petra did nothing to help him, muttered something sharp that widened his eyes and everyone else's.

She stamped away from the scene.

Her own damn fault, going for color.

3 Petra worked the case hard, doing all the usual procedural things as well as researching Baby Boy Lee on the Internet. Soon, she felt immersed in her victim's world, wondered what it had been like to be Edgar Ray Lee.

The bluesman had started out upper-middle class, the only child of two professors at Emory University in Atlanta. Ten years as a child prodigy on violin and cello had ended when Edgar's teenage rebellion aimed him at guitar and landed him on a Greyhound to Chicago, where he found a whole new lifestyle: Living on the streets and in borrowed cribs, sitting in with the Butterfield Blues Band, Albert Lee, B. B. King, and any other genius who happened to be passing through. Developing his chops but picking up bad habits.

The older musicians recognized the chubby kid's talent right away, and one of them gave him the nickname that stuck.

Baby Boy spent two decades scratching a living as a sessions sideman and a bar-band front man, endured big promises that petered, cut records that went nowhere, finally recorded a top-40 hit with a Southern band called Junior Biscuit. The song, penned, sung and guitar-riffed by the big man, was a gut-wrenching lament entitled "A Cold

Heart"—the very same ditty Baby Boy had played moments before his death.

The song made it to 19 on the Billboard Top 100, stayed on the charts for a month. Baby Boy bought himself a nice car and a whole bunch of guitars and a house in Nashville. Within a year, all the money was gone, as Lee kicked up his pattern of voracious womanizing and dining, and polydrug use. The next several years were a blur of fruitless rehab stints. Then: obscurity.

No relatives called about the case. Lee's parents were both dead, he'd never married or sired a child. That, God help her, made her care about him deeply, and the image of his corpse stayed in her head.

The usual procedural things were: having Baby Boy's apartment taped off before dropping in for a personal look-through, interviewing Baby Boy's band mates, his manager, the owner of the Snake Pit, bouncers and bartenders and cocktail waitresses, the few patrons who'd stuck around to gawk at the crime scene and had gotten their names on a list.

No one had any idea who'd want to hurt Baby Boy. Everyone loved Baby Boy, he was a great big kid, naïve, good-natured, would give you the shirt off his back—would give you his *guitar*, for God's sake.

The high point of usual procedure was an hour in a tiny, close interview room, in the company of star witness Linus Brophy.

When Petra first heard about an eyewitness, her hopes had surged. Then she'd talked to the homeless man and realized his account was next to worthless.

Brophy's description boiled down to a tall man.

Age? No idea.

Race? No idea.

Clothing? Not a clue.

It was real dark, Detective Lady.

If that wasn't enough to endear her to Brophy, the bum had a media jones, kept pestering her, wanting to know if someone from TV would be talking to him. Petra wondered how long till Brophy tried to peddle a screenplay. Hawking his story to the tabloids: I WATCHED ALIENS MURDER BABY BOY LEE.

Only problem was, the tabs couldn't care less. Because comeback attempt notwithstanding, Baby Boy was no celebrity. It had been eighteen years since the hit with Junior Biscuit, and in the age of rock-as-porn, Lee was just what MTV didn't want.

The gawkers from the scene said volumes. All were kids young enough to be Baby Boy's offspring and every single one admired him only by association: last year Baby Boy had played backup guitar on an album by a twentysomething band called Tic 439, a disc that had gone platinum and had fueled the big man's rebound attempt.

Still, Petra wondered if Baby Boy had taken in some heavy cash from the hit—big money was always a good motive. But that idea was quashed quickly when she spoke to Lee's manager.

"Nah, it didn't make Baby rich. Didn't make him squat." The former custodian of Lee's career was a big-haired, stoop-shouldered, denimed ferret named Jackie True, who spoke in a clinically depressed mumble.

"Why not, sir?"

"Cause it was bullshit, a scam," said True. "Those kids, they hooked him in by telling him they idolized him, he was God's answer to whatever. Then guess what they paid him: double scale. I tried to get a piece of the profits, at least the net, but . . ." True blew out air and shook his head. "I didn't even take my cut. Baby needed every penny."

"Too bad," said Petra.

"Too bad was Baby's theme song."

She was talking to True in the manager's crappy North Hollywood apartment. Jackie's boots were scuffed, and his nails were ragged. What did managers get—ten, fifteen percent? This one didn't come across like he had a stable full of thoroughbreds. Did Baby being gone mean that fresh footwear and manicures would remain dreams for Jackie? If so, scratch another motive.

No way Jackie True could be her man, anyway. The one thing Linus Brophy seemed sure of was that the killer had been tall, and True would be five-five after a session on the rack.

She moved on to the next name on her list: the soundman, a grad student at USC freelancing for the night, who'd barely heard of Baby Boy.

"Tell the truth," he said, "it really wasn't my thing. I'm into classical."

*   *   *

Petra visited Baby Boy's residence the afternoon following the murder. It turned out to be an apartment every bit as sad as Jackie True's, a ground-floor unit in a boxy white sixplex off Cahuenga, midway between Hollywood and the Valley. The building sat behind a cypress-lined parking lot. Oily pools dotted the asphalt and like Lee's thirteen-year-old Camaro, the resident cars were tired and dusty.

Given Lee's history, she'd expected dysfunctional clutter, poor hygiene, empty booze bottles, dope, whatever. But Baby Boy had been living clean, in every sense of the word.

The flat consisted of living room, kitchenette, bedroom, bathroom. Off-white walls, shag carpeting the color of Mexican limes, low, cracked ceilings, sixties-era light fixtures with a nod toward sparkle and gold paint. Petra started at the back and worked her way forward.

The bedroom smelled of stale sweat. Baby Boy had slept on a pillow-top, king-size mattress set upon a box spring that rested on the floor. No stash space underneath. Lee's clothes took up half the stingy closet: T-shirts, sweats, jeans, one huge black leather jacket so crackled it appeared ready to disintegrate. A nightstand drawer yielded a mostly empty date book and some overdue utility bills.

Petra took the book and continued to look around. No dope or alcohol anywhere, and the strongest nostrum she found in the bathroom was an economy-sized bottle of extra-strength Advil, the top left loose, indicating frequent use.

The avocado-colored fridge held yogurt, cottage cheese, decaf, nonfat Mocha Mix, some bruised peaches and plums, grapes that had started to pucker. In the freezer was a package of skinless chicken breasts and a dozen boxes of Lean Cuisine.

Dieting. Trying to better himself, the poor guy. And someone had gutted him like a fish.

The living room contained two straight-backed chairs, eight guitars on stands, and three amplifiers. Atop one amp was an obtrusive bit of elegance—a charming little cloisonné box, black enamel decorated with red dragons. Inside was an assortment of guitar picks.

And that was it.

Petra's cell phone tooted. The clerk at the station informed her that

Linus Brophy had called, wanted to know if she needed him for anything else.

She laughed and hung up.

More of the usual procedures took up the next few days—lots of perspiration, no inspiration. Petra's esophagus ached, and her head pounded. The case was starting to acquire that nasty whodunit reek.

At 1 A.M., Monday, sitting at her desk, she got to Baby Boy's datebook.

The black leatherette volume was virtually empty, save for scant reminders to shop for groceries, pick up laundry, or "call J. T."

Lee keeping in touch with Jackie True. Hoping for what?

Then Petra came to the week of the murder. A single notation spanned all seven days: the large, right-slanted block letters she'd come to know as Baby Boy's. But larger, penned in thick, black marker.

GIG AT S.P.

No exclamation points, but there might as well have been. Lee's excitement came across in the scale.

Petra flipped a page to today's date: Two notations, much smaller letters. Baby Boy planning a future that never arrived.

Gold Rush Studios? $$$?

That made sense. Jackie True had told her Baby Boy was still fired up, had intended to spend some of his Snake Pit fees on a recording session.

"Sad thing was," True had said, frowning, "Baby didn't realize how little studio time the gig was gonna buy him, once I paid the band and everything else."

"What's everything else?"

"Equipment rentals, the soundman, the kid who hauled our junk, you know." Moment's hesitation. "My cut."

"Not much left," said Petra.

"Not much to start with."

*   *   *

The second notation was for Wednesday and this one looked like an appointment:

RC on setup, Tele, J-45.

Petra had learned enough to know that Baby Boy played Fender Telecasters, so this was a date with an instrument repairman.

Then she flashed on the initials.

RC. Alex Delaware's lady friend, Robin Castagna built and fixed guitars, and from what Alex had told Petra, she was the one who got called when serious musicians needed work on their gear.

RC. Had to be.

Repair*man*, indeed.

Petra doubted Robin could shed any light on the case, but she had no other leads and made a note to phone tomorrow.

She went home early, thinking of Alex and Robin's cool, white contemporary house off Beverly Glen.

Those two, talk about a solid relationship.

Robin, unlike other people we know, had been smart enough to get herself a stable guy. Lucky break, especially cause the guy was a shrink, and Petra suspected most shrinks were high-maintenance.

Alex was good-looking to boot—another high-maintenance predictor. But despite all that, he had a what . . . a *solidity* about him. A little on the serious side, but that was better than the self-centered flakiness that seemed to afflict L.A. men.

Petra hadn't spoken to Alex for a while. She'd considered calling him when Billy's breaking-away had caused her to wonder about her skills as a . . . friend. Alex had been Billy's therapist. But she hadn't followed through. Too busy.

No, that wasn't the real reason. Solid or not, Delaware was still a shrink and Petra was worried she couldn't keep the sadness out of her voice and he'd pick up on it and want to do his thing. She was in no mood to be shrunk.

Now, shielded by homicide, she could make contact with impunity.

The next morning, at ten, she dialed the white house. Alex picked up and said, "Hey, Petra, what's up?"

They exchanged small talk, Alex inquired about Billy, Petra lied and said everything was going great. Then she said, "I'm actually calling Robin. Her name came up in the date book of the victim on a case I just picked up."

"Baby Boy Lee?"

"How'd you know?"

"Robin worked on his guitars. He's been here a few times. Sweet guy."

"You know him pretty well?"

"No," said Alex. "He came by once in a while. Friendly, always smiling. But a bluesman's smile."

"Meaning?"

"Sad, resigned. Robin told me he'd had some hard luck. A couple of times I walked in and found him playing. Best show I've seen all year. He had an incredible sense of phrasing—not a lot of notes but the right ones."

Talking like a music guy—nearly word for word, the same thing Petra had heard from the big man's band mates.

She remembered: Alex played guitar.

"Lots of hard luck," she said. "What else can you tell me about him?"

"That's about it. Robin worked on his guitars for free because he was always broke. He'd always make a show of writing out an IOU and handing it to her, but to my knowledge she never collected. Any idea who did it?"

"Nope. That's why I'm following everything up. Robin around?"

Several seconds passed. Then: "She doesn't live here anymore, Petra. We separated a few months ago."

"Oh."

"Mutual decision, it's working out," he said. But he didn't sound as if he meant it. "I'll give you her number."

Petra's cheeks had grown hot. Not embarrassment. Anger. Another castle crumbles.

"Sure," she said.

"She's got a place in Venice. Rennie Avenue, north of Rose. It's a side-by-side duplex, the studio's in the southern unit."

Petra copied the address and thanked him.

"I don't think she's in town, Petra. She spent a good part of last year touring with the Kill Famine Tour and has been moving around." Pause. "She met a guy."

"I'm sorry," Petra blurted.

"It happens," he said. "We'd agreed to . . . try out our independence. Anyway, this guy, he's a vocal coach, and he travels quite a bit, too. They're in Vancouver. I know because she called to let me know she's taking Spike to a vet, there. Toothache."

Petra remembered the pooch. Cute little French bulldog. A chance to change the subject. "Ouch. Hope he feels better."

"Me, too . . . anyway, they're due back tomorrow, I think."

"Okay, thanks."

"Sure. Good luck on the case. Say hi to Robin for me."

"Will do," said Petra, itching to break the connection. "You take care now."

"You, too."

He hung up. Petra shut out the call and went over the details of Baby Boy's demise for the umpteenth time. Then she left the station and got herself some lunch. Greasy hamburger at a Vine Street joint she was certain would disappoint.

4 The first time I made love to Allison Gwynn, I felt like an adulterer.

Totally irrational. Robin and I had been living apart for months. And now she was with Tim Plachette.

But when the touch, the feel, the smell of someone is imbedded in your DNA . . .

If Allison sensed my unease, she never said a word.

I met her shortly before my years with Robin started to unravel. I'd been helping Milo on a twenty-year-old murder. Years before, at the age of seventeen, Allison had been sexually abused by a man who figured in the case. Her college mentor was an old friend of mine, and he asked her if she'd talk to me. She thought about it and agreed.

I liked her right away—admired her courage, her honesty, her gentle manner. Her looks were too notable to miss, but back then I appreciated them as an abstraction.

Ivory skin, soft but assertive cheekbones, a wide, strong mouth, the most gorgeous, waist-length black hair I'd ever seen. Huge eyes, blue as midnight, projected a sharp curiosity. Like me, she was a psychologist. Those eyes, I figured, would serve her well.

She grew up in Beverly Hills, the only daughter of an assistant attorney general, went to Penn, continued there for a Ph.D. In her senior year, she met a Wharton whiz, fell in love, married young, and moved back to California. Within months of receiving her state license, her husband was diagnosed with a rare malignancy, and she was widowed. Eventually, she pulled herself together and built up a Santa Monica practice. Now she combined clinical work with teaching nights at the U, and volunteering at a hospice for the terminally ill.

Keeping busy. I knew that tune.

Seated, her high waist and willowy arms and swan neck implied height, but like Robin, she was a small, delicately built woman—there I go again, comparing.

Unlike Robin, she favored expensive makeup, considered clothes-shopping a recreational activity, had no problem flashing strategic glints of diamond jewelry.

One time she confessed it was because she'd been late to enter puberty, had hated looking like a child all through high school. At thirty-seven, she appeared ten years younger.

I was the first man she'd been with in a long time.

When I called her, it had been months since we'd spoken. Surprise brightened her voice. "Oh, hi."

I talked around the issue, finally asked her to dinner.

She said, "As in a date?"

"As in."

"I thought there . . . was someone."

"So did I," I said.

"Oh. Is this recent?"

"This isn't a rebound thing," I said. "I've been single for a while." Hating the awkwardness—the self-pity—of all that.

"Giving yourself time," she said.

Saying the right thing. *Trained* to say the right thing. Maybe this was a mistake. Even back in grad school, I'd avoided dating women in my field, wanting to know about other worlds, worried that intimacy with another therapist would be too confining. Then I met Robin, and there'd been no need to look anywhere . . .

"Anyway," I said. "If you're busy—"

She laughed. "Sure, let's get together."

"Still a carnivore?"

"You remember. Did I gorge myself that badly? Don't answer that. No, I haven't gone vegetarian."

I named a steakhouse not far from her office. "How about tomorrow night?"

"I've got patients until eight, but if you don't mind a late dinner, sure."

"Nine," I said. "I'll pick you up at your office."

"Why don't I meet you there?" she said. "That way I won't have to leave my car."

Setting up an escape plan.

I said, "Terrific."

"See you then, Alex."

A *date*.

How long had it been? Eons . . . Even though Allison would be bringing her own wheels, I washed and vacuumed the Seville, got compulsive about it, and ended up squatting at the grille wielding a toothbrush. An hour later, grubby and sweaty and reeking of Armor All, I took a long run, stretched, showered, shaved, shined up a pair of black loafers, and pulled out a navy blazer.

Soft, single-breasted Italian model, two Christmases old . . . a gift from Robin. I yanked it off, switched to a black sport coat, decided it made me look like an undertaker and returned to the blue. Next step: slacks. Easy. The featherweight gray flannels I usually wore when I testified in court. Add a yellow tab-collar shirt and a tie and I'd be— which tie? I tried on several, decided neckwear was too stuffy for the occasion, switched to a lightweight navy crewneck and decided *that* was too damn Hollywood.

Back to the yellow shirt. Open-necked. No, the tabs didn't look good that way. And the damn thing was already sweat-stained under the arms.

My heartbeat had kicked up, and my stomach was flipping around. This was ridiculous. What would I tell a patient in the same predicament?

Be yourself.

Whoever that was.

* * *

I reached the restaurant first, thought about waiting in the Seville and greeting Allison as she approached the door. I figured that might alarm her and went inside. The place was lit at tomb level. I sat at the bar, ordered a beer, and watched sports on TV—I can't remember the sport—had barely gotten through the foam when Allison arrived, freeing a black tide of hair from her sweater and looking around.

I got to her just as the maître d' looked up. When she saw me, her eyes widened. No look-over; just focusing on my face. I smiled, she smiled back.

"Well, hello." She offered her cheek, and I pecked. The sweater was lavender cashmere, and it matched the clinging dress that sheathed her from breastbone to knee. Matching shoes with big heels. Diamond earrings, diamond tennis bracelet, a short strand of silver pearls around her white neck.

We sat down. She ordered a glass of merlot, and I asked for a Chivas. The red leather booth was roomy, and I sat far enough away to avoid intrusiveness, close enough to smell her. She smelled great.

"So," she said, aiming those blue eyes at the empty booth next to us.

"Long day?"

Back to me. "Yes. Thankfully."

"Know what you mean," I said.

She played with a napkin. "What have you been up to?"

"After the Ingalls case quieted down, I took a little time off. Lately I've being doing court consultations."

"Crime consultations?"

"No," I said. "Injury cases, some child custody."

"Custody," she said. "That gets ugly."

"Especially when there's enough money to pay lawyers indefinitely, and you get stuck with an idiot judge. I try to limit myself to smart judges."

"Find any?"

"It's a challenge."

The drinks arrived. We clinked glasses and drank in silence. She twirled the stem, inspected the menu, said, "I'm starving, will probably gorge again."

"Go for it."

"What's good?"

"I haven't been here in years."

"Oh?" She seemed amused. "Did you pick it to indulge my carnivorous tendencies?"

"Yours and mine. Also, I recalled it as relaxed."

"It is."

Silence. My face warmed—Scotch and awkwardness. Even in the dim light I could see that she'd colored.

"Anyway," she said. "I don't know if I ever thanked you, but you made talking about my experience as easy as it could've been. So thanks."

"Thanks for helping. It made a difference."

She scanned the menu some more, gnawed her lower lip, looked up, said, "I'm thinking T-bone."

"Sounds good."

"You?"

"Rib eye."

"Major-league beefathon," she said. She looked at the empty booth again, brought her eyes back to the tablecloth, seemed to be studying my fingertips. I was glad I'd filed my nails.

"You're taking time off from crime cases," she said, "but you'll go back to it."

"If I'm asked."

"Will you be?"

I nodded.

She said, "I never got to ask you. What draws you to that kind of thing?"

"I could recite some noble speech about righting wrongs and making the world just a little bit safer, but I've stopped fooling myself. The truth is, I have a thing for unpredictability and novelty. From time to time, I need a shot of adrenaline."

"Like a race car driver."

I smiled. "That glamorizes it."

She drank wine, kept the glass in front of her lips, lowered it, and revealed her own smile. "So you're just another adrenaline junkie." She ran a finger around the base of her glass. "If it's all about thrills and chills, why *not* just run cars around the track or jump out of planes?"

The work I did had been a factor in the breakup with Robin. Would we still be together if I'd settled for skydiving?

As I framed my answer, Allison said, "Sorry, I didn't mean to put you on the spot. I'm just guessing that you crave more than novelty. I think you really do like making things right."

I didn't answer.

"Then again," she said, "who am I to utter pronouncements without a solid database? Being a behavioral scientist and all that."

She shifted her bottom, tugged her hair, drank wine. I tried to smile away her discomfiture but couldn't catch her eye. When she put her glass down, her hand landed closer to mine. Just a few millimeters between our fingers.

Then, the gap closed—both of us moving in concert. Touching.

Pretending it was accidental and retracting our hands.

The heat of skin against skin.

The blue shirt with which I'd replaced the sweat-ruined yellow one was growing sodden.

Allison began fooling with her hair. I stared into what remained of my Scotch. Breathing in the alcohol. I hadn't eaten much all day, and booze on an empty stomach should've set off at least a small buzz.

Nothing.

Too damned alert.

How was this going?

For the rest of the evening, we let loose a few more cautious bits of autobiography, ate well, drank too much, walked off the meal with a slow stroll up Wilshire. Side by side, but no contact. Her big heels clacked, and her hair flapped. Her hips rolled—not a vamp, just the way she moved, and that made it sexy. Men looked at her. Halfway through the first block, her hand slipped around my biceps. Breeze from the ocean misted the streets. My eyes ached with uncertainty.

Conversation fizzled and we covered the next few blocks in silence, pretending to window-shop. Back at our cars, Allison gave me a tentative kiss on the lips. Before I knew it, she'd gotten into her ten-year-old Jaguar and was roaring off.

Two days later, I called her and asked her out again.

She said, "I've got the afternoon off, was planning to relax at home. Why don't you come over and we can eat here? That is, if you're willing to take the risk."

"Big risk?"

"Who cares? You're the adrenaline-guy."

"Good point," I said. "Can I bring something?"

"Flowers are always appropriate. Not that I'm suggesting—I'm kidding, just bring yourself. And let's keep it casual, okay?"

She lived in a single-story Spanish house on Fourteenth Street, just south of Montana, within walking distance of her office. The alarm sign on the lawn was conspicuous, and the black Jag convertible was parked behind an iron gate that cut the porte cochere from the street. As I approached the front door, a motion-sensing light went on. Woman-living-alone precautions. Woman-who-had-been-molested-twenty-years-ago precautions.

As I parked, I thought about Robin moving back to Venice, all by herself. Correction: not alone anymore . . . *stop, fool.*

I rang the bell and waited, bouquet in hand. Figuring roses would be too forward, I'd chosen a dozen white peonies. Casual had come down to an olive polo shirt and jeans and running shoes.

Allison came to the door in a lime polo shirt and jeans and running shoes.

She took one look at me, said, "Do you *believe* this?" Then she cracked up.

As I sat in her compact white kitchen, she cooked mushroom and chicken liver omelettes and took a chilled salad out of the fridge. Sourdough, white wine, an ice bucket and a six-pack of Diet Coke filled out the menu.

The kitchen opened to a vest-pocket backyard and we ate outside on a trellis-topped patio. The garden was used-brick pathways and a patch of grass surrounded by high privet hedges.

I tasted the omelette. "Not much risk, here."

"It's one of the few things I can get through without disaster. Grandma's recipe."

"Let's hear it for Grandma."

"Grandma was ornery, but she knew her way around a stove." She talked about her family, and eventually I found myself parceling out bits of self-revelation. As the evening progressed, my shoulders loosened. Allison had relaxed, too, curling up on a couch, her feet tucked under her. Laughing a lot, blue eyes animated.

Pupils enlarged; those who study that kind of thing say it's a good sign. But shortly before eleven, her posture stiffened and she looked at her watch, and said, "I've got an early patient."

She stood and glanced at the door, and I wondered what had gone wrong.

When she walked me out, she said, "I'm sorry."

"For what?"

"For being so abrupt."

"Patients have their needs," I said, sounding like a stiff.

She shrugged, as if that wasn't it at all. But she said nothing more as she extended her hand for a shake. Her house had been warm, but her skin was cold and moist. In bare feet she was tiny and I wanted to take her in my arms.

I said, "Good to see you, again."

"Good to see you." I stepped out to her front porch. Her smile was painful as she began to close the door, then she came out and bussed my cheek.

I touched her hair. She turned her head and delivered another kiss, full on the lips but closed-mouthed. Hard, almost assaultive. I tried for another kiss, but she withdrew, and said, "Drive carefully," and this time she did close the door.

She phoned me the next day, at noon. "Wouldn't you know it, my early patient was a no-show."

"Too bad," I said.

"Yes . . . I . . . could we . . . would you like to . . . I'm free tonight at seven, if you're willing."

"Seven's fine. Want me to cook?"

"Alex, would you mind something other than just sitting around and eating? Maybe a drive? I've been so cooped up. Driving helps me unwind."

"Me, too." How many hundreds of miles, since Robin had left, had I put on the Seville? "We could take a spin up the coast to Malibu."

My favorite drive. All those night cruises along the Pacific with Robin—*shut up.*

"Perfect," she said. "If we get hungry, there are plenty of places to stop. See you at seven."

"Want me to meet you somewhere?"

"No, pick me up at my house."

I got there at 7:02. Before I reached the door, she opened it, stepped out onto the front path, and met me halfway, setting off the motion-sensing light. She had on a sleeveless, black cotton dress, no stockings, low-heeled black sandals. No diamonds, just a thin, gold choker that accentuated the length and whiteness of her neck. Her hair was clipped back in a ponytail. It made her look younger, tentative.

"I need to explain about last night," she said, talking fast, sounding breathless. "The truth is, the early patient was scheduled at nine-thirty. I had plenty of time, didn't need to kibosh everything. I was—let's call a spade a spade: I was nervous. Being with you made me very, very nervous, Alex."

"I—"

"It wasn't you." Her shoulders rose and fell. Her laugh was quick, just short of brittle, as she took my arm and ushered me into her house. Standing with her back to the door, she said, "If my patients could see me now. I'm a big-deal expert at helping others make transitions, but I am having the hardest time."

She shook her head. "Transitions. Now I'm being presumptuous—"

"Hey," I said. "The first time we went out I changed shirts three times."

She stared up at me. I touched her chin and raised it. She removed my hand.

"Saying the right thing," she said. "With people like us, you never know if it's the training."

"Occupational hazard," I said.

She threw her arms around me and kissed me deeply. Her tongue was gingery and nimble. I held her tight, stroked her face, her neck, her back, chanced roaming lower and when she didn't stop me, dropped both my hands and cupped her rear. She moved my right hand around to her front, sandwiched it between cotton-sheathed thighs. I explored her heat and she did something with her hips that was pure intent. Lifting the black dress, I peeled down her panties, felt the angle of her legs widen. I kissed her, I strummed her. One of her hands was tangled in my hair, holding fast. The other fumbled at my zipper. Finally, she freed me and we were on the hardwood floor of her living room and I was in her and she was clutching me and we were moving together as if we'd been doing it all our lives.

She kissed my face and said, "I'm going to go out on a limb. With you it's not just the training. You're a sweet man."

The feelings came later. After we'd slept and eaten leftovers and renewed our dehydrated bodies with gulps of water and were finally heading north on Pacific Coast Highway. Taking Allison's Jaguar because it was a convertible. I was at the wheel and Allison stretched out on the reclined passenger seat, bundled up in a big, white Irish sweater, hair loose, flapping like an ebony banner, face to the wind.

One hand rested on my knee. Beautiful fingers, long and tapered. Smooth and white.

No scars. Robin, though a master of tools, hurt herself from time to time.

I gave the Jag more gas, sped past black ocean and gray hillside, the headlights of other adventurers. Stealing peeks at Allison's face when the road straightened. My scalp still ached where she'd yanked my hair, and the stretch of brow from which she'd licked my sweat pinged with electricity.

I put on even more speed and she stroked my knee and I got hard, again.

Beautiful woman, sensuous woman.

Fast car, gorgeous California night. Perfect.

But this idiot's joy was muffled by the wagging finger of doubt—some notion that I'd cheated.

Beyond stupid. Robin's with Tim.

And now I'm with Allison.

Things changed. Change was good.

Right?

5 A hundred hours since Baby Boy had bled out in the alley and Petra had turned up nothing. The clammy, sour smell of whodunit permeated her sinuses. She found herself wishing for a slam-dunk bar stabbing but picked up no other cases. The crime drop that had become the department's big-time cap feather meant adequate staffing. It would be a while before the homicide dial rotated back to her.

She went over the file till her head hurt. Asked a couple of the guys if they had any ideas. A young D-I named Arbogast said, "You should listen to his music."

Petra had bought a few CDs, spent the early-morning hours with Baby Boy's bruised voice and wailing guitar licks. "For a clue?"

"No," said Arbogast. "Cause he rocked."

"Guy was a fucking genius," another detective agreed. An older one—Krauss. Petra would've never taken him for a blues fan. Then she realized he was around Baby Boy's age, had probably grown up with Baby Boy's music.

A genius dies but the mainstream press couldn't care less. Not even a phone call from the *Times*, despite uniformly good reviews of Baby Boy's music Petra found while surfing the Web. She left a message for the newspaper's music critic, on the off chance something in Baby Boy's past could point her in a new direction. Jerk never phoned back.

She did get pestered by a handful of self-styled "rock journalists," young-sounding guys claiming to represent outlets with names like *Guitar Buzz, Guitar Universe,* and *Twenty-first-Century Guitar,* each one wanting details for obituaries. No one had anything to say about Lee other than to praise his playing. The word "phrasing" kept coming up—Alex had used the term—and Petra figured out that meant how you put notes and rhythm together.

Her phrasing on this one stank.

The rock writers lost interest when she asked questions instead of answering theirs. Except for one guy who kept bugging her for details, a character named Yuri Drummond, publisher of a local magazine called *GrooveRat,* which had run a profile on Baby Boy last year.

Drummond alienated Petra immediately by calling her by her first name and proceeded to compound the annoyance by rooting around rudely for forensic details. *"How many stab wounds? How much blood did he actually lose?"*

Guy had the ghoulish curiosity and nasal voice of a hormonally stormed teenager, and Petra wondered about a prank caller. But when he asked her if anything had been scrawled on the alley wall, she stiffened.

"Why do you ask that?"

"Well, you know," said Drummond. "Like the Manson murders— Helter Skelter."

"Why would the Manson murders be related to Mr. Lee's murder?"

"I don't know. I just thought . . ."

"Have you heard anything about Mr. Lee's murder, Mr. Drummond?"

"No." Drummond's voice rose in pitch. "What would I know?"

"When did you interview Mr. Lee?"

"No, no, I never met him."

"You said you ran a profile on him."

"We ran an in-depth profile and listed his discography."

"You profiled him in depth without meeting him."

"Exactly," said Drummond, sounding cocky. "That's the whole point."

"What is?"

"*GrooveRat*'s into the psychobiosocial *essence* of art and music, not the cult of personality."

"Psycho-bio-social," said Petra.

"In plain words," said Drummond, condescending, "we don't care who someone screws, only the groove they put out."

"Hence the title of your magazine."

Silence.

Petra said, "Do you have information about who Baby Boy Lee was screwing?"

"You're saying there was a sexual angle to—"

"Mr. Drummond, what exactly was the focus of this profile?"

"The *music*," pronounced the little snip, letting the unspoken "*duh*" hang in the air.

"Baby Boy's phrasing," said Petra.

"Baby Boy's whole groove—the mind-set he put himself into to get the sound he did."

"You didn't think talking to him would help that?" Petra pressed, wondering why she was wasting time with this loser. Knowing the sad answer: nothing else on her plate.

"No," said Drummond.

"Did Baby Boy Lee turn down an interview with you?"

"No, we never asked him. So tell me, what kind of blade are we talking about—"

"What was Baby Boy's groove?" said Petra.

"Pain," said Drummond. "That's why his being killed is so—it fits. So what can you tell me about how it went down?"

Petra said, "You want gory details."

"Right," said Drummond.

"Do *you* have any idea who killed him?"

"Why would I? Listen, you really should help us. The public's got a right to know, and we're the best messenger."

"Why's that, Mr. Drummond?"

"Because we understood him. Were they? The details. Gory."

"Were you at the Snake Pit, Saturday night?"

"Nope."

"Not a big enough fan?"

"I was at the Whiskey—showcase for a bunch of new bands—hey, what're you saying?" Drummond's voice had climbed even higher, and now he sounded twelve. Petra visualized some acne-plagued scarecrow in a slovenly room. The kind of creepazoid with too much leisure time who'd phone the local supermarket, clutching the phone with sweaty hands: *"Excuse me, do you have pig's feet?" "Yes, we do." "Then wear shoes and no one'll notice yuka yuka yuka."*

Drummond said, "If I knew what was gonna happen, I'd have been there. Absolutely."

"Why's that?"

"To see his last show. What do they call that—a swan song?"

"Yuri," said Petra. "What is that, Russian?"

Drummond hung up.

On Friday, just after 6 P.M., the downstairs clerk beeped Petra's extension. "There's a Ms. Castagna here to see you."

"I'll be right down," said Petra, surprised.

When she got to the ground floor, Robin was by herself in the lobby, staring at some Wanted posters, hands on hips, her back to Petra. Her hair was longer than Petra remembered it, the mass of auburn curls trailing down her back like a heap of grapes. Alex's hair was curly, too. If the two of them had bred, they might've created another Shirley Temple.

Then Petra thought: all those years together, and they never *had* bred. Never tied the knot, either. Because of her own state, she found herself wondering about things like that.

She approached Robin, taking in Robin's outfit the way women do with other women. Black corduroy overalls over a red T-shirt with high-cut sleeves, black suede tennis shoes. Red bandana hanging out of a rear pocket.

Kind of a rock 'n' roll caj thing. On the wrong body the overalls could be deadly; Robin's curves made them look fine.

When Petra was a few steps away, she said, "Hi, there," and Robin turned and Petra saw that she'd been biting her lip and her dark eyes were moist.

"Petra," she said. They hugged. "I just got back to town, picked up your message this morning. I had to be in Hollywood for a session, so I figured I'd stop by. This is terrible."

"Sorry to tell you like that, but I didn't know when you'd be back."

Robin shook her head. "I heard about it yesterday, in Vancouver."

"Local papers cover it?"

"Don't know," said Robin. "I got it backstage. The music grapevine. I was shocked. We all were, I had no idea you were involved."

"I am, indeed," said Petra. "Anything you can tell me?"

"What can I say? He was such a sweetie-pie." Robin's words quivered and faded. She held back tears. "A big old sweet guy and a supremely talented man."

"Anything else on the grapevine buzz? Like who'd want to do this to him? Even the flimsiest rumor."

Robin gave another headshake, rubbed a smooth, tan arm. "Baby was the last person I'd peg with any enemy, Petra. Everyone liked him."

Not everyone, thought Petra. "As I said in the message, your name was in his book. What was it, an appointment to fix some guitars?"

"They're fixed. He was coming by to pick them up." Robin smiled. "I'm surprised he actually wrote it down. Time was a pretty plastic concept for Baby."

"You've been working on his gear for a while."

"Years. And often. Baby played so hard, his fingertips wore grooves in the fretboard. I was always planing boards down, refretting, doing neck-sets. These two were beyond that, needed complete new boards."

"A Fender Telecaster. And a J-45," said Petra. "Someone told me that's a Gibson."

Robin smiled. "Gibson acoustic. I'd already refinished it a couple of times because Baby let it get too dry and the lacquer cracked and flaked off and his pick nearly wore a hole in the top. This time I put in the second replacement fretboard. The Tele was simpler, just setup. I finished them both early, right before I left town, because I always tried to finish early for Baby."

"Why's that?" said Petra.

"Because Baby got sounds out of a guitar that no one else did, and I wanted to contribute my small bit. I knew I'd be traveling to Vancouver, so I left a message at his apartment to pick them up on Wednesday. He never got back to me, but that's not unusual. As I said, Baby and punctuality were strangers. Most of them are like that."

" 'Them' meaning musicians."

"Musicians," Robin repeated, and her lips curled upward.

Petra said, "So he never called, but he did jot down the appointment."

"Guess so. Typically, Baby just dropped in. Petra, what do I do with the guitars, now? They're not evidence, are they?"

"Are they worth anything?"

"Clean, they'd be very pricey. With all the modifications . . . a lot less."

"No value-added because Baby played them?" said Petra. "I read how Eric Clapton auctioned some guitars off, and they went way above estimates."

"Baby wasn't Clapton." Tears trickled from Robin's eyes. She produced the red bandana and dabbed them dry. "How could someone do this?"

"It stinks," said Petra. "I can't see how the guitars would be evidence, but sit tight. If I need them, I'll let you know."

Thinking: Maybe she should pick them up. On the slim chance she caught the bad guy and they brought him to trial and some defense attorney wanted to make a stink about the chain of evidence . . .

Robin was saying, "I hope you get whoever did it."

"What else can you tell me about Baby Boy?" said Petra.

"Easygoing. A big kid. People took advantage of his good nature. If he got hold of a dollar, it floated right out of his pocket."

"Doesn't seem as if he's made too many dollars, recently," said Petra, remembering what Alex had told her about Baby's perennial IOUs to Robin. Figuring quoting Alex right now might be a distraction.

"Things *were* tough for him," said Robin. "Had been for a while. He got a boost when a new pop band asked him to play on their album. Guys young enough to be his kids, but he was so up for it. Thought this might be a big break. The album did great, but I doubt they paid him much."

"Why's that?"

Robin kicked one suede tenny with the other. "He seemed broke—as usual. He hadn't paid me in a long time. Used to write out these elaborate IOUs—minicontracts, really. Both of us pretending we were being businesslike. Then he'd pick up his gear and offer a few dollars in partial payment and I'd say forget it and he'd argue but eventually give in. And that would be it till the next time. It went on for so long, I stopped expecting to get paid. But when he cut the album with those kids, he called me and promised he'd be settling up. 'Closing out my tab, sweet Lil Sis,' was the way he put it. He used to say if he'd had a little sister, he would've wanted her to be just like me."

Another swipe of the bandana.

"But the tab never got closed," said Petra.

"Not a penny. That's how I know the gig didn't produce serious money. If Baby'd been flush, I would've been high on his list, right after rent and food."

"His rent was paid up, and there was food in his fridge—diet food."

Robin winced. "That again? Onstage, he flaunted his weight—shook his belly, wiggled his butt, made jokes about being heavy. But the poor guy hated being big, was always resolving to trim down." She sniffed. "For all he'd been through, he never stopped wanting to better himself. Once, when he was feeling pretty down, he told me: 'God made a mess when he created me. My job's cleaning it up.' "

She broke down, crying, and Petra put an arm around her shoulder. A couple of uniforms walked through the front doors and swaggered across the lobby, jangling gear. Not even bothering to notice the weeping woman. They saw plenty of that.

6

The Thursday after Baby Boy Lee's murder, my doorbell rang. I'd been typing court reports all afternoon, ran out of words and wisdom, and called out for Chinese food.

Grabbing tip money, I trudged from my office to the living room, threw open the door, and faced Robin. She'd never surrendered her key but was acting like a guest.

Which, I suppose, she was.

She saw the tip money and smiled. "I can't be bought that easily."

I pocketed the bills. "Hi."

"Is this a bad time?"

"Of course not." I held the door open, and she stepped into the place we'd designed together. I watched her wander around the living room, as if reacquainting herself with the space. When she perched on the edge of a sofa, I took a facing seat.

"You know about Baby Boy," she said.

"Petra called me looking for you."

"I was just over at the Hollywood police station, talking to her." She stared at the ceiling. "I've never been close to someone who was murdered . . . all the years you and I were together, I stayed on the periphery."

"You didn't miss anything."

She played with an earring. "It's disgusting—the feeling of gone-ness. It brings back my father's death. It's not the same, of course. I was fond of Baby, but he wasn't family. Still, for some reason . . ."

"Baby was a good guy."

"Great guy," she said. "Who'd want to hurt him?"

She got up and walked around some more. Straightened a picture. "I shouldn't have barged in on you."

I said, "Does Petra have any leads?"

She shook her head.

"Any lifestyle issues? Had Baby gotten back into drugs?"

"Not as far as I know," she said. "The last few times when he came by he looked clean, didn't he?"

"Far as I could tell." Not that I'd paid much attention to Baby Boy's demeanor. The last time he'd dropped off some gear, music had drifted into the house from Robin's studio, and I'd gone over to listen. Baby Boy had left the studio door open and I stood there, watching, listen-ing, as he cradled his old Gibson acoustic like a baby, hammered some notes in a drop-D tuning, sang something low and pained and tender.

"But what do I know?" said Robin. "Maybe he had gotten back into the bad old days. What do any of us know about anyone?" She rubbed her eyes. "I shouldn't have come. It was inconsiderate."

"We're still friends."

"Right," she said. "That was the deal, walk away friends. Is that sit-ting right with you?"

"How're you doing with it?"

"Okay." She stood. "I'll get going, Alex."

"Things to do, places to see?" I said. Why *had* she had come? Shoulder to cry on? Was Tim's shoulder defective? I realized I was an-gry but also weirdly gratified—she'd chosen me.

"Nothing pressing," she said. "I don't belong here."

"I like you here." Why had I said that?

She walked over to me, tousled my hair, kissed the top of my head. "Once upon a time we'd be dealing with this you-know-how."

"How?"

She smiled. "Once upon a time, we'd be doing the two-backed beast. That's how we always ended up dealing with stress."

"I can think of worse ways to cope."

"Definitely," she said.

She lowered herself onto my lap and we kissed for a long time. I touched a breast. She emitted a low, sad sound, reached for me. Stopped herself.

"I'm so sorry," she said, as she ran for the door.

I got to my feet but remained in place. "Nothing to be sorry for."

"Lots to be sorry for," she said.

New adultery.

"How's Spike?" When in doubt, ask about the dog.

"Fine. You're welcome to come see him."

"Thanks."

The doorbell rang, and her head whipped around.

"I called out for food. That Hunan place in the Village."

She patted her hair in place. "Good place."

"Spicy but not hostile."

She gave a terrible smile and twisted the doorknob. An Hispanic kid who looked around twelve held out a greasy bag, and I jogged to the door, took the food, reached into my pocket for money, grabbed too many bills, thrust them at him.

"Thanks, man," he said, and hurried down the stairs.

I said, "Hungry?"

"Anything but," said Robin. As she turned to leave, I thought of a million things to say.

What came out was: "Petra's as good as they come. She'll keep working at it."

"I know she will. Thanks for listening. Bye, Alex."

"Anytime," I said.

But that wasn't true, anymore.

7 For two weeks of double shifts, most of which she neglected to file as overtime, Petra drove herself crazy, trying to track down as many members of Baby Boy's final audience as she could, coming up only with the few names on the freebie list—most of whom hadn't bothered to show up—and the stragglers she'd already talked to. She had a go with the Snake Pit's absentee owner—a dentist from Long Beach—reinterviewed the custodians, the bouncers, the cocktail waitresses, Lee's band—all pickup musicians—and the diminutive, poorly shod Jackie True. All useless.

She even tried to contact the members of Tic 439, the band that had sparked visions of comeback in Baby Boy's head. Here, she encountered another side of the music biz: layers of insulation, from the receptionists of record-company executives on up to the band's manager, an unctuous-sounding stoner named Beelzebub Lawrence, who finally deigned, after Petra called him a dozen times, to speak to her over the phone. Music pounded in the background, and Lawrence spoke softly. The two-minute conversation strained Petra's hearing and her patience.

Yeah, Baby Boy had been brilliant.

No, he had no idea who'd want to hurt him.

Yeah, the guys had dug jamming with him.

No, they hadn't had contact with him since the recording session.

Petra said, "He really added something to their sound, didn't he?" She'd bought the CD, found it an execrable mix of whiny lyrics and plodding rhythm. Only Baby Boy's guitar, sweet and sustaining, on two tracks, lent any sense of musicality to the mess.

Beelzebub Lawrence said, "Yeah, he was cool."

The coroner was finished with Baby Boy's corpse, but no one had come forward to claim it. Even though it wasn't her job, Petra did some genealogical research that led her to Edgar Ray Lee's closest living relative. A great-aunt named Grenadina Bourgeouis, ancient-sounding and feeble.

Senile, too, it soon became clear. The phone chat rattled the old woman and left Petra's head spinning. She called Jackie True and apprised him of the situation.

He said, "Baby wanted to be cremated."

"He talked about dying?"

"Doesn't everybody?" said True. "I'll handle it."

It was nearly 4 A.M. on a Monday, and she was mentally exhausted but too jumpy to sleep. She took a deep breath, sat back in her chair, drank cold coffee from the cup that had been sitting there for hours. Caffeine; that'll help the old nerves, smart girl.

The detective room was quiet, just her and a D II named Balsam pecking away at an antiquated computer. Balsam was Petra's age but carried himself like an old man. Old man's taste in music, too. He'd brought a boom box, but it wasn't booming. Tuned to an easy-listening station. Some eighties hair-band song redone with strings and a harp. Petra was transported to a department-store elevator. *Women's sportswear, floor three . . .*

Her notes on Baby Boy were spread out before her, and she gathered them up, began replacing them in the folder. Making sure each page was in its right place. You couldn't be too careful . . .

What difference did it make? This one wasn't going to close anytime in the near future.

Her phone rang. "Connor."

"Detective?" said a male voice.

"Yes, this is Detective Connor."

"Good, this is Officer Saldinger. I'm over at Western and Franklin, and we could use one of you guys."

"What's the problem?" said Petra.

"Your line of work," said Saldinger. "Lots of blood."

8 After Robin's drop-in, our contact was limited to polite phone calls and forwarded mail accompanied by even more polite notes. If she needed to talk about Baby Boy or anything else of substance, she'd found another audience.

I thought about visiting Spike. I'd adopted him, but he ended up disdaining me and competing for Robin's attention. No custody struggle, I knew the score. Still, from time to time I missed his little bulldog face, the comical egotism, the awe-inspiring gluttony.

Maybe soon.

I'd heard nothing about the murder since Petra's first call, and weeks later, I spotted her name in the paper.

Triple slaying in the parking lot of a dance club off Franklin Boulevard. Three A.M. ambush of a carload of Armenian gang members from Glendale, by members of a rival faction from East Hollywood. Petra and a partner I didn't know, a detective named Eric Stahl, had arrested a fifteen-year-old shooter and a sixteen-year-old driver after "a prolonged investigation."

Prolonged meant the case had probably opened shortly after Baby Boy's death.

Petra spending her time on something she could solve?

Maybe so, but she was driven; failure would stick in her gut.

For the next few weeks, I concentrated on spending time with Allison, helping kids, banking some income. One consultation kept me particularly busy: a two-year-old girl accidentally shot in the leg by her four-year-old brother. Lots of family complications, no easy answers, but things finally seemed to be settling down.

I convinced Allison to take off some time, and we spent a four-day weekend at the San Ysidro Ranch in Montecito, imbibing sun and great food. When we drove back to L.A. I convinced myself I was doing okay on all fronts.

The day after I got back, Milo phoned, and said, "Don't you sound chipper."

"Been working on chipper."

"Don't overdo it," he said. "Wouldn't want you to forget the morose underpinnings of our relationship."

"God forbid," I said. "What's up?"

"Something decidedly un-chipper. I've got a weird one, so naturally I thought of you."

"Weird in what way?"

"Apparently motiveless, but we psychologically astute types know better, don't we? An artist—a painter—murdered the night of her big opening. Last Saturday. Someone strangled her. Ligature—thin, with corrugations, probably a wound metal wire."

"Sexual assault?"

"There was some posing but no evidence of assault. You have time?"

"For you, always."

He asked me to meet him for lunch at Café Moghul, an Indian restaurant on Santa Monica, a few blocks from the West L.A. station. The place turned out to be a storefront blocked by gilt-flecked, madras curtains. An unmarked Ford LTD was parked near the entrance in a Loading Only space, and cheap plastic sunglasses that I recognized as Milo's sat atop the dashboard.

The place was magenta-walled and hung with machined tapestries of huge-eyed, nutmeg-skinned people and spire-topped temples. An ultra-soprano voice sang plaintively. The air was a mix of curry and anise.

A sixtyish woman in a sari greeted me. "He's over there." Pointing to a table along the rear wall. No need for guidance; Milo was the only customer.

In front of him was a quart-sized glass of what looked to be iced tea and a plate of fried things in various geometric shapes. His mouth was full, and he waved and continued masticating. When I reached the table, he half rose, wiped grease from his chin, washed down the baseball-sized bolus that orangutaned his cheeks, and pumped my hand.

"The mixed appetizers combo," he said. "Have some. I ordered entrees for both of us—the chicken tali, comes with rice, lentils, side vegetable, the works. The vegetable's okra. Which is usually about as appealing as snot on toast, but they do it good. Little mango chutney on the side, too."

"Hi," I said.

The shy woman brought a glass, poured me tea, and departed.

"Iced and spiced, lots of cloves," he said, "I took liberty there, too."

"How nice to be nurtured."

"How would I know?" He reached for a triangular pastry, muttered, "Samosa," and gazed at me from under heavily lidded, bright green eyes. Since Robin had moved out, I'd been trying to convince him I was okay. He claimed to believe me, but his body language said he was reserving judgment.

"No nurturance for the poor detective?" I said.

"Don't want it. Too tough." He winked.

"How're you doing?" I said, mostly to prevent him from focusing on my mood.

"The world's falling apart but I'm fine."

"Freelancing's still fun?"

"I wouldn't call it that."

"What would you call it?"

"Bureaucratically sanctioned isolation. I'm not allowed to have fun." He bared his teeth in what I knew was a smile; someone else might have taken it for hostility. I watched him toss another appetizer down his gullet and drink more tea.

Last year, he'd run afoul of the police chief before the chief retired, managed to play some cards, and ended up with a lieutenant's title and salary but not the desk job that came with promotion.

Effectively banished from the robbery-homicide room, he was given his own windowless office down the hall—a converted interrogation space, figurative miles from the other detectives. His official title was "clearance officer" for unsolved homicide cases. Basically, that meant deciding which cold files to pursue and which to ignore. The good news was relative independence. The bad news was no built-in backup or departmental support.

Now he was working a fresh case. I figured there was a back story, and he'd tell me when he was ready.

He looked in good trim, and the clarity in his eyes suggested he'd stuck to his resolution to cut down on the booze. He'd also resolved to start walking for exercise, but the last few times I'd seen him, he'd griped about his instep.

Today, he had on a coarse, brown, herringbone sport coat way too heavy for a California spring, a once-white wash-and-wear shirt and a green polyblend tie embroidered with blue dragons. His black hair was freshly cut in the usual style: long and shaggy on top, cropped tight at the temples. Sideburns, now snow-white, reached the bottoms of his fleshy ears. He called them his skunk stripes. The restaurant's lighting was kind to his complexion, rendering some of the acne pits as craggy contours.

He said, "The artist's name was Juliet Kipper, known as Julie. Thirty-two, divorced, a painter in oils. As they say."

"Who says?"

"Arty types. That's the way they talk. A painter in oils, a sculptor in bronze, an etcher in drypoint. Paintings are 'pictures' or 'images,' one 'makes' art, blah blah blah. Anyway, Julie Kipper: apparently she was gifted, won a bunch of awards in college, went on for an MFA at the Rhode Island School of Design and attracted New York gallery attention soon after graduation. She sold a few canvases, seemed to be moving forward, then things tightened up, and she ran into financial problems. She moved out here seven years ago, did commercial illustration for ad agencies to earn a living. A year ago, she got serious again about fine art, found herself gallery representation, took part in a couple of group shows, did okay. Last Saturday was her first solo show since she left New York."

"Which gallery?"

"Place called Light and Space. It's a cooperative run by a bunch of artists who use it mostly to showcase their own stuff. But they also support what they call distinctive talent, and Julie Kipper was deemed as such by their review committee. I get the feeling these people don't earn a living by their art. Most of them have day jobs. Julie had to pay for her own party—cheese and crackers and cheap wine, a jazz trio. About fifty people drifted in and out during the evening and six of the fifteen paintings were red-dotted—that means 'sold' in art lingo. They actually put little red dots on the title tag."

"Any of the co-op members twang your antenna?"

"They come across as a peace-loving bunch, nothing but good words about Julie, but who knows?"

Julie. Calling the victim by her first name early in the game. He'd bonded with this one. I said, "What happened?"

"Someone ambushed her in the ladies' room of the gallery. After hours. Close confines—just a sink and a toilet and a mirror. There was a bump on the back of her head—coroner says not serious enough to knock her out, but the skin was broken and traces of her blood were found on the rim of the sink. Coroner's guess is she was thrashing and her head knocked against it."

"Anyone else's blood?"

"I should be so lucky."

"A struggle," I said. "How big a woman was she?"

"Small," he said. "Five-four, hundred and ten."

"Any skin under her fingernails?"

"Not a molecule, but we did find some talcum powder. As in the stuff they use inside rubber gloves."

"If that's what it means," I said, "it implies careful preparation. How long after hours did it happen?"

"The show closed at ten, and Julie stayed behind to clean up. One of the co-op artists helped her, a woman named CoCo Barnes. Who I don't see as a suspect because A, she's in her seventies and B, she's the size of a garden troll. Just after eleven, Barnes went back to check and found Julie."

"Is she hard of hearing, as well?" I said. "All that thrashing around?"

"No mystery there, Alex. The gallery's one big front room, but the bathrooms are out back, separated by a solid-core door that leads to a small vestibule and a storage area that feeds to a rear alley door. Plus the bathroom door's also solid. Top of that, there was music playing. Not the jazz combo, they'd already packed out. But Julie had brought a stereo system and backup tapes for when the band took breaks. She switched it on while they straightened. Barnes not hearing a thing makes total sense."

The smiling woman brought shallow, round stainless-steel trays crowded with small saucerlike dishes. Basmati rice, lentils, green salad, okra, nan bread, tandoori chicken. A ramekin of mango chutney.

"Nice variety, huh?" said Milo, picking up a chicken wing.

"You're assuming the killer got in through the alley. Was the rear door forced?"

"Nope."

"How soon after ten did Julie go back to the bathroom?"

"CoCo can't recall. She remembers realizing Julie'd been gone for a while just before she checked. But the two of them had been busy cleaning. Finally, she had to go herself, made her way back there and knocked on the bathroom door and when Julie didn't answer, she opened it."

"Self-locking bathroom?"

He thought. "Yeah, one of those push-button dealies."

"So the killer chose not to lock up."

"Or forgot."

"Someone who brings gloves and ambushes his victim would remember."

He rubbed his face. "Okay, so what's the insight?"

"Showing off," I said. "Aiming for display. You said there was sexual positioning."

"Panties down to the ankles, legs spread, knees propped. No bruising or entry. Lying on her back between the toilet and sink. She had to be squeezed in there—it's not how you'd fall naturally." He brushed hair off his brow, resumed eating.

"What was her mood that night?"

"CoCo Barnes says she was flying high because of how well she'd done."

"Six out of fifteen paintings sold."

"Apparently that's great."

"Flying high," I said. "With or without aid?"

He put down his fork. "Why do you ask?"

"You said Julie's career flagged after her initial success. I'm wondering if personal habits got in the way."

He picked up what remained of the chicken wing, studied it, began crunching bones. He must've ground them fine enough to swallow, because nothing emerged. "Yeah, she had problems. As long as we're at it, Dr. Clairvoyant, got any stock tips?"

"Stash your money in the mattress."

"Thanks, . . . yeah, back in her New York days, she messed around with cocaine and alcohol. Talked openly about it, all the other co-op artists knew. But everyone I've talked to so far says she'd straightened up. I tossed her apartment myself and the most addictive thing in her medicine chest was Midol. Strongest thing in her system the night she was killed, according to the coroner, was aspirin. So it looks like she *was* flying on self-esteem."

"Until someone brought her down," I said. "And planned the fall carefully. Someone familiar enough with the gallery to know the bathroom would be a relatively safe place to get the job done. Is there any indication Julie arranged to meet someone after the party?"

"She didn't mention any appointment to anyone, and her book was clear except for the party."

"Posing but no assault. That could be someone wanted to make it look sexual."

"That's the vibe I get. The whole thing is too damned contrived for a rape-murder."

"Almost like an art piece," I said. "Performance art."

His jaws bunched.

I said, "Why'd you take this one?"

"Personal favor. Her family knew my family back in Indiana. Her dad worked steel with my dad. Actually, he was one of the guys my dad supervised on the line. He's dead, and so is Julie's mother, but the dad's brother—Julie's uncle—flew out to ID the body, got hold of me, and asked me to take it. Last thing I wanted was something with a personal connection, but what choice did I have? The guy was coming on like I was some goddamn Sherlock."

"You're famous in Indiana."

"Oh, joy," he said, forking a wad of okra, then changing his mind and flipping the gooey mess back on the plate.

"Was the wire ligament left behind?"

"No, that was the coroner's surmise from the marks on her neck. It sliced through the skin, but the killer took the time to remove it. We canvassed the area, found nothing."

"More careful planning," I said. "This is a smart one."

"Ain't we got fun."

9 We finished up and got into my car and Milo directed me to Light and Space's address on Carmelina, just north of Pico. I knew the neighborhood: storage facilities, auto body shops and small factories, just a stroll from L.A.'s western border with the city of Santa Monica. If Julie Kipper had been strangled a couple of blocks away, her uncle's appeal to Milo would've been futile.

As I drove, Milo balanced a toothpick between the tips of his index fingers and radar-scanned the passing world with cop's eyes. "Been a while since we did this, huh?"

Over the past few months we'd seen each other less and less. I'd put it down to his backlog of cold files and my workload. That was denial. There was mutual isolation going on. "Guess, you didn't have enough weird ones."

"Matter of fact, that's true," he said. "Just the usual, and I don't trouble you with the usual." A second later: "You doing all right? In general?"

"Everything's fine."

"Good." A block later: "So . . . everything with Allison's . . . things are working out?"

"Allison's wonderful," I said.

"Well, that's good." He picked his teeth, kept surveilling the city.

His first contacts with Allison had been professional: wrapping up the Ingalls file. She told me he'd been deft and compassionate.

His first reaction upon hearing that we were seeing each other had been silence. Then: *She's gorgeous, I'll grant you that.*

I'd thought: What won't you grant me? Then I figured I was being touchy and kept my mouth shut. A few weeks later, I cooked dinner for four at my place: a mild March evening, steaks and baked potatoes and red wine out on the terrace. Milo and Rick Silverman, Allison and me.

The surprise was Allison and Rick knew each other. One of her patients had been brought into the Cedars-Sinai ER after a car wreck and Rick had been the surgeon on duty.

They talked shop, I played host, Milo ate and fidgeted. Toward the end of the evening, he drew me aside. "Nice girl, Alex. Not that you need my approval." Sounding as if someone had prodded him to make the speech.

Since then, he'd seldom mentioned her.

"A few more blocks," he said. "How's the pooch?"

"I hear he's fine."

A moment later: "Robin and I got together a couple of times for coffee."

Surprise, surprise.

"Nothing wrong with that," I said.

"You're pissed."

"Why would I be pissed?"

"You sound pissed."

"I'm not pissed. Where do I turn?"

"Two more blocks, then a right," he said. "Okay, I keep my trap Crazy-Glued shut. Even though all these years you've been telling me I should express my feelings."

"Express away," I said.

"That guy she's with—"

"He has a name. Tim."

"Tim's a wimp."

"Give it up, Milo."

"Give what up?"

"Reconciliation fantasies."

"I—"

"When you saw her was she pining for me?"

Silence.

"Whoa," he said.

"Right turn here?"

"Yeah."

Light and Space's neighbors were a plating plant and a wholesaler of plastic signs. The gallery's warehouse origins were obvious: brick-faced, tar-roofed, three segmented steel overhead doors in front, instead of a window. Black plastic letters above the central door read LIGHT AND SPACE: AN ART PLACE. Stout combination locks secured the outer doors but the one in the middle was held in place by a single dead bolt that responded to a key on Milo's ring. He pushed, and the metal panel slid upward into a pocket.

"They gave you a key?" I said.

"My honest face," he said, stepping inside and flicking on lights.

The interior was five thousand square feet or so. Walls painted that vanilla white that brings out the best in art, gray cement floors, twenty-foot ceilings thatched by ductwork, high-focus spotlights fixed upon several large, unframed canvases.

No furniture except for a desk up front, bearing brochures and a CD player. The nearest wall was lettered in the same black plastic used on the outside of the building.

Juliet Kipper
Air and Image

Same title on the brochures. I picked one up, skimmed a few paragraphs of art-speak, flipped to a black-and-white headshot of the artist.

Juliet Kipper had posed in a black turtleneck and no jewelry, her face pallid against a gray matte background. Squarish face, not unpretty under chopped, platinum hair. Pale eyes, deep-set and watchful, challenged the camera. Her mouth was grim—tugged down at the corners. High, uneven bangs exposed a furrowed forehead. Concentrating hard. Or burdened. She'd made an effort to look the part of the troubled artist, or it had come naturally.

Milo was pacing the gallery, setting off echoes as he drifted from painting to painting. I began doing the same.

A smug psycho-prediction of Julie Kipper's art based upon the cheerlessness of her photo would have fallen flat. She'd created fifteen luminous landscapes, exuberantly colorful and textured, each marked by a master's control of composition and light.

Sere arroyos, fog-shrouded, razor-hewn mountains, furious waterfalls emptying to mirror-glass streams, deep green forests pierced by gilded bursts that promised distant discovery. Two ocean nocturnes were livened by cerulean blue heavens and lemon moonglow that turned the tide to froth. Every painting bore the confident brushstrokes of someone who'd known how to move pigment around the canvas. Layers of color seemed to fluoresce; in lesser hands, the work would've veered into tourist kitsch.

Prices ranged from two to four thousand. I examined the canvases with another eye, searching for familiar locales, but finding none. Then I read the title tags: *Dream I, Dream II, Dream III* . . .

Juliet Kipper had created her own terrain.

I said, "To my eye, she was a major talent." My voice bounced around the near-empty space.

Milo said, "I like her stuff, too, but what do I know? C'mon, let me show you where she died."

The bathroom was too small for both of us, and Milo waited outside as I checked out the grimy spot where Juliet Kipper had been strangled.

A nasty little space, windowless, dank. Cracked sink, oxidized spigots. Black threads of mold curled in the corners.

With all that dirt, the series of faint brown smudges on the cement floor would've escaped my notice if I hadn't known better.

I backed out of the room and Milo showed me the rest of the rear space. A large storage area to the left was filled with unframed paintings and office supplies and random pieces of cheap-looking furniture. The men's room was no more generous or attractive.

The gallery's rear door was striped by a push bolt.

"Another self-locking mechanism," I said. "Another deliberate attempt to invite discovery."

"Exhibitionist."

"But he keeps it in check. Someone very measured."

He pushed the bolt, propped the door open with a block of wood left there for that purpose, and we exited the building. An asphalt strip was backed by a ten-foot block wall. A Dumpster took up the far corner.

"What's on the other side of the wall?"

"Parking lot of a plumbing supplies outfit. The ground's higher on their side—two feet or so, but it would still be a climb. And there'd be no reason for the killer to scale it because all he had to do was walk right in." He led me around the north side of the gallery and pointed down another tarred passageway that bordered the plating plant and opened to the street. Fumes rose from the plant; the air smelled lethal.

"Not much security," I said.

"Why would a bunch of artists need any?"

We returned to the propped-open door, and I had a closer look at the lock.

"Same key as the front?"

"Yup."

"I assume all the co-op members have keys."

"Access is no mystery, Alex. Motive is. Like I said, I've already talked to all the co-op members, and none of them even remotely twangs my antenna. Fourteen out of twenty are women and of the six guys, three are of CoCo's vintage. The young ones seem like your basic, head-in-the-clouds creative type. We're talking the Venice crowd, here. Make art, not war. No one's being evasive. I ran checks on all of them, anyway. Clean. I've been fooled too often to think it can't happen again, but I'm just not picking up any serious vibes from this bunch."

We reentered the gallery, and I had another look at Julie Kipper's paintings.

Beautiful.

I wasn't sure that meant much in the art world, but it meant something to me, and I wanted to cry.

I said, "When was she divorced?"

"Ten years ago. Three years before she moved out here."

"Who's the ex?"

"Guy named Everett Kipper," he said. "He used to be an artist, too. They met at Rhode Island, but he switched careers."

"She kept his name."

"Julie told people the split was amicable. And Kipper was at the opening. Everyone I spoke to said they looked friendly."

"What career did he switch to?"

"Bond broker."

"From art to finance," I said. "Does he pay alimony?"

"Her bankbook shows monthly deposits of two grand, and she has no other obvious means of support."

"So with her gone, he saves twenty-four grand a year."

"Yeah, yeah, like any spouse he's the first suspect," he said. "I've got an appointment to talk to him in an hour."

"He's local?"

"Lives in South Pasadena, works in Century City."

"Why so long to get to him?"

"We played phone tag. I'm heading over there, next." He fingered the knot of his tie. "Businesslike enough for Avenue of the Stars?"

"No business I'd want a part of."

As we returned to the Seville, an old blue VW bus drove up to the gallery. SAVE THE WETLANDS sticker on the rear bumper. Above that: ART IS LIFE. A tiny white-haired woman sat low in the driver's seat. A yellow-and-brown dog on the passenger side stared at the windshield.

The woman waved. "Yoo-hoo, Detective!" and we approached the bus.

"Ms. Barnes," said Milo. "What's up?" He introduced me to CoCo Barnes, and she gripped my hand with what felt like a sparrow's talon.

"Just came by to see if you got in okay." Barnes glanced at the gallery's frontage. The dog remained in place, dull-eyed but tight-jawed. Big dog with a graybeard muzzle. Bits of dry leaves specked its coat.

I chanced petting the animal. It licked my hand.

Milo said, "We got in fine."

"You're all finished up in there?" CoCo Barnes's voice was scratchy, veering toward abrasive, tempered by a Southern inflection. She looked to be seventy. The white hair was cut in a boyish cap and trimmed unceremoniously. Her skin was the color and consistency of well-roasted chicken. Slate gray eyes—more acute than the dog's, but filmy, nonetheless—checked me out.

"What's his name?" I said.

"Lance."

"Nice dog."

"If he likes you." CoCo Barnes turned to Milo. "Any progress on Julie?"

"It's still early in the investigation, ma'am."

The old woman frowned. "Didn't I hear something about if you don't solve it quickly, you probably won't solve it at all?"

"It's not that simple, ma'am."

CoCo Barnes ruffled Lance's neck. "I'm glad I caught you, it saves me a phone call. Remember how you asked me to think about anything unusual that happened Saturday night, and I said there'd been nothing, it had just been your typical opening? Well, I thought about it some more, and there was something. Not at night and not at the opening, strictly speaking. And I'm not sure it's really what you're after."

"What happened?" said Milo.

"This was *before* the opening," said Barnes. "The day of the opening, around 2 P.M. Julie wasn't even here, yet. Just me and Lance, here. Clark Van Alstrom was here, too—the man who does those aluminum stabiles?"

Milo nodded.

CoCo Barnes said, "I brought Clark along because I can't lift that metal door by myself. Once I got in, Clark left, and I started setting up. Making sure everything was in order—a few months ago we had a power outage, and that was no good." She smiled. "Especially because the artist worked in neon . . . Anyway, I was checking things out, and I heard Lance bark. That doesn't happen often. He's a *very* quiet boy."

She smiled at the dog. Lance made a low, contented sound. "I'd set up a water bowl for him at the back, in the hallway near where Julie—just outside the bathrooms—but I'd left the door to the vestibule open, and I could hear him barking. He doesn't have much of a bark, mind you, he's fourteen years old and his vocal cords are pretty shot. What he produces is more of a cough." She demonstrated with a series of dry hacks. Lance's eyes shifted to her, but he remained inert. "He just kept it up, wouldn't stop, and I went back there to see what was wrong. By the time I got there he'd shlepped himself up on his feet and was facing the back door. I wondered if he'd heard rats—we'd had some rat problems a couple of seasons ago, an opening that was absolutely disastrous, where's the Pied Piper of Hamlin when you need him—so . . . where was I . . . oh, yes, I opened the door and had a look out back and there were no rats. But there was a woman. Foraging in the Dumpster. Obviously homeless, obviously quite mad."

"Mad as in angry?" said Milo.

"Mad as in disturbed, psychotic, mentally ill. I abhor labels, but sometimes they do get the picture across. This one was mad as the proverbial chapeau maker."

"You could tell this by—"

"Her eyes, for starts," said Barnes. "Wild eyes—scared eyes. Jumping all over the place." She tried to demonstrate with her own gray orbs, but they moved lazily. Blinking several times, as if to clear them, she turned to Lance and scratched behind his ear, and said, "Easy now, you're a *good* boy . . . then there was the way she carried herself, her clothes—mismatched, oversized, too many layers for the weather. I've lived in Venice for fifty-three years, Detective. I've seen enough mental illness to know it when it stares me in the face. Then, of course, there was the foraging. The moment the door opened she jumped back, lost her balance, and nearly fell. Such fear. I said, 'If you wait right here, I'll fetch you something to eat.' But she raised her hand to her mouth, chewed her knuckles, and ran off. They do that a lot, you know. Turn down food. Some of them even get hostile when you try to help them. They've got voices blabbering in their heads, telling them who-knows-what. Can you blame them for not trusting?"

She ruffled the dog some more. "It's probably nothing, but in view of what happened to Julie I don't suppose we can be too complacent."

"No we can't, ma'am. What else can you tell me about this woman?" said Milo.

The old woman's eyes sparked. "So you do think it's important?"

"At this stage, everything's important. I appreciate your telling me."

"Well, that's good to know. Because I almost *didn't* tell you, being as it was a woman and my assumption was a man killed Julie—the way she was . . ." The old woman's eyes clamped shut, then fluttered open. "I'm still trying to rid myself of the image . . . not that this woman couldn't have overpowered Julie. She was large—maybe six feet tall. Built big, too. Though with all that clothing, it was hard to tell, precisely. And we were only face-to-face for a second or so."

"Big bones," said Milo.

"Sturdy—almost masculine."

"Could it have been a man dressed up as a—"

Barnes laughed. "No, no, this one was pure girl all right. But a big girl. A lot bigger than Julie. Which got me thinking. It needn't have been a man at all, right? Especially if we're dealing with someone not in their right mind."

Milo's pad was out. "How old would you say she was?"

"I'd guess thirties, but it's a guess because that kind of misery—homelessness, mental illness—it overrides age, doesn't it?"

"In what way, ma'am?"

"What I mean," said Barnes, "is that people like that *all* look ancient and damaged—there's a coating of despair. This one, though, she'd managed to hold on to some of her youth; under the grime I could see some youth. I can't explain it any better than that."

CoCo Barnes ticked a finger. "In terms of other details, she wore a thick, padded military-type camouflage jacket over a red, black, and white flannel shirt over a blue UCLA sweatshirt. UCLA in white letters, the C was half-gone. On the bottom were heavy-duty gray sweatpants, and from the way they bulked, she had on at least one other pair of pants underneath. White, lace-up tennis shoes on her feet and a broad-brimmed black straw hat atop her head. The brim was shredded in front—pieces of straw coming loose. Her hair was bunched up in the hat, but some had come loose, and it was red. And curly. Curly red hair. Add a layer of grime to all of that, and you've got the picture."

Milo scribbled. "Ever see her before?"

"No," said Barnes. "Not on the walkway or kicking around the alleys in Venice or in Ocean Front Park or anywhere else you see the homeless. Maybe she's not one of the locals."

"Is there anything else you remember about the encounter?"

"It wasn't much of an encounter, Detective. I opened the door, she got scared, I offered to get her some food, she ran off."

Milo scanned his notes. "You've got a great memory, Ms. Barnes."

"You should've known me a few years ago." The old woman tapped her forehead. "I'm accustomed to taking mental snapshots. We artists view the world with a high-focus lens." Two rapid blinks. "If I hadn't chickened out of my cataract surgery, I'd be doing a lot better."

"Let me ask you this, ma'am: Could you draw me a picture of this woman? I'm sure it would be better than anything our police artist would come up with."

Barnes suppressed a surprised smile. "Haven't drawn in a while. Shifted to ceramics a few years ago, but, sure, why not? I'll do it and call you."

"Appreciate it, ma'am."

"Civic duty and art," said Barnes. "All in one swoop."

As I drove back to Café Moghul, I said, "How seriously do you take it?"

"You don't?"

"CoCo Barnes has cataracts, so who knows what she really saw. I still think the murder smacks of planning and intelligence. Someone well composed mentally. But that's just a guess, not science."

He frowned. "Tracking this redhead down means getting hold of the patrol officers where the homeless hang out, dealing with the social service agencies and the treatment centers. And if Barnes is right about the redhead not being local, I can't limit myself to the Westside."

"One thing in your favor," I said, "a six-foot woman with curly red hair isn't inconspicuous."

"Assuming I find her, then what? What I've got is a probable psychotic who Dumpster-dove in the alley five hours before Julie got strangled." He shook his head. "How seriously am I taking it? Not very."

A block later: "On the other hand . . ."

"What?"

"If I don't turn up anything else, soon, I can't afford *not* to chase it down."

I pulled up alongside the loading zone in front of the restaurant. A parking ticket was folded under the windshield wiper of his unmarked. He said, "Want to meet Everett Kipper?"

"Sure."

He eyed the citation. "You drive—long as I'm renting, I might as well occupy."

"Will the city reimburse me?"

"Oh, sure. I'll FedEx you a box of infinite gratitude."

Everett Kipper worked at a firm called MuniScope, on the twenty-first floor of a steel-and-concrete high-rise on Avenue of the Stars just south of little Santa Monica. Parking fees were stiff, but Milo's badge impressed the attendant, and I stashed the Seville for free.

The building's lobby was arena-sized, serviced by a dozen elevators. We rode up in hermetic silence. MuniScope's reception room was ovoid, paneled in bleached bird's-eye maple, softly lit and carpeted, and ringed by saffron leather modules. Milo's badge elicited alarm from the hard-faced, hard-bodied receptionist. Then she recovered and compensated with toothy graciousness.

"I'll ring him right away, gentlemen. Can I get you something to drink? Coffee, tea, Sprite, Diet Coke?"

We demurred and sank down in yellow-orange leather. Down-filled cushions. No corners in the egg-shaped space. I felt like a privileged unborn chick nestled in high-rent surroundings.

Milo muttered, "Cushy."

I said, "Put the client at ease. It works. I'm ready to peck through the shell and buy something."

A man in a black suit appeared from around a convex wall. "Detectives? Ev Kipper."

Julie Kipper's ex was a thin man with a big voice, a blond-gray crew cut and the smooth round face of an aging frat boy. Forty or so, five-eight, one-fifty. His bouncy stride suggested gymnastics or ballet training. The suit was a four-button model, tailored snug, set off by a sapphire blue shirt, gold tie, gold cuff links, gold wristwatch. His hands were manicured and smooth and outsized, and when we shook, I felt barely suppressed strength in his grip. Dry palms. Clear, brown eyes that made eye contact. A subtle bronze veneer to his complexion said outdoor sports or the tanning bed.

"Let's go in and talk," he said. Confident baritone, not a trace of anxiety. If he'd murdered his former spouse, he was one hell of a psychopath.

He took us to an empty boardroom with a view all the way to Vegas. Oyster-colored carpeting and walls, and a black granite conference table more than large enough for the thirty Biedermeier-revival chairs that surrounded it. The three of us huddled at one end.

"Sorry it took so long to get together," said Kipper. "What can I help you with?"

Milo said, "Is there anything about your ex-wife we should know? Anything that would help us figure out who strangled her?"

Putting emphasis on *wife* and *strangled* and watching Kipper's face.

Kipper said, "God, no. Julie was a wonderful person."

"You've maintained contact, despite the divorce ten years ago."

"Life took us in other directions. We've remained friends."

"Other directions professionally?"

"Yes," said Kipper.

Milo sat back. "Are you remarried?"

Kipper smiled. "No, still looking for Ms. Right."

"Your ex-wife wasn't her."

"Julie's world was art. Mine is slogging through bond prospectuses. We started off in the same place but ended up too far apart."

"Did you study painting in Rhode Island?"

"Sculpting." Kipper touched the face of his watch. The timepiece was thin as a nickel with an exposed skeleton movement. Four diamonds placed equidistant around the rim, crocodile band. I tried to estimate how many paintings Julie Kipper would have had to sell to afford it.

"Sounds like you've been researching me, Detective."

"Your marriage came up while talking to people who knew her, sir. People seem to know about your artistic origins."

"The Light and Space bunch?" said Kipper. "Sad crowd."

"How so, sir?"

"Maximally self-labeling, minimally talented."

"Self-labeling?"

"They *call* themselves artists," said Kipper. New edge in his voice. "Julie was the real thing, they're not. But that's true of the art world in general. There are no criteria—it's not like being a surgeon. Lots of pretense."

The brown eyes shifted down to his oversized hands. Square fingers, glossy nails. A well-tended hand. Hard to imagine it working a chisel, and the look in Kipper's eyes said he knew it. "That was my story."

"You were pretending?" said Milo.

"For a while. Then I gave it up." Kipper smiled. "I sucked."

"You were good enough to get into the Rhode Island School of Design."

"Well, what do you think of that?" said Kipper. Another layer of silk had been peeled from his voice. "Like I said, there are no criteria. What Julie and I had in common was we both won awards in high school and college. The only difference was, she deserved hers. I always felt like an impostor. I'm not saying I'm a total boob. I can do things with wood and stone and bronze the average person can't. But that's a far cry from art. I was smart enough to realize that, and got into something that fits me."

Milo glanced around the room. "Any artistic satisfaction in this?"

"Not a whit," said Kipper. "But I make a fortune and indulge my fantasies on Sunday—home studio. Most of the time my stuff never gets out of clay. Smashing it can be quite cathartic."

His face remained unlined, but his color had deepened.

Milo said, "How did your ex-wife feel about your switching careers?"

"That was years ago, how can it be relevant?" said Kipper.

"At this point, everything is, sir. Please bear with me."

"How'd she feel? She hated it, tried to talk me out of it. Which tells you something about Julie—her integrity. We were living like paupers in a hovel on the Lower East Side, doing odd jobs. Julie tried to tele-market magazine subscriptions, and I did janitorial duty in the building to make the rent. The day I got into finance was the first time we could count on a stable income. And not much of one, at that. I started off gofering for chump change at Morgan Stanley. But even that was a step up. Now we could buy food. But Julie couldn't have cared less. She kept yelling at me—I was talented, had sold out. I don't think she ever forgave me—not until she moved out here and looked me up and we reconnected. At that point, I think she could see that I was really happy."

"You moved here first."

"A year before Julie. After we divorced."

"And she looked you up."

"She called my office. She was really down—about failing to make it in New York, about having to draw stupid newspaper ads. She was also broke. I helped her out."

"On top of the alimony."

Kipper exhaled. "No big deal. Like I said, I do very well."

"So give me the chronology," said Milo. "Marriage, divorce, et cetera."

"Sum my life up in one sentence, huh?"

"A few sentences, sir."

Kipper unbuttoned his suit jacket. "We met right after we got to Rhode Island. Instant chemistry, within a week were living together. After graduation, we moved to New York and got married—fourteen years ago. Four years later, we got divorced."

"After the divorce, what was your contact with your ex-wife?" Milo'd avoided using Julie's name in Kipper's presence. Emphasizing the severed relationship.

Kipper said, "Our contact was occasional phone calls, even more occasional dinners."

"Friendly phone calls?"

"For the most part." Kipper's finger massaged the watch face. "I see where this is going. Which is fine. My buddies told me I'd be looked at as a suspect."

"Your buddies?"

"Some of the other brokers."

"They have experience with the criminal justice system?"

Kipper laughed. "Not yet. No, they watch too much TV. I suppose I'm wasting my time telling you I had nothing to do with it."

Milo smiled.

Kipper said, "Do what you have to do but know this: I loved Julie—first as a woman, later as a person. She was my friend, and I'm the last one who'd ever hurt her. I have no reason to hurt her." He slid his chair back several inches, crossed his legs.

"Friendly phone calls about what?" said Milo.

"Letting each other know what we were up to," said Kipper. "And I guess what you'd term business calls, too. Around tax time. I needed to account the alimony and any other money I sent Julie. And sometimes she needed extra."

"How much extra?"

"A bit here and there—maybe another ten, twenty grand a year."

"Twenty would be almost double her alimony."

"Julie wasn't good about money. She tended to get into tight spots."

"Trouble living within her means?"

Kipper's big hands lowered to the granite surface of the table and lay flat. "Julie wasn't good with money because she didn't care about it."

"So in total, you were giving her nearly forty thousand a year. Generous."

"I drive a Ferrari," said Kipper. "I don't expect any merit badges." His body shifted forward. "Let me explain Julie's history to you: Right after graduation she had an initial burst of success. Got placed in a high-quality group show at a midtown gallery and sold every single painting. She got great critical notice, too, but guess what: It didn't mean she made serious money. Her canvases were priced from eight to twelve hundred dollars, and by the time the gallery owner and her agent and every other gimme-type took their cuts, there was maybe enough to buy lunch at Tavern on the Green. The gallery kicked her price up to fifteen hundred a picture and told her to get productive. She spent the next six months working. Twenty-four hours a day, or it seemed that way." He winced.

"Tough regimen," said Milo.

"More like self-destruction."

"She have help keeping up her energy?"

"What do you mean?" said Kipper.

"We know about her drug problem. Is that when it started? Cocaine can be an energizer."

"Coke," said Kipper. "She was into it way before that—in college. But yes, it got intense when the gallery demanded she make instant art at an inhuman pace."

"What pace was that?"

"A dozen canvases within four months. A crap-monger could have splashed that together, no problem, but Julie was meticulous. Ground her own pigments, laid on layer after layer of paint, alternated with her own special glazes and varnishes. Was so picky that she sometimes made her own brushes. Could spend weeks making brushes. And frames. Each one had to be original—perfect for the painting. Everything had to be perfect. Everything became a project of immense significance."

"Her current works have no frames," I said.

"I saw that," said Kipper. "Asked her about it. She said she was concentrating on the image itself. I told her it was a good idea." One hand closed in a fist. "Julie was brilliant, but I don't know if she would have ever achieved real success."

"Why not?"

"Because she was *too* talented. What passes for art now is pure shit. Video-installations, 'performances,' crap put together with 'found materials'—which is art-bullshit language for garbage-picking. Nowadays, if you staple a dildo to a pop bottle you're Michelangelo. If you actually know how to draw, you're disparaged. Add to that Julie's absolute lack of business sense and . . ." Kipper's shoulders sagged. His black suit didn't pop a wrinkle.

"Not of this world," I said.

"Exactly," said Kipper. "She wasn't keyed into her surroundings. Take the money thing, for example. I tried to get her to invest some of the alimony in low-risk bond funds. If she'd started investing back when I did, she'd have built up a nice little nest egg, could have plied her art in the way she wanted. Instead, she had to lower herself by doing commercial gigs."

"She didn't like commercial art."

"She hated it," said Kipper. "But she refused to take the steps that would've freed her. I won't say she was masochistic, but Julie definitely had a thing for suffering. She was never really happy."

"Chronically depressed?" I said.

"Except when she was painting."

"Let's go back for a moment," said Milo, thumbing through his pad. "The New York gallery that took her on—the résumé on her brochure lists The Anthony Gallery—"

"That's the one. Bloodsucking Lewis Anthony."

"Not a nice man?"

"Few of them are," said Kipper.

"Gallery owners."

"Owners, agents, collectors." Both of Kipper's big hands had balled. "The so-called art world. We're talking profoundly ungifted people—people so far from personal talent they wouldn't recognize it if it chomped their gonads—living off the fruit of the gifted. Leeches on the body artistic. That's what Julie and I called them. Talent's a curse. Criminals get judged by their peers, but not artists."

His smooth, round face was deeply flushed.

Milo said, "So Lewis Anthony pressured Julie to produce, and that kicked her coke problem up a notch."

Kipper nodded. "She used coke and speed to keep herself working, booze and tranqs to bring herself down. Unless I forced her to eat and sleep, she didn't. It was hellish. I started staying away. Which was easy because I had my new career. Working my way up the corporate ladder and all that."

"Were you into drugs?"

Kipper hesitated. "I dabbled," he said, finally. "Everyone did, back then. But I never got hooked. I'm not an addictive personality. That probably has something to do with the lack of talent—not enough intensity up here." Touching his crew cut.

"The old genius-insanity link?" said Milo.

"Let me tell you, that's true. Show me a brilliant artist, and I'll show you one serious basket case. And yes, I'm including Julie in that. I loved her, she was a terrific person, but her resting state was turmoil."

Milo tapped the pad. "Tell me more about Lewis Anthony."

"What's to tell? The bastard pressured Julie, Julie doped herself to the gills and produced three canvases. Anthony berated her, sold all three, remitted a pittance back to Julie and told her he couldn't handle her unless she acquired a better work ethic. She came home, OD'd, and ended up in rehab."

Kipper's fingers opened and clawed black granite. "I've always felt guilty about that. Not being there when she needed me. When she came home with the check from Anthony, and I saw how puny it was, I went nuts—just lost it. Six months, watching her self-destruct—she lost twenty pounds preparing for that show—and all she had to show for it was two thousand bucks. I told her she was the chump of all chumps and went out to have a beer. When I came home, I found her stretched out in bed and couldn't revive her. I thought she was dead. I called the paramedics, and they took her to Beth Israel. A few days later, she was transferred to the psych ward at Bellevue."

"Involuntary commitment?" I said.

"For the first few days, whatever the law was. But she stayed there even after she could've left. Told me it was better being in the nut ward than living with someone who didn't care. What could I say? I'd bailed on her. Bellevue cleaned her up and sent her home, and I tried to re-connect with her. It was like talking to a block of stone. She couldn't work—no spark—and that freaked her out. She started doping again, we fought about it. Eventually, I moved out. I was the one who filed the divorce papers, but Julie didn't fight it—didn't do a damn thing to protect herself financially. I volunteered to give her half my income at the time as alimony, which was a thousand bucks a month. My attorney thought I was nuts." Kipper ran his hand through his crew cut. "As things got better for me, I upped it."

"Two thousand a month," said Milo.

"I know," said Kipper. "For a guy with a Ferrari, that's bullshit. But Julie refused to take any more. I offered to rent her a nice house—somewhere she could have a studio. But she insisted on living in that dump."

"The two of you stayed attached."

"Like I said, we had dinner once in a while." Kipper hung his head. "Sometimes we made love—I know that sounds weird, but sometimes chemistry reared its nasty little head. Maybe we were meant for each other. Wouldn't that be a laugh?"

"A laugh?"

"Living in a weird limbo," said Kipper. "I didn't want to cut her out of my life, why would I? And now she's gone. And you're wasting your time, here."

"Sir—"

"Hey," said Kipper, "you've got carte blanche. Come over to my house and tear up the fucking floorboards. But once you're through with that, would you do me a favor and get serious about nailing the motherfucker who really did it? And if you do get him, tell him he's a fucking savage who cut a chunk of beauty out of this fucking world."

Shouting. Red as a beet, the outsized hands white-knuckled.

Kipper exhaled and slumped.

Milo said, "I have a few more questions."

"Yeah, yeah, whatever."

"You attended the opening—"

"I attended and bought two paintings."

"Your ex-wife didn't mind that?"

"Why would she?"

"Being independent and all that," said Milo, "weren't you worried she'd view it as charity?"

"I would've been worried, except that Julie and I had discussed the paintings a while back. I'd seen them at her place and told her I really wanted two. She wanted to give them to me for free, but I refused. I said she should hang them at the show, red-dotted. As a strategic move—this is hot stuff, come and get it."

"How late did you stay at the opening?"

"Until a half hour before closing."

"Which would be?"

"Nine-thirty, -forty."

"Where'd you go after you left?"

"Ah," said Kipper. "The alibi. Well, I don't have one. I got into my car and took a drive. Sepulveda to San Vicente, over to Seventh and down into Santa Monica Canyon. I know the area because there's a gas station that sells 100-octane hi-test gas and a supplement that boosts it to 104. There's one in Pasadena, too. I thought of taking a beach drive, decided I wanted more curves—the Ferrari loves curves—turned around, took Sunset all the way to Benedict Canyon, had myself a little spin."

"Hi-test," said Milo. "How much do you pay for that?"

"Right now it's four-fifty a gallon."

Milo whistled.

Kipper said, "The Ferrari thrives on it."

"What model?"

"Testarossa."

"Work of art," said Milo.

"Oh, yeah," said Kipper. "High-maintenance. Like everything else in my life."

10

"The grieving ex-husband," said Milo, as I drove away from Century City, drifting past the ABC entertainment center.

"Angry ex-husband. Big, strong hands and a temper, and once he starts talking about the art world he heats up."

"Leeches on the body artistic."

"And Julie remained *in* the body artistic."

"He bothers you."

"He's worth looking at," I said. "Smart, powerful. And he'd been to the gallery. Even by his account his relationship with Julie was convoluted. A marriage full of upheaval, off-and-on physical intimacy ten years after the divorce. When intimates want to fake sexual assault, they generally fail to go all the way. Pulling the panties down, not off. Kipper claims he had to talk Julie into taking money, but who knows. He could also be a very frustrated guy. He used to have serious artistic aspirations. Letting go of dreams isn't always easy."

"Even with a Ferrari to soothe the angst?"

"As he reminded us three times. A Ferrari that he pumps full of high-octane gas. Think about that: He pays a hefty premium to beef up an already high-powered engine. We're talking an aggressive guy. Toss in a difficult ex-wife whom he continued to sleep with and money issues—"

"Julie told the other artists the split was amicable."

"How well did they know her? Did she tell anyone about her suicide attempts?"

"No," he said. "She talked about being in rehab, but didn't mention that. So, what, Julie reversed the terms and started hitting on Kipper for big money?"

"Maybe she got tired of the starving-artist bit, stepped back, and realized how well Kipper was doing and decided to up her own lifestyle. Kipper could've liked being generous when *he* was calling the shots. Julie's getting assertive would've been something else, completely. There was a good reason for Julie to take stock. She was entering middle age, and even her second try at art fame hadn't made headlines. I know she sold paintings, but Light and Space isn't a New York gallery, and the prices of her canvases haven't gone up much since she started out. In fact, in twenty-year-old dollars, they've dropped. So perhaps reality finally sank in: making it solely as a painter was going to be a struggle, and she was tired of scratching by. Kipper alluded to her living in a dump. How bad was it?"

"By his standards, a dump. By mine, basic. Two-bedroom apartment in Santa Monica, the east end, off Pico. The living room was her studio. Despite being an artist, she wasn't much for interior decorating."

"That's the tough part of Santa Monica," I said. "Gangs, drug traffic." Thinking about Robin's place on Rennie. Tim Plachette was a nice man, a mild man, always courteous to me. Would he be of any use if things got tough?

Milo was saying, ". . . I'll talk to the neighbors again. Take a closer look at hubbie."

"See what you can learn about his financial situation. Sometimes investment pros get overconfident and reckless with their funds. If Kipper leveraged heavily on a deal and lost some big bucks, ditching his obligation to Julie might be tempting."

"Strong hands," he said. "He's a little guy but still bigger than Julie. He'd be tough enough to overpower her in that bathroom."

"Maybe he didn't have to overpower her. She trusted him. That would've added to the element of surprise."

"Trusted him to what?"

"He told us they were still having sex."

"A tryst in that scuzzy place?"

"I've heard of stranger things," I said.

"So have I, but . . . I think your mind's gotten eviler than mine."

I made a U-turn and headed back to Santa Monica Boulevard. "When Julie's uncle asked you to take the case, did you talk to him about her?"

"Sure."

"Was he aware of her background?"

"To him she was just the sweet, talented niece who'd gone off to New York. Far as her family's concerned, she was Rembrandt."

"Nice to be appreciated."

"Yeah." A moment later, he said, "Strong hands. Whoever strangled Julie didn't rely on their hands, they used a wire."

"Good way to keep the hands clean," I said. "In addition to using gloves. Reduces the risk of leaving trace evidence."

"Clean hands."

"In a manner of speaking."

I dropped him off, drove home, and booted up the computer. Half a dozen search engines pulled up very little on either Everett or Julie Kipper.

Three hits for him: talks he'd given at private-client seminars run by MuniScope. The identical topic each time: for high-income individuals buying tax-free bonds, going for premiums rather than discount, could actually save money in the long run.

Julie's name came up only once: Six months ago, one of her early paintings had been sold at a Sotheby's Arcade auction. Eighteen hundred dollars for a ten-year-old oil-on-canvas entitled *Marie at Her Kitchen Table*. No accompanying photo. The sale had brokered low-ticket items, few of them illustrated.

The provenance of the painting told me little I couldn't have guessed: From the Lewis Anthony Gallery, N.Y., to a "private collector."

I looked up Anthony. Fifty references. He'd died five years ago, but the gallery was still in business.

I thought about the pathway Julie Kipper's life had taken. Putting herself through a drug-stoked work jag to meet the demands of the gallery owner. Three paintings.

And now one of them had been dumped by its owner for less than it had cost.

Demoralizing, if she'd known.

My bet was that she had. Somehow, someone would've told her.

Yet, she'd decided to chance a comeback. Perhaps the sale had *spurred* the comeback.

Had she created what she believed to be her best work, hoping for a second chance with another high-powered gallery, only to settle for Light and Space?

Low output meant no resale market.

Low demand for her work eliminated one possible motive for murder: someone trying to up the value of an investment because dead artists often fetch higher prices than live ones. That only applied to artists who mattered. As far as the art world was concerned, Juliet Kipper had never existed, and her death wouldn't elicit a blink.

No, this one had nothing to do with commercial intrigue. This one was personal.

A bright killer. Forward-thinking and outwardly composed, but inside . . . rage tempered to something cold and measured.

When he'd first called me, Milo had called it a "weird one," but the killer wouldn't see it that way. To him, twisting a wire around Juliet Kipper's neck would seem eminently reasonable.

I had a beer, thought some more about Julie's luminous paintings and snuffed-out talent, and got on the phone.

The Lewis Anthony Gallery was listed on Fifty-seventh Street in New York. The woman who answered the phone enunciated the way clippers snip through cuticles.

"Mr. Anthony passed several years ago." Her tone implied knowing such should be a prerequisite for American citizenship.

"Perhaps you can help me. I'm looking for works by Juliet Kipper."

"Who?"

"Juliet Kipper, the painter. She was represented by the gallery several years ago."

"How many is several?"

"Ten."

She snorted. "That's an eon. Never heard of her. Good day."

I sat there wondering what it would be like dealing with that kind of thing, full-time. Growing up with a head full of beauty and the gift of interpretation, being told how brilliant you were by the people who loved you—getting hooked on the oohs and ahs—only to enter what passed for "the real world" and learn that love didn't mean a damn thing.

Julie Kipper had faced a frigid universe that regarded the gifted as fodder.

The kindness of strangers, indeed.

Despite all that, she'd reached deep within herself again and produced works of transcendent beauty.

Only to be garroted and laid out and posed in a filthy bathroom.

Finding the person who'd done that suddenly seemed very important.

It wasn't until hours later—after finishing and mailing reports, paying some bills, making a run to the bank to deposit checks from lawyers—that something else hit me about Julie.

A gifted, damaged soul snuffed out violently, during the first blush of comeback.

The same could be said about Baby Boy Lee.

I compared the two cases. Both had been Saturday night, back-alley killings. Five weeks had lapsed between them. Neither Milo nor Petra—nor anyone else—had seen any link because there were no striking similarities. And as I checked off the differences a nice-sized list materialized on my scratch pad.

Male vs. female victim.

Late forties vs. midthirties.

Single vs. divorced.

Stabbing vs. strangulation.

Outdoor vs. indoor crime scenes.

Musician vs. painter.

I decided I was being overly analytic; no sense calling Milo. I went for a forty-minute run that challenged my heart and lungs but did little to clear my head, got back on the computer, and searched for murders of creative types within the last ten years.

Despite setting that arbitrary limit, a lot of extraneous material cropped up: scads of dead rock stars, mostly, almost every demise self-inflicted. The West Hollywood stabbing death of Sal Mineo, too. That had gone down in 1976, well before the one-decade cutoff. Mineo's murder, long a subject of film-biz intrigue and believed to be related to his homosexuality, had turned out to be a street burglary gone really bad.

The actor had been in the wrong place at the wrong time. Maybe that's how Baby Boy—and Julie—would shake out.

I kept searching and refining, ended up, hours later, with four possibles.

Six years ago, a potter named named Valerie Brusco had been bludgeoned in an empty field behind her studio in Eugene, Oregon. I found no direct reporting of the crime, but Brusco's name came up in a retrospective of Pacific Northwest ceramic artists, written by a Reed College professor, in which her violent end was noted. This one had been solved: Brusco's boyfriend, a cab driver named Tom Blascovitch, had been arrested and charged and incarcerated. But murderers get out of prison, so I printed the data.

The second case was the stabbing death of a saxophonist named Wilfred Reedy, outside a Washington Boulevard jazz club, four and a half years ago, documented in the obituary column of a musician union's magazine. The obit lauded Reedy's gentle nature and improvisational skills and noted that, in lieu of flowers, contributions to the widow could be made care of the union.

Reedy, sixty-six, had been a friend of John Coltrane and played with many of the greats—Miles Davis, Red Norvo, Tal Farlow, Milt Jackson. I logged into the *L.A. Times* archives and found a back-page squib on the crime and a single follow-up paragraph one week later. No leads or arrests. Anyone with information to call Southwest Division.

Homicide number three was the three-year-old stabbing of a twenty-five-year-old ballet dancer named Angelique Bernet in Cambridge, Massachusetts. Bernet had been part of a touring New York company performing in Boston, and she'd left her hotel around 2 A.M. Friday evening and never returned. Two days later, her body was found behind an apartment on Mt. Auburn Avenue, not far from the Harvard campus. Cross-references to the *Boston Herald* and the *Globe* pulled up brief accounts of the crime but no arrests. Something else the *Globe* reported caught my eye: Bernet had recently been promoted to stand-in for the prima ballerina and had, in fact, performed her first solo the night of her disappearance.

The final hit took place thirteen months later—another Hollywood murder. During an all-night recording session, a punk-rock vocalist named China Maranga had unleashed a drunken tirade at her backup band over what she viewed as lackluster playing, stomped out of the studio, and vanished. Two months later, her skeletal remains were discovered by hikers, not far from the Hollywood sign, barely concealed by brush. ID had been made using dental records. A broken neck and the absence of bullet holes or stab wounds suggested cause of death as strangulation, but that was about all the coroner could come up with.

China Maranga's teeth had been easy to identify—as a youngster, she'd undergone extensive orthodontic work. Her birth name was Jennifer Stilton, and she'd grown up in a big house in Palos Verdes, the daughter of a grocery-chain executive and an interior decorator. She'd earned good grades in prep school, where a sweet soprano earned her a starring role in the glee club. Admitted to Stanford, she majored in English Lit, got hooked on alternative music and whiskey and cocaine, amassed a collection of tattoos and piercings, and assembled a band of like-minded sophomores who joined her in dropping out. For the next several years, she and China Whiteboy toured the country, playing small clubs and garnering cult status but failing to get a record contract. During that period, China morphed her sweet soprano to a ragged, atonal scream. A tour in Germany and Holland garnered larger audiences and brought about a deal with an alternative label back in L.A. Sales of China Whiteboy's two albums were surprisingly brisk, the band began attracting attention from people-with-clout, rumors of a deal with a major label were rife.

China's murder ended all that.

China could barely play guitar, but she wielded one as a prop—a battered old Vox teardrop that she treated rough. I knew that because two members of the band—a pair of slouching, inarticulate wraiths named Squirt and Brancusi—were serious about their gear, and when they needed repairs, they came to Robin. When China snapped the Vox's neck during one of her more ebullient stage tantrums, the boys passed along Robin's number.

I remembered the day China dropped by. A particularly unpleasant July afternoon, strangled by West Coast pollution and East Coast humidity. Robin was working in back, and I was in my office when the doorbell rang. Eight times in a row. I padded to the front and opened the door on a pallid, curvaceous woman with spiked hair as black and shiny as La Brea tar. She hefted a guitar in a soft canvas gig bag and looked at me as if I was the intruder. Parked below the terrace was a big, dusty Buick the color of ballpark mustard.

She said, "Who the hell are you and am I as lost as I feel?"

"Where do you want to be?"

"In Paradise feasting on boy virgins—is this the guitar lady's place or not?"

She tapped her foot. Rolled her shoulders. Her left eye ticced. Her features were unremarkable but might've been pleasant if she'd relaxed. Some of the pallor came from ashy pancake makeup, laid on thick, and set off by kohl-darkened lids. The rest implied unhealthy habits.

Black ink tats—snaky, abstract images—covered what I could see of her left arm. A blue-and-black iron cross marked the right side of her face, where the jawline met the earlobe. Both ears sagged under an assortment of rings and plugs. All that and the eyebrow pierces and the nose studs said *Notice Me.* Her blue, pinpoint Oxford button-down shirt implied a forage in Daddy's Ivy League closet. The shirt was tucked into a plaid miniskirt—the kind parochial school girls are compelled to wear. Topped off by white knee socks stuffed into high, laced combat boots, the outfit said, *Don't even try to figure it out.*

"The guitar lady's out back," I said.

"Where out back? I'm not prancing around without knowing. This place freaks me out."

"Why?"

"There could be coyotes or some other shit."

"Coyotes come out at night."

"So do I—c'mon, man, my eyes hurt, show me."

I walked her down the terrace steps, around to the side of the house, and through the garden. She had very little stamina and was breathing hard by the time we reached the pond. As we approached the water, she overtook me and raced ahead, swinging the gig bag. Stopped and stared at the koi.

"Big fish," she said. "All you can eat sushi orgy?"

"Be an expensive meal," I said.

A grin turned her crooked mouth straight. "Hey, Mr. Yuppie, no need to reach for the Xanax, I'm not gonna steal your little babies. I'm a voodgetarian." She eyed the landscaping, licked her lips. "All this yummy yuppie greenery—so where is she?"

I pointed to the studio.

She said, "Okay, dollar-boy, you did your good deed for the day, go back to the stock pages," and turned her back on me.

Hours later, when Robin came into the house, alone, I said, "Charming clientele you've got."

"Oh, her," she said. "That's China Maranga. She shrieks in a band."

"Which one?"

"China Whiteboy."

"Squirt and Brancusi," I said, remembering two skinny guys with cheap electrics.

"They're the ones ratted me out to her. We're going to have a little chat."

She stretched and went into the bedroom to change. I poured myself a Chivas and brought her a glass of wine.

"Thanks, I can use that."

We sat on the bed and drank. I said, "Does the young lady shriek well?"

"She's got great range. From nails on chalkboard to nails on chalkboard even harder. She doesn't play, just swings her guitar around, like she wants to hurt someone. Last night, she assaulted a mike stand, and the neck broke off. I kept telling her it wasn't worth fixing, but she began crying."

"Literally?"

"Real tears—stomping her feet like a spoiled little kid. I should've sent her to talk to you."

"Outside my expertise."

She put down her glass and ran her fingers through my hair. "I'm charging her my max fee to bolt on one of those Fender necks I got at the bulk sale and taking my time about it. Next week, she'll have something even uglier to ruin, and she'd better pay cash. Now enough of this chitchat and let's get down to business."

"What business is that?"

"Something well within the range of your expertise."

When China came by to pick up the guitar a week later, I was in the studio having coffee with Robin.

This time she wore a greasy motorcycle jacket over a long lace dress, once white, now soup-bone beige. Pink satin high-heeled pumps. A black tam o' shanter capped the black spikes.

Robin fetched the hybridized Vox. "Here you go."

China held the instrument at arm's length. "Ugleee—I'm supposed to pay you for this?"

"That's the routine."

China stared at her, shifted her glare to me, then back to Robin. Reaching into a pocket of the leather jacket, she pulled out a crumpled mass of bills and dropped them on the workbench.

Robin counted the money. "This is forty dollars too much."

China marched to the door, stopped, flipped us off. "Buy yourself a fucking fish."

*　　*　　*

Her murder had elicited a headshake and a "How sad," from Robin.

China differed from Baby Boy and Julie Kipper in that she'd lacked substantial talent. But there was the matter of a rising star snuffed out mid-ascent.

I wondered if Robin had made any connection, years later, between the killings. Two clients of hers, one beloved, the other quite the opposite.

If she had, she hadn't let me know.

Why would she?

11 Juliet Kipper's house was one of two ugly gray boxes squeezed onto a skimpy lot. No backyard. The front was an oily mesa of concrete. Curling tar-paper roofs provided the only green in sight.

Bars on the windows. A rusted iron fence blocked entry to the property. Yellow tape across the rear unit billowed in the ocean breeze. I got out. The fence was locked. No doorbell or call box in sight. A shaved-head kid of sixteen or so sauntered down the street, walking a red-nosed pit bull leashed to a pinch collar. Both owner and dog ignored me, but the two older, shaved-head guys who drove by a few moments later in a chopped-and-lowered Chevy Nova slowed and looked me over.

No reason for me to be there. I returned to the car, took Pico to Lincoln, drove south to Rose Street, in Venice, where I crossed over to the good side.

Robin's place was a white cottage, shake-roofed and gabled, way too cute by half. Pretty flowers in front hadn't been there months ago. I'd never known Robin to garden. Maybe Tim had a green thumb.

His Volvo was parked in the driveway behind Robin's Ford truck. I considered leaving.

"To hell with that," I said, out loud. "Paternal rights and all that."

I was hoping she'd answer the door, but he did.

"Alex."

"Tim."

Tight smiles, all around. Cursory handshake. He had on his usual outfit: long-sleeved plaid shirt, khaki Dockers, brown moccasins. Mr. Laid Back. Rimless eyeglasses gave his blue eyes—true blue, deeper than my gray-tinged irises—a dreamy look.

He's a year younger than me, but I like to think he looks older because he's losing his hair. The strands that remain are fine and caramel-colored and too long—obvious overcompensation. There's gray in his beard. Soulful, those eyes.

Then, there's the voice. The smoothest, most sonorous basso profundo you'll ever hear. Every word rounded and plummy and cadenced. Walking advertisement for his craft.

He's a vocal coach, one of the best, works with opera singers and rock stars and high-priced public speakers, travels around a lot. Robin met him at a recording session a month after we separated. He'd been called in to help a diva whose larynx had frozen up, and he and Robin had started talking. She was there on an emergency call, too—several instruments knocked off kilter in transit.

I thought of the kind of emergencies the two of them faced. The two of them lived in a different world from mine.

From what I'd seen, Tim was easygoing, patient, rarely spoke unless he was spoken to. Divorced from another vocal coach, he had a twenty-year-old daughter studying at Juilliard who adored him.

A week after Robin met him, she called me up. Once we got past the hemming and hawing, I realized she was asking my permission.

I told her she didn't need it, wished her the best, hung up. Then I sank low. Within a month, she and Tim were living together.

"So," he said. The Voice making it sound profound. Maybe he was born with those pipes, but it set my teeth on edge.

"How's it going, Tim?"

"Well. With you?"

"Ditto."

He leaned against the doorjamb. "I'm on my way out, actually."

"On the road, again?"

"Indeed. The road to Burbank—sounds like a Hope and Crosby movie."

"Have fun."

He didn't budge. "You're here to . . ."

"See Spike."

"I'm sorry," he said. "He's at the vet. Having his teeth cleaned."

"Ah. There's also something I need to talk to Robin about."

No movement for a second, then he stepped aside.

I walked past him, through the small, dim living room furnished with his solid oak furniture and the few things Robin had taken with her. An old closet in the hallway had been turned into a passageway between the units. Through the door, I could hear the roar of a table saw.

"Alex?"

I stopped and turned. Tim remained in the doorway. "Please don't upset her."

"I wasn't intending to."

"I know—look, I'll be frank with you. The last time she spoke to you she was really upset."

"The last time she spoke to me was volitional. She dropped in on me."

He showed me his palms in a pacific gesture. "I know that, Alex. She wanted to talk to you about Baby Boy Lee. I thank you."

"For what?"

"Listening to her."

"Yet you think I upset her."

"No—look, I'm sorry. I shouldn't have said anything. It's just that . . ."

I waited.

He said, "Forget it," and turned to leave.

I said, "Did you know Baby Boy?"

The sudden change of topic made him flinch. "I knew of him."

"Ever work with him?"

"Never."

"What about China Maranga?"

"That name I don't know."

"She was a singer," I said. "More of a screamer, actually. Which is why I figured she might've consulted you."

"The screamers seldom do. Why are you asking about her?"

"She's dead. Murdered, like Baby Boy."

"That's what you're here for? Alex, I really don't think Robin should be exposed to any more—"

"I'll keep that in mind." I continued toward the connecting door.

"Fine," he called after me. "You're tough-minded. I concede. Now how about thinking of Robin, this time?"

This time. Dangling the bait. I swam by.

I stepped into the heat of machinery and the smell of hardwood. The floor was coated with sawdust. Several projects—guitars and mandolins in various stages of completion—hung on the wall. Robin's back was to me as she guided a block of rosewood through the whirring blade. Her hair was gathered under one of those bandanas she collects. She wore goggles, a dust mask, had on a tight, white tank top, loose black cotton yoga pants, white tennis shoes. The dark wood hissed and threw off what looked like chocolate chips. Startling her would be dangerous, so I stood there and watched and waited until she'd flipped the switch and stepped away from the saw and the roar died to a growl.

"Hi," I said.

She flipped around, stared at me through the goggles, pulled down the mask, laid the trimmed piece of rosewood on the bench.

"Hi." She wiped her hands on a rag.

"Just saw Tim on the way out. He's worried I'm going to upset you."

"Are you?"

"Maybe."

Flipping the mask over her back, she said, "C'mon, I'm thirsty."

I followed her into the tiny, old kitchen at the rear of the duplex. Old, white appliances, yellow tiles, several of them mended. The room was one-third the size of the spiffy new kitchen we'd designed together. But as in that room, all was spotless, everything in its place.

She got a pitcher of iced tea and poured two glasses and brought them to the Formica table that barely fit the room. Space for two chairs, only. Guess they didn't entertain much. Probably busy entertaining each other. . . .

"Cheers," she said, looking anything but cheerful.

We drank tea. She glanced at her watch.

I said, "If you're busy—"

"No, I'm tired. Been at it since six, ready for my nap."

In the old days, I'd have suggested a mutual nap. "I'll go," I said.

"No. What's on your mind, Alex?"

"China Maranga."

"What about her?"

"I was thinking," I said. "She and Baby Boy. There could be similarities."

"China? In what way?"

I told her, added the bare facts of Juliet Kipper's murder.

She got pale. "I guess—but really, there are so many differences."

"You're probably right," I said.

"You could say China's career was taking off," she said. "Her records were selling better than anyone expected. But, still . . . Alex, I hope you're wrong. That would be hideous."

"Murdering art?"

"Murdering artists because they're on the way up." Her color hadn't returned.

"Here I go again," I said, "bringing the bad stuff into your life." I stood. "I was wrong. Tim was right."

"About what?"

"The last time you saw me you were upset. I should know better."

She frowned. "Tim tries to protect me. . . . I was upset. But not by anything you did."

"What, then?"

"Everything. The state of the world—all this change. I know we did the right thing, but . . . then Baby Boy. One day I'm talking to him, the next day he no longer exists. At the time I guess I was especially vulnerable. I'm better now. Talking to you helped."

"Till now."

"Even now."

She took hold of my wrist. "You were there for me."

"For a change."

She let go and shook her head. "With all our history, you still need to fish for compliments?"

The spot where she'd touched me itched.

"Sit down," she said. "Please. Have more tea. We can be civilized."

I took a seat.

"Baby Boy was my friend," she said. "I had no relationship with China. My only contact with her was that one job, and she wasn't happy with it. Remember how she flipped me off?"

"Flipped *us* off," I said. "I think it was me she didn't care for. She kept calling me Mr. Yuppie."

"She was obnoxious . . . there's something she didn't have in common with Baby. He was the sweetest guy in the world. Another difference is that he had real talent. And her body was buried—no, I don't see it, Alex. My bet is she allowed herself to get picked up by the wrong person, maybe shot off her mouth and paid for it."

"Makes sense," I said. "She left the session angry. What about her band? Any of them ever display aggressive tendencies?"

"Those guys?" she said. "Hardly. They were like China. College kids playing naughty. And why would they kill China? When she died, so did the band. What does Milo think?"

"I haven't asked him, yet."

"You came here, first?"

"You're a lot better-looking."

"I guess that would depend on who you ask."

"No," I said. "Even Rick would say you're cuter." I got up again. "Thanks and sorry if I upset your biorhythm. Have a good nap."

I began walking toward the front of the house.

"They're hard, aren't they?" she called after me.

"What?"

"Changes in biorhythm. Tim's wonderful to me, but sometimes I still find myself starting to say something to *you* . . . are *you* okay?"

"I'm fine."

"She's treating you well?"

"Yes. How's Spike?"

"Too bad he's not here," she said. "Periodontal work."

"Ouch."

"They're keeping him overnight. You can visit. Call to make sure someone's here."

"Thanks."

"Okay," she said, standing. "Let me walk you out."

"Not necessary."

"Not necessary but polite. Mama raised me right."

She accompanied me to the curb. "I'll think more about China, ask around. If I come up with anything, I'll let you know." Big grin. "Hey, look at me: girl detective."

"Don't even think about it," I said.

She took my hand in both of hers. "Alex, what I said before is true. You didn't upset me. Not then, and not now."

"Big tough girl?"

She looked up at me and smiled. "I'm still pretty small."

Once upon a time, you took up a big corner of my heart.

"Not to me," I said.

"You could always do that," she said. "Make me feel important. I'm not sure I did that for you."

"Of course you did," I said.

She's wonderful. What the hell happened?

Allison's wonderful . . .

I dropped her hand, got into the car, started up the engine, and turned to give her a wave. She'd already gone inside.

12 A *partner*. The last thing Petra needed.

Not that she had any choice. Halfway through her shift, Schoelkopf had summoned her into his office and dangled a scrap of paper in her face. Transfer slip.

"From where?" she said.

"The Army. He's new to the department but he's got serious experience as a military investigator, so don't treat him like an idiot rookie."

"Captain, I've been doing fine solo—"

"Well, gee, that's great, Connor. I'm so glad the job's giving you intrinsic satisfaction. Here you go."

Waving the paper. Petra took it but didn't read it.

Schoelkopf said, "Go. He's due over in a couple of hours. Find him a desk and make him feel at home."

"Should I bake him cookies, sir?"

The captain's big black mustache spread as he flashed too-white caps. Last summer, he'd been gone for three weeks and had come back with a scary tan and new dentition and what looked like more hair in front.

He said, "If that's where your girlish talents lie, Detective, go ahead. My personal preference is oatmeal crunch." He waved Petra away.

When she reached his door, he said, "That Armenian thing squared away?"

"Seems to be."

"Seems to be?"

"It's all set with the D.A."

"What's on your plate, now?"

"The Nunes stabbing—"

"Which one's that?"

"Manuel Nunes. The bricklayer who troweled his wife—"

"Yeah, yeah, the bloody mortar. You on top of it?"

"It's not a whodunit," said Petra. "When the blues showed up Nunes was holding the trowel. I'm dotting the t's and crossing the i's." She resisted the temptation to cross her own eyes and give the bastard a goofy look.

"Well, dot and cross everything—speaking of whodunits, you ever accomplish anything on that musician—the fat boy, Lee?"

"No, sir."

"You're telling me it's ice-cold?"

"Afraid so."

"What," said Schoelkopf, "some nutcase just walked up and gutted him?"

"I can bring you the file—"

"Nah," said Schoelkopf. "So you got stuck. Guess what, it's good for you, once in a while. Gain a little humility." More caps. "Lucky for you he wasn't a big-time celebrity. Small potatoes like that, it goes cold, no one gives a shit. What about his family? Anyone squawking at you?"

"He didn't have much family."

"Lucky for you, again." Schoelkopf's big smile was polluted by anger. The two of them had gotten off to a bad start, and no matter what Petra did, she knew it would never improve. "You're a pretty lucky gal—'scuse me, lucky *woman*—aren't you?"

"I do my best."

"Sure you do," said Schoelkopf. "Okay, that's all. Show G.I. Joe the ropes. Maybe he'll turn out to be a lucky guy, too."

She returned to the detectives' room, calmed herself down, glanced at the scrap. Expecting a capsule background on her new partner. But all Schoelkopf had scrawled on the form was a name.

Eric Stahl

Eric. Cute-sounding. A military guy. Petra got herself a hot chocolate from the vending machine downstairs and climbed back up with her imagination in high gear. Picturing *Eric* as buff and cut, a Clint Eastwoody type, maybe one of those precision military buzz do's. An outdoor dude who surfed and biked, skydove, bungee-jumped, did all those adrenalized things.

A high-energy partner was fine with her. He could do the driving.

He showed up twenty minutes later. She'd been right about the haircut, but nothing else.

Eric Stahl was thirty or so, five-ten, tops, painfully thin, stoop-shouldered and gangly-limbed. The buzz was medium brown, prickly hairs riding the narrow, brooding face of a starving poet. Lord, this white boy was white! A too-many-hours-in-the-library complexion. Except for incongruous coins of pink on his cheeks—fever spots.

Sunken cheeks. Dagger-point chin, lipless mouth, the deepest-set eyes Petra had ever seen. As if someone had poked them with two fingers and pushed them back into his skull. Same matte brown as the hair. Static.

He said, "Detective Connor? Eric Stahl," without extending a hand or moving. Just stood by her desk, wearing a black suit, white shirt, and gray tie.

Petra said, "Hi, why don't you sit down."

Indicating a chair at the side of her desk.

Stahl considered the offer, finally accepted.

His black suit seemed to compound her own outfit: an ebony Vestimenta pantsuit she'd bought at the Barney's hanger sale two seasons ago. Funereal; the two of them looked like the welcoming committee at Forest Lawn.

Stahl didn't bat a lash. High energy, indeed. That face . . . grow out the buzz cut and dress him in leather pants and a bunch of other punky whatnot, and he'd fit right in with any of the dissolute hustlers you saw staggering down the boulevard.

Keith Richard's younger brother. Keith, himself, at the worst of his junkie days.

She said, "So, what can I do for you, Eric?"

"Cue me in."

"About?"

"Anything you think is important."

Up close, Stahl's skin was chalky. No inflection in the guy's voice. Only a throbbing vein at his left temple hinted at ongoing body function.

"You can use that desk," she said. "And that's your locker."

Stahl didn't move. He hadn't brought anything with him.

"How about," said Petra, "we drive around, and I show you the neighborhood."

Stahl waited for her to stand before he did. As they walked down the stairs, he lingered behind her. Creepy.

Schoelkopf had partnered her with a creepy robot.

They cruised down the dark boulevard. Hollywood at 4 A.M. was dotted meagerly with nightcrawlers and shadow-lurkers. Petra pointed out drug bars, illegal clubs, hangouts of known felons, taco joints where transvestite hookers congregated. If Stahl had an impression, he wasn't letting on.

"Different from the Army," she said.

No answer.

"How long were you in the military?"

"Seven years."

"Where were you stationed?"

Stahl thumbed his chin and grew contemplative.

It wasn't a trick question.

"All over," he finally said.

"All over domestic, or all over foreign?"

"Both."

"What," said Petra, smiling, "were you some top-secret op? If you tell me you have to kill me?"

She glanced at Stahl as she continued to drive. Expecting at least minimal levity.

Nothing.

Stahl said, "Overseas was the Middle East."

"Where in the Middle East?"

"Saudi Arabia, Bahrain, Djibouti, Dubai."

"The emirates," said Petra.

Nod.

"Fun?" said Petra.

Five-second digital delay. "Not much. They hate Americans. You couldn't bring a Bible in, or anything else that showed you were Christian."

Aha. A born-again.

"You're religious."

"No." Stahl turned away from her, stared out the window.

"Were you involved in the *Cole* bombing?" she said. "Stuff like that?"

"Nothing like that."

"Nothing like that," Petra echoed.

Stahl said, "I think that car over there is stolen."

Indicating a white Mustang two lengths ahead of them. Petra saw nothing fishy about the plates or the way the driver was handling the vehicle.

"Do you?" said Petra.

Stahl picked up the radio and phoned a cruiser. Totally comfortable with the equipment and the LAPD codes. As if he'd been working the division for years.

Petra's jaw hurt from conversational strain.

They rode around for another half hour in dead silence, and when Petra pulled into the parking lot, Eric Stahl said, "Anything I should do before tomorrow?"

"Show up," she said, making no attempt to hide her irritation.

"I will," said Stahl and he left the lot on foot, disappeared into darkness.

What, he took the bus? Or he doesn't want me to see what kind of car he drives?

Later, before she locked up her desk, Petra called Auto Theft and found out the white Mustang had been stolen.

13 After leaving Robin's house, I went home and got back on the computer, tried to track down China Maranga's band mates.

The guitarist who called himself Squirt was nowhere to be found in cyberspace, but the drummer, self-titled Mr. Sludge and the bass player, Brancusi, were easy to locate.

A year ago, Sludge, née Christian Bangsley, had been condemned on the "page of shame" Web site of a music zine called *misterlittle*: *Hot Flash: ex-Chinawhiteboy sells out, peddles junk-slop, ends up cap-pig cancerous bigtiiime!!!!*

During the three years since China's murder, Bangsley had made significant lifestyle changes: moving to Sacramento, investing a "small inheritance," and ending up the co-owner of a small chain of "family-style" restaurants called Hearth and Home. The zine noted Bangsley's plans to *"fester and postulate this tumor of phony-fuck normanrock-wellism into a malignant metastasizing !!!franchise!!!. Sludge dludes (sic) himself that he's cleeeen, now, but he's sludgier than ever."*

Along with the tirade, *misterlittle* ran before-and-after photos, and the contrast was so remarkable that I questioned the truth of the story.

During his band days, Sludge had been a scrawny, angry-eyed nightcrawler.

Christian Bangsley was well fed and Beatle-mopped, in a white shirt and tie. These eyes sparkled with contentment.

I found Brancusi on his personal Web site. His real name—shockingly—was Paul Brancusi. Local; he worked as an animator for Haynes-Bernardo, a Burbank studio, one of the major players in kids' TV.

Brancusi's bio listed two years as an art major at Stanford, an equal amount of time spent as a member of China Whiteboy, then another year at CalArts, where he'd picked up skills in computer graphics and animation.

He worked on a morning show called *The Lumpkins,* described as *"Edgy but kindly. Imaginary creatures live in a suburb that evokes some of the humor, nostalgia, and rib-tickling situations of a human neighborhood. But in Lumpkinville, imagination and fantasy reign supreme!"*

Home and Hearth's Sacramento corporate headquarters was listed. I called and asked to speak to Christian Bangsley.

The receptionist was cheerful—nourished by family-style food? "Mr. Bangsley's in a meeting. May I help you?"

"I'm calling about an old friend of Mr. Bangsley. China Maranga."

"Could you spell that, please?"

I did.

She said, "And what shall I tell Mr. Bangsley this is about?"

"A few years ago Mr. Bangsley played with Ms. Maranga in a band. China Whiteboy."

"Oh, that. She's dead, right?"

"Yes."

"So what message should I give Mr. Bangsley?"

I rattled off my L.A. police consultantship and told her I wanted to ask Bangsley a few questions.

"I'll be sure to tell him."

I reached Paul Brancusi at his desk.

He said, "All this time, and finally something's being done?"

"You don't feel enough was done at the beginning?"

"The cops never found out who did it, right? The thing that bothered me was that they didn't even want to talk to us. Even though we were close to China—closer than anyone, excepting maybe her father."

"Not her mother?"

"Her mother's dead," he said. "Died a year before China. Her dad's dead, too—you don't know much about it, do you?"

"Just starting out. How about filling me in? I can drop by your office anytime today."

"Let me get this straight: you're what—a shrink?"

I gave him a longer explanation than the one I'd offered the Hearth and Home receptionist.

"Why now?" he said.

"China's death might be related to another murder."

"Really," he said, stretching the word. "So now she matters. And I should talk to you because . . ."

"Because I *am* interested in talking to you."

"What a thrill."

"Just a brief talk, Mr. Brancusi."

"When?"

"You name it."

"In an hour," he said. "I'll be in front of the H-B building. I'm wearing a red shirt."

Haynes-Bernardo Productions occupied a massive, free-form, pink-brick-and-blue-tile structure on the east side of Cahuenga Boulevard, just before Universal Studios, where Hollywood gives way to the Valley.

The building had no corners. No symmetry of any kind. Just curves and swoops and parabolic adventurism, set off by odd-shaped windows placed randomly. A cartoonist's vision. Coco palms flanked a trapezoidal entry door the color of grape jelly, and a hundred feet of brick planter filled with struggling begonias ran along the front facade.

A man in an oversized red flannel shirt, baggy blue jeans, and grubby sneakers sat on the planter ledge, sucking on a cigarette.

As I approached him, he said, "You made good time," without looking up.

"Motivation," I said.

He studied me, and I returned the favor.

Paul Brancusi had changed less than Christian Bangsley. Still scrawny and sallow, he wore his hair long and uncombed, had tinted the natural dishwater color bronze.

His cigarette adhered to a chapped lower lip. A crusted cold sore was wedged below a hook nose. Blue-black iron cross tattoo on his right hand, stainless-steel stud in his left lobe. At least half a dozen healed-over pierces revealed themselves as tiny black dots on his nose, brow, and chin. Someone who'd never seen what he used to look like might have taken them for large pores.

John Lennon eyeglasses gave his eyes a faraway look, even as he checked me out.

He pulled out a pack of Rothman Filters and offered it to me.

"No, thanks." I sat down next to him.

"Who else got murdered?" he said.

"Sorry, can't give out details."

"But you want me to talk to you."

"You want China's murder to be solved."

"What I want and what's going to happen don't often coincide," he said.

The faraway eyes had grown dour. His back rounded as if under a terrible weight. He had a look and a sound that I recognized. Years of accrued disappointment. I thought of him hunched at his drawing table, bringing *The Lumpkins* to life. *Edgy but kindly. Rib-tickling situations.*

Brancusi fished out a cigarette and chain-lit. His cheeks hollowed as he devoured the smoke. "What do you want to know?"

"First of all, do you have any theories about who killed China?"

"Sure," he said. "Someone she pissed off. Which is about ten million people."

"Challenged in the charm department."

"China was a four-plus bitch. And guess what, you're the first cop-type to ever ask me about her personality. What's with those guys— retarded?"

"What did they ask?"

"Joe Dragnet stuff. The facts, just the facts. What time did she leave

the studio, what did she do the last few days before, who was she doping with, who was she fucking. No attempt to really get into who she
was."

Smoke exited his nostrils and dissipated quickly in the smoggy air.
"It was obvious they despised us and her, were blaming the whole
lifestyle thing."

"Do you think the lifestyle had anything to do with China's death?"

"Who knows? Listen, I really don't see the point of this."

"Bear with me," I said. "I need to get some context."

"Such as?"

"Such as, from what I can tell things were looking up for the band.
There was talk of a deal with a major label. That true?"

Brancusi sat up straighter, energized by nostalgia. "More than talk.
We had a decent shot. Had just done a showcase at Madame Boo,
where some of the better A & R guys were in the audience. We were
great that night—really rocked. Next day, we were called for an interview with Mickey Gittleson—any idea who he was?"

I shook my head.

"Big-time manager. Big-time clients." He rattled off a list of bands,
some of which I recognized. "He was hot to represent China Whiteboy.
If he'd have gotten behind us, things would've popped."

"You said 'he was.' "

"Dead," said Brancusi. "Last year, lung cancer. Idiot smoked too
much." He flicked ashes and cackled.

"What happened with Gittleson?"

"China broke the first appointment—pulled an absolute fit, said Gittleson represented everything evil about the music biz and she wasn't
going to sell out. Which was funny because during the showcase it was
she who'd freaked out when she saw Gittleson sitting there, told us
backstage that the guy was Mr. It. During the next act, she went over to
his table, chatted him up, just about gave him a lap dance. Couldn't
have hurt. The guy was a horny old goat, liked to fuck the talent."

"China flirting," I said, trying to picture that.

Brancusi laughed. "China was incapable of anything as light and
airy as femme flirtation. But she could put on the sexy act when she
wanted."

"Method acting?"

"What do you mean?"

"Was it real, or was she faking it? How sexually active was she?"

"She was plenty active," said Brancusi. "All with girls, she was into girls."

He stared at Cahuenga traffic, seemed to be losing interest.

I said, "So she was the one who got Gittleson involved but then she changed her mind."

"Typical China."

"Moody," I said.

He flicked the cigarette onto the sidewalk. It lay there smoldering.

I said, "You said the first appointment. Gittleson didn't cut you off after the first cancellation?"

"He was cool about it, we were a hot prospect, so he rescheduled. But a month later, he was traveling to Europe, arranged to meet us after he got back. Suggested we lay down some fresh tracks. That's the reason we were in the studio. Trying to burn a CD sampler that would really knock Gittleson's argyles off. And we were doing it. Hauling. China had changed her mind—now Gittleson was cool. She was on, she was motivated. That's the thing about her. Even when she was high, she was able to focus."

"Big-time high?"

"Is there any other kind?"

"So what happened?"

"The session's going great, China starts freaking out over something—maybe something someone said, the sound system—when she was like that it could've been the way the drapes were hanging. She pulls a fit, walks out on us, disappears."

"Not a word where she was going?"

"Nope. Just fuck-you's all around. We figured she'd be back, the way she always was. Tantrums were a way of life for her." He pulled out another cigarette and ignited it with a Donald Duck lighter.

"The opposition," he said, brandishing the lighter before snapping it shut.

I said, "What happened to the sides you cut that night?"

"They're worthless. I tried to peddle them, but without China to tour, no one—not Gittleson or any of the others—wanted to know us. A few months later, we were ancient history." Another cackle. "Serious pathos, huh? I coulda been a contender? Like that Swedish ship, the *Wasa*, ever hear of it?"

I shook my head.

"I was in Sweden last year, doing some business, they're maybe going to franchise *The Lumpkins* over there. So this Swedish animator is taking me around Stockholm. Weird city, all these big blond zombies lurching around looking like they haven't slept in years. Cause of the light thing they've got. Summertime, it never gets dark. Winter, it's dark all the time. This was summer, we get out of a club at midnight, and it's still broad daylight. Anyway, the next day this guy takes me to this ship, the *Wasa*. Big old wooden Viking warrior ship, built hundreds of years ago, huge, the Swedes loaded it with cannons for this war they were fighting with the Danes. Problem is, they over*loaded* it with cannons so when they launched it, the sucker sank right in the North Sea. They salvaged it forty years ago, pulled it up intact and built a museum around it. You can climb in and pretend you're Leif Ericson, get drunk and eat herring, whatever. Anyway, this guy who's taking me around, after we leave the museum, he turns to me with tears in his eyes, this incredible wistfulness, and says, 'Paul, my friend, if the *Wasa* hadn't sunk, Sweden would be a world power.' "

Three rapid drags on the fresh smoke. He held his breath, closed his eyes, broke out into a ragged coughing fit. Seemed comforted by the spasm. "We're the musical *Wasa*. If China hadn't been murdered, we would've been Aerosmith, ha-ha-ha."

"What else can you tell me about China?"

"She could've used *you*. Mentally unstable. We all were. I'm on lithium and antidepressants for bipolar. Four screwed-up personalities, and then we augmented it with endless dope."

Rib-tickling situations.

I said, "Christian Bangsley, too?"

"Mr. Corporate? Especially Chris. He was more thrashed than the rest of us. Had a very rich family and no moral fiber. As opposed to us, who merely had *weak* moral fiber."

"He sold out?"

"He didn't sell out," said Brancusi. "That's an asinine concept. What's the difference how you make your way through life—playing music or being a CPA or building warehouses or whatever? It's all one gray death march. Chris shifted gears, that's all."

"Where's Squirt?"

"Dead," he said, as if that made perfect sense. "Went over to Europe and OD'd on heroin. Some park in Switzerland. Living like a bum, it took weeks before they identified him."

"You're not surprised."

"Squirt was riding the needle pretty hard before China got killed. Afterward, he just started *shoveling* the stuff in."

"Traumatized by China's death."

"Probably. He was the most intense. Not counting China."

"Apart from China's general abrasiveness, was there anyone she had a run-in with during the week or so before her murder?"

"Not that I know about, but it wouldn't surprise me. She was just instinctually *unpleasant,* would get into this Greta Garbo mode—'I vant to be alone and fuck you for trying to relate to me.' "

"What about a stalker?"

He threw up his hands. "I don't think you *get* it. We weren't *stars,* no one *cared.* That's what *really* got to China. For all her talk about alienation, all that hermit posturing, she was a Palos Verdes princess who'd gotten tons of attention as a kid and still craved it. That's why it was monumentally *stupid* for her to blow off Gittleson. Ms. Schizo. One minute, she'd be seething because the band wasn't getting the respect it deserved, the next she'd be cussing out anyone who actually wanted to focus on the band—like journalists. She went out of her way to alienate them, called them butthole lickers, imposed a strict no-interview policy."

Out came the pack of Rothmans. Another chain light. "I'll give you an example: There was this zine, dinky little rag that wanted to do a story on us. China told him to fuck himself. They did the piece anyway, without talking to us. So what does China do? She phones the editor and gives it to him."

He shook his head. "I was there, listening to her end. 'Your mother fucks scabrous Nazi dicks and drinks Hitler's cum.' Granted she'd told them no, but what was the logic behind that?"

"Remember the name of the zine?" I said.

"You think some *journalist* type murdered China because she talked *mean* to him? Give me a break."

"I'm sure you're right," I said. "But if the editor was a fan, maybe he's got some ideas."

"Whatever," he said. "You've obviously got plenty of spare time . . . *Groove* something—*GrooveRut* or *GrooveRat*. He sent us a copy, and we chucked it. Cheap little desktop deal, probably out of business by now."

"What was the gist of the article?"

"We were geniuses."

"Did you keep a clipping?"

"Oh, sure," he said. "Along with my Grammys and my platinum records."

He shot to his feet, smoked and coughed and walked, hunch-shouldered to the grape-jelly door. Shoved it hard and went back to work.

14 I drove to a magazine stand on Selma Avenue off Hollywood Boulevard, and looked for *GrooveRat*. Fifty feet of stand, containing plenty of alternative publications and newspapers in two dozen languages, but no sign of the zine. I asked the turbaned Sikh proprietor, and he said he'd never heard of it but I might have some luck at the comics store/piercing parlor three blocks up the boulevard.

I cruised by the shop, found a CLOSED sign barely visible behind an accordion-grated front, and returned home wondering if Paul Brancusi's comment about too much leisure time had been on target.

The more I thought about it, the weaker the links between the cases seemed. I considered the three other murders I'd found Web-surfing.

The only other L.A. killing was the old saxophonist, Wilfred Reedy, and there'd been no suggestion he'd been on the verge of a comeback or career-climb. The killer of Valerie Brusco, the Oregon potter, had been caught and jailed, and Angelique Bernet, the ballet dancer—a young woman who *had* been offered a potential career boost—had died three thousand miles away in Massachusetts.

Subtotal: zero. Still no reason to bother Milo; he had his hands full investigating Everett Kipper—by my own reckoning the best bet for Julie's murderer.

The dinner hour was approaching, but I had no appetite. Another human voice would be palliative, but Allison was working at the hospice tonight.

I might do well by following her example: do some gut-wrenching clinical work that drew me miles from my own self—the kind of work I'd done years ago on the cancer wards of Western Pediatric Hospital.

I'd spent nearly a decade on those wards, a too-young, newly minted psychologist, pretending to know what he was doing. Seeing too much, too soon, feeling like nothing but an impostor.

Paying dues. But that was rubbish; oncologists and oncology nurses devote entire lives to the cause, so who the hell was I to self-aggrandize?

Allison's husband had died of cancer, and she spent one night a week with the terminally ill.

Not a comforting line of thinking. I returned to pondering China Maranga's death. Her verbal assault had been business as usual, but some people don't take well to abuse. And when I'd asked Robin to speculate about the case, her first instinct had been that China had run into someone on the street, accepted a ride, shot her mouth off one time too many.

Despite Paul Brancusi's dismissal, the stalker element couldn't be ignored. You didn't have to be famous to incite irrational attachment. And alternative zines were sometimes little more than glorified fan-club bulletins. *Fanatic*-club bulletins.

Had the editor adored China from afar? Had the way she'd treated him twisted his passions into rage she'd been ill equipped to handle?

I let my imagination run. Maybe he'd agreed to give China one last chance. Watching, waiting, outside the studio. China, stoned, unstable, angry at her band, leaves, and he follows her.

Pleased to be with someone who appreciated her, she accompanies him.

Then things turn.

China reverting to type.

And he's had enough.

Thin speculation, but it was that or introspection.

I booted up the computer and searched for *GrooveRat*. Not a single hit.

That surprised me. Every self-deluded purveyor of triviality has a Web site. So the zine had been beyond obscure. And, as Brancusi predicted, long out of circulation.

Already on-line, I set out to convince myself that there was nothing more to be learned about the other three murders.

Wilfred Reedy's name came up nearly a hundred times, mostly in discographies and laudatory reviews. Two references to his "tragic murder." No speculation. Neither Valerie Brusco nor Angelique Bernet merited notice beyond the hits I'd found initially.

I exited the virtual world, phoned Central Division, and asked for the detective who'd handled Reedy's case. The clerk had no idea what I was talking about and transferred me to a sergeant who said, "Why do you want to know?"

"I'm a consultant to the department—"

"What kind of consultant?"

"Psychologist. I work with Lieutenant Milo Sturgis in West L.A. Division."

"Then have him call."

"All I'm asking for is the name of the detective."

"You have a case number?"

"No." I repeated Reedy's name, gave him the date.

"That's four years ago," he said. "You got to call Records, downtown."

Dial tone.

I knew Records wouldn't give me the time of day and moved on to the Cambridge, Mass., police and Angelique Bernet. A Southie-accented man instructed me this was the new age of Homeland Security and there were forms to be filled out, requirements to be met. When he asked me for my Social Security number, I gave it to him. He said he'd get back to me and cut the connection.

A phone call to the Oregon State Penitentiary, where I inquired about the status of inmate Tom Blascovitch, Valerie Brusco's ex-boyfriend, evoked similar suspicion and resistance.

I put the phone down. Enough of amateur hour. Let Milo do his thing with Everett Kipper, and if he hit a brick wall, maybe I'd bring up the rest of it.

I was about to scavenge some dinner from the fridge when the phone rang.

"Tomorrow's fine," said Allison, "but guess what, so is tonight. The hospice is bringing in entertainment—a comedian and a bluegrass band. What's your schedule?"

I was waiting out in front of my house as she drove up in her Jag. She'd kept the top down and her hair was wild. When she got out I took her in my arms and kissed her hard.

"Wow," she said, laughing. "Good to see you, too."

She slid her arm around my waist and I looped mine over her shoulder as we climbed the stairs to the house.

Inside, she said, "Any of that Bordeaux left?"

"Whatever we didn't drink last time is still there."

We went into the kitchen, and I found the wine.

"Oh, my," she said, looking me over. "You really *are* happy to see me."

"You have no idea," I said.

Lying in darkness, I heard the sharp intake of Allison's breath.

"Everything okay?"

"Sure," she said, too quickly. Curled under the covers, her back to me.

I reached over and touched her face. Felt moisture on her cheek.

"What is it?" I said.

"Nothing." She began crying.

When the tears stopped, she said, "Are we at a point where it's safe to tell you anything?"

"Of course."

"I hope so," she said.

But she didn't speak.

"Allison?"

"Forget it. I'm fine."

"Okay."

Moment later: "Here I was, feeling so good, thinking what could be better than this, and Grant's face floated into my head. He looked happy—benevolent, happy for me. God, how I *need* to think of him as being happy."

"Of course."

"And then the thoughts came—all he'd missed, how I'd felt about him, how young he was. Alex, I miss him so much! And sometimes the way you touch me—the way you're tender with me when I need that—it makes me think about *him*."

She flipped onto her back. Covered her face with both hands. "I feel so *unfaithful*. To him, to you. It's been years, why can't I let *go*?"

"You loved him. You never stopped loving him."

"I never did," she said. "Maybe I never will—can you deal with that? Because it has nothing to do with you."

"I'm okay with it."

"You mean that?"

"I do."

"I understand your holding on to your feelings about Robin."

"My feelings," I said.

"Am I wrong?"

I didn't answer.

"You had years together," she said. "You'd have to be shallow to just toss it aside."

"Everything takes time," I said.

She let her hands drop from her face. Stared up at the ceiling. "Well, folks, I may just have made a giant goof."

"No," I said.

"I wish I could be sure of that."

I rolled closer and held her.

"Everything's fine," I said.

"I'm going to believe that," she said. "Given the alternative."

15 Ten days later, I heard from Milo. In the interim, I'd persisted with the Cambridge police and managed to talk to a detective named Ernest Fiorelle. He began by scoping me out, and we went through the old security bit. Finally, I satisfied his curiosity by faxing a copy of an old LAPD consultant's contract and a couple of pages of my deposition on the Ingalls case. Despite all that, Fiorelle ended up asking more questions than he answered about Angelique Bernet.

No serious leads had developed, and the case remained unsolved.

"My guess is some nut," said Fiorelle. "You're the shrink, you tell me."

"A sexual psychopath?" I said. "Was there evidence of rape?"

"I didn't say that."

Dead air.

I said, "What was crazy about it?"

"Cutting up a beautiful young girl and dumping her in an alley seems pretty crazy to me, Doc. Out there in L.A. does that pass for nahmul?"

"Depends on the day of the week."

His laughter was brief and harsh.

I said, "So none of Bernet's fellow dancers or musicians came under suspicion?"

"Nah, wimpy bunch, mostly females and gays. Scared witless. Everyone claimed to love the girl."

"Even though she'd been promoted."

"So what?" he said.

"I was wondering about jealousy."

"Doc, if you'da been to the crime scene, you wouldn't be wondering. This wasn't some . . . spat. This was ugly."

Still thinking about China's possible encounter with a stalking fan, I asked him about music conventions at the time of the murder.

"You kidding?" he said. "This is College-Town, Hahvuhd, the rest of them. We've got nothing but conventions going on all the time."

"Anything to do with the music business, specifically? A group of critics, journalists, fans."

"Nah, don't remember anything like that. And frankly, Doc, I don't know why you're bahkun up this tree."

"Nothing better to bark up."

"Well, maybe you should find something. And keep all that nutty stuff on the Left Coast. Nah, doesn't sound like any matches between the girl and your cases. Fact is, I found a better match in Baltimore, and that didn't pan out either."

"Who was the victim in Baltimore?"

"Some secretary cut up like Ms. Bernet. What's the difference, I just told you it didn't pan, Baltimore busted a lunatic and he hung himself. Gotta run, Doc. Have a nice warm L.A. day."

I searched for Baltimore homicides on the net but came up with nothing remotely familiar to Angelique Bernet or the other killings.

Nothing seemed to be the operative word.

During the same ten days, a few other things happened.

Tim Plachette called me one evening, and said, "Apologies for that ridiculous little mano-a-mano thing the other day."

"No big deal," I said. "You weren't out of line."

"Whether I was or not, I should've held my peace . . . I really care about her, Alex."

"I'm sure you do."

"You don't want to have this conversation," he said.

Something in his voice—desperation, anxiety that came from deep love, flipped my mood.

"I do appreciate your calling, Tim. And I won't get in the way."

"I'm not trying to be a censor, it's a free country. If you want to drop by, that's fine."

I flipped again: *Gee, thanks for permission, buddy.* But I knew he was right. Life would be a lot easier for all of us if I kept my distance.

"We all need to move on, Tim."

"It's good of you to say that. . . . Robin . . . and then there's Spike— I'm making an ass out of myself."

"That's the way it can be with women," I said.

"True."

We traded Y-chromosome chuckles.

"Anyway," he said.

"Be well, Tim."

"You, too."

Two days after that, Robin phoned. "I don't want to bother you, but I also don't want you to find out from someone else. *Guitar Player's* running a profile on me, and I must admit I think that's extremely cool. I know you buy it sometimes, so I thought you might see it."

"Beyond cool," I said. "Tell me the issue, and I'll be sure to buy it."

"This coming issue," she said. "They interviewed me a while back but never told me the piece was going to run. They called me today to say it was. It'll probably complicate my life by throwing me more business when I don't need it, but who cares; getting out in the limelight once in a while feels good. I'm such a baby, huh?"

"You deserve it," I said. "Enjoy."

"Thanks, Alex. How's everything?"

"Moving along."

"Anything new on Baby or that painter?"

"No," I said. When we were together she'd never wanted to know about that kind of thing. Maybe it was her affection for Baby Boy. Or the fact that what I did with my life no longer touched hers.

"Well," she said, "I'm sure if anyone can figure it out, it's you."

"Aw shucks, ma'am."

"Bye," she said, and the laughter in her voice put a little light in my day.

Milo reached me at home, the following Thursday, just after 9 P.M. Solitary end of a solitary day. I'd finished the last of my reports, collected tax information for my accountant, did a few handyman chores around the house. When the phone rang, I was doing the couch-spud bit: wearing grubby sweats, snarfing takeout ribs, a couple of Grolsches within reach. Dimming the lights and turning up the volume on the big screen as I watched both reels of *Magnolia*. Thinking, once again, that the film was a work of genius.

The previous two nights, I'd slept at Allison's place, waking up in her cozy, girly bedroom, smelling perfume and breakfast, resting the grizzle of my unshaven face against soft sweet sheets, dividing my brain between delight and disorientation.

No more talk about Grant or Robin, and she seemed content—or trying to fake it. She moved appointments around and took a day off and we drove up the coast, had lunch in Montecito, at the Stone House. Then we continued to Santa Barbara, walked along the beach, and up State Street to the art museum where a portraiture show was on display.

Black-eyed, too-wise Robert Henri children, the wistful, wounded women of Raphael Soyer, the dandies and dolled-up ladies of John Koch's New York arty crowd.

Pale, languid, dark-haired Singer Sargent beauties who made me look at Allison with new appreciation.

A late dinner at the Harbor, on the pier, stretched out to 11 P.M., and we got back to L.A. just before 1 A.M. For the last twenty miles I fought to stay awake. When I pulled up in front of Allison's house, I hoped she wouldn't invite me in.

She said, "This has been great—you're great for me. Want some instant coffee before you shove off?"

"I'll make it."

I kissed her and drove off. Now the night was mine.

The next morning, I rented the movie.

*   *   *

Milo said, "Am I interrupting something?"

"Beer and ribs and *Magnolia*."

"That, again? What is it, the tenth time?"

"Third. What's up?"

"You alone?"

"Yup."

"Then screw you for hoarding ribs."

"Fine," I said. "Come over and scavenge."

"Don't tempt me, Satan. No, Rick's cutting his shift early, and we're heading over to the Jazz Bakery. Larry Coryell's in town, and you know Rick. Anyway, CoCo Barnes sent over her drawing of the redhead. Afraid you were right. It's just this side of abstract—those cataracts scotch her as any kind of reliable witness. Also, here's the scoop on Everett Kipper. Not a popular guy."

"Among who?"

"His neighbors," he said. "He lives in a nice part of Pasadena—near the border with San Marino. Big craftsman place on a full-acre lot, lotsa house for one guy. The rest of the block's families and senior citizens. Both of Kipper's immediate neighbors are the latter—genteel old folk. They say he's unfriendly, keeps to himself, used to go out to his garage late at night, create a racket hammering marble or whatever. Finally, they called the cops, who went out and had a talk with Kipper. After that, things quieted down, but Kipper got downright unfriendly—doesn't answer when spoken to. The cops told him to cool it by ten, and the neighbors say Kipper makes a point of hammering up until the stroke of ten. Leaves his garage door open, making sure he can be heard."

"Hostile and vindictive," I said. "Sculpting and tearing it apart."

"I spoke to the Pasadena cops, but all they remember is the nuisance call. They sent me the report. Nothing illuminating. The neighbors also said Kipper rarely if ever entertains visitors, but every so often there was a blond lady around. I showed them Julie's picture, they thought maybe it was her."

"Maybe?"

"These are folks in their eighties and no one got a close look. Blond is what they remember—very, very light blond hair, the way Julie's was. So looks like Kipper was telling the truth when he said they'd maintained a relationship."

"How often was she there?"

"Irregularly. Sometimes once a month, sometimes twice. One of the old gals did tell me she's sure the blonde sometimes stayed the night because she saw her and Kipper getting into Kipper's Ferrari the next morning."

"Occasional intimacy," I said.

"Maybe she came by to pick up the alimony in person, and they forgot why they split up. That got me thinking about what you said— Julie's dependency. What if she decided she no longer wanted any part of that, told Kipper so, and things got nasty? He wouldn't kill her at his place. Not with the neighbors looking over his shoulder, that police report already on file. You've been talking about a smart, calculating guy, and he's a bright one. Do I have any way to prove it? *Nyet.* But there's nothing else in my scope."

"What's the state of Kipper's finances?"

"I'm light-years away from any kind of warrant on his accounts, but from all appearances, he's doing well. In addition to the Testarossa, he's got a vintage bathtub Porsche, an old MG, and a Toyota Land Cruiser. The house is stately and pretty, he keeps up the gardening and the maintenance—the place sparkles from the curb. Neighbors say he dresses sharp, even on casual days. One coot said he looked 'Hollywood.' Which in Pasadena is damn near felonious. Another one—an old lady— went on about Kipper liking black. Described it as 'an undertaker uniform.' Then her husband chimes in, and says, 'No, he looks like one of the stiffs.' Ninety-one, and he's cracking wise. Maybe it was the gin and tonic talking—they invited me in for a drinkie. I think I was the most exciting thing in the 'hood since the last Rose Bowl."

"Gin and tonics with the old folk," I said. "Refined."

"The Queen Mother drank gin and tonics and she lived to 101. But I had Coke. Let me tell you, it was tempting—they were pouring Bombay, and I haven't had much fun, recently. Virtue triumphed. Goddammit. Anyway, Kipper is still on my screen. The hostile, aggressive loner. Also, I did ask around about tall redheaded homeless gals. A few possibles surfaced on the Westside or Pacific Division, but all turned out to be wrong. One of the shelters in Hollywood does remember a woman named Bernadine or Ernadine who fits the description. Tall, big bones, crazy, midthirties or about. She drops in occasionally to dry out, but they haven't seen her in a while. The shelter supervisor had the feeling she'd fallen quite a ways."

"Why?"

"When her head cleared, she could sound fairly intelligent."

"No last name?"

"Unlike the public shelters, the privates don't always keep records— it's a church group, Dove House. Pure good deeds, no questions asked."

"When Bernadine sounded intelligent," I said, "what did she talk about?"

"I dunno. Why? This was just time-killing because I dead-ended on Kipper."

"Just wondering if she was a fan of the arts."

"All of a sudden you think it's worth pursuing?"

"Not really."

"What?"

"Forget it," I said. "I don't want to waste your time."

"Right now my time isn't exactly precious. Julie Kipper's uncle called this morning, politely inquiring as to my progress, and I had to tell him there was none. What's on your mind, Alex?"

I told him about the other killings I'd found, recounted my talk with Paul Brancusi.

"Wilfred Reedy I remember," he said. "Another of Rick's favorite jazz guys. I think that one was a dope thing. Reedy pissing off a dealer, or something like that."

"Reedy was an addict?"

"Reedy's kid was an addict. He OD'd and died and Reedy got hot about all the dealing near the South Central clubs, started making noise. I could be wrong, but that's what I remember."

"So it was solved?"

"Don't know, I'll find out," he said. "So . . . jealousy's become the motive?"

"It's the one point of consistency: artists struck down just as they're about to ascend. Four, if you include Angelique Bernet. But the differences outweigh any link."

"Wilfred Reedy wasn't ascending. He'd been admired for years."

"Like I said, wasting your time."

Silence.

"On the surface, it's not much," he said. "Still, I ain't sherlocking anything the old-fashioned way. Why don't I do this: make a few calls and try to disprove the theory. That's the scientific method, right? Blow up the whatchamacallit . . ."

"The null hypothesis."

"Exactly. I'll find out who handled Reedy, talk to Cambridge PD, see what's really gone down. I can also check whether or not that ceramicist's boyfriend is still behind bars, what are their names?"

"Valerie Brusco and Tom Blaskovitch," I said. "He was sentenced three years ago."

"Another creative type?"

"Sculptor."

"Same as Kipper—maybe another vindictive chisel man. Ah, the art world. Like I tell my mother, you never know when the job will elevate you to higher ground."

16 The next few weeks were a slow fade to futility. No new evidence on the Kipper murder surfaced, and Milo learned nothing about the other killings that excited him. He contacted Petra and learned she'd dead-ended on Baby Boy.

Tom Blaskovitch, the sculptor-killer, had been released from prison a year before, having earned good behavior points by setting up art classes for his fellow inmates. But he'd settled in Idaho, gotten a job as a handyman at a dude ranch, which was exactly where his boss was certain he'd been on the nights of the Kipper and the Lee murders.

Detective Fiorelle of the Cambridge police remembered me as a "pushy guy, one of those intellectuals—I know the type, plenty around here." The facts of Angelique Bernet's murder did nothing to support any link with Baby Boy or Julie: The dancer had been stabbed half a dozen times and dumped in an area of the college town that was well traveled during the day but quiet at night. No strangulation, no sexual posing; she'd been found fully clad.

The detective who'd worked the Wilfred Reedy case was dead. Milo got a copy of the file. Reedy had been gut-stabbed in an alley like Baby Boy, but strong indications of a drug-related hit had surfaced at the time, including the name of a probable suspect: a small-time dealer named

Celestino Hawkins, who'd fed the habit of Reedy's son. Hawkins had served time for assault with a knife. He'd been dead for three years.

China Maranga's file was thin and cold.

Milo phoned Julie Kipper's uncle and told him not to expect any quick solve. The uncle was gracious, and that made Milo feel worse.

Allison and I spent more time at each other's houses. I bought *Guitar Player* and read the profile on Robin. Spent a long time staring at the photos.

Robin in her new shop. No mention there'd ever been another one. Gorgeous carved guitars and mandolins and celebrity endorsements and big smiles. The camera loved her.

I wrote her a brief congratulatory note, received a thank-you card in return.

Two and a half months after Julie Kipper's murder, the weather warmed and the case file froze. Milo cursed and put it aside and re- sumed excavating cold cases.

Few of them were solvable, and that kept him grumbling and occupied. The times we got together, he never failed to mention Julie— sometimes with that forced blithe tone that meant failure was eating at him.

Soon after that, Allison and I drove up to Malibu Canyon to watch a meteor shower. We found an isolated turnoff, lowered the top of her Jaguar, reclined the seats, and watched cosmic dust streak and ex- plode. Shortly after we got home, at 1:15 A.M. the phone rang. I was skimming the papers, and Allison was reading V. S. Naipaul's *The Mimic Men*. She'd pinned her hair up. Tiny, black-framed reading glasses rode her nose. As I lifted the receiver, she looked over at the nightstand clock.

Most of the early-morning calls were hers. Patient emergencies.

I picked up.

Milo spit, "Another one."

I mouthed his name, and she nodded.

"Classical pianist," he went on, "stabbed and strangled after a con- cert. Right behind the venue. And guess what: This guy was on his way up, career-wise. Record deal pending. It wasn't my call, but I heard it on the scanner, I went over and took over. Lieutenant's prerogative. I'm here at the scene. I want you to see it."

"Now?" I said.

Allison put the book down.

"Is there a problem?" he said. "You're not a night owl anymore?"

"One sec." I covered the phone, looked at Allison.

"Go," she said.

"Where?" I asked Milo.

"Hop, skip, and jump for you," he said. "Bristol Avenue, Brent-wood. The north side."

"Moving up in the world," I said.

"Who, me?"

"The bad guy."

Bristol was lovely and shaded by old cedars and marked by circular turn-arounds every block or so. Most of the homes were the original Tudors and Spanish Colonials. The murder house was new, a Greek Revivalish thing on the west side of the street. Three square stories, white and columned, bigger by half than the neighboring mansions, with all the welcoming warmth of a law school. A flat green lawn was marked by a single, fifty-foot liquidambar tree and nothing else. High-voltage lighting was blatant and focused. A stroll away was Rockingham Avenue, where O. J. Simpson had dripped blood on his own driveway.

A black-and-white with its cherry flashing half blocked the street. Milo had left my name with the uniform on duty and I got smiled through with a "Certainly, Doctor."

That was a first. Lieutenant's prerogative?

Four more squad cars fronted the big house, along with two crime-scene vans and a coroner's wagon. The sky was moonless and impene-trable. All the shooting stars gone.

The next uniform I encountered offered standard-issue cop distrust as he called on his walkie-talkie. Finally: "Go on in."

A ton of door responded to my fingertip—some sort of pneumatic assist. As I stepped inside, I saw Milo striding toward me, looking like a day trader whose portfolio had just imploded.

Hurrying across a thousand square feet of marble entry hall.

The foyer had twenty-foot ceilings, ten percent of that moldings and dentils and scrollwork. The floor was white marble inset with black granite squares. A crystal chandelier blazed enough wattage to power a third-world hamlet. The walls were gray marble veined with apricot, carved into linen-fold panels. Three were bare, one was hung with a frayed brown tapestry—hunters and hounds and voluptuous women. To the right, a brass-railed marble staircase swooped up to a landing backed by gilt-framed portraits of stoic, long-dead people.

Milo wore baggy jeans and a too-large gray shirt and a too-small gray herringbone sport coat. He fit the ambience the way a boil fits a supermodel.

Beyond the entry hall was a much larger room. Wood floors, plain white walls. Rows of folding chairs faced a raised stage upon which sat a black grand piano. Several scoop-shaped, gridlike contraptions hung from the corners of the curved wooden ceiling—some sort of acoustic enhancement. No windows. Double doors at the rear blended with the plaster.

A pedestal sign to the left of the piano read SILENCE PLEASE. The piano bench was tucked under the instrument. Sheet music was spread on the rack.

The double doors opened and a thickset man in his sixties burst forth like a hatchling, trotting after Milo.

"Detective! Detective!" He waved his hands and huffed to catch up. Milo turned.

"Detective, may I send the staff home? It's frightfully late."

"Just a while longer, Mr. Szabo."

The man's jowls quivered and set. "Yes, of course." He glanced at me, and his eyes disappeared in a nest of creases and folds. His lips were moist and purplish, and his color was bad—mottled, coppery.

Milo told him my name but didn't append my title. "This is Mr. Stefan Szabo, the owner."

"Pleased to meet you," I said.

"Yes, yes." Szabo fussed with a diamond cuff link and offered his hand. His palm was hot and soft, so moist it verged on squishy. He was soft and lumpy, bald but for red-brown fuzz above floppy ears. His face was the shape of a well-bred eggplant and the nose that centered it a smaller version of the vegetable—a pendulous, plump, Japanese eggplant. He wore a white silk, wing-collared formal shirt fastened by half-carat diamond studs, a ruby paisley cummerbund, black, satin-striped tuxedo pants, and patent loafers.

"Poor Vassily, this is terrible beyond terrible. And now everyone will hate me."

"Hate you, sir?" said Milo.

"The publicity," said Szabo. "When I built the odeum, I took such pains to go through every channel. Wrote personal notes to the neighbors, assured everyone that only private affairs and very occasional fund-raisers would be held. And always, the ultimate discretion. My policy's always been consistent: fair warning to everyone within a two-block radius, ample parking valets. I took *pains*, Detective. And, now this."

He wrung his hands. "I need to be especially careful because of you-know-who. During the trial, life was hell. But beyond that, I'm a loyal Brentwoodite. Now *this*."

Szabo's eyes bugged suddenly. "Were *you* involved in *that* one?"

"No, sir."

"Well, that's good," said Szabo. "Because if you were, I can't say I'd have any great confidence in you." He sniffed the air. "The poor odeum. I don't know if I'll be able to continue."

"Mr. Szabo built a private concert hall, Alex. The victim was tonight's performer."

"The *victim*." Szabo placed a hand over his heart. Before he could speak, the doors opened again and a young, lithe Asian man in snug black satin pants, a black silk shirt, and a red bow tie hurried toward us.

"Tom!" said Szabo. "The detective says a while longer."

The young man nodded. He looked to be thirty at most, with pore-less, tight skin glowing ivory under a dense blue-black cirrus of hair. "Whatever it takes, Stef. Are you okay?"

"Not hardly, Tom."

The young man turned to me. "Tom Loh." His hand was cool, dry, powerful.

Szabo hooked his arm around Loh's biceps. "Tom designed the odeum. Designed the house. We're partners."

"In life," said Tom Loh.

Szabo said, "Is the caterer doing anything or just standing around? As long as she's stuck here, she might as well tidy up."

Milo said, "Mr. Szabo, let's hold off on cleanup until the crime-scene people are through."

"Crime-scene people," said Szabo. Tears filled his eyes. "Never in my life did I imagine that term would be relevant to our *home*."

Tom Loh said, "Is the—is Vassily still here?"

"The body will be removed as soon as we're finished," said Milo.

"Sure, fine, whatever. Is there anything else I can tell you? About Vassily, the concert?"

"We've already been through the guest list, sir."

"But as I told you," Szabo broke in, "the guest list is only part of the audience. Eighty-five out of a hundred and thirteen people. And you must take my word: every one of those eighty-five is beyond reproach. Twenty-five are our faithful season-ticket holders—neighbors whom we grant free admission."

"Stroking the neighbors," explained Loh. "So we could get the odeum through zoning hassles."

"Eighty-five out of one thirteen," said Milo. "Leaving twenty-eight strangers."

"But surely," said Szabo, "anyone who'd be interested in Chopin would be too refined to . . ."

Loh said, "Let them do their job, Stef." His hand rested atop the older man's shoulder.

"Oh, I know you're right. I'm just a fellow trying to make the world a more beautiful place, what do *I* know about *this* kind of thing?" Szabo smiled weakly. "Tom reads mystery novels. He *appreciates* this kind of thing."

"Only in fiction," said Loh. "This is hideous."

Szabo seemed to take that as a reproach. "Yes, yes, of course, I'm babbling, don't know what I'm saying. Go about your business, Detective." He touched his chest. "I need to sit down."

Loh said, "Go upstairs, I'll bring you a Pear William." Taking Szabo's arm, he guided the older man toward the landing, stopped and watched as Szabo trudged the rest of the way by himself, then returned to us.

"He's traumatized."

"How long have you had the odeum?" said Milo.

"Same time as the house," said Loh. "Three years. But the project was over a decade in the making. We began right after Stef and I moved from New York. We were together two years before that. Stef was in the hosiery business, and I was in urban design, did public and private spaces. We met at a reception for Zubin Mehta. Stef had always been a classical music freak, and I was there because I'd done some work for one of the maestro's friends."

Dark, almondine eyes focused on Milo. "Do you think this will jeopardize the odeum?"

"I couldn't say, sir."

"Because it's vital to Stef." Loh plinked one end of his red bowtie. "I really don't think there'd be any legal basis to stop it. The neighbors have been supportive. Stef buys their children's school raffle tickets by the score, and we contribute heavily to every neighborhood project. We're on good terms with the zoning board, and believe me that took some doing."

"Zoning board raffle tickets?" said Milo.

Loh's eyes rolled, and he smiled. "Don't ask—the point is, I'd hate for it to end. It means a lot to Stef, and he means a lot to me."

"How often do you throw concerts?"

"Throw concerts," said Loh, amused by the image. "Stef schedules four a year. Last year, we added an extra one at Christmas, as a benefit for the John Robert Preston School."

"Neighbor's kid?"

Loh's smile widened. "I can see why you're a detective."

Milo said, "I went over the till and counted thirteen checks from people not on the guest list. That leaves another fifteen who paid cash. The cash balance matches perfectly. Any idea who those fifteen are?"

Loh shook his head. "You'd have to ask Anita—the girl at the door."

"I did. She doesn't recall."

"Sorry," said Loh. "It's not as if we were looking for—as if this could've been anticipated."

"What can you tell me about Vassily Levitch?"

"Young, intense. Like all of them. Stefan would know more. Music is his passion."

"And you?"

"I keep things organized."

"Is there anything you can say about Levitch's demeanor?"

"Very quiet, nervous about the performance. He barely slept or ate, and I heard him pacing in his room just before the recital. But really, Detective, that's how it usually is. These people are gifted, and they work harder than can be imagined. Vassily arrived two days ago and practiced seven hours each day. When he wasn't playing, he was holed up in his room."

"No visitors?"

"No visitors and two phone calls. From his mother and his agent. He'd never been to L.A. before."

"Gifted," said Milo. "And on his way up."

"That's Stefan's thing," said Loh. "He seeks out rising stars and tries to help their ascent."

"By offering them recital time, here?"

"And money. Our foundation issues grants. Nothing lavish, each artist receives a fifteen-thousand-dollar stipend."

"Sounds generous to me."

"Stef's the soul of generosity."

"How does Mr. Szabo locate the artists—how did he find Vassily Levitch, specifically?"

"From Vassily's agent in New York. Now that the concerts have achieved a certain reputation, we get contacted frequently. The agent sent Stefan a tape, and Stefan listened to it and decided Vassily would be perfect. Stefan tends to favor soloists or small ensembles. We're not exactly set up for an orchestra."

"How long before the concert were the arrangements made?"

"A while back," said Loh. "Months. We need ample time for preparation. The acoustics, the lighting, choosing the caterer. And, of course, the advance publicity. Such as it is."

"Which is?"

"Occasional mention on selected radio stations. KBAK—the classic station mentions us twice a day for two weeks prior. That fits our budget as well as our aspiration. We can't handle a large crowd, nor do we wish one."

"Eighty-five on the guest list," said Milo. "Why not prearrange all the seats?"

"Stefan left a few extras for outsiders in order to be public-spirited. Music students, teachers, that kind of thing."

"Any publicity other than radio?"

"We don't try for that," said Loh. "Even the small bit of exposure we get means more seat requests than we can handle."

"Was that true tonight?"

"I'd assume so." Loh frowned. "You can't seriously believe a member of the audience did this."

"At this point, I'll entertain any theories, sir."

"Here's mine: Someone intruded. The truth is, anyone could've gone back there behind the poolhouse and stabbed Vassily. Bristol's an open street, we don't like living behind walls and gates."

"What would Levitch have been doing back there?"

Loh shrugged. "Possibly walking off his tension after the recital."

"Any idea when he left the reception?"

"Not a clue. People were milling. Stefan suggests that the artists stick around. For their sake—making connections. Generally, the artists comply. Obviously, Vassily slipped away."

"Shy type?" said Milo. "Holing up in his room."

"Yes. But he did like to stroll the garden at night. After he finished practicing. By himself."

"Were there guests milling outside, too?"

"We discourage that, try to keep them indoors. Trampling the plants and all that. But it's not as if we post armed guards."

"No armed guards," said Milo. "Just one security man."

"For the neighbors—they prefer that Bristol be free of a Gestapo ambience. And there's never been any need for an army of guards. This is one of the safest neighborhoods in the city. Despite you-know-who."

"The only fence is at the rear property line."

"Correct, behind the tennis court," said Loh.

"How big's the property?"

"A little over two acres."

"What was the security guard's specific assignment?"

"To provide security, whatever that means. I'm sure he wasn't pre-pared for any . . . serious eventuality. This wasn't exactly a rap concert. The average age of the audience had to be sixty-five. We're talking per-fect behavior."

"That include the outsiders?"

"When it comes to the concerts, Stefan can be a bit of a martinet. He *insists* on dead silence. And his tastes run to soothing music. Chopin, Debussy, all that good stuff."

"Do you share Mr. Szabo's tastes?"

Loh grinned again. "I'm more into technorock and David Bowie."

"Any David Bowie concerts scheduled for the odeum?"

Loh chuckled. "Mr. Bowie isn't exactly within our price range. Nor would Stefan's sensibilities survive the experience." He shot a sleek black cuff and consulted a sleek black watch.

Milo said, "Let's have a look at Levitch's room."

As we climbed the stairs, Milo said, "Big house."

Loh said, "Stefan's family escaped from Hungary in 1956. He was a teenager, but they managed to cram him into a large steamer trunk. We're talking *days* without food or toilet facilities, a few air holes for breathing. I'd say he's entitled to his space, wouldn't you?"

The right side of the landing was taken up by two enormous bedrooms—Szabo's and Loh's. Open doors to both revealed flashes of brocade and damask, polished wood, soft lighting. To the left, were three guest suites, smaller, less opulent, but still stylishly turned out.

The room where Vassily Levitch had spent the past two nights was taped off. Milo broke the tape, and I followed him inside. Tom Loh stood in the doorway, and said, "What should I do?"

"Thanks for your time, sir," said Milo. "Feel free to go about your business."

Loh went back down the stairs.

Milo said, "Stay there while I toss, if you don't mind. The evidentiary chain and all that."

"Got to be careful," I said. "Especially in light of you-know-who."

The guest suite was papered in red silk, furnished with a canopied queen bed, two Regency nightstands, and an ornate, inlaid Italian chest of drawers. Empty drawers, as was the closet. Vassily Levitch had lived out of his black nylon suitcase. Even his toiletries had remained in the valise.

Milo examined the contents of the pianist's wallet, went through the pockets of every garment. A kit bag produced aftershave, a safety razor, Advil, Valium, and Pepto-Bismol. A manila envelope in a zippered compartment of the suitcase contained photocopied reviews of other recitals Levitch had given. The critics lauded the young man's touch and phrasing. He'd won the Steinmetz Competition, the Hurlbank Competition, the Great Barrington Piano Gala.

No driver's license. A check-cashing ID card put him at twenty-seven years old.

Milo said, "Zero plus zero."

I said, "Can I see the body?"

A rear patio as large as the odeum emptied to the rolling lawn and widely spaced birch trees walled by a twelve-foot-tall ficus hedge. A gothic arch cut into the hedge led the way to a fifty-foot lap pool, a tennis court, a cactus garden, a shallow pond devoid of fish and, tucked into the rear, right corner, a four-car garage.

I could see no driveway or any other direct access from the street to the garage, and asked Milo about that.

"They use it for storage—antiques, clothing, lamps. You should see the stuff; I could live off their castaways."

"They leave their cars in front?"

"His and his Mercedes 600s. Concert nights they park on the street. Want the house to look 'aesthetically pure.' Nice life, huh? C'mon."

He led me behind the garage to where a female cop guarded Vassily Levitch's corpse. The body lay on a narrow strip of soiled concrete backed by another high ficus hedge, sharing space with five plastic garbage cans. A battery-op LAPD floodlight turned everything bilious. Milo told the policewoman to take five. She looked grateful as she headed toward the cactus garden.

He stood back and let me take in the details.

A mean, putrid space; even the grandest of estates have them, but on this estate, you had to make your way through two acres of beauty to find it.

Best kill spot on the property. Someone who'd been here before and knew the layout?

I raised the point. Milo chewed on it but said nothing.

I got closer to the body, stepping into greenish light.

In life, Levitch had been a handsome young man—a golden-haired boy, literally. His sculpted face stared up into the night, topped by a mass of curls that caressed his shoulders. Prominent nose, chin, cheek-bones, an aggressive forehead. Long-fingered hands were frozen in palms-up supplication. The tails of his cutaway coat had crumpled under him. A starched white shirt, now mostly crimson, had been ripped open, exposing a hairless chest. A seven-inch slit, the edges curling, ran vertically from umbilicus to the hollow beneath the pianist's sternum. Something pale and wormy peeked out from the wound. A curl of bowel.

Levitch's white pique bow tie was also blood-splotched. His eyes popped, a distended tongue flopped from one corner of his mouth, a bloody ring necklaced his gullet.

I said, "Paramedics rip the shirt?"

He nodded.

I stared at the corpse some more, moved away.

"Any thoughts?"

"Baby Boy was stabbed, Julie Kipper was strangled, and this poor guy endured both. Was the cut pre- or postmortem?"

"Coroner says probably pre because of all the blood spray. Then the wire was looped around his neck. So what are you saying? A serial with escalation?"

"Or strangulation is the killer's goal and sometimes he needs to make concessions. Sadists and sexual psychopaths enjoy choking out their victims because it's intimate, slow, and feeds the power lust incrementally. Julie was an easy target because she was tiny, and the cramped space of the bathroom trapped her, so the killer was able to go straight for his fun. Levitch, on the other hand, was a strong young guy, so he had to be disabled first."

"What about Baby Boy? Far as I've heard, there was nothing around his neck."

"Baby Boy was a huge man. Choking him out would've been a challenge. And Baby Boy's kill spot was public—a city alley, easy for someone to walk by. Maybe the killer was being careful. Or he got spooked before he could finish."

"Be interesting to know how Levitch's stab wounds match up with Baby Boy. I'll check with Petra. Till now we didn't think our cases had anything in common."

He stared at me, shook his head. Took another look at Levitch.

"However this shakes out, I need to do the routine, Alex. Which in this case is major-league scut: IDing audience members, canvassing the neighborhood for sightings of suspicious strangers, checking the files for recent prowler calls. Too much for one noble soldier. The guys who pulled the case initially are a couple of D-Is, green, no whodunit experience, claim they're interested in getting their feet wet. They actually seem grateful for Uncle Milo's council. I'll sic 'em on the grunt work, get on the phone tomorrow with Levitch's agent in New York and see what I can learn about him."

"Hey, boss-man," I said.

"That's me," he said. "Chairman of the Gore. Seen enough?"

"More than enough."

We walked back to the house, and I thought about Vassily Levitch left to die in the company of garbage cans. Baby Boy, dumped in a back alley, Juliet Kipper's life terminated in a toilet.

"Demeaning them is the thing," I said. "Reducing art to trash."

17 The next day Milo asked me to a meeting. Five P.M. in the back room of the same Indian restaurant.

"I'll be there. Anything new?"

"Levitch's agent and mother had nothing to offer. She mostly sobbed, all the agent could say was Vassily was a beautiful boy, amazing talent. The reason I want to put heads together is Petra said Levitch's wound sounds like a perfect match to Baby Boy's. Plus, the coroner's telling me the ligature used on Levitch is the same gauge and consistency as the one used to choke out Julie. And guess what—your idea about Baby Boy's killer being spooked might be right-on. Turns out there was a witness in the alley, some homeless guy. Pretty well booze-blasted, and between that and the darkness, his description didn't amount to much. But maybe the killer sensed him and split."

"What's the description?"

"Tall guy in a long coat. He came up to Lee, shmoozed, then moved in for what looked like a hug. Guy walks away, Lee falls down. The killer made no move on the homeless guy—Linus Brophy—but you never know."

"The killer wouldn't go for Brophy."

"Why not?"

"Out of his focus," I said. "We're talking about someone with very specific goals."

I gathered together my notes and drove to Café Moghul. The same amiable sari'd woman beamed as she ushered me through the restaurant and over to an unmarked door next to the men's room. "He is here!"

The windowless, green room had probably once served as storage space. Milo sat at a table set for three. Behind him was a sleeper couch pushed up against the wall. On the couch was a tightly curled bedroll, a stack of Indian magazines, and a box of tissues. Curry smells drifted in through a ceiling grate.

I sat down as he dipped some kind of wafer into a bowl of red sauce. The sauce tinted his lips liverish.

"Our hostess seems quite impressed with you."

"I tip big. And they think my presence offers protection."

"They've had problems?"

"Just the usual—drunks wandering in, unwanted solicitors. Couple of weeks ago I happened to be here when some idiot peddling dried flowers for an instant nirvana cult got unruly. I engaged in diplomacy."

"And now the U.N.'s requesting your résumé."

"Hey, those clowns could use the help—here she is."

He stood and greeted Petra Connor.

She looked around and grinned. "You really know how to treat a girl, Milo."

"Only the best for Hollywood Division."

She had on the usual black pantsuit, the brownish lipstick and pale matte makeup. Her short, black hair was glossy, and her eyes shone. Like Milo, she'd brought a bulging, soft attaché case. His was cracked and gray, hers, black and oiled.

She gave me a wave. "Hi, Alex." Then she half turned as a round-shouldered man stepped into the room. "Guys, this is my new partner, Eric Stahl."

Stahl wore black, too. A baggy suit over a starched white shirt and skinny gray tie. He had collapsed cheeks, eyes recessed as deeply as those of a blind man. His spiky crew cut was a deep brown shade one half tone lighter than Petra's ebony coif, but, hue-wise, that was a fine distinction. A few years older than Petra, but like her, thin with fair skin. In Stahl's case, a tallowy pallor rendered sickly by contrast to Petra's crisp, cosmetic kabuki. But for rosy spots on his cheeks, he might've been fashioned of wax.

He appraised the room. Flat, inert eyes.

Milo said, "Hey, Eric."

Stahl said, "Hey," in a low voice and shifted his gaze to the table.

Three place settings.

Milo said, "I'll get you fixed up."

"Just get a chair, Eric won't be eating," said Petra.

"Oh, yeah?" said Milo. "Don't like Indian, Eric?"

"I ate already," said Stahl. His voice matched his eyes.

"Eric doesn't eat," said Petra. "He claims he does, but I've never seen it."

The smiling woman brought platters of food. Milo snarfed, Petra and I picked, Eric Stahl placed his hands flat on the table and stared at his fingernails.

Stahl's presence seemed to discourage small talk. So did the situation, and Milo got right down to business, passing around Julie Kipper's case file, then summarizing the little he had on Vassily Levitch.

Both Hollywood detectives took it in without comment. Milo said, "Could you recap Baby Boy?"

Petra said, "Sure." Her account was concise, focused on the relevant details. The precise delivery emphasized how little she'd unearthed, and when she finished, she seemed bothered.

Stahl remained mute.

Milo said, "Sounds like a match to Levitch, at least. How about the psych wisdom, Alex?"

I summarized the out-of-town cases quickly, glossed over Wilfred Reedy because his murder sounded like a drug hit, and moved on to China Maranga. As I put forth the suggestion that she might've been stalked without knowing it, the three of them listened but didn't react.

A trio of blank faces; if I was right, they were faced with monumental work.

"The night China disappeared," I said, "she left the studio in a foul mood and quite possibly stoned. Under the best of circumstances, she had a bad temper, was known to unload on people without warning. Here's a prime example: She refused an interview with a fanzine, but the editor was persistent and ran the story anyway. A puff piece. China's thanks was to phone the guy and abuse him. Viciously, was the way her band mate put it. She had no sense of personal safety, lived high-risk. That and a major tantrum in the wrong setting could've proved fatal."

"What was the name of the fanzine?" said Petra.

"Something called *GrooveRat*. I looked for it but couldn't—"

Her slim, white fingers on my wrist stopped me midsentence.

"*GrooveRat* did a piece on Baby Boy," she said. She opened her attaché case, drew out a blue murder book, and began paging. "The editor was persistent with me, too. Real pest, kept calling, bugging me for details . . . here we go: Yuri Drummond. I didn't take him seriously because he sounded like an obnoxious kid. He told me he'd never actually met Baby Boy but ran a profile on him."

"Same as China," said Milo. "Baby Boy turn him down, too?"

"I didn't ask. He claimed interviews weren't the magazine's style, they were into the essence of art, not the persona, or some nonsense like that. He sounded about twelve."

"What did he want from you?" I said.

"The gory details." She frowned. "I figured him for an adolescent ghoul, shined him on."

Milo said, "Be interesting to know if he ever wrote up Julie Kipper."

"Wouldn't it," said Petra.

I said, "I tried to find a copy of *GrooveRat* at the big newsstand on Selma, but they didn't carry it. The owner suggested a comics store on the boulevard, but they were closed."

"Probably a dinky fly-by-night deal," said Milo.

"That's what China's band mate said. He didn't save a copy, either."

"Yuri Drummond . . . sounds like a made-up name. What, he wants to be a cosmonaut?"

"Everyone reinvents themselves," said Petra. "It's the L.A. way." Glancing at Stahl. He didn't respond.

"Especially if they're running from something," I said.

"*GrooveRat*," she said. "So what does this mean? A fan gone psycho?"

"Someone overinvolved in the victims' careers. Maybe someone whose identity became enmeshed with the creativity of others. 'Leeches on the body artistic' is how Julie Kipper's ex-husband described critics and agents and gallery owners and all the other ancillaries of the creative world. The same can be said of fanatical followers. Sometimes attachments morph into business arrangements—presidents of fan clubs selling memorabilia—but the core remains emotional: celebrity by association. For most people, fandom's a fling that ends when they grow up. But certain borderline personalities never mature, and what starts out as a harmless ego-substitution—the kid standing in front of a mirror playing air guitar and imagining himself to be Hendrix—can turn into a psychological hijacking."

"Hijacking what?" said Milo.

"The adored one's identity. 'I know the star better than he knows himself. How dare he get married/sell out/not listen to my advice?' "

"How dare he refuse my generous offer to be interviewed," said Petra. "Adolescents are the biggest fanatics, right? And Yuri Drummond sounded adolescent. The fact that he published a zine makes him hard-core."

"Desktop publishing's elevated hard-core," I said. "Buy a computer and a printer, and you, too, can be a media-master. I know these victims vary demographically, but I've thought all along that the crucial element is their career status: poised for a jump. What if the killer became attached to them precisely *because* they weren't stars? Entertained rescue fantasies—he'd be the star-maker by writing about them. They rejected him, so he interrupted the climb. Maybe he convinced himself they sold out."

"Or," said Petra, "since we're talking about vicarious talent, maybe he was an aspiring artist himself and simply got consumed with jealousy."

Milo said, "Aspiring guitarist, painter, singer, and pianist?"

"A real megalomaniac," she said.

All three detectives looked at me.

"It's possible," I said. "A dilettante who bounces from game to game. I had a patient years ago, a successful writer. Scarcely a week went by when he didn't meet someone who planned to pen the Great American Novel if only they had time. This guy had written his first four books while holding down two jobs. One thing he told me stuck: When someone says they want to be a writer, they'll never make it. When they say they want to write, there's a chance. That could fit with our bitter-fan scenario: someone who gets off on the external trappings of creativity."

Petra smiled. "Leeches on the body artistic." Years ago, she'd worked as a painter. "I like that."

"So we're talking two possibilities," said Milo. "A rescue fantasy turned on its head or pathological jealousy."

"Or both," I said. "Or, I'm dead wrong."

Petra laughed. "Don't say that up on the witness stand, Doctor." She picked up a piece of wafer bread, cracked a corner between sharp, white teeth, chewed slowly. "Yuri Drummond went on about his zine capturing the essence of art. When he started nagging me for the gories, it could've been revisiting the scene—psychologically."

"Ego trip," said Milo. "Like arsonists standing around watching the flames."

"Did Drummond write the story on Baby Boy?" I said.

"I think he told me a writer did," said Petra. "All I copied down was the guy's name. At the time it seemed irrelevant." She placed her napkin on the table. "Time to check the guy out, earn my salary. This was good, Milo. Let me split the check with you."

"Forget it. I run a tab here."

"You're sure?"

"I'm a rajah," he said. "Go detect. Stay in touch."

Petra touched Milo's shoulder briefly, favored me with a smile, turned and headed for the door.

Stahl got up and followed her out. During the entire discussion, he hadn't said a word.

18

The silent type. Some women thought they liked that.

Petra had thought she liked it. But working with Stahl was proving to be a trying experience.

The guy never spoke unless spoken to, and even then, he drew upon his verbal bank account one scroogy syllable at a time.

Now here they were, driving away from the meeting with Milo and Alex, when there should've been animated discussion. Stahl just stared out the passenger window, inert as dirt.

What? Looking for another stolen car? He'd spotted two GTAs in one week, and the second had contained a passenger with a felony manslaughter warrant, so brownie points for the two of them. But if that's what floated Stahl's dinghy, he should've asked for an assignment to Auto Theft.

Why he'd chosen Homicide puzzled her. Why he'd given up the security of an Army gig for the streets was an even bigger question mark.

She'd hazarded a few polite questions. Every attempt to crack the shell revealed a granite egg.

Not that old Eric was any big old stoic macho man with obvious dominance needs or glory lust. On the contrary, he'd made it clear, right from the beginning, that Petra was the senior partner.

And unlike most men, he knew how to apologize. Even when it wasn't necessary.

Two days into their partnership, Petra had arrived early and found Stahl at his desk, reading a folded newspaper and sipping herbal tea—that was another thing, he didn't drink coffee, and if anything contravened the detective code of ethics, it was caffeine phobia.

When he saw her he looked up and Petra sensed unease—the merest hint of restlessness—in his flat, brown eyes.

"Evening, Eric."

"This wasn't my idea," he said, handing her the paper. A two-paragraph article toward the back had been circled in black marker.

Summary of the Armenian gang killing. Her name in print, as the investigator. Along with Stahl's.

The case had been wrapped up well before Stahl's arrival. Someone—maybe a departmental PR doofus, or even Schoelkopf digging at Petra intentionally—had doled out cocredit.

"Don't worry about it," said Petra.

"I don't like it," said Stahl.

"Don't like what?"

"It was your case."

"I don't care, Eric."

"I thought I'd call the *Times*."

"Don't be ridiculous."

Stahl stared at her. "Okay," he said, finally. "I wanted to clarify."

"You have."

He returned to his tea.

A mile before the Hollywood station, Petra said, "So what do you think?"

"About what?"

"Dr. Delaware's theory."

"You know him," said Stahl. A statement, not a question.

"If you're asking whether he's good, he is. I've worked with him and Milo before. Milo's the best—top solve-rate in West L.A., maybe the department."

Stahl tapped his knee.

"He's gay," said Petra.

No answer.

"Delaware's smart," she said. "Brilliant. I usually don't have much faith in shrinks, but he's come through."

"Then I like his theory," said Stahl.

"So what next? Check out comics stores for *GrooveRat* or try to find it with phone work?"

"Both," said Stahl. "There are two of us."

"Which would you prefer?"

"Your call."

"State a preference, Eric."

"I'll do the phone work."

Big surprise. Eric at his desk, avoiding real-live *people*.

She dropped him off and cruised Hollywood for alternative bookstores. Inquiries about *GrooveRat* produced blank stares from the clerks, but most of them looked blasted to begin with. On her fifth try, the pimply kid at the counter hooked a thumb toward a cardboard box to his left. Red ink scrawl on the flap said OLD ZINES, ONE BUCK.

The carton smelled moldy and was crammed with paper and loose sheets—spindled and mutilated magazines.

Petra said, "You definitely have *GrooveRat* in here?"

The kid said, "Probably," and stared off into space.

Petra began pawing through the box, raising dust that grayed her black jacket. Most of the zines seemed to be little more than adolescent hobby junk. Several were printed on pulp. She skimmed. A world of incoherence, fluctuating from bored to breathless, mostly to do with music and movies and dirty jokes.

Nearly at the bottom of the pile, she found a coverless copy of *GrooveRat*. Ten pages of poorly typed text and amateurish cartoons. The date on the masthead was the previous summer. No volume or number listings.

Not much in the way of staff, either.

Yuri Drummond, Editor & Publisher
Contributing Writers: The Usual Gang of Miscreants

The second line reminded Petra of something—ripoff of a *Mad* magazine line. All four of her brothers had collected *Mad*. Something about the usual gang of idiots . . .

So Mr. Drummond was unoriginal, as well as pretentious. That fit with Alex's theory.

The bottom of the masthead listed an address for mailing subscription checks. The zine promised "irregular publication," and charged forty dollars a year.

Delusional, as well. Petra wondered if anyone had bitten. She supposed if idiots were willing to pay three bucks a minute for phone tarot, anything was possible.

The address was right here in Hollywood—on Sunset east of Highland, just a short drive away.

She scanned the table of contents. Four pieces on rock bands she'd never heard of and a write-up of a sculptor who worked in plastic-coated dog poo.

The author of the art piece, nom-du-plumed "Mr. Peach," really appreciated fecal art, terming it *"primally satisfying and gut-wrenching (Duchamp-Dada-yuk yuk, kids.)"* Petra was surer than ever that she was dealing with an adolescent mind, and that didn't synch with the careful planning of the murders. Still, the zine cropping up in two cases bore attention.

A careful check of the remaining pages revealed nothing on Baby Boy Lee, Juliet Kipper, or Vassily Levitch. Nothing on the Boston case Alex had found, either—Bernet, the ballerina. Petra had her doubts about that one, but you didn't want to ignore Alex's gut.

She paid for the rag and headed for *GrooveRat* headquarters.

Strip mall at Gower and Sunset. A Mail Boxes N' Stuff. Big shock.

"Suite 248" was really Box 248, now leased to Verna Joy Hollywood Cosmetics. Petra knew that because as she waited for the woman in charge to stop fussing with a cuticle and give her the time of day, two bound stacks of mail on the counter caught her eye. Lots of interest in Verna Joy; too much for one box.

The top envelope was pink, with a return address in Des Moines. Neat, feminine cursive writing advertised *"Payment Inside."*

The mail-drop woman finally put away her emery board, spotted Petra studying the stacks, snatched them up, and jammed them under the counter. A peroxide blonde in her sixties, she'd gone overboard with the brown eye shadow and the black liner, left the rest of her tired, splotched, drinker's face unpainted. Emphasizing the eyes— bringing out the despair.

Petra showed her ID and the woman's expression shifted from irritation to outright contempt. "What do *you* want?"

"A magazine named *GrooveRat* used to lease Box 248. How long has it been since they vacated, ma'am?"

"Don't know and wouldn't tell you if I did." The woman's jaw jutted.

"Why's that, ma'am?"

"It's the law. Bill of Rights. You need a warrant."

Petra relaxed her posture, tried a soft smile. "You're absolutely right, ma'am, but I don't want to search the box. I'd just like to know how long it's been since the tenant vacated."

"Don't know and wouldn't tell you if I did." The woman's smile was tight-lipped and triumphant.

"Were you working here when *GrooveRat* occupied the box?"

Shrug.

"Who picked up *GrooveRat*'s mail?"

Ditto.

"Ma'am," said Petra. "I can come back with a warrant."

"Then you do that," said the woman with sudden savagery.

"What's the problem, ma'am?"

"I got no problem."

"This could be related to a homicide investigation."

The smudgy eyes remained resolute. Petra fixed on them, mustered a hard stare. The woman said, "You don't impress me."

"Homicide doesn't impress you?" said Petra.

"It's always homicide," said the woman. "Everything's homicide."

"What?"

The woman jabbed a finger. "This is my place, and I don't have to talk to you." But she followed that with: "Protect yourself, and it's *homicide*. Stand up for your rights, and it's *homicide*."

Battle of stares.

"What's your name, ma'am?"

"I don't have to tell—"

"You sure do, or you'll be arrested on an obstruction charge." Petra reached for her cuffs.

"Olive Gilwhite," said the woman, jowls flittering.

"Are you sure you don't want to cooperate, Ms. Gilwhite?"

"I'm not saying nothing."

Rather than deliver a grammar lesson, Petra left the mail drop and drove back to the station. Eric Stahl was at his desk phoning and taking notes. She ignored him and played with the computers, plugging in Olive Gilwhite's name and the mail drop's address and finally coming up with something.

Two years ago, the proprietor of a Hollywood Mailboxes N' Stuff, a man named Henry Gilwhite, had been busted for homicide.

Petra fished in the files and found the case summary. Gilwhite, sixty-three, had shot a nineteen-year-old male trannie prostitute named Gervazio Guzman to death in back of the mail drop. Gilwhite had claimed self-defense in an attempted mugging, but his semen on Guzman's dress told a different story. The case had been pled down to manslaughter, and Gilwhite was serving time at Lompoc. Five to ten, but at his age, that might very well mean life.

Leaving Mrs. Gilwhite to run the store and drink herself to death.

Protect yourself, and it's homicide.

Petra resolved to find some way to lean on the nasty old biddy.

As she thought about it, Stahl got up and approached her desk.

"What's up, Eric?"

"I've got a few possibles on Yuri Drummond."

"Possibles?"

"There's no Yuri Drumonds anywhere in the state, so I looked up all the Drummonds in our zip codes."

"Why limit it to Hollywood?" said Petra.

"It's a place to start. If Drummond's a star-chaser, maybe he wants to live in the hub."

"Eric, the stars live in Bel Air and Malibu."

"I was speaking metaphorically," said Stahl. He drew a three-by-five index card from his suit jacket. Still wearing his black suit coat. Every other detective was in shirtsleeves.

Petra said, "What'd you come up with?"

"DMV has twelve Drummonds listed, five of them females. Of the seven males, four are older than fifty. These are the three remaining."

The longest speech she'd ever heard from him. His flat eyes had acquired a murky glow, and the coins in his cheeks had deepened to vermilion—this one got *off* on *tedium*. He handed her the index card. Neat printing in green ink; a list.

1. *Adrian Drummond, 16.* (A Los Feliz address that Petra recognized as a gated street in Laughlin Park. Rich kid? That fit, but 16 seemed young to be publishing anything, even a low-level zine.)
2. *Kevin Drummond, 24.* (An apartment on North Rossmore.)
3. *Randolph Drummond, 44.* (An apartment on Wilton Place.)

"The first two have no records," said Stahl. "Randolph Drummond has a five-year-old prior for vehicular manslaughter and DUI. Should we start with him?"

"Bad car crash?" said Petra. "It's not exactly serial murder."

"It's antisocial," said Stahl. Something new came into his voice—harder, more intense. His eyes had narrowed to slits.

Petra said, "Still, my money's on the second one—Kevin. The voice I heard was younger than forty-four, and the zine's got an immature flavor. Of course, all this assumes any of these are our guy. For all we know our Drummond lives out in the Valley." But even as she said that, she doubted it. The *GrooveRat* POB had been rented in Hollywood. Stahl's instincts were good.

He said, "Okay."

"For all we know his name's not even Drummond," said Petra.

"Yuri's probably fake and so why not the surname?" The incident with Olive Gilwhite had left her combative.

Stahl didn't answer.

"Let's go," Petra said, shoving the card at him and grabbing her purse.

"Where?"

"On a Drummond-search."

19 Kevin Drummond's Rossmore address matched an eighty-year-old, three-story brick-faced, mock Tudor just below Melrose, where the street turned into Vine and commercial Hollywood began.

The mansions of Hancock Park were a brief stroll south, and between that high-priced real estate and Drummond's block, sat the Royale and the Majestic and other elegant, doorman-guarded buildings. Gorgeous old vanilla-colored dowagers, facing the green velvet links of the Wilshire Country Club, built when labor was cheap and architecture meant ornament. Petra had heard that Mae West had lived out her days in one of them, clad in satin gowns and keeping company with young men till the end. God bless her.

But any vestiges of glamour had faded by the time you got to Drummond's street. The bulk of the buildings were ugly boxes knocked into place during the fifties, and the remaining older structures appeared ill tended, like Drummond's. Several bricks were missing from the facade and a warped slat of cardboard shielded a second-story window. On the ground floor, protection was provided by rusty security grates across the front door and the street-level windows. The alarm sign on the scrubby little lawn was that of a shoddy company Petra knew had been out of business for years. The hub, indeed.

To the right of the entrance were twenty call buttons, most with the tenant IDs missing from the slots. No identification for Drummond's second-story unit. The names that remained in place were all Hispanic or Asian.

Petra pushed Drummond's button. No answer. She tried again, leaned on the buzzer. Nothing.

Unit One was the manager, *G. Santos*. Same result.

She said, "Let's try the other two."

Randolph Drummond's place on Wilton was a sixty-unit, pink-stucco monster built around a cloudy swimming pool. Drummond's apartment was at street level, facing the traffic. No security here, not even a symbolic gate across the cutout that led to the complex, and Petra and Stahl walked right in and up to Drummond's door.

Petra's knock was answered by a boomy "Hold on!" The lock turned and the door opened and a man leaning on aluminum elbow crutches said, "What can I do for you?"

"Randolph Drummond?"

"In the flesh. Such as it is." Drummond's torso canted to one side. He wore a brown v-neck sweater over a yellow shirt, spotless khakis, felt bedroom slippers. His hair was white, neatly parted, and a snowy beard bottomed a full face. Weary eyes, seamed skin, mild tan. Hemingway on disability.

Petra would have guessed his age as closer to fifty-four than forty-four.

Massive forearms rested on the crutches. A big man above the waist, but skimpy legs. Behind him was a bed-sitting room—the bed open and covered with a silk throw. What Petra could see appeared military-neat. The sounds of classical music—something sweet and romantic—streamed toward the detectives.

Waste of time. Handicap aside, this was no zine guy. She said, "May we come in, sir?"

"May I ask why?" said Drummond. Jovial smile but no give.

"We're investigating a homicide and looking for a man who calls himself Yuri Drummond."

Drummond's smile expired. He shifted his weight on the crutches. "Homicide? Lord, why?"

His reaction made Petra's heart beat fast. She smiled. "Could we talk inside please, sir?"

Drummond hesitated. "Sure, why not? Haven't had a visitor since the last wave of do-gooders."

He stamped backward on his crutches and cleared space, and Petra and Stahl stepped into the apartment. Inside, the music was louder, but barely. Kept at reasonable volume—issuing from a portable stereo on the floor. One room, just as Petra had thought, outfitted with the bed and two armchairs, a cubby kitchen. A tiny bathroom could be seen behind the arch in the rear wall.

Two plywood bookcases perpendicular to the bed were filled with hardcovers. Literary fiction and law books. Drummond had been busted for manslaughter; a jailhouse expert?

Petra said, "Do-gooders?"

"Disability pimps," said Drummond. "State grants, private foundations. Your name gets on a list and you become a potential customer. Go on, make yourselves comfortable."

Petra and Stahl each took a chair, and Drummond lowered himself to the bed. Keeping that smile pasted on during what looked like a painful ordeal. "Now who got homicided and why would I know anything about it?"

Petra said, "Have you heard of Yuri Drummond?"

"Sounds Russian. Who is he?"

"What about a magazine called *GrooveRat*?"

Drummond's chunky knuckles whitened.

"You know it," said Petra.

"What interest do you have in it?"

"Mr. Drummond, it would be better if we asked the questions."

"Yes, I've heard of it."

"Are you the publisher?"

"Me?" Drummond laughed. "No, I don't think so."

"Who is?"

Drummond inched his bulk toward the bed cushions, took a long time to get comfortable. "I'm happy to cooperate with the police, but you really need to let me know what's going on."

"We really don't," said Stahl.

Stahl's voice seemed to spook Drummond. Drummond paled and licked his lips. Then his eyes brightened with anger. "I put myself here. In this situation." Tapping the crutches. "Little drinking-and-driving problem. But you probably know that."

No answer from the detectives. Petra glanced at her partner. Stahl looked furious.

"Inscrutable public servants," said Drummond. "I got caught— thank God. Served time in a hospital ward, did AA." Another tap. "I'm telling you this because I've been trained to confess. But also so you'll understand: I'm a fool but not an idiot. My head's been clear for ten years, and I know that nothing I've done abrogates my rights. So don't try to intimidate me."

"Abrogate," said Stahl, reaching out and touching the spine of a law book. "You like legal terminology."

"No," said Drummond. "On the contrary. I despise it. But I used to be an attorney."

"Is Yuri Drummond your son?" said Petra.

"Not hardly. I told you I've never heard that name."

"But you have heard of *GrooveRat*. The magazine Yuri Drummond edits."

Drummond didn't reply.

"Mr. Drummond," said Petra. "We found you, we'll find him. Why add to your roster of poor decisions?"

"Ouch," said Drummond, stroking his beard.

"Sir?"

Drummond chewed his cheek. "I didn't know he was calling himself 'Yuri.' But, yes, I have heard of the so-called magazine. He's my brother's kid. Kevin Drummond. So now he's Yuri? What's he done?"

"Maybe nothing. We want to talk to him about *GrooveRat*."

"Well, you've come to the wrong place," said Drummond.

"Why's that?"

"Don't see Kevin," said Drummond. "Let's just say it's not a close-knit family."

"Any idea why he took on the name Yuri?"

"Hell if I know—maybe he fancies himself subversive."

"When's the last time you spoke to your nephew?"

"I *never* speak to him." Drummond's smile was sour. "His father—my brother—and I used to be law partners, and my indiscretions cost Frank quite a bit of business. After I was paroled and discharged from rehab, he fulfilled his brotherly obligation by finding me this place—ten units set aside for state-funded cripples—then proceeded to shut me out completely."

"How do you know about *GrooveRat*?"

"Kevin sent me a copy."

"How long ago?"

"Years—couple of years ago. He'd just graduated college, announced he was a publisher."

"Why would he send it to you?" said Petra.

"Back then, he liked me. Probably because no one else in the family did—wild, alkie uncle and all that. Brother Frank's a bit stuffy. Growing up with him couldn't have been fun for Kevin."

"So you were Kevin's mentor."

Drummond chuckled. "Not remotely. He sent me the rag, I wrote him a note and told him it was dreadful, he should study accounting. Mean old uncle. I never liked the kid."

"Why not?" said Petra.

"Not a charming lad," said Drummond. "Mumbly, ninety-eight-pound-weakling type, kept to himself, always going off on some project."

"Publishing projects?"

"The fancy of the moment. Tropical fish, lizards, rabbits, trading cards, God knows what. Those little Japanese robots—of course he had to have every single one. He was always collecting crap—toy cars, computer games, cheap watches, you name it. Frank and his mother indulged him. Frank and I grew up with no money. Sports was our thing, we both lettered in football in high school and college. Frank's other boys—Greg and Brian—are super athletes. Greg's got a scholarship to Arizona State and Brian's playing varsity in Florida."

"Kevin's not athletic."

Drummond smirked. "Let's just say Kevin's an indoor type."

Talking about his nephew had brought out the cruelty. Petra thought: Drunk, this guy would be ugly. "Do you have kids of your own, Mr. Drummond?"

"No. I used to have a wife." Drummond's eyes squeezed shut. "She was next to me in the car when I hit the pole. My lawyer used my grief as a defense and got me a lighter sentence."

His eyes opened. Moist.

Stahl watched him. Rigid. Unimpressed.

Petra said, "So when's the last time you saw Kevin?"

"Like I said, years ago. I couldn't hazard a precise guess. After my review of his so-called publication, he never called me. It wasn't really a magazine, you know. Just something Kevin cranked out in his bedroom. Probably cost Frank another chunk of change."

"Do you recall anything about the content?"

"I didn't read it," said Drummond. "I took one look, saw it was crap, and tossed it."

"Crap about what?"

"Kevin's take on the art world. People he considered geniuses. Why?"

"Did Kevin write the whole thing himself?"

"That's what I assumed—what, you think he had a staff? This was *amateur* hour, Detective. And what the hell does it have to do with homicide?"

Petra smiled. "So you never see Kevin. Despite the fact that he lives close to you."

"Does he?" Drummond seemed genuinely surprised.

"Right here in Hollywood."

"Hooray for Hollywood," said Drummond. "Makes sense."

"Why's that?"

"Kid always was a star-fucker."

They spent a while longer in the apartment, going over the same territory, rephrasing, the way detectives do, when trolling for inconsistencies. Refusing Randolph Drummond's offers of soft drinks but fetching a Diet Coke for the man when he began licking his lips. Petra did most of the talking. The few times Stahl spoke, Drummond grew uneasy. Not evasiveness, as far as Petra could tell. Stahl's inflectionless tone seemed to spook the guy, and Petra found herself empathizing.

The interview produced home and business addresses and phone numbers for Franklin Drummond, Attorney at Law, both in Encino, and the fact that, two years ago, Kevin Drummond had graduated from Charter College, a small, expensive private school near Eagle Rock.

"They sent me an invitation," said Drummond. "I didn't attend. It was an insincere offer."

"What do you mean?" said Petra.

"No offer to drive me there. I wasn't going to take the damn bus."

It was nearing 4 P.M. by the time they got back to Kevin Drummond's building. Still, no one home.

Time for Encino. As they drove north over Laurel Canyon, Petra said, "Randolph D. bother you?"

"He can't stand his nephew," said Stahl.

"Angry man. Estranged from his entire family. But can't see any link to our case. Can't see him moving round town on those crutches and offing artistic types."

"He killed his wife."

"You see that as relevant?" said Petra.

Stahl's pale fingers interlaced. A stricken look washed over his face, then it was gone so fast that Petra wondered if she'd really seen it.

"Eric?" she said.

Stahl shook his head. "No, he has nothing to do with our case."

"Back to Kevin, then. That comment about his being a star-fucker would tie in with Delaware's theory. So would the history of failed projects. And attraction to fads. This could be one pathetic little loser who just couldn't take not being talented and decided to act out against those who were."

Stahl didn't answer.

"Eric?"

"Don't know."

"What's your intuition?"

"I don't rely on intuition."

"Really?" said Petra. "You've been pretty good with GTAs."

As if taking that as an invitation, Stahl's head swiveled toward the passenger window, and he studied the traffic flow. He stayed that way during the entire trip to the Valley.

They tried Franklin Drummond's Ventura Boulevard office first. The "firm" was a one-lawyer affair on the tenth floor of a bronzed-glass high-rise. The waiting room was cozy, bathed in the same type of romantic music Randolph Drummond had played. The young receptionist was friendly enough when she informed them that Mr. Drummond was in court. Her nameplate said DANITA TYLER, and she looked busy.

"What kind of law does Mr. Drummond practice?" said Petra.

"General business, real estate, litigation. May I ask what this is about?"

"We'd like to talk to him about his son, Kevin."

"Oh." Tyler was puzzled. "Kevin doesn't work here."

"Do you know Kevin?"

"By sight."

"When's the last time you saw him?"

"Is he in trouble?"

"No," said Petra. "We need to talk to him about his publishing business."

"Publishing? I thought he was a student."

"He graduated college a couple of years ago."

"I mean a graduate student. At least that was my impression." The young woman fidgeted. "I probably shouldn't be talking about it."

"Why not?"

"The boss has a thing for privacy."

"Any particular reason?"

"He's a private man. Good boss. Don't get me in trouble, okay?"

Petra smiled. "Promise. Could you please tell me where Kevin attends grad school?"

"Don't know—that's the truth. I'm not even sure he *is* in grad school. I really don't know much about the family. Like I said, Mr. Drummond likes his privacy."

"When's the last time Kevin was here, Ms. Tyler?"

"Oh, my . . . I couldn't tell you. The family almost never comes in."

"How long have you been working here, Ms. Tyler?"

"Two years."

"During that time have you ever met Randolph Drummond?"

"Who's he?"

"A relative," said Petra.

"Publishing, huh?" said Tyler. "The police . . . what, some kind of porno—no, don't answer that." She laughed, ran a finger across her mouth. "I *don't* want to know."

They had her call Franklin Drummond's cell phone, but the attorney didn't answer.

"Sometimes," she said, "he turns it off during the ride home."

"The man likes his privacy," said Petra.

"The man works hard."

They drove out onto Ventura Boulevard. Petra was hungry, and she looked for a semi-inviting, cheap eatery. Two blocks west, she spotted a falafel stand with two picnic tables. Leaving the unmarked in a loading zone, she bought a spiced lamb shwarma in a soft pita and a Coke and ate as Stahl waited in the car. When she was halfway through the sandwich, Stahl got out and took a seat across from her.

Traffic roared by. She munched.

Stahl just sat. His interest in food matched his hunger for human discourse. When he did eat, it was always something boring on white bread that he brought from home in a clean, brown bag.

Whatever home was for Eric.

She ignored him, enjoyed her food, wiped her lips, and stood. "Let's go."

Ten minutes later they pulled up to the home where Kevin Drummond had pursued his ever-shifting fancies.

*   *   *

It was a beautifully tended, extrawide ranch house perched on the uppermost lot of a hilly street south of Ventura Boulevard. Jacarandas shaded the sidewalks. Like most nice L.A. neighborhoods, not a sign of humanity.

Lots of wheels. Three or four vehicles for each house. At Franklin Drummond's, that meant a new-looking, gunmetal Baby Benz sharing circular-driveway space with a white Ford Explorer, a red Honda Accord, and something low-slung under a beige car cover.

The man who opened the door was loosening his tie. Midforties, stocky build, a broad, rubbery face topped by wavy salt-and-pepper hair, a nose that looked as if it had spent some time in the ring. Gold-rimmed eyeglasses sat atop the meaty bridge. Behind the lenses, cool brown eyes looked them over.

With three grown sons, Franklin Drummond had to be older than his brother's forty-four. But he looked younger than Randolph.

"Yes?" he said. The tie was royal blue silk. It loosened easily, and Frank Drummond let it drape over his barrel chest. Petra noticed a wee gold chain dangling from the back. Brioni label. Drummond's shirt was tailored and baby blue with a starched white collar, and his suit pants were gray pinstripe.

Petra told him they were looking for his son.

Frank Drummond's eyes narrowed to paper cuts, and his chest swelled. "What's going on?"

"Have you heard from Kevin recently, sir?"

Drummond stepped out of the house and closed the door behind him. "What's this about?"

Wary but unruffled. This guy was a working lawyer. A one-man firm, accustomed to taking care of his own business. Any sort of subterfuge would bounce right off him, so Petra kept it straight and simple.

"It's Kevin's magazine we're interested in," said Petra. "*GrooveRat*. A couple of the people he covered have been murdered."

As she said it, it sounded far-fetched. All this time searching for a nerdy little wanna-be, and it would probably turn into nothing.

"So?" said Frank Drummond.

"So we'd like to talk to him," said Stahl.

Drummond's eyes tilted toward Stahl. Unlike his brother, he was unimpressed by Stahl's zombie demeanor. "Same question."

"These are general inquiries, sir," said Petra.

"So find him and inquire away," he said. "He doesn't live here anymore."

"When's the last time you saw him?" said Petra.

"Why should I get into this?"

"Why not, sir?"

"General principles," said Frank Drummond. "Keep your mouth shut, flies don't enter."

"We're not flies, sir," said Petra. "Just doing our job, and it would really help us if you could direct us to Kevin."

"Kevin lives by himself."

"In the apartment on Rossmore?"

Drummond glared at her. "If you know that, why are you here?"

"Does Kevin pay his own rent?"

Drummond's lips pursed. He clicked his tongue. "I don't see that Kevin's financial arrangements are relevant to your investigation. If you want to read the magazine, go ask him, and I'm sure he'll be happy to share. He's proud of it."

The tiniest rise in pitch on "the magazine" and "proud."

"He wasn't home," Petra said.

"So try again. It's been a long day—"

"Sir, if you're paying his rent, we thought you might know about his comings and goings."

"I pay," said Drummond, "and that's the extent of it."

Petra smiled. "The joys of parenthood?"

Drummond didn't take the bait. He reached for the door handle.

"Sir, why does Kevin call himself 'Yuri'?"

"Ask him."

"No idea?"

"He probably thinks it sounds cool. Who cares?"

"So you don't see your son, at all?" said Petra.

Drummond retracted his arm, began to fold both limbs across his chest and changed his mind. "Kevin's twenty-four. He has his own life."

"You wouldn't happen to have any copies of *GrooveRat*, would you?"

"Not hardly," said Drummond. The two words were ripe with scorn—the same flavor of contempt Petra had just heard from Uncle Randolph.

Macho-man put-down of Kevin's latest nonsense.

This father, that uncle, two jock brothers. Growing up eccentric and unathletic would've been tough for poor Kevin. Traumatic enough to twist him in the worst possible way?

" 'Not hardly'?" said Petra.

"Kevin took all his things with him when he moved out."

"When was that?"

"After he graduated."

Randolph Drummond had received a copy of the zine around then. At the advent of the maiden issue, Junior and Dad had experienced a parting of the ways. Creative differences, or Dad tired of Junior slacking off?

"Is Kevin in school, sir?"

"No." Frank Drummond's mouth got tight.

"Is there some reason these questions bother you, sir?"

"*You* bother me. Because I think you're bullshitting me. If you're after the magazine, why all these questions about Kevin? If he's under suspicion for something—well, that's just crap. Kevin's a gentle kid."

Making that sound like a character flaw.

Twenty-four-year-old *kid*.

Petra said, "Any idea who, besides Kevin, wrote for *GrooveRat*?"

Drummond shook his head and worked at looking bored.

"How did Kevin finance his baby?"

Drummond's right hand moved to the lovely blue tie, squeezed it into a ribbon, let go. "If you want copies, I'm sure Kev's got some in his apartment. If you see him, tell him to call his mother. She misses him."

"As opposed to," said Stahl, as they drove away.

"What do you mean?"

"His mother misses him. His father doesn't."

"Dysfunctional family," said Petra. "Kevin was the resident sissy. So where does that take us?"

"Frank was evasive."

"Or just a lawyer who likes asking questions, not answering them. We made it pretty obvious we're after more than back issues. Which is fine with me. Shake things up a bit, see what happens."

"What could happen?" said Stahl.

"I don't know. What bothers me is we're spending all this time chasing a kid and his stupid magazine."

"You said he was a ghoul."

"I did?"

"At the meeting," said Stahl. "You said Yuri wanted the gory details. Was a ghoul."

"True," said Petra. "So?"

A half block of silence.

Stahl said, "Let's give his apartment another try."

It was close to 6 P.M. Petra, used to working nights, often found herself showering at this hour, then wolfing a bowl of cereal. All the paper and meetings on the Armenian case and breaking in Stahl and today's lunch with Milo and Alex and this entire futile afternoon had played havoc with her bio clock. She felt queasy and fatigued.

"Sure," she said. "Why not?"

Kevin Drummond was still out, but a press of the manager's button produced a high-pitched "Yes?"

Petra identified herself and the door buzzed open and the detectives found themselves face-to-face with a short, stout woman in her fifties, wearing a white blouse over black leggings and sneakers. Eyeglasses dangled from a chain around her neck. A jumbo roller topped a mass of too-black hair. Freshly waved locks hung down to her shoulders. She said, "Is everything okay?"

"Mrs. Santos?"

"Guadalupe Santos." Open smile. Someone with a pleasant demeanor. Finally.

"We're looking for one of your tenants, Mrs. Santos. Unit fourteen, Kevin Drummond."

"Yuri?" said Santos.

"That's what he calls himself?"

"Yes. Is everything okay?"

"What kind of tenant is Yuri?"

"Nice boy. Quiet. Why do you want him?"

"We'd like to talk to him as part of an investigation."

"I don't think he's here. I saw him . . . hmm . . . maybe two, three days ago. I met him out back, taking out the garbage. I was. He got into his car. His Honda."

DMV had reported a five-year-old Civic. But remembering the red Accord in Frank Drummond's driveway, Petra said, "What color?"

"White," said Guadalupe Santos.

"So Mr. Drummond's been gone for three days."

"Maybe he goes in and out when I'm sleeping, but I never see him."

"No problems from him."

"Easy tenant," said Santos. "His daddy pays his rent six months in advance, he don't make noise. Wish they were all like that."

"He have any friends? Regular visitors?"

"No girlfriends, if that's what you mean. Or boyfriends." Santos smiled uneasily.

"Is Yuri gay?"

Santos laughed. "No, just kidding. This is Hollywood, you know."

Stahl said, "No visitors at all?"

Santos turned serious. Stahl's contagious amiability. "Now that I think about it, you're right. No one. And he doesn't come and go much. Not the neatest guy, but that's his business."

Petra said, "You've been up to his apartment."

"Twice. He had a leaky toilet. And another time I had to show him how to work the heater—not too mechanical."

"A slob, huh?" said Petra.

"Not like dirty," said Santos. He's just one of those—howyoucallit—holds on to everything?"

"Pack rat?"

"That's it. It's a single, and he's got it all filled up with boxes. I couldn't tell you what's in them, it just looked like he never throws anything out—oh yeah, I did see what was in one of them. Those little cars—Matchboxes. My son used to collect them but not as many as Yuri's got. Only Tony outgrew it. He's in the Marines, over at Camp

Pendleton. Training sergeant, he spent time over in Afghanistan, my Tony."

Petra offered a congratulatory nod and a moment of respect for Sergeant Tony Santos. Then: "So Yuri collects stuff."

"Lots of stuff. But like I said, not dirty."

"What kind of work does he do?"

"I don't think he does any," said Guadalupe Santos. "With his daddy paying the rent and all that, I figured him for . . . you know."

"What?"

"Someone with . . . I don't want to say problems. Someone who can't work regular."

"What kind of problems?" said Petra.

"I don't want to say . . . he's just real quiet. Walks with his head down. Like he doesn't want to talk."

Big difference from the pushy guy who'd hectored Petra. Kevin chose his moments.

She showed Kevin Drummond's DMV picture to Santos. Blurred picture, five years old. Skinny kid with dark hair and a nondescript face. *Brown and brown, 6'2", 150, needs corrective lenses.*

"That's him," said Santos. "Tall—he wears glasses. Not such good skin—some zits here and here." Touching her jawline and her temple. "Like he had it bad when he was younger, you know, and it didn't all heal up?"

Six-two fit Linus Brophy's description of Baby Boy's killer. Would a skinny kid have been able to overpower Vassily Levitch? Sure, given the element of surprise.

"Shy," said Petra. "What else?"

"He's like one of those—someone who'd like computers, want to be by himself, you know? He's got tons of computer stuff up there, too. I don't know much about that kind of thing, but it looks expensive. With his daddy paying the rent, I just figured . . . he's a good tenant, though. No problems. I hope he isn't in trouble."

"You'd hate to lose him as a tenant," said Stahl.

"You bet," said Santos. "This business, you never know what you're gonna get."

*   *   *

On the way back to the station, just as the sun began to set, Petra spotted an elderly man and woman walking slowly up Fountain Avenue followed by a large, white, yellow-billed duck.

Blinking to make sure she wasn't hallucinating, she stopped, backed up until she was even with the couple. They kept plodding, and she coasted at their pace. Two munchkins in heavy overcoats and knit caps, veering toward androgynous twinhood, the way very old people sometimes do. Ninety or close to it. Each step was labored. The duck was unleashed and trailed them by inches. Its waddle looked a trifle off-balance.

The man looked over, took the woman's arms, and they stopped. Nervous smiles. Probably some animal regulation being violated, but who cared about that.

"Nice duck," said Petra.

"This is Horace," said the woman. "He's been our baby for a long time."

The duck lifted a foot and scratched its belly. Tiny black eyes seemed to bore into Petra's. Protective.

She said, "Hey there, Horace."

The duck's feathers ruffled.

"Have a nice day," she said, and pulled away from the curb.

Stahl said, "What was that?"

"Reality."

20

Two days after the meeting with Petra and Stahl, Milo asked me to come along for a second interview with Everett Kipper.

"It's a drop-in, this time," he said. "I called ahead, but Kipper's in meetings all day."

"Why the renewed interest?" I said.

"I want to talk to him about *GrooveRat*, see if Yuri Drummond ever expressed an interest in interviewing Julie. Petra and Stahl haven't been able to get hold of actual copies, but Drummond's looking more interesting. He's a twenty-four-year-old loner, real name of Kevin, lives in a one-bedroom pad on a scruffy part of Rossmore. Hasn't been seen for several days—isn't that intriguing? The zine sounds like a vanity deal, delusional. Daddy's a lawyer, pays the rent and probably the printing costs. He wouldn't give Petra the time of day. I'm talking a real clam-up."

"He's a lawyer," I said.

"Petra picked up definite family tension. Kevin sounds like the family weirdo, and Daddy was definitely not pleased to be discussing him."

"A loner," I said.

"What a shock, huh? He's got a history of jumping from project to project—from obsession to obsession. Exactly the fanatical personality you described. He's also a pack rat, his landlady says his apartment's piled high with boxes. Including toys. So maybe kill trophies are part of his collection. He started doing the zine in his senior year. Petra found one partial copy, and Drummond lists himself as the entire editorial staff. He asked an outrageous subscription price, but there's no evidence anyone ever paid."

"Where'd he go to school?"

"Charter College, which is pretty selective, so he's probably smart—just like you've been saying. And he's tall—six-two—which would synch what the wino witness saw. All in all, it's not a bad fit. Stahl's staking out his apartment, and Petra's still trying to learn more about *GrooveRat*—to see if anyone distributed it. If we can locate back issues and find the articles on Baby Boy and China and hopefully Julie, we'll ask for a warrant and won't get one. But it's something."

The orchestration of the murders had set me thinking of a killer in his thirties or forties, and twenty-four seemed young. But maybe Kevin Drummond was precocious. And for the first time since the Kipper case had opened, Milo's voice was light. I kept my mouth shut. Drove to Century City.

The same ovoid waiting room, the same toothy woman at the front desk. No initial alarm, this time, just a chilly smile. "Mr. Kipper's gone to lunch."

"Where to, ma'am?"

"I wouldn't know."

Milo said, "You didn't make the reservation?"

"No reservation," she said. "Mr. Kipper prefers simple places."

"Business lunches at simple places?"

"Mr. Kipper prefers to eat by himself."

"What about the people he's been meeting with all morning?"

The receptionist bit her lip.

Milo said, "It's okay. He pays your salary, you need to do what he tells you. The city pays mine, and I'm just as determined."

"I'm sorry," she said. "It's just . . ."

"He doesn't want to talk to us. Any reason?"

"Not that he mentioned. He's like that."

"Like what?"

"Not much of a talker." She bit her lip. "Please . . ."

"I understand," said Milo. Sounding as if he really did.

We left the office, took the elevator down to street level. Dark-suited men and women streamed in and out of the building.

"If she's telling the truth about a simple place," he said, "my guess is one of the food stands in the Century City Mall a block away. Meaning he probably walked and will return this way."

Three massive granite planters filled with rubber trees punctuated the plaza in front of Kipper's building. We chose one and sat on the rim.

Twenty minutes later, Everett Kipper appeared, walking alone. This time his suit was the color of a blued revolver, tailored snug, also four-button. White shirt, pink tie, a flash of gold at his cuffs as he moved toward his building with that bouncing stride. The business crowd in front had thickened, and he passed us, unmindful.

We got off the ledge and jogged toward him. Milo said, "Mr. Kipper?" and Kipper whipped around with the practiced tension of a martial arts fighter.

"What now?"

"A few more questions, sir."

"About what?"

"Could we talk up in your office?"

"I don't think so," said Kipper. "Cops in the office is bad for business. How long will this take?"

"Just a few moments."

"Step over here." He led us behind one of the rubber trees. The plant cast spatulate shadows on his round, smooth face. "What?"

Milo said, "Ever hear of a magazine called *GrooveRat*?"

"No. Why?"

"We're trying to trace any articles that might have been written about Julie."

"And this magazine wrote one?" Kipper shook his head. "Julie never mentioned it. Why's that important?"

"We're conducting a careful investigation," said Milo.

Kipper said, "The answer's still no. Never heard of it."

"Are you aware of any publicity Julie received recently?"

"She got none, and it bugged her. Back in New York, when she had her gallery show at Anthony, she got plenty. The *New York Times* mentioned the show in their arts section, and I think some of the other papers did, too. She remembered that. Being obscure was part of what was painful."

"What else was painful?"

"Failure."

"No publicity at all for the Light and Space show?"

Kipper shook his head. "She told me Light and Space sent a notice of the group show to the *L.A. Times,* but they didn't deign to run it . . . wait a second, there was one magazine that did want an interview— not the one you mentioned. Nothing with Rat in the title . . . what was it . . . shit. Not that it mattered. Julie was pretty jazzed about it, but in the end they crapped out."

"Canceled?"

"She waited, but the writer stood her up. She was not happy, called the editor and bitched. In the end they ran a piece—something short, probably to mollify her."

"Review of the show?" I said.

"No, this was before the show, maybe a month. For all I know Julie called them herself. She was trying to drum up publicity for herself. For the comeback." Kipper tweaked his nose. "She really believed she had a shot."

"She didn't?"

Kipper looked as if he wanted to spit. "The art world, I . . . what was the name of the magazine . . . *Scene* something, a wiseass name . . . she showed me a copy. Looked vapid to me, but I didn't say anything because Julie was excited . . . *Scene* . . . *SeldomScene* something. Now, I'm out of here."

He turned and walked away. The flaps of his suit coat billowed. No breeze blew through the plaza. Creating his own turbulence.

SeldomSceneAtoll was listed in West Hollywood, on Santa Monica near La Cienega, and the address turned out to be a genuine office building—two-story, chocolate brick, squeezed between a florist and a strip mall full of cars and short tempers. Milo left the unmarked in a loading space in the mall lot, and we entered the building through a door emblazoned with a NO SOLICITORS sign.

The directory listed theatrical agencies, nutritionists, a yoga school, business managers, and JAGUAR TUTORIALS/SSA in a second-floor suite.

"Sharing space," I said. "No media empire."

"Jaguar Tutorials," said Milo. "What, they train you to become a predator?"

The ambience said none of the occupants had made it to stardom/health/wealth: shabby gray halls, filthy gray carpeting, dehydrated plywood doors, a reek that said quirky plumbing, an elevator whose lights didn't respond to a button push.

We took the stairs, breathing in insecticide and dancing around sprinkles of dead roaches.

He knocked on the Jaguar/SSA door, didn't wait for a reply, and twisted the knob. On the other side was a smallish single room set up with four movable workstations. Cute little computers in multicolored boxes, scanners, printers, photocopiers, machines I couldn't identify. Electrical cord linguini coiled atop the vinyl floor.

The walls were covered with enlargements of framed *SSA* covers, all of a type: maliciously lit, photos of young, malnourished, beautiful people lolling in body-conscious clothing and radiating contempt for the audience. Lots of vinyl and rubber; the duds looked cheap but probably required a mortgage.

Male and female models, Nefertiti eye makeup for both. Slashes of purplish cheek blush for the skinny women, four-day beards for their male counterparts.

A dreadlocked, dark-skinned man in his late twenties wearing a black and bumblebee yellow striped T-shirt and yellow cargo pants hunched at the nearest PC, typing nonstop. I glanced at his screen. Graphics; Escher by way of Tinkertoys. He ignored us, or didn't notice. Miniearphones produced something that held his attention.

The two central stations were unoccupied. At the rearmost computer, a young woman in her midtwenties, also plugged in aurally, sat reading *People*. Chubby and baby-faced, she wore a black patent-leather jumpsuit and red moonwalker shoes, bobbed in time to what seemed to be a three-four beat. Her hair was unremarkable brown, sprayed into a fifties bouffant. She turned toward us, arched an eyebrow—an eyebrow tattoo—and the beefy steel ring piercing the center of the arch flipped up, then clicked down. The loop in her upper lip remained stationary. So did the score of studs lining her ears and the painful-looking little knoblet parked in the center of her chin.

"What?" she shouted. Then she yanked out the earphones, kept bobbing her head. One two three one two three. Waltz of the young and metallic.

"What?" she repeated.

Milo's badge elicited twin tattoo arches. The outlines of her mouth had been inked in permanently, as well.

"So?" she said.

"I'm looking for the publisher of *SeldomSceneAtoll.*"

She thumped her chest and made ape sounds. "You found her."

"We're looking for information on an artist, Juliet Kipper."

"What's up with *her*?"

"You know her?"

"Didn't say that."

"Nothing's up with her, anymore," said Milo. "She was murdered."

The eyebrow ring drooped, but the face below it remained bland.

"Whoa whoa whoa," she said, and she got up, walked over to the graphics guy, jabbed his shoulder. Looking regretful, he pulled off his phones.

"Juliet Kipper. Did we feature her?"

"Who?"

"Kipper. Dead artist. She got murdered."

"Um," he said. "What kind of artist?"

The girl looked at us.

Milo said, "She was a painter. We've been told you wrote about her, Ms. . . ."

"Patti Padgett." Big smile. A not-small diamond was inlaid in her left frontal incisor.

Milo smiled back and took out his pad.

"There you go," Patti Padgett said. "Always wanted to be part of the official police record. When did we supposedly write about the late Ms. Kipper?"

"Within the last few months."

"Well that narrows it down," she said. "We've only put out two issues in six months."

"You're a quarterly?"

"We're a broke." Patti Padgett returned to her desk, opened a drawer, began rummaging. "Let's see if whatshername Julie merited our . . . how'd she die?"

"Strangled," said Milo.

"Ooh. Any idea who did it?"

"Not yet."

"Yet," said Padgett. "I like your optimism—the greatest generation and all that."

Bumblebee-shirt said, "That was World War II, Patricia, he's Vietnam." He glanced at us, as if waiting for confirmation. Received blank stares and put his earphones back on and bopped, dreadlocks swaying.

"Whatever," said Padgett. "Here we go. Three months ago." She placed the magazine in her lap, licked her thumb, turned pages. Not many pages between the covers. It didn't take long for her to say, "Oka-ay! Here she is right in our 'Mama/Dada' section . . . sounds like someone liked her."

She brought the article to us.

"Mama/Dada" was a compendium of short pieces on local artists. Juliet Kipper shared the page with an emigrant Croatian fashion photographer and a dog trainer who moonlighted as a video artist.

The piece on Julie Kipper was two paragraphs, noted the promising New York debut, the decade of "personal and artistic disappointments," the "would-be rebirth as an essentially nihilistic conveyor of California dreamin' and ecological schemin.' " Nothing I'd seen in Kipper's landscapes had connoted nihilism to me, but what did I know?

Kipper's work, the writer concluded, "makes it obvious that her vision is more of a paean to the paradoxical holism of wishful thinking than a serious attempt to concretize and cartograph the photosynthetic dissonance, upheaval, and mulchagitation that has captivated other West Coast painters."

Author's credit: *FS*

"Mulchagitation," mumbled Milo, glancing at me.

I shook my head.

Patti Padgett said, "I think it means moving dirt around, or something like that. Total foggoma, right?" She laughed. "Most of the art stuff we print is like that. Would-bes with no ability hitching a ride on the talent train."

Milo said, " 'Leeches on the body artistic.' "

Padgett stared up at him with naked worship. "You want a gig?"

"Not in this rotation."

"Hindu?"

"*Make*-do."

Padgett told Bumblebee: "Be threatened, Todd. I'm in love."

Milo said, "If you don't like the writing, why do you print it?"

"Because it's *there, mon gendarme*. And some of our readership digs it." She spit out another laugh, set off a metal whirligig. "With our budget, we ain't exactly *The New Yawker*, honeybunch. Our focus—*my* focus, cause what *I* like is what flies—is lots of fashion, some interior design, a little film, a little music. We toss in the finesy-artsy shitsy because some people think it's cool and in our niche market, cool is everything."

Milo said, "Who's FS?"

"Hmm," said Padgett. She returned to Bumblebee and lifted an earphone. "Todd, who's FS?"

"Who?"

"The credit on the Kipper story. It's signed 'FS.' "

"How would I know? I didn't even remember Kipper."

Padgett turned to us. "Todd doesn't know, either."

"Don't you keep a file of contributors?"

"Wow," said Padgett, "this is getting seriously *investigative*. What's the deal, a serial vampire killer?"

Milo chuckled. "What makes you say that?"

"I dig the *X-Files*. C'mon, tell Patti."

"Sorry, Patti," he said. "Nothing exotic, we're collecting information." He smiled at her. "Ma'am."

"Ma'am," she said, placing a black-nailed hand over a generous breast. "Be still my fluttering heart—hey, how about you guys let me follow you around and write up what you do—day in the life and all that. I'm a kick-ass writer, MFA from Yale. Same for Todd. We're as dynamic a duo as you could hope to encounter."

"Maybe one day," said Milo. "Do you keep a contributor file?"

"Do we, Todd?"

Off came the earphones again. Padgett repeated the question. Todd said, "Not really."

"Not really?" said Milo.

"I've got a quasi file," said Todd. "But it's random—data inputted as it comes in, no alphabetization."

"In your computer?" said Milo.

Todd's stare said, *Where else?*

"Could you please call it up?"

Todd turned to Padgett. "Isn't there a First Amendment issue, here?"

"Puh-leeze," said Padgett. "These guys are going to let us ride with them, we'll do a kick-ass law enforcement issue—use that strung-out Cambodian model for the cover, whatshername with the sixteen-syllable name, doll her up in a *tight* blue uniform, give her a riding crop, a gun, the works. We'll *rock*."

Todd cleared his screen of graphics.

It took a second. "Here it is. FS—Faithful Scrivener."

Milo hunched lower and stared at the screen. "That's it? No other name?"

"The proverbial 'what you see,' " said Todd. "This is how the submission came in, this is how I log it."

"When you paid, what name did you put on the check?"

"Right," said Todd.

"Ha-ha-ha," said Padgett.

"You don't pay."

Padgett said, "We pay the cover models and the photographers as little as we can. Sometimes if we get someone with a genuine résumé—a screenwriter with a credit—we can scratch up something—like a dime a word. Mostly we don't pay because no one pays us. Distributors refuse to advance us the wholesale price until returns are caculated—we get royalties only for issues sold, and that takes months." She shrugged. "It's a sad day for entrepreneurship."

Todd said, "She was an undergrad econ major at Brown."

"As a sop to Daddy," said Padgett. "He runs cor-po-ra-tions."

"How long have you been publishing?" I said.

"Four years," said Todd. Adding with pride: "We are currently four hundred thousand in the hole."

"In hock to my daddy," said Padgett. "To appease him, we maintain a job."

"Jaguar Tutorials," said Milo. "Which is?"

"SAT preparation," said Padgett, lifting a business card from her desk and flashing it at us.

Patricia S. Padgett, B.A. (Brown) MFA (Yale)
Senior Consultant, Jaguar Tutorials

"Our mission should we accept it," she said, "is to educate the offspring of anxiety-ridden social climbers in the fine points of college entrance exams."

Milo said, "Jaguar as in . . ."

"The connotation," said Todd, "is of mastery and swiftness."

"Also," said Padgett, "of upscale. As in Jag-oo-ar motorcars. We can't afford Beverly Hills rent, but we want to pull in the B.H. kids."

Todd said, "The Ivy League thing helps."

Padgett said, "Todd did his undergrad at Princeton."

"So," said Milo, turning back to the screen, "this Faithful Scrivener person sent you a piece under a pseudonym, and you printed it and never paid."

"Looks that way," said Todd. "This notation—OTT—means an over-the-transom submission."

Padgett said, "That's publishing-speak for we didn't solicit it, it just showed up."

"You get a lot of that?"

"Plenty. Mostly garbage. Real garbage—I'm talking illiterate."

"Has 'FS' written any other pieces for you?"

"Let's see," said Todd. He scrolled. "Here's one. All the way back at the beginning." To Padgett: "Back in Issue Two."

Milo read the date. "Three and a half years ago."

She said, "The halcyon days—look at this: evidence, clues, red herrings—we're stylin' and sleuthin', Todd—hey, Officer, can we get cool badges, too?"

She went and got a copy of Issue Two. Faithful Scrivener's first piece was in a section entitled "Pits and Peaches." Brutal reviews alternating with mindless raves.

This one, a Peach. Two paragraphs singing the praises of a promising young dancer named Angelique Bernet.

Review of a ballet concert at the Mark Taper, in L.A. Experimental piece by a Chinese composer entitled "The Swans of Tianenmen."

Two months before Bernet's murder in Boston.

The company had been to L.A., first.

Angelique had been part of a trio of ballerinas featured during the final act. FS had picked her out because of "slap-in-the-face cygnian grace so fully synched with the tenor of the composition that it tightens one's scrotum. This is DANCE as in paleo-instinctuo-bioenergetics, so right, so real, so unashamedly erotic. Her artistry sets her apart from the palsiform pretendeurs that comprise the rest of *la compagnie allegement*."

"Ouch," said Padgett. "We really need to be more selective."

" 'Cygnian,' " said Milo.

Todd said, "It means swanlike. It's on the advanced SAT vocab list."

" 'Tight scrotum,' " said Padgett. "He had the hots for her. What are we dealing with, some kind of sexual psycho?"

Milo said, "Could you print copies of both articles? And as long as we're at it, have you ever run anything by someone named Drummond?"

Padgett pouted. "I ask, he doesn't answer."

"Please?" said Milo, smiling at her again, but talking in the low, threatening tones of a bear emerging from its cave.

Padgett said, "Yeah, yeah, sure."

"First name?" said Todd.

"Check any Drummond."

"Check Bulldog," said Padgett.

No one laughed.

No record of Kevin or Yuri or any other Drummond showed up in the SSA contributor files. No articles on Baby Boy Lee or China Maranga, either, but Todd did find a write-up of a recital given by Vassily Levitch. Another "Pits and Peaches" entry, one year ago. Levitch had played one piece at a group recital in Santa Barbara.

"Another Over The Transom," said Milo.

The byline: E. Murphy.

The hyperbolic, sexually loaded prose evoked Faithful Scrivener: Levitch was "lithe as a harem houri" as he "stroked Bartok's tumescent etude" and "squeezed every drop from the time/space/infinity between notes."

Padgett rotated her chin stud. "Boy, do we print crap, this walk down memory lane is not making me proud."

Todd said, "Keep your perspective, Patti. Your old man markets toxic chemicals."

Patti Padgett photocopied the articles and walked us to the door. Sticking close to Milo.

He said, "Ever hear of *GrooveRat*?"

"Nope. Is it a band?"

"A zine."

"There are hundreds of those," she said. "Anyone with a scanner and a printer can do one."

Her smile began fresh, ended up old, sad, defeated. "Anyone with a rich dad can take it a step higher."

21 As we got back in the car, Milo's cell phone chirped the first seven notes of *Für Elise*. He slapped it to his ear, grunted, said, "Yeah, I'll be there ASAP, treat her nice."

To me: "Vassily Levitch's mother flew in last night from New York and is waiting for me at the station. Maybe she'll know something that ties Levitch to Drummond beyond 'E. Murphy'— so what was *that* all about? Drummond using pen names? And if he's got his own zine, why send stuff to Patti and Todd?"

"The Bernet piece was written before *GrooveRat* was started—if Kevin was the author, he would've still been a sophomore. Maybe he sent the others because Patti and Todd were getting distribution and he wasn't."

"The need for exposure," he said. "Lots of sex in the prose. He wants to screw them."

"He wants to *own* them," I said. "And he traveled to do it. Levitch's recital was in Santa Barbara. Angelique Bernet was reviewed in L.A. but murdered in Boston. If you could verify his presence in Boston at the time, that would be grounds for a warrant."

"Yeah," he said, "but how do I verify *without* a warrant? The airlines have tightened up big-time, and Kevin's family isn't going to volunteer the info."

We traveled west on Santa Monica. When we reached Doheny, I said, "If Drummond freelanced for *SeldomScene*, he may very well have submitted to other magazines."

His hands clenched around the wheel. "What if the bastard uses a dozen pseudonyms? What do I do—find some expert to conduct linguistic analysis of every fringe mag in the country?"

"I'd start with Faithful Scrivener and E. Murphy bylines, see where that leads."

"Extracurricular reading. Meanwhile, a grieving mother waits."

A few blocks later, he said, "Any other insights? From the writing?"

"It's the type of inflated prose you see in college papers. Writing to impress. If it's Kevin we're dealing with, he didn't get strokes at home, channeled his energies into projects, came to see himself as a maven of the art world. I'd check his college newspaper for reviews, see if the writing matches."

"You keep saying that. 'If it's Kevin.' "

"Something bothers me," I admitted. "Even at twenty-four, Kevin seems young for these killings. If he murdered Angelique Bernet he did it at the age of twenty-one. There are elements of Angelique that fit a novice: multiple stab wounds that could mean a blitz attack, the body left out in the open. But traveling three thousand miles from his comfort zone's pretty calculated."

"What about this," he said. "He sees Bernet dance in L.A., gets the hots, writes her up, checks the ballet company's travel schedule, takes a trip to Boston. Maybe he's not even sure why. All sorts of feelings bouncing around in his head. Then he stalks her, follows her to Cambridge, makes contact with her—he could've even come on to her and she rejected him. He freaks out, does her. Flies home. Sits thinking about it—realizes what he did. That he got away with it. Finally, he's *succeeded* at something. Thirteen months after that, China disappears. The killer takes time to bury her, and no one finds her for months. Because now he's being careful. Plotting it out. And he's close to home. Make any sense?"

"If he's a gifted boy."

"Excitable boy," he said. "Like that song."

"The recent murders fit with rising confidence," I said. "All three were done right at the venues. In Baby Boy's and Levitch's cases with the audience still present, in Julie's with CoCo Barnes in the next room. That stinks of audaciousness. Could be he's practiced his craft, is feeling like a virtuoso."

"Practiced—meaning other murders we don't know about."

"Thirteen months lapsed between Angelique and China, then nothing for nearly two *years* until Baby Boy. After that, we've got six weeks to Julie and nine weeks to Levitch."

"Great," he said.

"The alternative is he managed, somehow, to suppress his urges for years and now he's losing control."

"How could he suppress?"

"By obsessing on a new project."

"GrooveRat."

"Being a publisher could grant serious illusions of power. Perhaps he's finally realized that the zine's a failure. Yet another one."

"Daddy pulled the plug?"

"From what Petra says, Daddy was never enthusiastic."

"The art world fails him," he said. "So he takes it out on the artists. Let's get back to the sexual angle. We've got male and female victims? What's that say? A bisexual killer?"

"Or a sexually confused killer," I said. "Certainly, a sexually inadequate killer. In no case was there any penetration. He's intimidated by the clash of genitalia, substitutes the eroticism of talent. Targeting talent on the rise, he captures their essence at its peak. How's that for a cheap Freudian shot?"

"You're talking about an artistic cannibal," he said.

"I'm talking," I said, "about the ultimate critic."

Back at my house, alone.

Allison was in Boulder, Colorado, for a conference. After that, she'd be traveling to attend her former father-in-law's birthday.

I'd driven her to the airport, and she'd spent the night at my house. After I stashed her suitcases in the car, she removed something from her purse and handed it to me.

Petite, chrome-plated automatic. As I took it, she said, "Here's the clip," and gave me that, too.

"Forgot to leave it at home," she explained. "Can't get on the plane with it. Could you keep it for me?"

"Sure." I placed the gun in my pocket.

"It's registered, but I have no carry permit. If that bothers you, you can put it in the house."

"I'll chance it. Ready to go?"

"Yup."

As we neared the 405 South, she said, "You're not going to ask?"

"I figure you've got a reason."

"The reason is after what happened to me, when I finally got my head straight, I told myself I'd avoid feeling that helpless again. I started with the usual stuff—self-defense courses, basic safety manuals. Then, years later, when I was a postdoc, I treated a woman who'd been raped twice. Two separate incidents, years apart. The first time she blamed herself. She'd been out-of-her-mind drunk, got picked up by a lowlife in a bar. The second time was some monster managing to jimmy a closed bedroom window. I did all I could for her, looked up gun shops in the yellow pages, bought my little chromium friend."

"Makes sense."

"Does it?"

"You kept it."

"I like it," she said. "I really think of it as my friend. I'm a pretty good shot. Took basic and intermediate training. Still go to the range once a month. Though I've missed a couple of months because we've been spending time."

"Sorry to distract you."

She touched my face. "Does it bother you?"

"No."

"You're sure."

Within ten years, I'd shot two men to death. Both had been out to kill me. Evil men, self-defense, no option. Sometimes I still dreamed about them and woke up with acid in my stomach.

I said, "In the end we look out for ourselves."

"True," she said. "I didn't really forget to leave it home. I wanted you to know."

22 Eric Stahl sat and drank water.

Tap water in a half-gallon Sprite bottle. He'd brought it from home.

Watching Kevin Drummond's apartment on Rossmore.

He'd arrived before sunrise, checked out the rear of the building. Treading cat-light on old sneakers sure not to squeak.

No sign of Kevin Drummond's car.

No surprise.

He found himself a good spot, catercornered from the dingy brick building. Nice oblique angle; he could study the entrance without straining his head, a passerby would have no idea what he was after.

Not that a passerby would be likely to notice. Plenty of vehicles on the block, and Stahl had brought his personal wheels: a beige Chevy van with windows tinted way beyond the legal limit.

All the comforts of . . . during the first hour, a blue jay had swooped and cast a shadow across the building. Since then, very few signs of life.

Seven hours twenty-two minutes of watching.

Torture for someone else; Stahl was as close to content as he could be.

Sit. Drink bottled water. Sit. Stare.

Put the pictures out of your head.

Keep it clear, keep everything clear.

23

I volunteered.

A visit to Charter College, where I'd try to find a sample of Kevin Drummond's writing.

"Thanks," Milo said. "Good idea, you being professorial and all that."

"I'm professorial?"

"You can be—it's a compliment, I've got great respect for academia."

Before I started out, I took care of some unfinished business: second attempt to reach Christian Bangsley, née Sludge, now CEO of Hearth and Home restaurants. It had been months since the first call. This time the young-sounding receptionist put me through. As I introduced myself, Bangsley cut me off.

"I got the first message," he said. "Didn't call back because I have nothing to tell you."

"Was anyone stalking China?"

Silence.

He said, "Why, after all these years?"

"It's still an open case. What do you know?"

"I never saw anyone bugging China."

Tension in his voice made me persist. "But she did tell you something."

"Shit," he said. "Look, I've put all that past me. But there are assholes out there who don't want me to."

Recalling the Internet flames—*"ex-Chinawhiteboy sells out . . . ends up cap-pig cancerous bigtiiime"* I said, "Are you being stalked, yourself?"

"Nothing regular, but sometimes I get letters. People who claim to be fans and don't like what I'm doing. People living in the past."

"Have you contacted the police?"

"My lawyers say it's not worth it. That people telling me they're unhappy with how I'm running my life is no crime. Free country and all that. But I *don't* want publicity. The only reason I'm talking to you now is my lawyers said if you tried again, I should. That if I didn't, you'd think I was being evasive. Which I'm not. I just can't help you. Okay?"

"I'm sorry you're being harassed. And I promise to keep anything you tell me under wraps."

Silence.

I said, "What happened to China went well beyond harassment."

"I know, I know. Jesus—okay here it is: China bitched once about someone bugging her. Following her. I didn't take it seriously because she was always paranoid about something. High-strung. The band used to joke she'd been weaned on chili peppers."

"When did she start complaining?"

"A month or two before she disappeared. I told the cops, they blew me off, said I needed more details, it was worthless."

"What exactly did China complain about?"

"She was convinced she was being peeped, stalked, whatever. But she never actually saw someone, couldn't describe anyone. So maybe the cops were right. She talked about it being a *feeling*, but China had lots of feelings. Especially when she was high, which was most of the time. She could get paranoid over nothing, just blow up."

"She never went to the police."

"Right," said Bangsley. "China and the police. The thing is, she wasn't *scared*, she was *pissed*. Kept saying if the asshole ever showed his face, she'd break it, claw out his eyes, and shit in the sockets. That was China. Always aggression."

"Was it real?" I said.

"What do you mean?"

"Was she really that fearless or was it a cover?"

"I don't know," he said. "I really don't. She was hard to read. Had this wall around her. Drugs were the mortar."

Paul Brancusi had mentioned nothing about any stalker. I said, "Did China tell anyone else about being followed? The other members of the band?"

"I doubt it."

"Why?"

He hesitated. "China and I were . . . closer. She was officially gay, but for a while we had a thing going on—shit, this is exactly what I didn't want. I'm married now, expecting my second kid—"

"No one's interested in your love life," I said. "Just what you know about China's stalker."

"I don't even know if there *was* a stalker. Like I told you, she never actually saw anything."

"A feeling," I said.

"Exactly," said Bangsley. "China had a vivid mind. When you were with her you had to be careful to step back, put things in perspective."

"At the time did you believe her?"

"I fluctuated. She could be convincing. One time we were up in the hills, late at night, smoking weed, doing other good stuff and suddenly she went rigid and her eyes got scary and she grabbed my shoulders—hard, it hurt. Then she stands up and says, 'Fuck, he's *here*! I can *feel* him!' Then she starts walking around in circles, like a gun turret on a tank—like she's aiming herself at something. And she starts screaming into the darkness. *'Fuck you you asshole fuck, come out and show your fuckshit face.'* Waving her fist, crouching down like she's ready to go karate-nuts. At that moment, I believed her—the darkness, the quiet, how *certain* she was, convinced me. Later, I said to myself, 'What was *that*?' "

"What happened after she screamed?"

"Nothing. I got worried someone would hear her, tried to get her down the hill and into my car. She made me wait until she convinced herself whoever was up there was gone. We crashed at my place. The next morning she was gone. She'd eaten all the munchies in my fridge and split. A month or two later, she disappeared, and when they finally found her, I freaked out. Because the place she was buried wasn't far from where we were sitting that night."

"Did you tell the cops?"

"After the way they treated me?"

"China was found near the Hollywood sign."

"Exactly," he said. "That's where we were. Under the sign. China loved the sign, liked the story of some actress throwing herself off. There used to be a riding ranch up there, one of those rent-a-horse deals. China told me she liked to sneak in at night, talk to the horses, smell the horseshit, just wander around. She said she got off on walking around other people's property. Made her feel like a Manson girl. She went through this phase where she was *into* the Manson family, talked about writing a song dedicated to Charlie, but we told her we wouldn't play it. Even then we had some kind of standards."

"Enamored of serial killers."

"No, just Manson. And she wasn't serious about that. It was just another China thing—something came into her head, it poured right out of her mouth. Anything for attention, she loved attention. Which was Manson's thing, right? I remember thinking how weird it was that maybe she'd been murdered by some Manson type. Ironic, you know?"

Charter College was 150 acres nestled in the northeast corner of Eagle Rock, set apart from that bedroom community's blue-collar, mostly Latino, bedrock sensibilities by ivy-covered stucco walls and grandiose trees.

The college had been established 112 years ago, when Eagle Rock's twelve-hundred-foot elevation and clean air had led developers to frame it "The Switzerland of the West." Over a century later, the surrounding hills were pretty on the uncommon clear day, but chain motels were the closest Eagle Rock came to resort living.

I drove up Eagle Rock Boulevard, a broad, sun-bleached haven for garages and auto parts emporia, turned onto College Road, and entered a residential neighborhood of small, craftsman bungalows, and chunky stucco cottages. An arch emblazoned with the school's crest fed into Emeritus Lane, a broad, spotless strip heralded by a shield-shaped flower bed spelling out the institution's name in red and white petunias.

The campus buildings were Beaux-Arts and Monterey Colonial visions, all painted the same gray-dun and set, gemlike, in the jewel box of old-growth greenery. I'd treated a few Charter students, over the years, was familiar with the school's basic flavor: selective, expensive, established by Congregationalists, but decidedly secular now, with a bent toward activist politics and community involvement.

Visitor parking was easy and free. I picked up a campus map from a Take-One stand and made my way to the Anna Loring Slater Library. A good number of the handsome kids I passed were smiling. As if life tasted delicious, and they were ready for the next course.

The library was a two-story, twenties masterpiece with a mediocre, four-story, eighties addition tacked to its south wing. The ground floor was all hush and computer-click, a hundred or so students glued to their screens. I asked a librarian the name of the school paper and where I'd find back copies.

"The *Daily Bobcat*," he said. "Everything's on-line."

I found a computer station and logged on. The *Bobcat* file contained sixty-two years of back issues. For the first forty, the paper had been published as a weekly.

Kevin Drummond was twenty-four, meaning he'd probably enrolled six years ago. I backed up a year to be careful and set about scrolling thousands of pages and scanning bylines. Nothing with Drummond's name on it showed up for the first three years. No pieces by Faithful Scrivener or E. Murphy, either. Then, in the March of what turned out to be Drummond's junior spring semester, I got my first hit.

Kevin Drummond, Communications, had penned a review of a showcase at the Roxy on Sunset. Seven new bands doing their thing in hopes of a breakthrough. Thumbnail reviews of every act; Kevin Drummond had liked three, hated four. His prose was straightforward, uninspired, with none of the puffery or the sexual imagery of the *SeldomScene* pieces.

I found eleven more articles, spread out over a year and half, ten write-ups of rock acts, similarly bland.

The exception was interesting.

May of Drummond's senior year. Faithful Scrivener byline. A retrospective look at the career of Baby Boy Lee.

This one, longer, gushing, termed Baby Boy, "a manifest icon, whose elephantoid shoulders may sag Atlassly under the ponderous mantle of Robert Johnson, Blind Lemon Jackson, the entire pantheon of Delta-Chicago-craw-aching royalty but whose soul is whole and will never be sold. Baby Boy deserves the weight and the pain of genius's crushing burden. He is an artist with too much emotional integrity and psychopathology to ever achieve long-lasting popular acclaim."

The essay ended by quoting lyrics from "the totemic, aorta-straining lament 'A Cold Heart,' " and concluded that, "to a bluesman, the world will always be a coldhearted, unwelcoming, treacherous place. Nowhere does the adage 'no gain without pain,' apply more than in the noir universe of smoky bars, loose women, and sad endings that has fed the genius of every scurvied picker and addicted string-bender from time immemorial. Baby Boy Lee may never be a happy man, but his music, raw and vital and resolutely uncommercial, will continue to warm the hearts of many.' "

A year later, Lee had put the lie to that thesis by sitting in on the sessions that produced Tic 439's monster pop hit.

Cognitive dissonance, but on the face, not much of a motive for murder.

I needed to know more about Kevin Drummond.

Charter College's Communications Department was housed in Frampton Hall, a majestic, Doric-columned affair, separated from the library by a five-minute stroll. Inside were worn mahogany walls, a domed ceiling, and cork floors that muted footsteps. The building also hosted the departments of English, History, Humanities, Women's Studies, and Romance Languages. Communications shared the third floor with the latter two.

Three faculty members were listed on the directory: Professor E. G. Martin, Chair; Professor S. Santorini; Professor A. Gordon Shull.

Start at the top.

Chairperson Martin's corner suite was fronted by an empty reception area. The door leading to an inner office was six inches ajar and a keyboard click-clack solo in the same key as the library sound track leaked into the anteroom. Sepia photos of Charter College in its infancy decorated the walls. Big, clean buildings dominating twiggy saplings; grim, celluloid-collared men and high-buttoned women with the resolute look of the heaven-sent. A sign above the nearest file spelled out the chair's full name. ELIZABETH GALA MARTIN, PH.D.

I approached the inner office. "Professor Martin?"

A sentence worth of key-presses, then silence. "Yes?"

I stated my name and appended my academic appointment at the med school downtown and cracked the door another couple of inches.

Professorial.

A very dark black woman in a calf-length, topaz silk dress and matching pumps came around from her desk. She had cold-waved, hennaed hair, wore a string of pearls and matching earrings. Forty or so, plump, pretty, puzzled. Sharp licorice eyes above gold, half-moon glasses looked me over.

"Professor of pediatrics?" An alto that might have been mellow under other circumstances, sectioned each word into precise syllables. "I don't recall any appointment."

"I don't have one," I said, showing her my LAPD consultant ID. She came closer, read the small print, frowned.

"Police? What's this all about?"

"Nothing alarming, but if you'd be kind enough to spare me a moment?"

She stepped back and appraised me again. "This is irregular, to say the least."

"I apologize. I was doing research in your library, and your name came up. If you'd rather set up an appointment—"

"My name came up how?"

"As chair of Communications. I'm looking into one of your alumni. A man named Kevin Drummond."

"You're looking *into* him," she said. "Meaning the police are."

"Yes."

"What, exactly, is Mr. Drummond suspected of?"

"Do you know him?"

"I know the name. We're a small department. What has Mr. Drummond done?"

"Maybe nothing," I said. "Maybe murder."

Elizabeth G. Martin removed her glasses. Dull thumps sounded from the corridor. Shoes on cork. Youthful chatter crescendoed and diminished.

She said, "Let's not stand out here."

Her office was Persian-carpeted, book-lined, compulsively neat, with two walls of windows that looked out to luxuriant lawns. California impressionist landscapes, probably valuable, probably college-owned, hung wherever the bookshelves left off. Elizabeth Martin's Berkeley Ph.D. and ten years of ensuing academic honors were heralded on the wall behind her carved, gilded-age, partner's desk. On the desk were a smoke gray laptop and an assortment of crystal office niceties. A green marble fireplace hosted a rack of cold, scorched logs.

She sat down and motioned me to do the same. "What exactly is going on?"

I tried to be forthcoming with as few details as possible.

"Well, all that's dandy, Professor Delaware, but there are First Amendment issues here, not to mention academic freedom and common courtesy. You don't really expect to waltz in here and have us throw open our files simply because that would abet your investigation. Whatever it's alleged to be."

"I'm not interested in confidential information about Kevin Drummond. Just anything that might be relevant to a criminal investigation, such as disciplinary problems."

Elizabeth Martin remained impassive.

I said, "We're talking multiple murders. If Drummond turns out to be involved in criminal activities, that will become public. If he posed problems here, and Charter hushed it up, the college will be drawn in."

"Is that a threat?"

"No," I said. "Just a statement of how these things play themselves out."

"Police consultant . . . your academic department's comfortable with your activities? Do you keep them fully apprised?"

I smiled. "Is that a threat?"

Martin rubbed her hands together. A silver-framed photo on the mantel showed her in a formal red gown, next to a tuxedoed, gray-haired man ten years older. Another shot pictured her in casual clothes, with the same man. Behind them, gold-and-rust tile-roofed buildings in the background. A diagonal stretch of teal canal, the curve of a gondola prow. Venice.

She said, "Whatever the contingencies, I can't go along with this."

"Fair enough," I said. "But if there's something I should know—that the police should know—and you do eventually find a way of helping, it will make a lot of people's lives easier."

She picked a gold pen from a leather box and drummed the desk. "I can tell you this: I can't recall Kevin Drummond posing any problems for the department. There was nothing . . . homicidal about him at all." The pen tapped her in-box. "Really, Professor Delaware, this all sounds quite outlandish."

"Did you teach Kevin, personally?"

"When did he graduate?"

"Two years ago."

"Then I'd have to say yes. Two years ago, I was still teaching my mass-media seminar, and every Communications major was required to take it."

"But you have no specific recollection of teaching him?"

"It's a popular class," she said, without hubris. "Communications is an arm of Charter's Humanities Nexus. Our students take core classes in other departments and vice versa."

"I assume Kevin Drummond had a faculty advisor."

"I wasn't his advisor. I work with the honor students."

"Kevin wasn't an honor student."

"If he was, I'd have a specific recollection." She began typing on the laptop.

Dismissed.

Stepping down the hall to seek out Professors Santorini and Shull was unlikely to escape her scrutiny. I'd find some other way to contact her colleagues. Or have Milo do it.

I'd gotten up when she said, "His advisor was Gordon Shull. Which is lucky for you, because Professor Susan Santorini's doing research in France."

Astonished by the sudden turn, I said, "May I talk to Professor Shull?"

"Be my guest," she said. "If he's in. His office is two doors to the left."

Outside in the mahogany corridor, several students lounged. Down a ways, near Romance Languages. No one congregating at Communications.

A. Gordon Shull's office door was locked, and my knock was answered by silence. I was writing a note when a hearty voice said, "Can I help you?"

A man wearing a backpack had just come up the rear staircase. Midthirties, six feet tall, well-built, he had ginger hair buzzed to the skull and an angular, heavy-browed, wind-toughened face. He wore a red-and-black plaid shirt, black tie, black jeans, brown hiking boots. The backpack was Army green. Pale blue eyes, craggy features, five day stubble-beard; handsome in a coarse way. A *National Geographic* photographer, or a naturalist adept at obtaining grants to study rare species.

"Professor Shull?"

"I'm Gordie Shull. What's up?"

I repeated the spiel I'd given Elizabeth Martin.

A. Gordon Shull said, "Kevin? It's been what . . . a couple of years. What's the problem?"

"There may be none. His name came up in an investigation."

"What kind of investigation?"

"Homicide."

Shull stepped back, loosened the pack, scratched his big chin.

"You're kidding. Kevin?" He flexed his shoulders. "This is mind-blowing."

"When Kevin was your student did he pose any problems?"

"Problems?"

"Disciplinary problems."

"No. He was a little . . . how can I put this . . . eccentric?"

He pulled a large chrome key ring out of his jeans and unlocked the door. "I probably shouldn't be talking to you. Privacy . . . and all that. But homicide . . . I guess I should check this out with my boss before we go further." His eyes traveled down the hall to Elizabeth Martin's office.

"Professor Martin directed me to you. She's the one who told me you were Kevin Drummond's advisor."

"Did she? Hmm . . . well, then okay . . . I guess."

His office was a third the size of the boss's, mocha-walled and gloomy-dark until he raised the blind on a single narrow window. The panes were blocked by a massive, knobby tree trunk, and it took Shull's flicking the lights on to brighten the room.

Faculty status was clearly demarcated at Charter College. Shull's desk and bookshelves were almost-wood Danish modern, his side chairs gray-painted metal. No California impressionism, here, just two posters for contemporary art exhibitions in New York and Chicago.

Two black-framed diplomas hung askew behind the desk. A bachelors' degree fifteen years ago from Charter College and a masters' four years later from the University of Washington.

Shull tossed his backpack in a corner and sat down. "Kevin Drummond . . . wow."

"In what way was he eccentric?"

He swung his feet atop his desk and placed his hands behind his head. His basic-training hairdo revealed a large knobby skull beneath the ginger stubble. "You're not actually saying the kid's a murderer?"

"Not at all. Just that his name came up during an investigation."

"How?"

"I wish I could tell you."

Shull grinned. "No fair."

"What can you tell me about him?"

"You're a psychologist? They sent you because someone thinks Kevin's psychologically disturbed?"

"Sometimes the police feel I'm right for a specific task."

"Incredible . . . for some reason your name's familiar."

I smiled. He smiled back. "Okay, Kevin Drummond's eccentricity . . . for starts, he kept to himself—at least from what I saw. No friends, no campus involvement. But not a scary kid. Quiet. Thoughtful. Medium-bright, not too socially adept."

"How much contact did you have with him?"

"We met from time to time for curriculum guidance, that kind of thing. He seemed to be drifting . . . seemed not to be enjoying the college experience. Which is nothing unusual, lots of kids get down."

"Depressed?" I said.

"You're the psychologist," said Shull. "But yes, I'd have to say so. Now that I think about it, I never saw him smile. I tried to draw him out. He wasn't much for casual conversation."

"Intense."

Shull nodded. "Definitely intense. Serious kid, no sense of humor that I ever noticed."

"What were his interests?"

"Hmm," said Shull. "I'd have to say pop culture. Which would describe half our students. They're products of their upbringing."

"What do you mean?"

"The zeitgeist," said Shull. "If your parents were anything like mine, you got some grounding in books, theater, art. Today's undergrads are likely to grow up in homes where episodic TV's the entertainment of choice. It's a little tough getting them jazzed about quality."

My childhood had been grounded in silence and gin. I said, "What aspects of pop culture interested Kevin?"

"All of it. Music, art. In that sense, he fit the department perfectly. Elizabeth Martin dictates that we take a holistic approach. Art as a general rubric, the interface of the art world with other aspects of the culture."

"Medium-bright," I said.

"Don't ask me to tell you his grades. That's a definite no-no."

"How about a ballpark appraisal?"

Shull turned toward the tree-filled window, rubbed his head, loosened his tie. "We've moved onto touchy ground, my friend. The college is adamant about protecting grade confidentiality."

"Would it be fair to call him a mediocre student?"

Shull laughed very softly. "Okay, let's go with that."

"Was there a change in his grade pattern over time?"

Shull hesitated. "I might possibly recall a slight drop in effort toward the end of his stay here."

"When?"

"The last couple of years."

Right after Angelique Bernet's murder. Sometime before he'd graduated, Kevin Drummond had conceived *GrooveRat*.

I said, "Are you aware that Kevin tried his hand at publishing?"

"Oh, that," said Shull. "His *zine*."

"You saw it?"

"He talked to me about it. In fact, it was the only time I ever saw him get animated."

"He never showed you the zine?"

"He showed me some articles he'd written." Shull's smile was crooked, rueful. "He was needy for praise. I tried to comply."

"But his writing wasn't praiseworthy," I said.

Shull shrugged. "He was a kid. He wrote like a kid."

"Meaning?"

"Sophomoric—junioromoric, seniormoric. I get a steady diet of it. Which is fine. Any craft takes time to develop. The only difference between Kevin and hundreds of other kids is that he thought he was ready for the big time."

"Did you let him know he wasn't?"

"Lord, no," said Shull. "Why would I shatter his confidence, a troubled kid like that? I knew the world would do that to him, all by itself."

"A troubled kid," I said.

"You're telling me he's involved in murder." Shull returned to his chair. "I really don't want to bad-mouth him. He was quiet, a little weird, a little delusional about his talent. That's all. I don't want to make him sound like a maniac. He wasn't that different from other nerdy-types I've seen."

He placed his elbows on the desk and looked at me earnestly. "There's no way you could give me any details, is there? My old journalistic impulses are coming to the fore."

"Sorry," I said. "So you went from journalism to academia."

"Academia has its charms," said Shull.

"What else can you tell me about Kevin?"

"That's really it. And I've got office hours in a few minutes."

"I won't take much more of your time, Professor. What else can you tell me about Kevin's publishing dreams?"

Shull pulled on his chin. "Once he got on the publishing kick—his senior year—it was all he could talk about. Kids are like that."

"Like what?"

"Obsessive. We accept them to college and call them adults but they're really still adolescents, and adolescents obsess. Entire industries have been built on that fact."

"What was Kevin obsessed with?"

"Success, I suppose."

"Did he have a particular point of view?"

"With regard to what?"

"Art."

"Art," echoed Shull. "Once again, we're talking adolescent attitudes. Kevin adhered to the seminal sophomoric belief."

"What's that?"

"Anticommercialism. If it sells, it sucks. Basic dorm-debate stuff."

"He told you that."

"More than once."

"You feel differently?"

"My job is to nurture the little ducklings, not pepper them with the buckshot of criticism."

"When Kevin showed you his articles, did you do any editing?"

"Not his articles. On papers I'd assigned, I suggested minor revisions."

"How'd he take criticism?"

"Well." Shull shook his knobby head. "Very well as a matter of fact. Sometimes he asked for more. I guess he looked up to me. I got the feeling he wasn't getting much support anywhere else."

"Are you aware Kevin wrote arts reviews for the *Daily Bobcat*."

"Those," said Shull. "He was quite proud of them."

"He showed them to you."

"Showed them off. I suppose he came to trust me. Which didn't mean pizza-and-beer, anything outside of office hours. Kevin wasn't that type of kid."

"What type is that?"

"The kind you'd enjoy having a beer with."

I said, "Did he tell you about his pen names?"

Shull's eyebrows arced. "What pen names?"

" 'Faithful Scrivener,' " I said. " 'E. Murphy.' He used them to write for his zine and other arts magazines."

"Did he," said Shull. "How curious. Why?"

"I was hoping you could tell me, Professor."

"Enough with the title. Call me Gordie . . . pen names . . . you're implying Kevin was concealing something?"

"Kevin's motivations are still a mystery," I said.

"Well, I wouldn't know about any pen names."

"You said his grades dropped over time. Did you notice any change in his writing style?"

"How so?"

"He seems to have gone from simple and direct to wordy and pretentious."

"Ouch," said Shull. "You're the critic, not me." He pulled down his tie, opened the collar of his plaid shirt. "Pretentious? No, on the contrary. The little I saw of Kevin's development seemed to indicate improvement. A little more elegance. But I guess that would make sense. If you're right about Kevin being disturbed. If his mind deteriorated, that would show up in his writing, wouldn't it? Now, I'm sorry, but I do have an appointment."

When we reached the door, he said, "I don't know what it is you think Kevin did—probably don't want to know. But I have to say I feel sorry for him."

"Why's that?"

Instead of answering, he opened the door and we stepped out into the hallway. A pretty Asian girl sat on the floor a few feet away. When she saw Shull she got to her feet and smiled.

He said, "Go in, Amy. Be with you in a sec."

When the girl was gone, I said, "Why do you feel sorry for Kevin?"

"Sad kid," he said. "Lousy writer. And now you're telling me he's a psycho killer. I'd say that qualifies for pitiable."

24

I left the college, got on the 134 East and was headed back toward L.A. when my cell phone beeped.

Milo said, "Last couple hours, I could've used you. Grief counseling with Levitch's mom. Vassily was a wonderful son, boy prodigy, total genius, apple of Mama's eye, who in the world would want to hurt him. Then I got a prelim report from my Ds. Nothing turned up on the Bristol Street neighborhood canvass, and all the audience members they've talked to noticed nothing out of the ordinary. Ditto for the security guard and the parking valets. So whoever offed Vassily either blended in or slipped in unnoticed."

"You said the audience was older. Wouldn't a kid like Kevin Drummond stand out?"

"Maybe he went in disguise. Maybe he took a back-row seat in the darkness. Plus, you attend a piano recital, you're not exactly looking for suspicious characters. There are still some personal checks from the nonmembers to go over. Get over to the college, yet?"

"I did. Kevin Drummond wrote a few arts reviews for the student paper, for the most part nothing illuminating. But during his senior year—shortly before he started *GrooveRat*—his style shifted suddenly. From straightforward prose to what we found in the *SeldomScene* pieces. Maybe he experienced some sort of psychological change at that time."

"Going schizo?"

"Not if he's our guy. These crimes are too organized for a schizophrenic. But a mood disorder—mania—would fit with the overheated prose and the delusions of grandeur. Which is how Drummond's faculty advisor described his publishing plans. Mania can mean a loosening of boundaries—and inhibitions. And periodic departures from usual demeanor. The advisor describes Kevin as quiet, unassertive. He had no friends, was very serious, a mediocre student with high aspirations. Not fun to be around. All of which could be the depressive component of a bipolar disorder. Another thing that synchs with mania is the hoarding behavior his landlady described. The history of flitting from fad to fad may very well have been a precursor to a manic break. Mania's not often associated with violence, but when it is, the violence can be serious."

"So now we've got a diagnosis," he said. "But no patient."

"Tentative diagnosis. The advisor also said Kevin felt strongly that commercial success and quality were incompatible. By itself that means little—he termed it dorm-room doctrine, and he's right. But most college students move past dorm life and develop autonomy. Kevin doesn't seem to have made big strides in that direction."

"Arrested development . . . success is corrupt, so nip it in the bud. Meanwhile, no sign of him, and it's looking more and more as if he's rabbited. Petra says Stahl's been on the apartment like a rash, hasn't caught a glimpse of the guy. I'm putting a BOLO on Drummond's Honda but without declaring him an official suspect, it'll be prioritized at the bottom of the basket."

"Despite the missing car, it's possible Drummond's holed up in his apartment," I said. "A loner like that, some canned soup and a laser printer could sustain him for a while. Has Stahl checked?"

"He had the landlady knock. No answer, no sounds of movement on the other side of the door. Stahl thought of having her use her master key—go in on pretense of a gas leak, whatever. But he thought better of it, called Petra, she called me, and we all decided to wait. Just in case a search does pull up something serious. Kevin's daddy is a lawyer. We ever bust the kid, he's gonna be represented by a shark, no sense jumping the gun and risking an evidentiary mess. Just to make sure, I had a chat with an assistant D.A. who leans toward permissive about grounds for warrants. She listened to what I had, asked me if I was taking my routine to open-mike night at the Comedy Store."

"So what's the plan?"

"Stahl keeps watching, and Petra continues checking out Hollywood spots, clubs, alternative bookstores, to see if anyone knows Kevin. I'm going over the file on Julie Kipper to see if there's anything I missed. I also called Fiorelle in Cambridge and suggested he scour hotel registers for Drummond. He said he'd try, but that was a lot to ask for."

"One more thing," I said. "I spoke to Christian Bangsley, China Maranga's other living band mate. He says China was certain someone was stalking her." I recounted the incident near the Hollywood sign. "It made her angry, not frightened. The night she disappeared, she was enraged at the band. Throw in drugs and her aggressive personality, and it could add up to a volatile situation."

"With a guy like Kevin."

"With any wrong guy. China being buried near the sign is consistent with a stalker. She had a thing for the sign, went up there regularly. Someone watched her, learned her patterns. Maybe she wasn't picked up walking the streets. Maybe she chose that night to hike, was followed and ambushed. Bangsley said when she screamed, no one heard. Up there in the hills, the sound of a struggle would be muted."

"What kind of thing did she have for the sign?"

"The story of that starlet flinging herself to her death appealed to her."

"Unfulfilled dreams," he said. "Sounds like she and Drummond would've had some common ground."

"Sure," I said. "Until they didn't."

25 After a futile double shift combing Hollywood for someone who recognized Kevin Drummond, Petra went to bed at 3 A.M., got up at nine, and did phone work from her apartment, lying in bed, hair pinned, still in her T-shirt and panties.

Milo had filled her in on Alex's visit to Drummond's college. Drummond's professor's description, firming up the profile.

Your basic loner; big shock.

One heck of a loner—not a single club owner or bouncer or patron or bookstore employee remembered his face.

The only people she found who responded to Drummond's DMV photo at all, were the owner of a Laundromat within two blocks of Drummond's apartment and the clerk at a nearby 7-Eleven who thought, yeah, maybe the guy came in there and bought stuff from time to time.

"What kind of stuff?"

"Maybe Slim Jims?" The clerk was a skinhead with a vulnerable face who reacted with the edgy eagerness of a game show contestant.

"Maybe?" said Petra.

"Maybe pork rinds?"

The Laundromat owner was a Chinese man who barely spoke English and smiled a lot. All Petra could get from him was "Yeah, mebbe wash." She resisted the impulse to ask if Drummond had rinse-cycled a load of bloody duds, trudged back to her car, and returned to the station, where she decided to work Drummond's pen names.

No chance Faithful Scriveners would be in the system, but she found plenty of felonious E. Murphys. Too late to deal with it at this hour, so she put it off for tomorrow.

Now, here she was all comfy and beddy-bye, working the phones.

Two hours later: none of the *E. Murphys* looked promising.

She located Henry Gilwhite, the transsexual-murdering husband of obnoxious Olive, the POB lady, and by 12:35 P.M. she knew that Gilwhite had begun his sentence at the state penitentiary at San Quentin only to be transferred to Chino within a year. A three-minute conversation with an assistant warden told her why.

She thanked the A. W., brewed coffee, ate a hollowed-out bagel, showered, dressed, drove to Hollywood.

She found a parking space in the strip-mall lot that afforded a clean view of the mail drop. A few scuzzy types entered and exited, then nothing for ten minutes. Petra made a smiling entrance and earned a brown-lidded glare from Olive.

"Hi, there, Mrs. Gilwhite. Heard from Henry, recently?"

Olive went scarlet, the splotches on her face knitting into a rosaceous mask. "You."

Never had a pronoun sounded more hostile.

"Have you?" said Petra.

Olive mumbled something foul under her breath.

Petra put her hands in her pockets and stepped closer to the counter. Rolls of stamps sat at Olive's dimpled elbow. She snatched them up and turned her back on Petra.

"Nice for you that Henry got transferred, Olive. Chino's a lot closer than San Quentin, easier to visit. And you do get there regularly. Every two weeks, like clockwork. So how's he doing? The old blood pressure under control?"

Olive half turned, revealing a flabby profile. Her lips bunched, as if gathering spit. "What's it to you?"

"Chino's a lot safer, too," said Petra. "What with Armando Guzman, a cousin of Henry's victim incarcerated at Quentin *and* being a big deal in the Vatos Locos gang. Turns out, there's a large contingent of V.L.s in Quentin, but only a few at Chino, so it's easier to segregate someone like Henry. What they tell me, though, is that Chino's getting overcrowded. Situation like that, you can never tell when things are going to change."

Olive wheeled around. Pale. "You *can't.*" Hostility had been sucked from her voice, replaced by a nerve-scratching whine.

Petra smiled.

Olive Gilwhite's cheeks fluttered. The peroxide thatch above her drinker's face thrummed. Living with this harridan must've been fun for Henry. Then again, there were always trannies available for back-alley trysts.

Olive Gilwhite said, "You can't."

"The thing is," said Petra, "Henry being a convicted murderer, even at his age, even with the hypertension, he's not going to garner much sympathy from the prison administration. The fact that he's refused any psychological counseling isn't helping him in the brownie-points department, either. Stubborn fellow, your Henry."

Olive picked at the platinum bird's nest. "What do you *want?*"

"Box 248. What do you remember?"

"A loser," said Olive. "Okay? Like all of them. What the hell kinda clientele you think I deal with? Movie stars?"

"Give me details on the loser," said Petra. "What did he look like? How'd he pay for the box?"

"He looked like . . . young, skinny, tall. Big glasses. Bad skin. One of those what-they-call nerds. A nerd fag."

"Gay?" said Petra.

"That's what I said."

"What makes you think that?"

"I don't think it, I know it. He got fag stuff in the mail," said Olive, sneering again.

"Gay magazines?"

"No, an invitation from the Pope. Yeah, magazines. What do you think these are for?" Gesticulating at the wall of boxes. "Not too many Bibles coming in." Olive laughed, and even at this distance Petra could smell juniper berries on her breath. Midday gin.

"Did he give you his name?"

"Who remembers."

"He did give you a name."

"He had to fill out a form."

"Where is it?"

"Gone," said Olive. "Once the box changes hands, I toss out the paperwork. You think I got space to keep it all?"

"Convenient," said Petra.

"That's my middle name. Threaten me all you want, but it's not gonna change facts." Olive cursed under her breath and Petra made out *fuckin' bitch.* "You should be ashamed, so-called officer of the so-called law, threatening me. I should report you. Maybe I will." Olive folded her arms across her bosoms, but she stepped back, as if readying herself for a blow.

Petra said, "What threat are we talking about?"

"Right," said Olive. "Overcrowding. Things change."

"I don't hear any threat, ma'am, but feel free to complain about me to anyone you choose." Petra flashed her ID. "Here's my badge number."

Olive eyed a pen but didn't move toward it.

"What name did the nerd give?" said Petra.

"I don't remember."

"Try."

"I *don't* remember—something Russian. But he wasn't. I figured him for a nut."

"Did he act nuts?"

"Sure," said Olive. "He came in drooling and shaking and seeing Martians."

Petra waited.

"He was a *weirdo,*" said Olive. "Get it? What, I'm supposed to be some kind of psychiatrist? He was a nerd-fag, didn't talk much, kept his head down. Which was fine with me. Pay the fee, collect your filthy little secrets, get the hell outta here."

"How'd he pay?"

"Cash. Like most of them."

"By the month?"

"No way," said Olive. "I got a space problem. You want to take up space, you guarantee me three months. So that's at least what I got from him."

"At least?"

"Some of them, I ask for more."

"Which ones?"

"The ones I figure I can get it from."

"Was he one of them?"

"Probably."

"How long did he have the box?"

"A long time. Coupla years."

"How often did he come in?"

"I hardly ever saw him. We've got twenty-four-hour access. He came in at night."

"You're not worried about theft?"

"I clean out the cash drawer, lock everything up. They want to steal a few pens, who cares? Too much pilferage, I raise the fees on the box, and they know it. So they behave. That's capitalism."

Henry Gilwhite's transsexual encounter had taken place late at night. Petra pictured Olive back home at the double-wide in Palmdale. What had Henry's cover story been? Going to the neighborhood tavern for a couple of beers?

Suddenly, she felt sorry for the woman.

"I won't trouble you much longer—"

"You've already troubled me plenty."

"—was the Russian name Yuri?"

"Yeah, that was it," said Olive. "Yuri. Sounds like urine. What'd he do to piss you off?" She cackled, slapped the counter, exploded into phlegmy laughter that morphed into uncontrollable coughing.

Nasty-sounding wheezes accompanied Petra as she left the maildrop.

26 At 4 A.M., two days into his surveillance of Kevin Drummond's building, Eric Stahl left his van and sneaked around to the back of the apartment structure. The night was blue, whipped by transitory, biting gusts from the east. The neon glow to the north—the Hollywood glow—was misted and dim.

Drummond's block had been quiet for a while. Nearly two hours remained until sunrise.

Stahl had thought for a long time before deciding this was right. He'd been doing nothing but sitting and thinking for nearly fifty hours. He and Connor had spoken by cell phone three times. She'd learned nothing.

During the fifty hours, Stahl had observed plenty of comings and goings, including a dog-beater he would've loved disciplining, a shifty-eyed heathen with an eye for a near-new Toyota parked halfway up the block—that one he would've called in but the guy thought better of jacking the car and left—and a couple of furtive tête-à-têtes between drug dealers and customers.

The busiest dealer lived in the building north of Drummond's. Stahl noted his address for a later report to Narcotics. Anonymous tip; that would keep things simple.

Most of Drummond's neighbors seemed to be law-abiding His-panic folk.

Quiet. The last vehicle to rumble by was a yellow cab, twelve min-utes ago.

Stahl zipped up his black windbreaker, stashed his kit in a button pocket of his black cargo pants, got out of the car, appraised the street, stretched, breathed, jogged the diagonal trajectory to the building on well-padded black running shoes. Old shoes, the squeak pounded out of them on the fifteen-mile runs that had become a thrice-weekly com-ponent of his routine.

His new routine . . .

The space between Drummond's building and its southern neigh-bor was a mess of weeds, nice and soft on the feet, and quiet. No lights on in any of the units.

As the city slept . . .

He continued to the back, scoped out the parking slots. He'd made several passes back there, but just in case. No sign of the white Honda, Drummond's space was empty.

Stahl hustled over to the building's rear entrance.

Locked, single dead bolt. An alarm sticker was pasted across the wood, but Stahl knew, from prior research, that it was false advertis-ing. No wires, no open account at the alarm company. He removed his kit, pulled out his high-focus, narrow-beam penlight, inspected his col-lection of key specimens, eyeballed the slit in the bolt. Two blanks looked promising. The first one fit.

The Army had taught him how to play with locks. And all sorts of other skills.

He'd used these particular skills only once. In Riyadh, the heat and the sand nearly unbearable, the relentless sun bleaching his retinas. Despite all the high-rises and conspicuous consumption, the avail-ability of American food on the base, the city had never been anything to Stahl but a desert hellhole.

The lockpick assignment in Riyadh had been part of a bigger plan: breaking into the penthouse of a Saudi prince who'd seduced the eighteen-year-old daughter of one of the military attachés at the U.S. embassy.

Skinny, plain-looking blond girl, borderline I.Q., subterranean self-esteem. The prince, handsome, rich, soft-spoken, had sweet-talked her into sex-on-demand at his place and fed her dope. Now feathers were being ruffled. Royal *family* feathers: consorting with a girl of such obvious inferiority could prove harmful to the prince's image, but no way would the Saudis move on their golden boy. Dirty work was always left to foreigners.

"Think of it this way," Stahl's C.O. told him. "She's getting off easy, being American. She was Saudi, they'd stone her to death."

Officially, the prince lived with his family in a palace. His fuck pad was a white marble paradise atop one of the highest-rises, the delivery door of which just happened to have been left open and unguarded on a certain night.

Same night the prince was due to dine with a couple of the State Department flunkies everyone despised. Accompanied by one of his three wives, but that afternoon he'd stashed the American girl in the f pad, plied her with pills, left her there, supervised by one female Filipina servant, to be available when he dropped in for a sexual nightcap.

Stahl staked out the high-rise and saw the prince stash his slut: a yellow Bentley Azure pulled around to the building's delivery entrance. The prince, dressed in a white silk shirt and cream slacks, got out of the car, leaving the driver's door open. An attendant rushed to close it, but the car didn't move. Five minutes later, the left passenger door opened and two men in suits emerged with a bundled figure that they hustled into the building. The same attendant was ready for them, too, holding the door.

An hour later, the prince, decked out in long, white Arab robes and a gold-banded *kaffiyeh*, got behind the wheel of the Azure and sped off.

Twenty minutes later, the two men in suits left on foot, got into a black Mercedes parked nearby, and drove away.

Soon after dark, Stahl was inside the building, lifting the skirts of his own robe and climbing twenty-eight flights to the prince's digs.

A sleepy guard was stationed on the other side of the stairwell door. Stahl walked toward him, muttered a few memorized Arabic phrases, flipped the guy around, put on the chokehold, dragged him into the stairwell and bound his arms and legs with plastic ties. Then he pulled out his pick kit and flipped the lock. Expensive digs, but cheap lock. No reason for Talal to feel insecure.

The girl was in plain sight, lolling on a purple brocade sofa, naked, stoned, eyes fixed on satellite-delivery MTV.

"Hi, Cathy."

The girl stroked her breasts and licked her lips.

The Filipina maid appeared. Stahl gave her a puff of whatever was stored in the little blue inhalator the med officer had slipped him and she nodded out and he placed her in a chair. Peeling off the Arab robes, he continued working in his black T-shirt and jeans. Wrapping Cathy in the same blanket the prince's guys had used, slinging her over his shoulder and getting the hell out of there.

He carried the girl down twenty-eight flights. A car was waiting behind the building. No Bentley, not even a Mercedes, just a plain old unmarked Ford. Had she been awake, Cathy would have seen it as a comedown. Talal liked to do her in the Bentley, and she'd told her sister she loved it.

Riyadh had been nothing but deceit . . . stay on task, no time to get distracted.

The lock kit was one of the few things Stahl had taken with him when he'd entered civilian life.

Such as it was.

He entered the apartment's ground floor. Drummond's flat was on the second floor toward the back, but a staircase ran from the front. He made his way up the thinly carpeted hallway.

The building smelled of bug spray and hot sauce. Under the carpet was old wood flooring that sagged and creaked; he trod carefully. Two light fixtures in the ceiling; only the one in front was operative. The steps were tile over cement and silent under his rubber soles.

Within seconds, he was at Drummond's unit, unnoticed. Kit out, penlight on the keyhole. Same make as the back door, the same master popped it.

He shut the door, locked it, removed his Glock from the black nylon holster that rode his hip, stood in the darkness, waiting for a life vibration—some nuance of occupancy—to disturb the silence.

Nothing.

He took a step forward. Whispered, "Kevin?"

Dead air.

He scanned the room. One room, not large. Two small windows, both shaded, looked out to the building next door. Turning on the room light would yellow the shades, so Stahl relied on his other flashlight, the black Mag with the wider beam.

He swept it over the room, careful to avoid the windows.

Kevin Drummond's living space was occupied by an unmade single bed, a crappy-looking nightstand, and a folding chair positioned in the center of a low, wide desk. Closer inspection revealed the desk to be an unpainted door laid over two sawhorses. Lots of work-space. The right side, bordering the bed, was taken up by a hot plate and provisions. Three cans of generic chili, a bag of potato chips, a jar of mild salsa, two six-packs of Pepsi. A toothbrush in a glass.

To the left were three computers with nineteen-inch flat screens, a pair of color printers, a scanner, a digital camera, a stack of toner-cartridge replacements for the printers, twelve reams of white paper.

Past the equipment a door led to the bathroom. To get there, Stahl had to manipulate his way around piles of magazines. Nearly every free inch of floor space was taken up by boxes.

He checked the lav first. Shower, sink, toilet, no signs of recent usage, but the room smelled stale. Mold in the shower, rings of grime around the sink drain, and Stahl wouldn't have used the blackened toilet on a bet. No medicine cabinet, just a single glass shelf above the sink. Carelesly squeezed toothpaste tube, OTC sinus remedy, ladies' hand cream—probably a masturbatory aid—aspirin, Pepto-Bismol, prescription acne pills dispensed three years ago at an Encino pharmacy. Three pills left. Kevin had stopped paying attention to his skin.

No soap in the shower, no shampoo, and Stahl wondered how long it had been since Kevin had been here.

Did he have another crib?

He returned to the front room, stepped among the boxes. Anything he came up with tonight would be useless—worse than useless, if the break-in came to light, he'd have screwed the investigation.

He began checking the boxes' contents.

Expecting Drummond's cache of *GrooveRat* back issues.

Wrong; not a single copy of the zine anywhere in the apartment. The guy was a pack rat, but he collected other people's creations.

From what Stahl could tell, the junk was divided into two categories: toys and magazines. The toys were Hotwheels cars, some still in their boxes, *Star Wars* and other action figures, stuff that wasn't familiar. The pages were *Vanity Fair, The New Yorker, InStyle, People, Talk, Interview*. And gay pornography. Lots of it, including some bondage and S & M stuff.

The mail-drop lady had told Petra that Drummond was gay. Stahl wondered if she'd told Sturgis. How Sturgis would take to learning about Kevin's proclivities.

She'd told *him* about *Sturgis's* proclivities. Probably wanting to make sure he didn't let loose some homophobic remark.

Which was ridiculous because he never remarked about anything, even this early in their partnership she should've seen that.

He made her nervous; when they rode together, she was jumpier than a sand flea.

This case was working out well. Both of them, happy to be going their separate ways.

Connor wasn't a bad sort. Career woman. No family ties.

Superficially tough, but new situations made her antsy.

He made her antsy.

He knew he did that to people.

He couldn't have cared less.

He completed the search of Kevin Drummond's apartment, finding no personal papers or trophies, nothing criminal or suggestive of criminality. Hoarding all that paper was consistent with the guess the shrink had worked up: Drummond was highly obsessive. Drummond's choice of magazines said the obsession was personality, celebrity.

The break-in had accomplished two things: Stahl knew, now, that the lack of a warrant wasn't hurting them. All this search would've added to the mix was verification of Drummond's homosexuality, and he couldn't see where that fit in . . . maybe the S & M stuff? Drummond being into his own S, other people's M?

The other thing: spending time in Drummond's digs, feeling the cold solitude, he was willing to bet Drummond had rabbited a while back, had no intention of returning. Even with all that computer equipment left behind.

Daddy's dough, easy come, easy go.

No copies of *GrooveRat* left behind said Kevin had another storage space. Or he didn't care about publishing anymore.

Moving on to a new hobby?

Flicking off the Maglite, he stood in Drummond's pathetic little room, making sure no one had been alerted by his presence. Just in case, he pulled out the mask and slipped it over his face. Army-issue, black Lycra, two eyeholes. This way, if anyone accosted him during his departure, all they'd remember would be a central-casting, night-stalking burglar.

The mask would scare any rational person off and lessen the chance of confrontation.

Stahl would do anything to protect himself. But he preferred not to have to hurt anyone.

27 The call came in as Milo and I were having breakfast on the Third Street Promenade in Santa Monica. A sky the color of lint promised rain, and few pedestrians passed our outdoor table. The weather didn't dissuade a scrawny man playing bad guitar for spare change. Milo slipped him a ten, told him to find another spot. The man moved twenty feet down and resumed howling. Milo returned to his Denver omelette.

It was two days after my visit to Charter College, Kevin Drummond still hadn't shown up at his apartment, and Eric Stahl's feeling was that he wouldn't be returning soon.

"Why not?" I said.

"Stahl's gut feeling, according to Petra," he said.

"Is that worth much?"

"Who knows? Meanwhile, the only new thing we've learned about Drummond is that he's gay. Petra found out that he used his POB primarily to get gay porn." He put his fork down. "Think that's relevant?"

"We were talking about someone sexually confused—"

"So maybe he resolved his confusion. What about Szabo and Loh? Rich gay men living the good life. There's a focus for jealousy."

"Szabo and Loh weren't targeted, and their house was the scene of only one murder. Whoever killed Levitch was after what Levitch had."

"Talent." He glanced at the howling guitarist. "There's a guy in no danger."

"Anything new on Kipper?" I said.

"He has a girlfriend. Much younger—late twenties, very good-looking, name of Stephanie. She works as a legal secretary for a firm in his building. For the last few days, Kipper's been squiring her around in public. This one's blond, too, so Kipper's neighbors could've been mistaken about his visitor being Julie. If I didn't have the *SeldomScene* articles linking Julie to the others and a tentative match between the ligatures used on her and Levitch, I'd be wondering about Kipper's considering a second try at marriage. Ex-spouses can make things messy, financially as well as emotionally. And we know from Kipper's neighbors that he can be vindictive."

"Julie makes waves, he shuts her up."

"Yeah," he said. "Too bad. I don't like the guy—something about him . . ."

He forked omelet, gulped coffee.

"Stephanie," I said. "You spoke to her?"

"I heard her friend call her that when they went to the ladies' room."

"You've been staking out the building?"

"At the time, it seemed prudent." He shrugged. His phone went off. "Sturgis . . . hi . . . *really* . . . yeah, okay, I've got Alex with me, might as well bring him along . . ." He read his Timex. "From where we are, forty-five minutes. Yeah. Thanks. Bye."

He clicked off, pocketed the phone, looked at my half-eaten toast. "That was Petra. How about taking that to go?" Pinning money under his plate, he waved to the waiter, pushed away from the table.

"What's up?" I said, following him out to the Promenade.

"Dead woman," he said. "Dead redhead."

The autopsy room was spotless tile and stainless steel, silent and pleasantly cool. Petra and Milo and I stood next to a shrouded mass on a stainless table as a soft-spoken attendant named Rhonda Reese checked paperwork. Reese was thirtyish, chestnut-haired, curvy, with the open face of a tour guide.

I'd sailed to Boyle Heights on the 10, but Interstate 5 had been jammed by the proverbial jackknifed big rig, and the backlog had turned the drive to the coroner's office to an hour-long ordeal. During that time, Milo had dozed, and I'd thought about women. Petra met us in the lobby.

"I've already checked us in," she said. "Let's go."

Rhonda Reese drew the sheet back and folded it neatly at the foot of the table. The corpse was long and rawboned and female, waxy flesh tinted that unique green-gray. Eyes and mouth, shut. Peaceful expression, no obvious signs of violence. A scatter of pimples and fibroid lumps filled a flat expanse of chest between small, deflated breasts. Inverted, corrugated nipples, sharp hips, wide pelvis, skinny legs covered with curly, auburn down. The ankles crusted by red skin, hardened and crackled like alligator hide.

Street ankles.

The woman's soles were black, as were the dirty, ragged nails on her toes and fingers. Fungus grew between the toes. An unruly rusty pubic thatch was littered with dandruff. A few white hairs sparked the thatch.

Red hair on top, as well, but much brighter, with claret roots and overlay of purple at the tips. Long, matted hair, filthy and dense, crowned a swollen face that might've been pretty once upon a time.

No needle marks.

"Any guesses?" said Milo.

Rhonda Reese said, "I can't speak for Dr. Silver, but if you open her eyes you'll see petechiae."

"Strangulation." He moved closer to the body, checked the eyes, squinted. "The neck's a little rosy, too, but no ligature marks." He glanced at Petra, and she nodded. Not like the others.

I said, "Gentle strangulation?"

Petra stared at me. Milo shrugged. The term was obnoxious but well-established jargon for a murderous ploy: using a broad, soft ligature to blunt the outward evidence of strangulation. Some people choke themselves that way to achieve heightened sexual pleasure and accidentally die.

Milo and I had worked a gentle strangulation case a few years ago. No accident, a child . . .

He said, "When's the autopsy, Rhonda?"

"You'll have to ask Dr. Silver. We're pretty booked."

"Dave Silver?" said Petra.

Reese nodded.

"I know him," said Petra. "Good guy, I'll talk to him."

Milo eyed the body again. "When did it happen?" he asked Petra.

"Yesterday, early A.M. Two of our uniforms found her off the boulevard, on the south side of the street. Alley behind a church that had once been a theater."

"That Salvadoran Pentecostal place?" said Milo. "East end?"

"That's the one. She was propped sitting against the wall, garbage service came by, she was blocking their truck from getting close to the Dumpster and they thought she was asleep, so they tried to wake her." To Reese: "Tell them about her clothes."

"We removed layers," said Reese. "Lots of them. Junky old clothes, really filthy." She wrinkled her nose. "That rash on her legs, you know what it is, right? Circulation problems. She's got tons of stuff growing on and in her. We cultured God-knows-what from her feet and nose and throat. On top of the body odor, you could smell the alcohol, the whole room reeked. Her blood work won't be back till later today, but I'll lay odds she's a .3 or higher."

The recitation wasn't without compassion, but the facts remained cruel.

Milo remained expressionless as he inspected the body again. "No tracks that I can see."

"There aren't any," said Reese. "Looks like drink was her main thing, but we'll see what the tox screen pulls up."

"Did you list the articles of clothing?"

"Right here," said Reese, turning pages of the coroner's file. "Two pairs of woman's panties, two pairs of men's boxers, three T-shirts, a bra over that, blue UCLA sweatshirt."

"Was the C half gone on the sweatshirt?" said Milo.

"Doesn't say," said Reese. "Let me go look."

A cardboard carton sat atop a stainless-steel counter. Reese gloved up, bent over the box, retrieved a large, paper bag that she opened.

Wrinkling her nose again, drew out a blue sweatshirt fuzzed with dirt and leaves. "Yup, half a C."

Milo turned to Petra. "The old lady at Light and Space described her Dumpster diver as wearing that. The drawing she did was useless, so I figured cataracts. Guess she could see okay, after all, just a lousy artist. Is this officially your case?"

Petra said, "No, Digmond and Battista caught it, I just happened to hear them talking about it, and I recalled what you said about a tall redhead homeless-type nosing around. No ID yet, her prints are being run as we speak."

Rhonda Reese said, "Can I put this back?"

Milo said, "Sure, thanks. Where are the crime-scene snaps?"

Petra said, "Dig and Harry have a set, and there's a copy here."

"Rhonda, if it's no trouble, we could use some dupes."

"I can do that," said Reese. She left the room and returned a while later with a white envelope.

Milo thanked her, and she said, "Good luck, Detectives."

He said, "Feel like solving a few 187s for us, Rhonda?"

Reese laughed. "Sure, why not. Do I get to talk to someone alive?"

We reconvened in the morgue parking lot.

Milo said, "Digmond and Battista gonna give you any space on this?"

"They're booked solid, would be *thrilled* to shunt it to me. But I want to wait and see if it actually ties in to the others. For all we know, it's not even homicide."

"Petechiae?"

"She could've choked or had a seizure or vomited hard. Anything that bugged her eyes hard enough would do it, and you know how prone street people are to catastrophe. If the hyoid or the thyroid cartilages are messed up, that'll be a different story. The sweatshirt says she was at the gallery, but if she's connected to the other victims, why the lack of aggression to her body? No cuts, not even a scratch. And if it is strangulation, it doesn't match what we saw on Kipper and Levitch. That deep ligature ring—wire biting into the neck, someone really angry. Serials get more violent over time, not less, right, Alex?"

I said, "This could be tied in with the others but result from a different motivation. This victim could mean something different to the killer."

"Like what?" said Milo.

"She was behind the gallery casing the place for the killer."

"Advance woman?" he said. "Drummond chooses a homeless woman for an accomplice? And now he gets rid of her?"

"He would if she became a liability. A homeless woman, alcoholic, possibly mentally ill, might've served a purpose for him when he wasn't under threat. But if he knows he's the object of investigation, he might have decided to cover his tracks."

"He might very well know he's the object," said Petra. "We've talked to his family and his landlady. He hasn't been seen for days, all the evidence says he's rabbited."

I said, "A broad ligature is sometimes used when the killer has some level of sympathy for the victim. Also, she's a big woman. If she drank herself into a stupor, that would've made his job a lot easier, no need to confront or struggle. The way she was propped is almost respectful. Were her legs spread?"

Milo opened the envelope, drew out color photos, shuffled through until he found a full-length body shot.

"Legs tight together," said Petra.

"No sexual positioning, but it could still be a pose," I said. "Strangulation, even with no struggle, can set off spasms. This looks too orderly to be natural."

The two of them studied the photo. Milo said, "Looks posed to me."

Petra nodded.

I said, "There's no intent to demean, here. Just the opposite, he's _guarding_ her sexuality."

"Kevin's gay," said Milo. "Maybe women aren't sexual objects to him."

"Julie was posed sexually. Kevin may be leaning toward gay, but if he's our guy, he's still plenty confused."

"That makes sense," said Petra. "Macho dad and brothers, all that emphasis on sports and being manly. It couldn't have been easy for him."

She glanced at Milo, and I noticed a spark of unease in her dark eyes. Wondering if she'd offended him.

He nodded, as if to reassure her.

"Whatever the motive," I said, "the killer took care to make this victim look comfortable. Relative to the other cases, it's an indication of respect."

"Accomplice but not a girlfriend?" said Milo.

Petra said, "Even if Kevin does have an interest in girls—even if he's quirky in ways we don't know—I can't see a young guy associating with a diseased homeless woman. What motive would he have to hang with her?"

"Kevin's an isolate," I said. "Probably sees himself an outcast from way back. On top of his sexual issues, he's set himself up as a white knight fighting a lonely battle for art in its pure form. With that kind of alienation, I can see him gravitating toward other outsiders."

"Which means I should be scoping out the street people, not the bookstores."

Milo said, "Hanging with the homeless, offing the talented. It's like a war against the bright side of life."

I said, "There's something else I find interesting. This body showed up behind a former theater. What if that's a sneaky little allusion to the death of the performing arts?"

"They're still performing there," said Milo. "The church. Isn't that what preaching is? Or maybe, he's being sacrilegious."

Petra said, "This is veering into serious weirdness." She gnawed her lip. "Okay, what next?"

Milo said, "We're ninety-nine percent sure this is the redhead CoCo Barnes saw, but let's see if I can get a positive ID from the old lady. Main thing is find out who she is, woman like this is gonna be in the system somewhere. When do the prints come in?"

"You know prints. Could be today or next week. I'll talk to Dig and Harry, see if we can speed things up."

"Once we know who she is, we trace her movements. And maybe

we don't need to wait for prints. After Barnes told me what she saw, I did some asking around, found a shelter in your bailiwick—Dove House—where they knew of a tall redhead who dropped in from time to time. Bernadine something. They also said they figured her for someone who'd lived better once upon a time, because when her head cleared, she talked intelligently."

I said, "Maybe that's the side the killer saw. He knew he needed to get her blind drunk to render her helpless."

Petra said, "I know Dove House, brought kids there. They've got a pretty good success rate."

Milo looked at the death shot. "No one's perfect."

28 We found CoCo Barnes spinning an amorphous pot in her garage studio. Lance the dog snored at her feet.

It took her one glance to say, "That's her— just like my drawing. Poor thing, what happened to her?"

"We don't know yet, ma'am," said Milo.

"But she's dead."

"Yes, ma'am."

"Oh, boy," said Barnes, wiping clay from her hands. "Do me a favor, we ever meet again, call me CoCo, not 'ma'am.' You're making me feel paleolithic."

Milo phoned Petra and reached her out in the Valley. When he asked if we could hit the shelter without her, she said fine.

"What's she doing?" I said.

"Keeping an eye on Kevin's folks' house. Stahl's still watching the apartment, but that's looking pretty useless."

I turned the car around, noticed my gas gauge was near empty.

"All the back-and-forth," he said. "I'll pay to fill it up."

"Spring for dinner instead."

"Where?"

"Somewhere expensive."

"Double date?" he said.

"Sure." I pulled into a gas station on Lincoln.

He jumped out, used his credit card to activate the pump, hooked up the nozzle, bounced his eyes around, ever the detective. I felt like stretching, so I wiped the windows.

"So how's Allison?" he said.

"She's in Boulder."

"Skiing?"

"Psych convention."

"Oh . . . okay, all filled up." He replaced the hose. "When's she getting back?"

"Few days. Why?"

"We need to wait for her," he said. "To schedule the double date."

Dove House occupied a run-down, cloud-colored apartment building on Cherokee, just north of Hollywood Boulevard. No sign or identifying marks. The front door was open, and the ground-floor unit to the left was labeled OFFICE.

The director was a young, clean-shaven black man named Daryl Witherspoon, working alone at a battered desk. Cornrows lined his skull. A silver crucifix swung as he got up and walked toward us. His gray sweats smelled freshly laundered.

Milo showed him the picture, and he placed a palm against his cheek. "Oh, my. Poor Erna."

"Erna who?"

"Ernadine," said Witherspoon. "Ernadine Murphy."

"E. Murphy," I said.

Witherspoon regarded me curiously. "What happened to her?"

Milo said, "I called here about a week ago, spoke to a woman who thought she knew Ms. Murphy."

"That was probably Diane Pirello, my assistant. Was Erna—did this happen a week ago?"

"Last night. What can you tell us about her?"

Witherspoon said, "Let's sit down."

Milo and I perched on a thrift shop sofa that stank of tobacco. Witherspoon offered us coffee from a bubbling machine, but we declined. Footsteps sounded from above. The room was painted a bright yellow that seared the eyes. Inspirational messages taped to the plaster were the art du jour.

Witherspoon pulled up a chair and said, "Are you able to tell me what happened?"

"That's still unclear," said Milo. "She was found in an alley just a few blocks away. Behind the Pentecostal church."

"The church . . . she wasn't religious," said Witherspoon. "That's one thing I can tell you."

"Resistant?" I said.

He nodded. "Very. Not that we lean hard on them. But we do try to get through to them. Ernie had no desire to embrace the Lord. She really wasn't one of our regulars, just checked in from time to time when things got bad for her. We never turn anyone away unless they're violent."

"Was she ever violent?"

"No, never."

Milo said, "What made things go bad for her?"

"It all came down to alcohol. She was drinking herself to death. We've known her off and on for the last couple of years, and lately, we could see significant deterioration."

"Such as?"

"Health problems—persistent cough, skin lesions, stomach problems. One time she slept here and the next morning her sheets were splotched with blood. At first we figured it was . . . you know, the time of the month. There's no shortage of tampons here, but some of the women forget. As it turned out, Erna was bleeding from . . ." Witherspoon flinched . . . "her rear end. Internally. We called in one of our volunteer doctors and finally convinced Erna to be examined. She said it was nothing critical, but that Ernie did have some fissures that should be looked into. She also said there were probably intestinal problems that should be looked into. We offered to send Erna to a specialist, but she left and didn't return for months. That was her pattern. In and out. For a lot of them, we're a depot."

"What about mental problems?" said Milo.

"That goes without saying," said Witherspoon. "For most of our people, that's a given."

"What kind of specific mental problems did Ernadine Murphy have?"

"As I said, it all came down to drink. I figured she finally went too far—organic brain syndrome they call it. Going dull. And when she'd sleep here, she'd sometimes wake up and hallucinate. Korsakoff's syndrome, it's a vitamin B deficiency they get." He frowned. "Folks joke about pink elephants, but there's nothing funny about it."

I said, "What was she like before she deteriorated?"

"Hmm . . . I can't say she was ever really . . . normal. I'm not saying she was stupid. She wasn't. Once in a while, when we could dry her out long enough and she talked, you could see she had a good vocabulary—our sense was she'd once been educated. But when we tried to ask her about it, she'd clam up. Lately, those dry periods were few and far between. For the last year or so she was still pretty dysfunctional."

"Aggressive?" said Milo.

"Just the opposite—passive, spaced-out, slurred speech, trouble focusing. Her motor skills were affected, too. She'd stumble, trip—is that what happened to her? Did she fall and hit her head?"

"Doesn't look like it," said Milo.

"Someone did this to her."

"We don't know yet, sir."

"Oh, Lord," said Witherspoon.

Milo took out his pad. "Who's the doctor who evaluated her when she bled on the sheets?"

"We use several, all volunteers. I think this time it was Hannah Gold. She's got an office on Highland. It was only one time, she never established a relationship with Erna. No one did. We could never reach her."

Witherspoon's shoulders rose and fell. "God gives and takes away, but there's plenty we humans do in the interim that affects the journey."

"What do you know about Ms. Murphy's family history?"

"Nothing," said Witherspoon. "She never opened up."

I said, "Did she have any friends? Connect with any of the other residents?"

"Not that I saw. To be honest, most of the other women were afraid of her. She was large, could come across threatening if you didn't know."

"How so?"

"Lurching around," said Witherspoon. "Mumbling to herself. Seeing things."

"What did she see?" said Milo.

"She never put it into words, but from the way she behaved—standing there and pointing and moving her lips—you could tell she was frightened. Was seeing something that frightened her. But she wouldn't accept comfort."

"So the other women were afraid of her."

"Maybe I overspoke," said Witherspoon. "More nervous than afraid. She never caused a problem. Sometimes she'd go off in a corner, get agitated, start mumbling and shaking her fist. When she did that, everyone gave her space. But she never aggressed against anyone. Sometimes she'd punch her own chest, rap her head with her knuckles. Nothing serious, but you can see how that would be scary. A woman of her size."

"Those lucid periods," I said. "What made you think she was well educated?"

"Her vocabulary," said Witherspoon. "The way she used words. I wish I could remember a specific example but I can't. It's been a while since I've seen her."

"How long?" said Milo.

"Maybe three, four months."

"Could you please check your records and be more specific, sir?" said Milo.

"Sorry. The only records we keep are for the government. Tax-exempt status and all that. Shuffling government paper takes up a lot of my time, so I don't add to my burden."

"A good vocabulary," I said.

"It was more than that—good diction. Something about the way she talked could be . . . sophisticated."

"During her clear periods what did she talk about?"

Witherspoon fingered a cornrow. "Let me ask Diane." He strode to his desk, punched a phone extension, talked in a low voice, said, "She'll be right down."

Diane Petrello was in her sixties, short and stout with clipped gray hair and big, round, tortoiseshell glasses even wider than her face. She wore a pink sweatshirt that said *Compassion*, a long denim skirt, and sneakers.

When Milo told her about Erna Murphy, she said, "Oh my God," in a soft, high voice. Tears rolled down her cheeks as he added a few details. As she sat down opposite us and wiped her eyes, Daryl Witherspoon fixed her a cup of tea.

She warmed her hands on the cup, and said, "I hope the poor thing finally finds some peace."

"Tortured soul," said Milo.

"Oh, yes," said Diane Petrello. "Aren't we all?"

He went over some of the same ground we'd covered with Witherspoon, then repeated my question about Erna Murphy's lucid periods.

"What she talked about," said Petrello. "Hmm, I'd say mostly art. She could spend hours looking at pictures in art books. One time, I went out and bought some old art books for her at a thrift shop but when I brought them back, she was gone. She was like that. Restless, wouldn't stay put. In fact, that was the last time I saw her. She never got to see the books."

"What kind of art did she like?" said Milo.

"Well . . . I guess I couldn't tell you. Pretty pictures, I suppose."

"Landscapes?"

Julie Kipper's pretty pictures.

Diane Petrello said, "Anything pretty. It seemed to calm her down. But not always. Nothing really worked when she was all wound up."

"She could be pretty agitated," said Milo.

"But she never caused problems."

"She have any friends here at Dove House?"

"Not really, no."

"Anyone on the outside?"

"Not that I ever saw."

"She talk about any outside friends?"

Petrello shook her head.

Milo said, "Specifically, ma'am, I'd be interested in a young man in his early twenties. Tall, thin, dark hair, bad skin, eyeglasses."

Petrello looked at Witherspoon. They both shook their heads.

Witherspoon said, "Is he the one who did this?"

"We don't know if anyone did anything, sir. What else can you tell us about Ms. Murphy?"

"That's all I can think of," said Petrello. "She was so alone. Like so many of them. That's the main problem, really. Aloneness. Without Divine Grace, all of us are alone."

Milo asked if we could show Erna Murphy's picture to the other residents, and Darryl Witherspoon frowned.

Diane Petrello said, "There are only six women in residence this week."

"Any men?" said Milo.

"There are eight men."

Witherspoon said, "It's been a tough couple of weeks, everyone we've got is kind of fragile. Those pictures you showed me would be too much."

Milo said, "How about this: no picture, we just talk. And you come along to make sure we do it right."

Another glance passed between Witherspoon and Petrello. He said, "Guess so. But at the first sign of trouble, we quit, okay?"

Witherspoon returned to his desk as Milo and I trailed Diane Petrello up a flight of protesting stairs. The upper floors were divided into single rooms that lined a long, bright, turquoise hallway. Women were housed on the second floor, men on the third. Each room was set up with two bunk beds. Bibles on the pillow, a tiny portable closet, more religious posters.

Half of the residents were sleepy. Erna Murphy's name elicited only blank looks until a young, dark-haired woman named Lynnette with the face of a fashion model and old needle tracks in the crooks of her pipe-stem arms, said, "Big Red."

"You know her?"

"Roomed with her a couple of times." Lynnette's eyes were huge and black and wounded. Her hair was long and dark and greasy. A tattooed star the size of a sheriff's badge decorated the left side of her neck. A vein ran through the center of the body art, pulsing the blue ink. Slow pulse, steady, unperturbed. She sat on the edge of a lower bunk, Bible at one arm, bag of Fritos at the other. Her back curved like that of an old woman. The downturn of her mouth said she'd given up on personal safety. "What happened to her?"

"I'm afraid she's dead, ma'am."

Lynnette's pulse remained sluggish. Then her eyes drooped with amusement.

Milo said, "Something funny, ma'am."

Lynnette shot him a crooked grin. "Only thing funny is *'ma'am.'* So what, someone offed her?"

"We're not sure."

"Maybe her boyfriend did it."

"What boyfriend would that be?"

"Don't know. She just told me she had one and that he was real smart."

"When did she tell you this?" said Milo.

Lynnette scratched her arm. "Had to be a long time ago." To Petrello: "Had to be not the last time I was here, maybe a few times before that?"

"Months," said Petrello.

"I been traveling," said Lynnette. "Had to be months."

"Traveling," said Milo.

Lynnette smiled. "Seeing the U.S.A. Yeah, had to be months— could be six, seven, dunno. I just remember it cause I thought it was bullshit. Cause like who'd want her? She was a skank."

"You didn't like her."

"What was to like?" said Lynnette. "She was a whack job, would start off having a conversation with you, then space out, start walking around, talking to herself."

"What else did she say about this boyfriend?" said Milo.

"Just that."

"Smart."

"Yeah."

"No name?"

"Nope."

Milo stepped closer to the bed. Diane Petrello interposed herself between him and Lynnette, and he retreated. "If there's *anything* you can tell us about the boyfriend, I'd greatly appreciate it."

Lynnette said, "I don't know nothin'." A second later: "She said he was smart, that's it. Bragging on herself. Like, *he's* smart so *I'm* smart. She said he was gonna come take her out of here." She puffed her lips. "Right."

"Out of Dove House?"

"Out of *here*. The *life*. The *street*. So maybe he did. So look what happened to her."

We got back in the car. Milo said, "What do you think?"

"Erna Murphy liked pretty art," I said. "That would be a point of contact with someone like Kevin, the self-assigned arbiter of art. Julie Kipper's paintings certainly qualified as pretty. Erna would've been attracted to them. Maybe he directed her to the show. Used her as some sort of distraction."

"CoCo Barnes opens the back door and maybe she forgets to lock it." He rubbed his face. "A psychotic advance woman. Think he could've used Erna for more than just that? What if he had her actually do Julie? Erna was big enough to overpower someone Julie's size, especially in the closed confines of that bathroom. A woman would also explain the lack of semen or sexual assault. And we just heard she could be lucid."

"Relatively lucid," I said. "Julie's murder was too well planned and thought out for a psychotic. Not a shred of forensic evidence was left at the scene. Erna can't have been counted on to be that meticulous. No, I can't see that. There's something else going on here—'E. Murphy' wrote a review of Vassily Levitch a year ago. The prose was florid but not confused enough to be Erna's. Her name was expropriated. It's a kind of identify theft."

"Smart boyfriend," he said. "Lynnette was sure Erna was being delusional about that."

"In terms of a romantic bond, she probably was. But there was a relationship. Erna's aesthetic interests, the fact that she'd been educated, was periodically articulate, could've made her appealing to someone like Kevin Drummond. A tragic figure who'd hit rock bottom, the ultimate outsider. Even her *psychosis* would have appealed to him. Some fools still think being crazy is glamorous. But whatever bond they had, Kevin was careful to keep her at arm's length. His landlady never saw her around his apartment, and no one Petra's talked to has linked the two of them."

"He idealizes her, then he kills her."

"She ceased fitting into his worldview, became a threat."

"Cold," he said. "That's one thing that does fit all of it. Cold-hearted. Like Baby Boy's song. I bought one of his CDs, been listening to it, trying to get some insights."

"Any success?"

"He was one hell of a player, even a tone-deaf philistine like me can hear his soul pouring outta that guitar. But no big insights. Did you know your name's on the album?"

"What are you talking about?"

"Tiny print, on the bottom, where he thanks everyone from Jesus Christ to Robert Johnson. Big list, Robin's in there. He calls her 'the beautiful guitar lady,' thanks her for keeping his instruments happy. Then he tacks you on. Something along the lines of 'Thanks to Dr. Alex Delaware for keeping the guitar lady happy.' "

"Been a while since that was true."

"Sorry," he said. "I thought you'd get a kick out of it."

I pulled away from the curb, drove west on Hollywood Boulevard. Construction brought us to a halt. Hard-hatted crews running amok. Graft kings rejuvenating the neighborhood. Maybe one day, the shiny, sterile, franchised Hollywood the civic fathers lusted for would emerge. Right now, glitz coexisted with sleaze in an uneasy balance.

A few miles away, north, in the hills, was the Hollywood sign, where a starlet had ended her life decades ago, and China Maranga's body had been left to rot. I didn't suggest driving up there, and neither did Milo. Too long ago to matter.

We crawled to Vine Street. He said, "Erna. Another soul expropriated."

I said, "A user. That's what this is all about."

29 Encino. Petra digested the details of Milo's call. The E. Murphy ID meant the redhead's murder would end up in her basket, too.

She phoned Eric Stahl and filled him in.

"Okay," he said, in that infuriating, flat voice. *Nothing impresses me.*

"You going to keep watching Kevin?" she said.

"Probably a waste of time."

"Why's that?"

"I don't think he'll be coming by soon," said Stahl. "Whatever you want."

"I'm still watching his parents' house. No action yet, but I want to stick with it. Meantime, I think we should start delving into Erna Murphy's history. If you really think Kevin's crib is a zero, feel free to start on that."

"Sure."

Silence.

Petra waited him out. He said, "Anywhere you want me to start?"

"The usual data banks—hold on, a woman just drove up to the house, could be Kevin's mother—doesn't look like a happy camper—just do the usual, Eric, I'll talk to you later."

*   *   *

She remained in her Accord and watched the woman climb out of her baby blue Corvette. The low-slung, covered thing she and Stahl had seen during their first visit to Franklin Drummond's home.

The red Honda was registered to Anna Martinez—an Hispanic maid who appeared to live in; the other three vehicles were registered to Franklin Drummond. His daily drive was the gray Baby Benz, the 'Vette was the missus's toy, no one seemed to bother with the white Explorer. Maybe spare wheels for the two younger sons when they visited from college.

Kevin drove cheap wheels. Not the favored child.

The woman flipped her hair, wiggled her butt, and alarm-locked the Corvette. Middle-aged, tall, skinny, long-legged. Big, thick features. Homely, but in a not-unsexy way. The hair was a bright, orange helmet— same color as Erna Murphy's, isn't *zat* interesting Dr. Freud? She wore a baggy white jersey sweater embroidered with rhinestones that bobbled her big boobs, black leggings with footstraps, backless sandals with hypodermic heels.

Fuck-me shoes. Aging bimbo?

Was Kevin's mommy doing someone other than Kevin's daddy?

Petra watched her walk up to the front door, fool in her Gucci purse, remove a ring of keys.

Definitely Kevin's mom. He hadn't inherited his lanky frame from fireplug Franklin.

The car, the heels, the rest of it said Mama liked to party. A woman in touch with her sexuality. Toss that into the family mix and Petra could only imagine what Kevin's childhood had been like.

This afternoon, Mama looked miserable. Tense. Tight neck, croquet wicket mouth. She dropped the key ring, bent, and retrieved it.

Petra got out of her car as the woman's key aimed at the lock. Made it to the woman's side before she made contact and twisted.

The woman turned. Petra flashed the badge.

"I have nothing to say to you." Smoker's voice. Tobacco mixed with Chanel 19 emanated from the redhead's clothing.

"You are Mrs. Drummond," said Petra.

"I'm Terry Drummond." Fear in the voice.

"Could you spare a moment to talk about Kevin?"

"No way," said Terry Drummond. "My husband warned me you'd be by. I have no obligation to talk to you."

Petra smiled. The rhinestones on Terry's shirt formed the crude outline of two terriers. Kissing. Sweet. "You certainly don't, Mrs. Drummond. But I'm not here to persecute you."

Terry Drummond's key arm tightened. "Call it what you want. I'm going inside."

"Ma'am, Kevin hasn't been seen for nearly a week. As a mother, I'd think you'd be concerned."

Studying the woman for a hint that Kevin had made contact.

Tears welled up in Terry Drummond's eyes. Soft brown eyes, flecked with gold. Gorgeous eyes, really, despite the too-generous application of shadow and mascara. Petra revised her appraisal. Despite the thick features, Terry was more than attractive; even in her anxiety she exuded oodles of sensuality. As a young woman, she'd probably been dead-on sexy.

What would it be like to have a mother like that?

Petra knew nothing about mothers; hers had died giving birth to her.

She relaxed her posture, gave Terry Drummond time to think. Terry wore big gold jewelry, a three-carat rock on her ring finger. Up close the Gucci bag looked real.

Petra saw her as someone whose body heat and flashy looks had snagged an up-and-coming lawyer. Someone who'd climbed a few notches socially, probably given up whatever entry-level career she'd had, raised three boys, immersed herself in suburban motherhood, only to see her oldest son turn out . . . different.

Now she was terrified. Kevin hadn't phoned home.

She said, "It's got to be worrying, ma'am. No one's saying Kevin's guilty of anything, he's just someone we need to talk to. He could be in danger. Think about it: Has he ever disappeared like this before? Don't you think it's important that we find him?"

Terry Drummond bit back tears. "*I* haven't heard from him, so how could *you* find him?"

"How long has it been, ma'am?"

Terry shook her head. "That's all I'm going to say."

"Do you have any idea why we're interested in him?"

"Something to do with murder. Which is ridiculous. Kevin's gentle." Terry's voice rose on the last word, and she flinched. Petra had a sense someone had used it as an insult when referring to Kevin.

The gentle one.

"I'm sure he is, Mrs. Drummond."

"Then why are you hounding us?"

"Not trying to, ma'am. I'm sure you know Kevin better than anyone. You care about him more deeply than anyone. So if he does get in touch, you'll offer him good advice."

Terry Drummond cried. "I don't need this. I don't need this one bit. If my idiot brother-in-law hadn't finked on Kevin, I wouldn't have to be dealing with this—why don't you look at *him*? He already *killed* two people."

"Randolph?"

"His wife and child, the dirty drunk," snarled Terry. "Frank was always telling Randy to stop drinking. He nearly ruined us—the lawsuits. It's only cause Frank's so smart that he managed to climb back up to the top. So you can see why Randy'd have it in for us."

"All Randy did was confirm he was Kevin's uncle," said Petra. "We'd have found out, anyway."

"Why?" said Terry. "Why are you harassing my boy? He's good, he's kind, he's smart, he's gentle, he'd never hurt anyone."

The woman's entire body had gone rigid, and Petra shifted gears.

"Did Kevin have a friend named Erna Murphy?"

"Who?"

Petra repeated the name.

"Never heard of her. Kevin never had any—I don't know his friends."

Asocial Kevin. The admission made Terry blanch, and she tried to cover: "They move out, go their own way. Creative people especially need their space." That sounded like a well-practiced rationalization for Kevin's oddness.

"Yes, they do," said Petra.

"I paint," said Terry Drummond. "I started taking art lessons, and now *I* need *my* space."

Petra nodded.

"Please," said Terry. "Let me be."

"Here's my card, ma'am. Think about what I said. For Kevin's sake."

Terry faltered, then took it.

"One more thing," said Petra. "Could you just tell me why Kevin called himself Yuri?"

Terry's smile was abrupt, blinding, and it made her gorgeous. She touched her breast, as if remembering what it had nourished. "He's so cute. So clever. I'll tell you, and then you'll see how off base you are. Years ago, when Kevin was little—just a little guy, but he was always bright—Frank was telling him about the space race. About Sputnik, which was a big thing when *Frank* was a little guy. The Russians got there first, showed us Americans how we got soft and lazy. Frank used to talk to Kevin like that all the time. Kevin was Frank's firstborn and he really spent time with him, took him everywhere. Museums, parks, even the office, everyone called Kevin 'a little lawyer' because he talked so great. Anyway, Frank was telling Kevin about the Russians and Sputnik and this Russian astronaut—whatever they call them, cosmo-something . . ."

"Cosmonauts."

"Cosmonauts beating out the astronauts, the first one was a guy named Yuri something. And Kevin, little as he was, was just listening to Frank, and then when Frank finished, Kevin piped up, 'Daddy, *I* want to be first. *I* want to be a Yuri.'"

Terry's tears flowed anew. One long-nailed hand plucked at a rhinestone terrier. "After that, whenever he did something good, got a good grade on a test, anything, I called him Yuri. He liked that. It meant he'd done a good job."

30
Two messages on my machine.

Allison, two hours ago. Robin, a few minutes later. Both asking me to call back when I had a chance. I phoned Allison's hotel. She picked up on the fourth ring, sounded out of breath. "It's you, great. You caught me out the door."

"Bad time?"

"No, no, excellent time. On my way to another seminar."

"How's the conference?"

"Boulder's pretty," she said. "Thin air."

"Thin, hot air?"

She laughed. "Actually, there've been some good papers, stuff you might enjoy. PTSD in victims of terrorism, a good survey of depression in kids . . . how's the case coming along?"

"Not much progress," I said.

"Sorry . . . wish you were here. We could've had some fun on the slopes."

"There's still snow?"

"Not a lick. I canceled Philadelphia, will be coming home tomorrow. Want to get together tomorrow night?"

"You bet."

"I didn't offend Grant's folks," she said. "To tell the truth, they seemed relieved. Everyone knows it's time to cut the ties. Shall I take a cab directly from the airport?"

"I can pick you up."

"No, work on the case. I should make it by eight."

"Should I cook?"

"If you want, but it's not vital. One way or another we'll obtain nourishment."

I put off phoning Robin. When I finally did and heard the tension in her voice, I regretted the delay.

"Thanks for calling back."

"What's wrong?"

"I didn't want to bother you, but I thought you should know— you'd have found out eventually. Someone broke into my place, vandalized the shop, made off with some instruments."

"God, I'm sorry. When?"

"Last night. We were out, got back around midnight, found the lights on and the door to the studio ajar. The police took three hours to arrive, wrote a report, called in detectives who wrote another report. Technicians came and dusted for fingerprints. Strangers in my house— all those procedures you and Milo always talk about."

"Was it a forced entry?"

"The back door's bolted and grated but they just shoved it off the hinges. Looks like they were rusted. The alarm was set, but the detectives said the lead must have worn down, wasn't making proper contact. It's an old house . . . I should've checked but the landlord lives in Lake Havasu, everything's a drawn-out process."

"How much damage?"

"They took a bunch of stuff, but what's worse is they smashed whatever was on the bench. Beautiful old things, an ivory-bridge Martin, Clyde Buffum's Lyon & Healy mandolin, a Stella twelve-string. My insurance will cover it, but my poor clients, those instruments mean more than money . . . you don't need to hear this, I don't know why I called. Tim installed a new door, then he had to fly up to San Francisco."

"You're alone?"

"Just for a few days."

"I'll be right over."

"Don't, Alex . . . yes, do."

She was waiting for me, sitting in a white plastic chair on her tiny front lawn, wearing a green sweater and jeans.

Her arms were around me before I made contact.

She said, "They took Baby Boy's guitars." Her body trembled. "I'd been talking to Jackie True about buying them so I could give them to you, Alex. He checked with Christie's and they told him neither would fetch a premium. He was about to agree."

She looked up at me. "I knew you'd enjoy them. It was going to be my birthday present to you."

Her birthday was coming up in a month. I hadn't thought about it.

I stroked her curls. "It was a sweet thought."

"That's what counts, right?" She smiled and sniffled. "Let's go inside."

Her living room looked the same but for some missing pieces of china. I said, "Detective have any ideas?"

"Gang bangers. They obviously weren't pros. Left some prime stuff behind—a gorgeous D'Angelico Excel and a forties F-5—thank God I had those in a closet. Other than Baby's Gibson, they went for the electrics. Couple of seventies Fenders, a Standell bass, a Les Paul gold-top reissue."

"Going for the flash," I said. "Kids."

"That and all the wanton destruction says immaturity, according to the detectives. Like what kids do when they break into schools. The gangs are active south of Rose. Until now we haven't felt it."

South of Rose was two blocks away. Another arbitrary L.A. boundary, as genuine as a movie.

Maybe Robin suddenly realized that because she began shivering, clung harder to me, buried her head in the folds of my shirt.

"Tim's trip up north was an emergency?" I said.

"He didn't want to go, I insisted. He got a contract to work with the kids in a new *Les Miserables* production. Two weeks of prep before opening night. With kids you have to be careful not to stress the vocal cords."

"Thought you'd only be alone for a couple of days."

"I'm going up there as soon as I take care of this."

I said nothing.

"Thanks for coming, Alex."

"Need help straightening up?"

"I don't even want to go in there."

"How about a breather, then. Let's go somewhere for a cup of coffee."

"I can't leave," she said. "The locksmith's coming."

"When?"

"He was due an hour ago. Just sit with me. Please."

She brought out a couple of Cokes, and we sat opposite each other drinking.

"Some cookies?"

"No, thanks."

"I'm being selfish. I'm sure you're busy."

I said, "Where are you going to sleep tonight?"

"Here."

"You'll be okay?"

"Yes," she said. "I don't know."

"Why don't we do this: Once the new locks are in, we'll tidy up, bring the instruments to my place for safekeeping, then you can fly up to San Francisco tonight."

She placed her hands in her lap.

"I could do that," she said.

Then she cried.

When she was ready to face the damage we entered the studio. Robin's pin-neat organization had been reduced to trash. The two of us swept and straightened, collected shreds of ravished instruments, tuning pegs, bridges, salvaging what we could, discarding the rest.

Uncoiling and discarding kinked guitar strings. Hurting myself a couple of times on the sharp ends of the wires because I was working fast, with a blank mind.

The ordeal left Robin short of breath. She dusted the workbench, hopped up, said, "It's fine, don't do any more," stretched an arm.

I stood there, broom in hand.

"Come here," she said.

I put the broom down and walked toward her. When I was a foot away, she hooked a hand behind my neck, drew me in, kissed me.

I turned my head and her lips grazed my cheek.

Her laughter was dry. "All those times you were inside me," she said. "And now it's wrong."

"Boundaries," I said. "Without them, there's not much to civilization."

"Feeling civilized, are you?"

"Not particularly," I said.

She grabbed me and kissed me harder. This time, I let her tongue work its way into my mouth. My cock felt like an iron bolt. My emotions lagged well behind.

She knew it. Touched my cheek with the flat of her hand, and for a moment I thought she'd slap me. Instead she just drew away.

"At the core," she said, "you were always a good boy."

"Why doesn't that feel like a compliment?"

"Because I'm scared and alone and have no use for boundaries."

She kept her arms at her side. Her eyes were a strange mix of cool and wounded.

"Tim says he loves me," she said. "If he only knew—Alex, I'm behaving badly. Please believe me: When I called you all I really wanted was comfort. And to tell you about Baby's guitars. God, I think that's what bothers me the most about the break-in. I really wanted you to have them. I wanted to *do* something for you." She laughed. "And the funny thing is, I don't really know why."

"What we had," I said, "isn't just going to vanish."

"Do you ever think of me?"

"Of course."

"Does she know?"

"Allison's smart."

"I try hard not to think of you," she said. "Mostly, I succeed. I'm happy more often than you might think. But sometimes you stick to me. Like a burr. Mostly, I deal with it very well. Tim's good to me."

She gazed around the ravished studio. "Pride, the fall. I really didn't wake up yesterday thinking, 'Hey, girl, how about a little despair.' " She laughed, this time with some fervor. Touched my cheek gently. "You're still my friend."

"I am."

"Will you tell her? About coming here?"

"I don't know."

"You probably shouldn't," she said. "Ignorance being bliss and all that. Not that you did anything wrong. *Au contraire.* So there's nothing to tell. That's my advice. As a girl."

Gang bangers. As good a theory as any. I wanted her up in San Francisco, anyway.

My erection hadn't flagged. Positioning myself so she wouldn't see, I moved toward the closet where she stored the most expensive instruments. "Let's get everything out to your truck."

31 "A guitar string," I said.
Milo and Petra and Eric Stahl stared at me.
The second group meeting. No Indian food,
a small conference room at the West L.A. Division. Seven P.M. and the phones were ringing.

Cleaning up Robin's studio—handling the strings—had given me the idea. When I'd told Milo about the break-in, he said, "Shit. I'll check with Pacific, make sure they're taking it seriously."

I went on: "The size, the corrugations. Check a low E or A string against the marks on Juliet Kipper's and Vassily Levitch's necks. It also fits with the idea of our boy as a would-be artiste."

"He plays them," said Petra.

Milo grumbled, opened the case files, found the photos, passed them around. Stahl inspected the pictures without comment. Petra said, "Hard to tell from these. I'll go out and buy some strings, bring them over to the coroner. Any particular brand?"

I shook my head.

"Artiste," said Milo. "Wonder if Kevin has guitar strings in his pad."

Stahl's eyes drifted briefly to the floor.

Petra said, "I spoke to Kevin's mom. Very uptight but no revelations. Kevin's gentle, et cetera. Her anxiety level could mean she has no idea where her boy is. Or that she does. One thing did catch my eye: she's a flaming redhead."

"Like Erna Murphy," said Milo. "Interesting. What do you think about that, Alex? The old Oedipal connection?"

"What's the mother like?" I said.

"Curvy, voluptuous, flashy dresser," said Petra. "More flash than class. Probably a looker in her youth. Not too shabby now."

"Seductive?"

"I'm sure she could be. I didn't pick up any weird vibes vis à vis Kevin, but it was only a three-minute conversation. The lady definitely did *not* want to talk to me."

I said, "It's possible Erna's red hair evoked something in Kevin."

"Guitar string," said Milo. "What's next, he stabs them with a fiddle bow? Kevin's got a history of false starts. Wonder if he tried to be a guitar hero, too."

Petra said, "Let's get in his apartment—smell a gas leak and get the landlady to check. Meanwhile, we're there to ensure her safety."

Stahl said, "I'll do it."

Milo said, "About the break-in. Robin's name appeared on the liner notes to Baby Boy's CD, and Baby Boy's guitars were taken."

Putting into words what had gnawed at me.

"Your name was on there, too, Alex."

"It was a long list," I said. "And even if there is a connection, I have nothing to worry about. Not an artist. You going to call Robin?"

"I don't want to freak her out, but I do want her to be careful. It's good she's in San Francisco . . . yeah, I'll call her. Where's she staying?"

"Don't know. Her boyfriend's working with some kids on a *Les Miz* production, should be easy enough to find out."

His lips twisted, and he played with the cover of the pad.

Her boyfriend.

The wall clock said seven-ten. If Allison's flight was on time, she'd be landing in twenty minutes.

Milo said, "Anything new on Erna Murphy."

Stahl said, "No criminal history, no state hospitalizations."

"We haven't been able to track down any family to inform," said Petra.

"Most of the state mental hospitals closed down years ago," I said. "She could've been committed and we wouldn't know it."

Stahl said, "I'm open to suggestions, Doctor."

Milo said, "Even if she was hospitalized at Camarillo or someplace like that, it tells us nothing. We already know she's mentally ill. We need something more recent, some connection to Drummond. She has no record at all?"

Stahl shook his head. "Not even a traffic violation. She never got a driver's license."

"That probably means she's been impaired for a while," I said.

"Impaired but bright and educated?" said Milo.

"Driving can be frightening for disturbed people."

"Driving scares me, sometimes," said Petra.

"What paper *does* she have?" said Milo.

Stahl said, "A Social Security number, and state welfare says she got on their rolls about eight years ago but didn't put in for benefits. The only employment record I can find is eight years before that. She worked at a McDonald's from June through August."

"Sixteen years ago," said Milo, "she was seventeen. High school summer job. Where?"

"San Diego. She went to Mission High, there. The school lists her parents as Donald and Colette Murphy but says they have no other records. S.D. County assessor has Donald and Colette living in the same house for twenty-one years, then selling it ten years ago. No indication where they moved. No record of their buying another house. I took a trip down there. The neighborhood's working-class, civilian military employees, retired noncoms. No one remembers the Murphys."

"Maybe when Daddy retired, they moved out of state," said Milo. "It would be nice to find them for *their* sake." A half-second grimace tightened his face; imagining another bad-news call. "But the picture I'm getting is Erna was long gone from hearth and home, so it's unlikely they can tell us anything relevant." He looked to me for confirmation.

"The lack of social connections," I said, "would make Erna the perfect acquaintance for our boy. Someone he could talk to without fear of her confiding his secrets to another friend. Someone he could dominate, whose identity he could borrow."

"The lack of connections," said Petra, "made her an easy victim." She brushed nonexistent lint from the lapel of her black pantsuit. To Milo: "What, now?"

"Maybe another visit to Kevin's parents?" said Milo. "Shake the family tree a bit and see what falls out?"

"Not right now," she said. "Dad's overtly hostile, very clear he wants nothing to do with us. It's possible Mrs. D. could be made more pliable, but he's calling the shots. And his being an attorney makes it riskier than usual. One wrong move, he makes lawyer noise, there goes the evidentiary chain. If we had infinite manpower, I'd stick a surveillance on the house. What I figured I'd do in the real world is work the streets some more. Keep looking for anyone who remembers Erna or Kevin." She glanced at Stahl. "No harm trying to trace her parents."

He said, "Donald and Colette. I'll go national."

"A guitar string," said Milo. "So far, we're playing out of tune."

"So far," said Petra, "we don't even know what the song is."

32 Allison arrived by taxi, an hour and a half late, freshly made-up but looking exhausted. I had a couple of steaks on the grill, spaghetti with olive oil and garlic in the sauté pan, was mixing a butter lettuce salad.

"I was wrong," she said. "Food at hand seems like a great idea."

"No peanuts on the plane?"

"We were lucky to *land*. Some guy got drunk and rowdy. For a while it looked as if it was going to be ugly. A bunch of us subdued him, and finally he fell asleep."

"A bunch of us?" I said.

"I got hold of one ankle."

"Sheena, Queen of the Jungle."

She flexed a biceps. "It was terrifying."

"Brave girl," I said, holding her.

"When it happens, you don't even think," she said. "You just act . . . I need to sit down. Is wine on the menu?"

We took a long time eating, chatting, slipping into the fuzz of light intoxication. Later, undressed, in bed, we held each other without making love and fell asleep like roommates. I awoke at 4 A.M., found Allison's side of the bed empty, and went to look for her.

She was in the kitchen, sitting in dim light, wearing one of my T-shirts and drinking instant decaf. Hair tied up carelessly, face scrubbed of makeup, bare legs smooth and white against the dark oak floor.

"Biorhythm must be off," she said.

"From Colorado?"

She shrugged. I sat down.

"Hope you don't mind," she said, "but I was wandering around, trying to tire myself out. What are all those guitar cases in the spare bedroom about?"

I told her.

She said, "Poor Robin, what a trauma. Nice of you."

I said, "It seemed the right thing to do."

A clump of black hair came loose, and she slipped it behind her ear. Her eyes were bloodshot. Without makeup she looked a bit faded, but younger.

I leaned over and kissed her lips. Sour breath, both of us.

"So she's back in San Francisco?"

"Yup."

"Helping her *was* the right thing to do," she said. "Now do something for me."

She got up, crossed her arms, raised the T-shirt from her slim, white body.

I was up by seven, wakened by her light snoring. I watched her chest rise and fall, studied her pale, lovely face scrunched between two pillows. Mouth agape in what could have been a comical expression. Long-fingered hands gripped the covers.

Tight grip. Frantic movement behind her eyelids. Dreams. From the tension in her body, maybe not good ones.

I closed my eyes. She stopped snoring. Started again. When she opened her eyes and saw me, the blue irises were clogged with confusion.

I smiled.

She said, "Oh," sat up, stared at me, as if encountering a stranger.

Then: "Good morning, baby." She knuckled her eyes. "Was I snoring?"

"Not a bit."

*   *   *

She had a morning full of patients and left at eight. I tidied up, thought about Robin in San Francisco, Baby Boy Lee's instruments gone and what that meant, if anything.

Three blocks south, the gangs were active . . .

But Baby's Gibson had been the only acoustic instrument taken.

The phone rang. Milo said, "The ligature marks on Julie and Levitch are a perfect match to a light-gauge low E guitar string. Now what does that mean?"

"It means nothing about these killings is accidental," I said. "And that worries me. Talk to the Pacific detectives about Robin's break-in?"

"They see it as a routine burglary."

"Are they good?"

"Average," he said. "But no reason to think they're wrong. Robin's neighborhood, there's plenty of that."

I thought of Robin living with me, up in the Glen. Higher-priced neighborhood. Safer. Except when it wasn't. A few years ago, a murderous psychopath had burned down the house.

Our house . . .

Milo said, "I asked them for a uniform drive-by for the next few weeks."

"The usual two passes a day?"

"Yeah, I know, but it's better than nothing. I also gave them Kevin Drummond's vehicle and plates, told them to keep a special lookout. Meanwhile, Robin's in San Francisco, so don't worry. Stahl and the landlady got into Drummond's apartment last night. He collects toys and magazines, has a slew of computer and printing equipment. No guitars, no strings, no creepy trophies, nothing incriminating. And not a single copy of *GrooveRat*. That's what I find interesting."

"Covering his tracks," I said. "Or he's got another storage space."

"Stahl's calling U-rent places."

"Wonder if it was Stahl's second entry."

"What do you mean?"

"Normally he's got the demeanor of a statue. Yesterday, when you talked about going in, his eyes got jumpy, and he looked at the floor."

"Did he . . . he's a strange one, that's for sure . . . the magazines included gay porn. Rough stuff. Stahl said Kevin's been living spartan, just a few bits of clothing, no personal effects of any consequence. That could be because he split for the long run or there is another stash spot."

"It could also mean psychological deterioration," I said. "Drawing inward. Spitting on his parents' values."

"Petra decided she will give the parents another try—specifically the father. I'm heading over to Ev Kipper's office building, see if I can learn more about his girlfriend. Because one of his neighbors called me. Claims Ol' Ev's been looking especially angry. Pounding away late at night, past the curfew. They're afraid to call the cops. Also the girlfriend's been looking rather down the last coupla days, eating alone. I can't see any easy link to the cases, but I don't have a lead in any other direction. The more I think about Erna Murphy, the more I want to know about her, but all Petra's found, so far, are a few merchants who vaguely remember Erna on the street. No buddies or boyfriends, she was always by herself."

"What about the doctor the Dove House folks called in when she bled on the sheets? Could be Erna opened up to her."

"The Dove House folks said the doctor just met Erna once."

"The Dove House folks admitted they don't stay in touch with the women once they leave the shelter. And Erna was out of there more than she was in. If she got sick again, maybe she returned to the person who'd cared for her."

"Well," he said, "nothing else looks promising, might as well check it out—you mind doing it? I'm on my way to Century City."

"Sure," I said. "What's the doctor's name?"

"Let me check my notes . . . here it is . . . Hannah Gold."

"I'll call her now."

I phoned Dr. Gold, got a male receptionist, used my title.

He said, "She's with a patient, Doctor."

"It's about a patient. Ernadine Murphy."

"Is this an emergency?"

"It's important."

"Hold on, please."

Moments later: "Dr. Gold wants to know what it's about?"

"Ernadine Murphy was murdered."

"Oh. Hold on, please."

Longer wait, this time. The same man came on the line. "Dr. Gold will be free at noon. You can come by then."

* * *

The office was a sand-colored bungalow next to a Fiat mechanic. A black plastic sign to the right of the door said:

Vrinda Srinivasan, M.D.
Hannah R. Gold, M. PH., M.D.
Angela B. Borelli, M.D.
Internal Medicine, Obstetrics-Gynecology,
Women's Health Issues

I arrived at noon, but Dr. Gold wasn't free. Three patients sat in the waiting room—two elderly women and a starving girl around fifteen. All of them looked up as I entered. The kid kept staring until my smile made her frown in disgust and she returned to picking her cuticles.

Small, overheated waiting room, furnished with clean but faded castoffs. Framed photos of Machu Picchu and Nepal and Angkor Wat hung on the walls. Enya sang sweetly on tape.

A handwritten sign taped to the reception counter said:

We take Medi-Cal from you—
and sometimes we even get paid by the State.
Cash won't be refused—pay what you can, or don't
worry about it.

No glass blocking the reception area, just a cramped space occupied by a young man in his early twenties with neatly cut, prematurely gray hair. He pored over *Principles of Accounting* as if it were a thriller. A name tag on his plaid, short-sleeved shirt read ELI.

When I stepped up, he put the book down reluctantly.

"I'm Dr. Delaware."

"She's running late." He lowered his voice: "She's very upset by what I told her. You might not be able to tell, but she is. She's my sister."

Twenty-five minutes later, all three patients were gone, and Eli announced he was going to lunch.

"She'll be right out," he said, tucking the textbook under his arm and leaving the bungalow.

Five minutes after that, a woman in a buttoned white coat stepped into the waiting room, holding a medical chart. Young face, foxlike, the kind of bronze skin that glows naturally. Not much older than thirty but her thick, brushy, shoulder-length hair was snow-white. Genetics; Eli would get there soon. She had pale, green eyes that could've used some rest.

"I'm Dr. Gold." She held out a hand, gripped my fingers defensively, the way delicately boned women learn to do so as not to be crushed. Her skin was dry and cold.

"Thanks for meeting with me."

The sea-colored eyes were down-slanted, wide, and curious. Broad mouth, strong, square chin. An exceedingly handsome woman.

She locked the waiting room door, sat down on a worn, olive green, herringbone chair that matched nothing else in the room, crossed her legs. Beneath the white coat, she wore black jeans and gray boots. Enya's voice mourned in Gaelic.

"What happened to Erna?" she said.

I gave her the basics.

"Oh, my. And you're here because . . . ?"

"I consult to the police. They asked me to talk to you."

"Meaning the murder has psychological overtones as opposed to a dumb street crime."

"Hard to say, at this point," I said. "How well did you know her?"

"You don't really know someone like Erna. I saw her a few times."

"Here or at Dove House?"

"Once there, twice here."

"She returned after your emergency call to the shelter."

"I gave her my card," she said. "I was shocked to find out she'd actually kept it." She flipped the chart open. Inside was a single page. Upside down, I made out small, neat handwriting. "Both times were drop-ins. The first was a little over two weeks after I saw her at Dove House. Her anal fissures had started bleeding again, and she was complaining of pain. It didn't surprise me. All I'd done the first time was a superficial exam. Someone like that, you can only imagine what's going on internally. I urged her to get scoped, offered to arrange it for free at County. She refused, so I gave her salve and analgesics and the basic lecture on hygiene—not laid on too thickly. You have to know your audience."

"Know what you mean," I said. "I trained at Western Peds."

"Really?" she said. "I did my training at County but rotated through W.P. Do you know Ruben Eagle?"

"I know him well."

We exchanged names, places, other petty commonalities, then Hannah Gold's face turned grave. "The second time I saw Erna was a lot more alarming. It was at night. She burst in here just as I was closing up. The staff had gone home and I was turning off the lights and the door opened and there she was, waving her hands, really out of sorts. Then her eyes got a panicked look and she reached out."

She shuddered. "She wanted physical comfort. I'm afraid I stepped away from her. She was a big woman, my reflexive response was fear. She gave me this look, just collapsed on the floor in tears. I eased her to her feet, brought her back to my office. She was muscularly rigid and babbling incoherently. I'm not a psychiatrist, I didn't want to fool with Thorazine or anything else heavy. Calling Emergency Services would have been a betrayal—I no longer felt threatened. She was pathetic, not dangerous."

She closed the chart. "I gave her an IM injection of Valium and some herb tea, sat there with her for—had to be almost an hour. Finally, she calmed down. If she hadn't, I *would* have called the EMTs."

"Any idea what had upset her?"

"She wouldn't say. Got extremely quiet—almost mute. Then she apologized for bothering me and insisted on leaving."

"Almost mute?"

"She answered simple yes-or-no questions about nonthreatening top-ics. But nothing about what had brought her to the office or her physical problems. I wanted to check her out physically, but she'd have none of that. Yet, she kept apologizing—lucid enough to know she'd been inap-propriate. I suggested she return to Dove House. She said that was a dandy idea. Those were her exact words. 'That's a dandy idea, Dr. Gold!' When she said it she was almost . . . perky. She'd do that, turn cheerful without warning. But it was an upsetting cheerfulness—overwrought. Using phrases that were . . . too refined for the context."

"The people at Dove House felt she'd been well educated."

Hannah Gold thought about that. "Or faking it."

"What do you mean?"

"Haven't you seen psychotics do that? They latch on to phrases and spit them back—like autistic children?"

"Was that your sense of Erna?"

She compressed her lips. "I really can't claim to have a sense of her." The down-slanted eyes narrowed. "Do you have any idea who did this to her?"

"It could be someone she trusted. Someone who used her."

"Sexually?"

"Was she sexually active?"

"Not in the classic sense," she said.

"What do you mean?"

She licked her lips. "When I examined her, her vaginal area was raw, and she had body lice and old scars—fibrosed lesions. Those are things you expect in a street person. But then I did a pelvic and couldn't believe what I found. Her hymen was intact. She was still a virgin. Women on the street get used in the worst ways imaginable. Erna was a big woman, but a violent man—a group of men—could've subdued her. I find the fact that she was never entered remarkable."

Unless her companion had no interest in heterosexual intercourse.

"Her genital area was raw," I said. "She could've been assaulted without being penetrated."

"No," she said, "this was more like poor hygiene. There were no lacerations, no trauma of any sort. And she didn't get upset when I checked her out. Just the opposite. Stoic. As if she was totally cut off from that part of her."

I said, "When she was lucid—refined—what did she talk about?"

"The first time she was here I got her to talk about things she liked, and she started going on about art. How it was the best thing in the world. How artists were gods. She could name painters—French, Flemish, artists I've never heard of. For all I know, she made them up. But they sounded authentic."

"Did she ever mention friends or family?"

"I tried to ask her about her parents, where she was from, where she went to school. She didn't want to talk about that. The only thing she admitted to was a cousin. A really smart cousin. He liked art, too. She seemed to be proud of that. But that's all she'd say about him."

"Him," I said. "A male cousin."

"That's my recollection." She shook her head. "It's been a while. You said someone she trusted might've abused her. There really is a cousin? I assumed it was all delusion."

"I haven't heard of one," I said. "The police are thinking she might've been lured by someone she knew. When did her two visits take place?"

She consulted the chart. Erna Murphy's first drop-in had been five months ago. The second had taken place on a Thursday, two days before Baby Boy's murder.

"The cousin," she said. "She talked about him as if she was really impressed. If I'd known . . ."

"No reason to know."

"Spoken like a true psychologist. When I was in med school I dated a psychologist."

"Nice guy?"

"Terrible guy." She suppressed a yawn. "Ex*cuse* me! Sorry, I'm bushed. And that's really all I can tell you."

"Kissing cousin," said Milo, by cell phone.

"Nothing beyond kissing." I gave him the results of Erna Murphy's pelvic exam.

"Last virgin in Hollywood. If it wasn't so pathetic . . ." He was on his cell, calling from the car, reception fading in and out.

"More like virgin sacrifice," I said. "She was used and discarded."

"Used for what?"

"Good question."

"Theorize."

"Adoration, submissiveness—listening to his fantasies. Running chores—as in scoping out murder scenes and reporting back. An asexual relationship is consistent with Kevin's being gay. The interest in art drew them together. Maybe she called him her cousin because he represented her surrogate family. She refused to say a word about her real family."

"Or," he said, "Kevin's really her cousin."

"That, too," I said. "Red hair, just like his mother." I laughed.

"Hey, sometimes it helps not to be too brilliant."

"How would you know?" I said.

"Pshaw. No luck on Erna's folks, yet. Stahl's working with the military. But guess what: Kevin's Honda showed up. Inglewood PD tow yard. Parked illegally, it got hauled in two days ago."

"Inglewood," I said. "Near the airport?"

"Not far. I'm heading there as we speak. Gonna flash Kevin's picture at the airline desks, see if anyone remembers him."

"You're canvassing LAX by yourself?"

"No, me and my baby Ds, but it's still a needle in the proverbial you-know-what. The Honda's being transferred to our motor lab, but it's been pawed over pretty thoroughly. What finding it does, though, is firm up Kev as our bad boy. He did bad things, found out we were asking about him, cut town. There were no trophies in his pad because he took them." His voice was engulfed by static. ". . . any ideas about which airline to start with?"

"Check with Passport Control and eliminate foreign flights."

"My first stop," he said, "not that it's gonna be a snap, those guys love paperwork. Let's assume domestic, though. Where would you begin?"

"Why not Boston?" I said. "He's been there before. Enjoyed the ballet."

33 Eric Stahl spent two days dealing with the various branches of the United States armed forces. Thousands of Donald Murphys in the Social Security files. Military service would winnow it down, but Pentagon pencil pushers weren't spitting out the information without putting him through the usual.

The fact that he knew the sublanguage made it a little easier.

How he felt about the military was another thing.

He'd started with Erna's mother, first, because Colette was a less common name. One hundred eighteen SSI records with forty-three fitting the approximate age range. He began with the Western states, came up empty. Wondering all the while if this chasing down Erna was fruitless, even if he found her family.

Even so; he'd do what he was told.

He worked his way east, found a Colette Murphy in Saint Louis whose evasive tone and repeated denials made him wonder. From her accent Stahl guessed a black woman. He didn't ask. You didn't do that anymore.

The Army had taught him racial sensitivity. As in treat the Saudis like gods and smile as they shit on you.

He traced Saint Louis Colette with her local police, found out she had a record for petty larceny—which explained the caginess—and that she'd never been married to any Donald.

At 8:30 P.M. he reached a Colette Murphy in Brooklyn.

Eleven-thirty, her time. She said, "You woke me up."

"Sorry, ma'am." Not expecting much, Stahl gave her the line—tracing Donald on a routine investigation, no mention of Erna's name.

She said, "Christ, at this hour? That's not me, it's my sister-in-law. My husband's brother married her, and they had a crazy kid. I'm Colette, and Donald finds himself a Colette, too. Weird, right? Not that it's any great shakes being in this family. They're both bums. My Ed and his brother."

"Donald?"

"Who else."

"Where's your sister-in-law?"

"Six feet under," said Brooklyn Colette.

"Where's Donald?"

"Who knows, who cares?"

"Not a nice guy."

"A bum," she said. "Like Ed."

"Could I talk to Ed?"

"You could if you were six feet under."

"Sorry," said Stahl.

"Don't be. We weren't close."

"You and your husband?"

"Me and any of them. When Ed was alive, he beat the hell out of me. I finally got some peace. Until you woke me up."

"Any idea where I can find Donald?"

"Thanks for the apology," she said.

"Sorry for waking you, ma'am."

"I think he was out in California. What'd he do?"

"It's about his daughter Erna."

"The crazy one," said Brooklyn Colette. "What'd she do?"

"Got murdered," said Stahl.

"Oh. Too bad. Well, good luck finding him. Check bum places. He drank like a fish. Same as Ed. Navy never cared. Made him a sergeant, or whatever they call them in the Navy—petty something. No big war hero, he shuffled papers. Made himself out like he was a hero. Liked to wear that uniform of his, go to bars, try to pick up women."

"Military types do that."

"You're telling me?" said Brooklyn Colette. "I was married to one for thirty-four years. Ed was Coast Guard. Then he joined the Port Authority, sat at a desk, and made like he was an admiral." She cackled. "Finally, his ship came in, and I'm on high ground. I'm going back to sleep—"

"One more thing, ma'am," said Stahl. "Please."

"It's late," she snapped. *"What?"*

"Do you recall what Navy bases your brother-in-law was stationed at?"

"Somewhere in California. San Diego, or something. I remember we visited them one summer. Sat around doing nothing, some hosts. After that they got to go to Hawaii, Navy sent 'em to Hawaii, can you believe that? Like a paid vacation."

"How long were they in Hawaii?"

"A year or so, then Donald retired, got the pension, they moved back to California."

"San Diego?"

"Nah, somewhere near L.A., I think. We lost contact. Me, I'da stayed in Hawaii."

"Why didn't they?"

"How would I know? They were stupid. Talking about that side of the family is bringing back bad memories. Good-bye—"

"Any idea where near L.A.?" said Stahl.

"Didn't you just *hear* me, mister? Where do you get off, asking all these questions, this hour of the night. Like you got a right. You sound military—you did military time, am I right?"

"I served, ma'am."

"Well goody for you, oh-say-can-you-see-by-the-dawn—enough of you, soon *I'm* gonna see the dawn."

San Diego to Hawaii made it easy. Back to the SSI list. Donald Arthur Murphy, sixty-nine years old.

Somewhere near L.A. Despite her problems, Erna hadn't strayed far from home.

It was too late to access Navy or county property files, so Stahl drove to his one-room flat on Franklin, removed his clothes, folded them neatly, got on his bed, lay atop his blanket, masturbated briefly while thinking of nothing, showered, and scrubbed himself raw. Then he placed pre-washed, precut salad greens on a paper plate, added a can of tuna because he needed protein, ate quickly without tasting, went to sleep.

The next morning, he used his home phone.

Donald Arthur Murphy owned no real estate in L.A. County. Same for Orange, Riverside, San Bernadino, all districts south, to the Mexican border. Stahl worked his way through the northern counties up to Oregon. Still no hits.

A renter.

He phoned the Navy office in Port Hueneme, finally obtained the address where Murphy's pension check was sent each month.

Sun Garden Convalescent Home. Palms Avenue, in Mar Vista.

A half hour car ride. Connor hadn't called him in a while, but he wanted to keep things orderly, so he phoned her at the station. Knowing she wouldn't be in. He left a message—document everything. Tried her home number, got no answer.

Was she sleeping in and letting the phone ring? Or out, already, working the streets? Maybe neither and she was recreating—out on a date, she was cute enough. A girl with a social life.

Intellectually, he understood the need for pleasure.

Viscerally, it left him cold.

34

Petra got up early to work the streets. Last night's shift had been spent with the after-dark crowd: clubbies, bouncers, parking valets, boulevard evangelists, dope-zombies, curb trawlers, assorted other miscreants. Crazies, too. Hollywood at night was an open-air asylum.

She stared into dead eyes, sniffed rancid auras, felt revulsion and pity and futility. These were Erna Murphy's compatriots, but no one coherent enough to talk admitted knowing the big redhead.

Today would be more mundane: covering merchants she'd missed the first time around. Hopefully some good citizen would recall Erna.

It was a miscreant who came through. A pallid, twenty-two-year-old meth shooter and petty pill dealer named Strobe, with matted, oatmeal-colored hair that hung past his shoulder blades. Real name: Duncan Bradley Beemish. A country kid—a hick—from somewhere down South, Petra couldn't remember where. He'd run away years ago, come to Hollywood, rotted like so many of them.

Petra had worked him as a small-time informant. Very small-time and only once. She'd run into Beemish while working a bar shooting and the speedfreak had provided ambiguous info that led Petra to someone who knew someone who *might've* heard something about something that *might've* gone down but hadn't.

That fiasco had cost her seventy bucks, and she'd had enough of Strobe. But he found her as she talked to the owner of a joint on Western that advertised "Mediterranean Cuisine." On Western, that meant kabobs and felafel and charcoal fumes that leaked to the sidewalk.

The proprietor was a Middle-Easterner with a big gold frontal incisor and a too-friendly attitude—the unctuous type that could turn quickly. The food stand had a B rating from the health department, which meant rodent droppings had topped the acceptable level. Gold Tooth denied ever seeing Erna Murphy and offered Petra a free sample. As she begged off and turned to leave, a reedy voice said, "I'll take the sanwich, 'Tective Connor."

She turned, saw Strobe's twitchy face. The kid never stood still, and his long hair vibrated like electric filament.

The falafel guy's swarthy complexion purpled. "You!" To Petra; "Geet him offa my brawberty, he alla time take the hot bebber."

"Fuck you, Osama," said Strobe.

Petra said, "Work on the charm, Duncan."

Strobe hacked and blew tobacco breath at her and slapped his knee. " 'Tective Connor! Whuz up—wuz *that*?" Twitchy fingers wiggled at the photo in Petra's hand.

"Dead woman."

"Cool. Lemme see."

The falafel king ordered: "*You. Police.* Geet him offa my *brawberty!*"

Strobe bent his knees in a crouch, filthy hair strands swinging like vines as he put body English into a fulminating one-finger salute. Before he could complete the gesture, Petra ushered him off the property, away from Gold Tooth's shouts, and over to her car.

"Fuckin' towelhead," said Strobe in a suddenly scary voice. "If I come back and cut him, you gonna bother to investigate?" Before Petra could answer, the freak's meth-attenuated attention span snapped his coyote eyes back to Erna Murphy's photo. Merriment in the eyes— mean-spirited. The kid's cold side lurked just beneath the surface. "Hey—I know her."

"Do you," said Petra.

"Yeah, yeah, yeah, yeah, yeah, saw her—what—lemme see—hadda be a few days ago."

"Where, Duncan?"

"How mutchez it worth?"

"A sandwich," said Petra.

"Ha. Hahahahahahaha. Get serious, 'Tective Connor."

"How can I know what it's worth until you tell me what you know, Duncan?"

"How can I tell you what I know unless you *pay* me, 'Tective Connor?"

"Duncan, Duncan," said Petra, unclasping her purse and pulling out a twenty.

Strobe snatched the bill like a zoo animal grabbing a peanut. He pocketed the money, squinted at the photo. "Hadda be a few days ago."

"You already told me that. When, exactly? And where?"

"When exactly was . . . three days ago. Maybe three . . . could be two . . . could be three."

"Which is it, Duncan?"

"Oh, man," said Strobe. "Time . . . you know. Sometimes, it . . ." He chuckled. Finishing the sentence in his head and deeming it witty.

Two versus three was a crucial distinction. Erna Murphy had been killed three days ago. Two would mean Strobe had zero credibility.

"Two or three, choose one," said Petra.

"I'd hafta say three."

"Where'd you see her, Duncan?"

" 'Roun Bronson, Ridgeway, 'roun there, you know."

Not far from where Erna's body had been found. Petra squinted at Strobe, took in his scrawny frame, the double bags under his eyes, incipient wrinkles. The kid had what, five more years?

Strobe fidgeted under her scrutiny, rocked on his heels, twisted his hair. Girlish gesture, but nothing feminine about this kid. He was a victim turned to predator. On a dark, secluded street Petra wouldn't have approached him without backup.

"What time was this?" she said.

"Like I said . . . late." Another chuckle. "Or early, depending."

"What time?"

"Two, three, four."

"A.M."

Strobe stared at her, stunned by the idiocy of the question. "Yeah," he said.

"What were you doing there, Duncan?"

"Hanging."

"Who were you hanging with?"

"No one."

"Hanging all by yourself."

"Hey," said Strobe, "least I know I got good company."

Hollywood near Bronson was only a short stroll from Hospital Row on Sunset. Perfect place to score pills from some corrupt doctor or nurse or pharmacist, then back to the boulevard for resale. More than theory. Petra knew last year Narcotics had busted a surgical resident playing wholesaler. Idiot studies that hard, gets that far, only to blow it.

She said, "I'm figuring you were doing a little trading."

Strobe knew exactly what she meant and he flashed a gap-toothed grin. Green stuff grew on his gums. Lord.

Petra said, "Tell me exactly what you saw."

"She's a crazy, right?"

"Was."

"Yeah, yeah, yeah. That's what I saw, a crazy, acting crazy, walking up and down crazy, talking to herself. Like any other crazy. Then some car picked her up. A john."

"You're saying she was hooking?"

"What else do bitches do at night when they're walking back and forth." Strobe laughed. "So what, he cut her? We got a Jack Ripper or something?"

"You're amused by all this, Duncan."

"Hey, you get your laughs where you get 'em."

"Do you know for a fact that she was hooking?"

"Well . . . sure. Why not?"

"There's 'sure' and there's 'why not,' " said Petra.

"I gotta choose one again?"

"Cut the crap, Duncan. Tell me what you know for a fact and there's another twenty in it for you. Keep this up, and I take back the first bill and book you on something."

"Hey," said Strobe, in that same scary voice. Petra figured she'd probably averted something nasty between him and the hot-tempered falafel vendor. For the time being.

Strobe's eyes were all over the place, and his emaciated frame had tightened up. Checking out an escape route.

Or planning something aggressive?

Then he glanced at Petra's purse.

Her gun was inside, right on top. Her cuffs were on her belt, riding the small of her back.

He wouldn't be that nuts—would he?

She smiled, said, "Duncan, Duncan," grabbed him, spun him, bent his arm back, fumbled with the cuffs, got one wrist, then the other.

"Aw, 'Tective!"

A quick frisk produced a crumpled, half-empty pack of Salems, a baggie of pills and capsules, and a rusted pocketknife.

"Aw," he repeated. Then he began bawling, like a baby.

She put him in the backseat of her car, stuffed the cigarettes in his shirt pocket, ditched the dope down a sewer drain—sorry, Pacific Ocean—pocketed the knife, got in front, unzipped her purse, placed her hand on her gun.

Tears drizzled from the kid's eyes.

"I'm real sorry, 'Tective Connor," he said, sounding around twelve. "I ain't trying to jerk you aroun', I'm just hungry, is all, need a sandwich."

"Not enough business?"

Strobe looked in the direction of the storm drain. "Not no more."

"Look," she said, "I don't have time for games. Tell me exactly what you know about Erna Murphy and what you saw three nights ago."

"I don' know nothing about her, don' even know her name," said Strobe. "I just seen her like I told you, I know she's one a the crazies—"

"She hang with any other crazies?"

"You gonna arrest me?"

"Not if you cooperate."

"You gonna take these off?" Shifting his arms. "It hurts."

His wrists were tiny, and she'd ratcheted the cuffs tight. But no way was he in pain. She'd been careful, she always was. Everyone an actor . . .

"They come off when we're finished."

"Ain't this illegal?"

"Duncan."

"Sorry, sorry—okay okay okay what I know . . . what was the question?"

"Did she hang with other crazies."

"Not any I saw. It's not like she was there all the time, like a part of the scene. She'd be there, then she wouldn't. Know what I mean? I never talked to her, no one talked to her, she didn't talk to no one. She was crazy."

"Do you know for a fact that she was hooking?"

Strobe's fuzzy tongue traveled along the meager, parched strip of grayish tissue that passed for his lower lip. "No. I can't say that. I just assumed. Cause she got in the car."

"What kind of car?"

"Just a car," he said. "Nothing fancy—no Beemer or Porsche."

"Color?"

"Light."

"Big or small?"

"Small, I guess."

Kevin Drummond drove a white Honda. Milo's call about the car turning up near the airport firmed Kevin up further as their guy. The plan was to wait until the vehicle was processed, then she'd be bracing Kevin's parents, again.

Strobe's story kicked things up several notches. Time and place, a perfect fit.

Kevin decides Erna's expendable, picks her up, drives her a few blocks away, plies her with booze, does the deed, ditches the car in Inglewood, makes the short hike to LAX and is heavenward.

Milo had called her early this morning, before she left. No sightings of Kevin at the airport, yet.

"The car," she said. "Give me a brand, Duncan."

"I dunno, 'Tective Connor."

"Nissan, Toyota, Honda, Chevy, Ford?"

"I dunno," Strobe insisted. "That's the truth, I don't wanna give you some bullshit and then you find out different and you think I'm lyin' and you come back for me—could you please take these *off*, I can't *stand* being tied up."

Something in the kid's tone—a genuine plaintiveness that spoke of past indignities—tugged at her heart. Runaways came to Hollywood for a reason. For a horrible moment, Petra visualized a younger, rosy-cheeked Duncan Beemish tied up at home by some pervert.

As if sensing her unease, Strobe broke down and cried even louder. Petra cut him off mentally. "Not a van? Definitely a car?"

"A car."

"Not an SUV?"

"A car."

"Color?"

"Light."

"White, gray?"

"I dunno, I ain't lying to you—"

"Why'd you assume she was hooking, Duncan?"

"Because she was on the street and the car pulled up and she got in."

"How many people in the car?"

"Dunno."

"What did the driver look like?"

"Didn't see him."

"How far were you from the car?"

"Um um um, maybe half a block."

"This happened right on the boulevard?"

"No, a side street."

"Which one?"

"Um . . . Ridgeway, yeah I think it was Ridgeway, yeah yeah Ridgeway. It's real dark there, go there and check, all these broken streetlights."

Ridgeway was a block from where the surgeon had been busted. The city had probably fixed the lights, only to have them vandalized by the freelance pharmacists.

Petra said, "Before she got in the car, did she talk to the driver?"

"No, she just got in."

"No negotiating? No scoping out for a U.C. cop? That doesn't sound like a hooker, Duncan."

Strobe's eyes widened. Speedfreak insight. "Yeah, you're right!" He squirmed some more. "Can you take these off? Please?"

She pumped him a while longer, got nothing, left the car, returned to Mr. Gold Tooth and ordered a jumbo kabob combo with double hot peppers and an XL cola. Once again, he tried to freebie her, once again she insisted on paying in full, and Tooth's dark eyes clouded.

Some ethnic insult, no doubt. "I give you *extra* bebbers."

Returning to the Honda, she placed the food on the trunk, pulled Strobe out, uncuffed him, had him sit on the curb, a few feet away. He complied readily and she brought him the food and another twenty-dollar bill.

A few feet away, Gold Tooth glared.

Strobe's claws were on the sandwich before Petra took a breath. Snarfing audibly. Making animal sounds.

With a mouth full of meat and bread and tahina dripping down his chin, he said, "Thanks, 'Tective."

"*Bon appétit,* Duncan."

35 Milo followed the blonde. He'd been watching her building for an hour, tailed her as she and a group of coworkers left and walked a block west to the Century City Mall. Her companions were three other women, all dressed like the blonde in somber-colored suits. All were older than the blonde, who appeared to be twenty-five or -six.

Everett Kipper's young squeeze, Stephanie.

She was shapely, of medium height, a good deal of it legs. She made no attempt to capitalize on that, her skirt was knee length. But she couldn't prevent the way she moved naturally.

The blond hair was long and straight, platinum with an overlay of gold. From the back, she looked like every straight guy's dream.

Milo appreciated her figure the way he enjoyed a good painting.

He followed the four women to the Food Court, where the coworkers veered into the warren of fast-food booths after one of them said, "You're sure, Steph?"

Stephanie nodded.

Her friend said, "See you later."

She continued walking, past the Brentano's bookstore and the multiplex theaters, stopping to window-shop at Bloomingdale's and several boutiques, then continuing until she reached a plaza at the south end of the mall. Benches and food vendors were scattered around a big square of sun-brightened stone.

Gorgeous day. Perfect for a meeting with someone you loved.

The complex was jammed with shoppers and tourists and white-collar types from the neighboring office buildings taking lunch. Milo bought a jumbo iced tea, melted into the throng, and strolled leisurely while keeping his eye on that pretty blond head.

When Stephanie stopped in the center of the plaza and didn't move for a moment, he kept himself behind a corner, then ventured out on foot and stood with his back to her sipping tea through a straw. Positioned so he could watch her reflection in a shop window.

She tossed her hair, smoothed it over her ears. Removed her sunglasses, put them back on.

Waiting for the boyfriend? Milo was curious why Kipper had been looking so angry.

He kept his eye on the walkway. Kipper's likely approach.

Stephanie bought a hot pretzel with mustard and a cup of something from a pushcart vendor, took a bench, and began eating.

Munching away, tossing crumbs to the pigeons.

Crossing those long legs.

Finishing most of the pretzel and the drink, she got up and bought an ice-cream cone from another cart and sat back down in the same spot.

Not a single glance at her watch.

Fifteen minutes passed, and she didn't look the least bit impatient.

Another five. She yawned, stretched, looked up at the sun.

She removed her shades again. Took midday heat on her face.

Eyes closed. Mellowing out.

Not waiting for anyone.

Milo crossed the plaza, made a long, wide, circle, and approached her from the back. She wouldn't see him until he was ready.

His badge was in hand, concealed by his fingers. She was sure to be startled by the sight of a big man bearing down on her, and he hoped the shield would focus her, avoid a scene.

She didn't hear him coming, didn't look up and open her eyes until he'd walked around to the front of her bench, was nearly on top of her.

Dark eyes, surprised. He looked past that, focused on the bruise that swelled her left cheekbone. She'd done well with her makeup, had almost concealed the purpling, but a bit peeked through—a rosy splotch deepening her smooth, tan complexion. The entire left side of her face was enlarged. Cosmetics couldn't handle edema.

The badge scared her, and he pocketed it. "Sorry to bother you, ma'am. Especially today."

"I don't understand," she said in a small voice. "Today?"

He sat down beside her, recited his title, emphasizing all the buzzwords. *Lieutenant. Police. Homicide.*

That did nothing to squelch Stephanie's fear level, but it did focus her anxiety.

"This is about Julie, right?" she said. Trembling lips. "You can't be serious."

"Serious about what, Ms. . . . ."

"Cranner. Stephanie Cranner. Ev told me you'd been asking him lots of questions about Julie. That you probably suspected him because he was the ex." Her hand rose toward the bruised cheek, then stopped and dropped into her lap. "That's ridiculous."

"He told you we suspected him," said Milo.

"It's true, isn't it?" said Stephanie Cranner. Pleasant voice—youthful, lilting, but strained by anxiety. Everything about her radiated youth and health. Except the bruise.

"Did Mr. Kipper do that to you?"

The brown eyes dropped. "I don't want to make a big deal out of it. It has nothing to do with Julie—not her murder, anyway."

Milo slumped, made himself as small as possible, nonthreatening.

Stephanie Cranner sat up straighter. "I've got to get back to the office."

"You just got here," said Milo. "Usually you take forty minutes for lunch."

Her mouth dropped open. "You've been watching me?"

He shrugged.

"That's outrageous," she said. "I haven't done anything. I just happen to be in love with Ev." A beat. "And he loves me."

Milo eyed the swollen cheek. "First time he's done that?"

"Yes. Absolutely."

"Ah."

"It is," she said. "Absolutely the first time. That's why I don't want to make a big deal. Please."

"Sure," said Milo.

"Thank you, Lieutenant."

He made no move to leave.

She said, "May I go now, Lieutenant? Please?"

Milo swiveled, eased himself a little closer, made eye contact. "Ms. Cranner, I have absolutely no desire to make your life difficult. I work Homicide, not Domestic Violence. Though I should tell you, the two aren't always unrelated."

Stephanie Cranner gaped at him. "This is unbelievable. You're saying . . ."

"I'd be less concerned about your well-being if I knew what happened."

"What happened was Ev and I had . . . words. A fight. It was my fault, I lost it. Got physical and started shoving at him, kept shoving, really shoving hard. He took it for a while, then finally he shoved me back."

"With his fist?"

"With his hand," she said, showing Milo a smooth palm. She wore two rings on each hand. Cheap stuff—thin gold, semiprecious stones. No diamond solitaire.

"His open hand did that?"

"Yes, it did, Lieutenant. Because I was charging him and the movement—all the force, we collided. Believe me, he was a lot more upset than me. Got down on his knees and begged forgiveness."

"Did you grant it?" said Milo.

"Of course, I did. There was nothing to forgive." She thumped a firm bosom. "I started it. He was defending himself."

Milo sipped iced tea and let several moments pass.

"Lunching alone, today," he said.

"He's in a meeting."

"Ah." Using the old shrink word, again. After riding Alex about it for years, he'd found it a useful tool.

"He is," said Stephanie Cranner. "If you don't believe me, you can check."

"And you were in the mood to be alone."

"Is that a crime?"

"What got you so upset that you shoved him, Ms. Cranner?"

"I don't see why I have to talk about it."

"You don't."

"Then I won't."

Milo smiled.

She said, "You're not going to let go of this."

"I've got a job to do."

"Look," she said, "if you *have* to know, the fight was about Julie. Which is exactly why you're wasting your time looking at Ev."

She folded her arms across her chest, looked smug. As if that explained it all.

Milo said, "You lost me, Ms. Cranner."

"*Pu-leeze,*" she said. "Don't you get it? Ev *loved* Julie. Still does. That's what ticked me off. He loves me but he also—he can't get Julie out of his head. Even with her being . . . since she died, he can't . . ." A blush spread from her neck to her hairline, a reaction so sudden and deeply pigmented that it appeared cartoonish.

"Since she died he can't what?" said Milo.

Stephanie Cranner mumbled.

"Pardon?"

"You know."

Milo said nothing.

"Shit," said Stephanie Cranner. "Me and my big mouth." Her fingertips grazed his sleeves. She batted her lashes and flipped her hair and shot him a sick smile. "Please, Lieutenant, don't tell him I said anything about . . . please don't tell him, he'd . . ."

She stopped herself.

Milo suppressed his own sick smile, knowing what had been coming. *He'd kill me.*

"He'd be unhappy," she said, too emphatically. "I had no right to tell you, you've got me to say things I don't mean."

"Let's leave it at this: Since Julie, Mr. Kipper's changed."

"No. Yes. Not just in that way. Mainly emotionally. He—he's distant. It's all part of the same thing."

"Emotionally," he said. Another shrink's trick. Echoing.

She said, "Yes! Ev cared for Julie so much that he can't put her out of his mind and . . . give himself over."

She drew back her arm, hurled the remaining piece of pretzel across the plaza. More of an assault than altruism; pigeons scattered. The mustard-crusted dough rolled, teetered, came to a halt.

She said, "I knew about Julie when I started going with him."

"Knew what?"

"That they still saw each other once in a while. I was cool with that. I figured it would fade. And Ev tried. He wanted to give himself to me, but . . ."

She blinked away tears, put on her sunglasses, showed Milo her profile.

"They kept seeing each other," he said.

"It was nothing sneaky, Lieutenant. Ev was always open about it. It had always been part of the deal." She turned abruptly, faced Milo, again. "Ev loved Julie so deeply that he couldn't let go of her. There's no way he would have done anything to hurt her, let alone kill her."

He managed to keep her there for another fifteen minutes, shifted the topic to her work and learned she was a U. grad, working as a secretary while she studied, nights, for a Pepperdine MBA. Smart, with big plans.

Seeing herself and Kipper as a potential power couple in the financial world.

She gave him nothing more about Kipper and Julie. He handed her his card.

She said, "I really have nothing else to tell you."

Figuring she'd toss it the moment he was gone, he left the plaza, amazed that someone so young and good-looking and bright would accept the contingencies Ev Kipper had saddled her with.

Probably something to do with her own upbringing, but that was

Alex's world. Back in his unmarked, he phoned Alex at home, recounted the interview.

Alex said, "I'm inclined to agree with her."

"That level of passion? Julie and Kipper get divorced but nine years later Kipper can't let go? His feelings for her are so intense that once she's dead, he can't get it up? Doesn't all that imply an unhealthy emotional situation, Alex? Toss in Kipper's temper—and now we know he acts out physically—and doesn't that add up to an explosive situation? Like I told Cranner, domestic violence and homicide ain't strangers."

"I'm not saying Kipper couldn't have lost it and gotten violent with Julie. But that's not the crime scene we've got. Julie's murder was thought-out, cold and calculated just like all the others. Stalking, an optimal kill site, the use of a preselected weapon, pseudosexual posing. If Kipper had done it, he wouldn't have demeaned Julie. On the contrary, he'd have arranged her body in as dignified a manner as possible. The only thing that would get me to change my mind is some link between Kipper and Erna Murphy. Also, the same type of guitar string was used on Julie and Levitch. That would mean Kipper murdered Levitch to cover for Julie. And that sounds like a bad movie."

"Life sometimes imitates bad art," said Milo. "Why not? A well-dressed man like Kipper would blend in with the concert crowd at Szabo and Loh's. And Julie and Levitch were the only ones the string was used on."

"You have your doubts about the psychic-cannibal scenario? What about Faithful Scrivener? All those reviews of our victims."

"Artistic types get reviewed . . . it's not a matter of doubt, I'm exploring alternatives."

"Okay," said Alex.

"I'm sure you're right. But Kipper being that freaked out over Julie bugs me. Not just the impotence but his defying the cops by hammering late at night. To me that says boundaries are loosening. I wouldn't want to be Stephanie. I'm not sure she sees the danger."

"Your instincts are good. If you think she's in serious danger, warn her."

"Basically, I did . . . okay, I'm gonna check in with Petra, then see how the motor lab's doing on Kevin Drummond's Honda. Thanks for listening."

"My pleasure."

"Robin still in San Francisco?"

"Last I heard," said Alex.

Keeping his voice even, but Milo knew the question had been out of line. No time to get distracted. Stay on course.

If only he could decide what "on course" meant.

He didn't apologize, no sense apologizing. Instead he said, "Anything turns up, I'll let you know."

"I'd appreciate that," said Alex, back to his friendly voice. "This one's a twister, isn't it?"

Always, the therapist.

36 Eric Stahl snapped off fifty one-handed pushups, followed by another four hundred conventionals. That level of exertion seldom made him sweat, but this time, he was soaked—anticipation of the visit to Donald Murphy?

Stupid, he should be able to control it. But the body didn't lie.

He showered, dressed in one of his four black suit–white shirt–gray tie combos and drove to Sun Garden Convalescent Home in Mar Vista.

The place was a coffee-colored two-story building with dark brown trim. Inside was a lobby covered in flocked green paper. Ancient people lolled in wheelchairs.

Then: the hospital smell.

Vertigo stabbed Stahl. He fought the urge to bolt, kept his posture boot-camp rigid, yanked his lapels in place, and walked to the front desk.

The woman in charge was a middle-aged Filipina who wore a white coat over her floral dress. In Saudi Arabia, a lot of the servants had been Filipinas—little more than slaves, really. People in a worse situation than him.

This one's badge said she was CORAZON DIAZ, UNIT ASSISTANT.

Hospital lingo for clerk.

Stahl smiled at her, worked hard at being a regular guy, told her what he was after.

"Police?" she said.

"Nothing serious, ma'am. I just need to speak with one of your patients."

"We call them guests."

"The guest I'm looking for is Donald A. Murphy."

"Let me check." Computer clicks. "Floor two."

He rode a very slow elevator up to the second floor. More flocked walls but no mistaking this for anything but what it was: a ward. A nursing station was positioned at the center, and a couple of women in red uniforms stood around chatting. Then one long corridor lined by rooms. Two gurneys in the hall. Rumpled bedding on one.

Stahl struggled to maintain.

Even as he approached the nurses, they didn't stop talking. He was about to ask them for Donald Murphy's room number when he noticed a whiteboard above the station. Names inked in with blue marker, not unlike the case list at the station.

Two-fourteen.

He made his way up the hall, passing rooms occupied by very old people, some in wheelchairs, others bedridden. Waves of television noise hit him. The click-click of medical apparatus.

The smell, even stronger up here. The generic chemical reek, mixed with vomitus, fecal stench, sick sweat, and a host of odors he couldn't identify.

His skin had turned clammy, and another attack of imbalance nearly doubled him over. He stopped midway up the corridor, pressed a palm against the fuzzy wallpaper, breathed in, out, in, out. Felt light-headed but a little better, and kept going to 214.

Open door. He went in and closed it behind him. The man on the bed had tubes running in and out of his nose and arms. A bank of monitors above his pillow proved he was alive. Catheter hosing trailed from under the sheets to a bottle on the floor filled with amber fluid.

The Navy said CPO Donald Arthur Murphy (ret.) was sixty-nine years old but this guy looked a hundred.

Stahl checked the patient's wrist bracelet. D.A. MURPHY, the correct birth date.

His own heart pounding, he forced his way past the anxiety and studied the man on the bed. Erna's father had a withered, triangular face topped by dry, wild white hair. A few of the hairs bore the remnants of their original color: a faint ginger at the roots. Murphy's hands were large and thick and liver-spotted. His nose was a mass of gin blossoms. His toothless mouth had collapsed.

Eyes closed. Still as a mummy. No respiration Stahl could make out, but the monitors said otherwise.

He said, "Mr. Murphy?"

No reaction from the body on the bed or the equipment.

All the effort for nothing. He stood there, wondering who to talk to when another wave of vertigo hit him and a full-body sweat washed over him like hard surf—too strong to control, shit, this one was going to get him.

He spotted a chair. Made it over just in time. Closed his eyes . . .

A foghorn brought him out of it.

"Who are *you* and *what* do you think you're *doing* here?"

Stahl's eyes opened, traveled to the clock above the medical monitors. He'd been out for just a few minutes.

"Answer me," demanded the same voice. Brassy, female—a blaring tuba of a voice.

He turned, faced the source.

Older woman—mid to late sixties. Big, broad-shouldered, heavyset.

Her face was a near-perfect sphere, topped by a puffy, sprayed bulb of champagne-colored waves. Made up heavily, way too much rouge and eye shadow. Burgundy lipstick did little to enhance her rubbery lips. She wore a grass green knit suit that had to be expensive, with big crystal buttons and white piping on the lapels. Too tight for her linebacker's frame, she seemed to be bursting out of it. Matching shoes and purse. Crocodile purse with massive rhinestone clasp. The rock on her sausagelike ring finger was no rhinestone. Blinding white, humongous. Diamond earrings, a pair of stones in each. A string of huge black pearls encircled a turkey-ringed neck.

"Well?" she blared. Glaring down at him as she planted both hands on barn-wide hips. Another massive ring sparkled from her right hand. Emerald solitaire even bigger than the diamond. Enough jewelry on her to finance Stahl's retirement several times over.

"I'm going to call Security, right now." Her jowls shook, and her bosoms expressed sympathy.

Stahl's head hurt; the sound of that merciless voice was ground glass in an open sore. He fumbled in his pocket, flashed the badge.

"You're the police?" she said. "Then what in blazes were you doing sleeping in Donald's room?"

"Sorry, ma'am. Not feeling well. I sat down to catch my breath, must've passed out for a second—"

"If you're sick, then you *certainly* shouldn't be here. Donald's very ill. You'd better not have given him anything. This is outrageous!"

Stahl got to his feet. No more vertigo. Annoyance at having to deal with this battle-ax had vanquished his anxiety.

Interesting . . .

He said, "What relationship do you and Mr. Murphy have?"

"No, no, no." A finger wagged. Diamonds glinted. *"You* tell *me* why *you're* here."

"Mr. Murphy's daughter was murdered," said Stahl.

"Erna?"

"You knew her?"

"Knew her? I'm her aunt. Donald's baby sister. What happened to her?" Irritated, demanding, not a trace of sympathy. Or shock.

"You're not surprised?" said Stahl.

"Young man, Ernadine was psychiatrically disturbed, had been for years. Donald had no contact with her, nor had I. No one in the family had." She regarded the man on the bed. "As you can see, there's no point in bothering Donald."

"How long has he been this way?"

Her expression said, *What's it to you?* "Months, young man, months."

"Coma?"

The woman laughed. "You must be a detective."

"What's wrong with him, Ms. . . ."

"*Mrs.* Trueblood. Alma F. Trueblood."

Murphy's *baby sister.* Stahl couldn't imagine this one ever being small.

He said, "Ma'am, is there anything you can tell me about—"

"No," snapped Alma Trueblood.

"Ma'am, you didn't hear the question."

"Don't need to. There's nothing I can tell you about Ernadine. As I just said, she's been disturbed for years. Her death was a long time coming, if you ask me. Living on the street, like that. Donald hadn't seen her in years. You'll just have to take my word on that."

"How many years?"

"Many. They lost contact."

"You say her death was a long time coming?"

"I certainly do. Ernadine refused help, went her own way. Lived on the *streets.* She was always a strange little girl. Wild, sullen, odd habits—strange eating habits—chalk, dirt, spoiled food. She picked at her hair, walked around in circles talking to herself. Drew pictures all day but had not a *whit* of talent."

Alma Trueblood drew herself up. "I never liked having her around. She was a bad influence on my children and I must tell you, Officer, I won't have the family drawn into anything sordid."

"Wow," said Stahl.

"What is *that* supposed to mean, young man?"

"You seem pretty angry."

"I am *not* angry! I am *protective.* My brother *needs* protection— look at him. First his heart, then his liver and his kidneys. Everything's failing. *I'm* footing the bill for this place, and, believe me, it adds up to a pretty penny. If I wasn't, Donald would end up in some Veterans Affairs hospital. No, I won't hear of that. The Good Lord's been kind to me, and my big brother will rest here for however long it takes. Now, don't think me cruel. I regret hearing about Ernadine. However, she left the family years ago, and I won't have her ruining things."

"Ruining things by dying?"

"By . . . associating us with whatever sordid life she led. We—my husband and I, William T. Trueblood—are well respected in the community. We endow many worthy causes, and I won't have Mr. Trueblood's name dragged into anything unsavory. Is that clear?"

"Very."

"I'll thank you to leave, then." Alma Trueblood popped the clasp on the green croc purse, offering Stahl a view of the contents. Lots of stuff inside, but everything neatly arranged—parcels wrapped in filmy tissue paper. First time he'd seen a purse that organized.

"Ever spend time in the military, Mrs. Trueblood?"

"Why would you ask that? Ridiculous." Thick fingers probed the bottom of the purse, found a small gold case that she opened. Out came a cream-colored calling card. "Have someone inform me as to Ernadine's burial arrangements. I'll be footing the bill. Of *course*. Good day, young man."

Stahl slipped the card in a jacket pocket. Great paper, heavy weight, silky gloss.

Baby sister had climbed socially.

He headed for the door.

Alma Trueblood said, "You'd better do something about that narcolepsy of yours. I'm sure your superiors wouldn't be pleased to hear about it."

37 Milo called late in the afternoon. "Petra and I figured it's time to give Drummond's parents another try. No prints in the Honda other than Kevin's on the steering wheel and the driver's door handle, and a few scattered smudges from various Inglewood tow-yard folk. No blood, no body fluids, no weapons. No link to Erna Murphy, either, but Petra did find someone who saw her getting into a small, light car the night she was killed. Walking distance from the kill spot. Kevin's car wasn't towed till the next day."

"Who's the witness?" I said.

"Speedfreak hustler," he said. "It's not sterling, but it does firm up the time frame: Kevin picks her up, finishes her off, cuts town."

"After wiping Erna's prints from his car. Had it been washed recently?"

"Hard to tell with it sitting in the yard all this time. Lab guys did say the passenger door appeared to be too clean, as in wipedown. That's an indication of criminal intent, which is why we want to lean on Mommy and Daddy. Your suggestions and your presence would be appreciated. Psychological strategy and all that."

"When?" I said.

"After dark. Couple of hours. I'll pick you up, Petra'll meet us there."

"Not Stahl?"

"Petra's got him on the computer. See you in two. Start warming up the old insight machine."

When it comes to dealing with people, you can only rehearse so much. But the three of us tried, sitting in Petra's Accord on a quiet, Encino street. The spot was two blocks west of Franklin and Teresa Drummond's house, in the shade of a shaggy, anthropomorphic pepper tree. The moonlight was feeble, just enough to transform branches to grasping limbs. From time to time a car drove by, but no one noticed us.

Petra filled us in on the Drummonds. "Does any of that sound like breeding ground for a psycho killer, Alex?"

"So far," I said, "it sounds like upper-middle-class suburban life."

She nodded, ruefully. "I figure we focus on Frank—his being dominant and all that. If we ignore him, we run the risk of alienating him right from the start."

"He'll come to the door alienated," I said. "You can start off being polite, but at some point you may need to get more assertive."

"Threatening?" said Milo.

"If they do know where Kevin's gone, they're vulnerable to an aiding and abetting charge," I said. "Frank's an attorney. He may try to bluster his way through it, but I'd watch for signs of anxiety. As well as too much hostility—overreacting can be a cover."

"So, what, we ask them to sell out their kid to save their own butts?"

"However they feel about Kevin, they may not be willing to put themselves in criminal jeopardy. At some point, I'd also focus on the financial angle. They bankrolled Kevin's magazine, so they bear indirect responsibility for whatever flowed from that. At the least, it won't help Frank's practice. In that regard, the mother might also be your target. Work on her guilt by showing her Erna's photos."

"Who is maybe Cousin Erna," said Milo. To Petra: "Stahl still hasn't come up with any link, there?"

"Nope," she said. "Like I told you, he located Erna's dad, but he's comatose, on his way out. While he was at the rest home, he did run into a relative. Donald Murphy's sister, a real battle-ax named Alma Trueblood. More like she ran into Stahl. She says Erna had been strange all her life, refused family help."

She turned to me. "So we study their reactions. Three of us, two of them should make that feasible. Do we tell them Alex is a psychologist?"

"What for?" said Milo.

"Let them know the case has kicked up a notch, Kevin's being thought of as a psycho."

Both of them waited for my answer.

I said, "No, I'll just stay in the background. If you don't mind giving me some leeway, I'll cut in if I feel the timing's right."

"Fine with me," said Petra.

Milo nodded.

She said, "You guys ready?"

A stocky man in a too-tight red Lacoste shirt, baggy khakis, black socks and bedroom slippers came to the door. Fleshy face, broad nose, wavy graying hair, keen, angry eyes. A tightly coiled man, ready to pounce.

Petra said, "Evening, Mr. Drummond."

A ripple coursed through Frank Drummond's jaw. He looked at Milo and me.

"A battalion? What now?"

Petra said, "We found Kevin's car."

Franklin Drummond blinked. I'd hung back, kept most of my body concealed behind Milo's bulk, but I was studying Drummond intently. He must've sensed it because his eyes fixed on mine, and his mouth worked.

"Where?" he said.

"It was impounded, sir," said Petra. "Parked illegally near LAX. We're canvassing various airlines, right now, to find out where Kevin's gone. If you know . . ."

"LAX," said Drummond. Sweat broke at his hairline. The brown eyes were seized by a clutch of rapid blinks. "Goddamn."

"May we come in, please?"

Drummond rolled his meaty shoulders and stood taller. Snapping back into litigator stance. "I have no idea where Kevin is."

Petra said, "That must concern you, sir."

Drummond didn't answer. She went on: "At this point, Kevin's disappearance is being regarded as a criminal matter."

"You people are ridiculous."

Petra edged closer to Drummond. Milo and I followed. Full-court press. "If you know where your son's gone, it's in his interest and yours that you tell us."

Drummond's jaws clenched.

A voice behind him called out, "Frank?" Rapid footsteps. Muffled, yet percussive.

"It's all right," he said. But the footsteps continued, and Terry Drummond's face appeared over her husband's right shoulder. Half her face. She was an inch or so taller than him. Boosted by high-heeled backless sandals. Four-inch heels, not much thicker than darning needles. The percussion.

Plush carpeting contributed the muffling.

I looked at the heels again. Putting herself through foot agony in the privacy of her own home.

"Go back in," Frank Drummond ordered her.

"What?" she insisted.

Petra told her about the Honda.

"Oh, no!"

Frank said, "Terry."

"Frank, please—"

"Ma'am, Kevin could be in danger," said Petra.

Frank wagged a finger in her face. "Now, you listen—"

"Frank!" Terry Drummond reached around, grabbed his hand, pushed down, and lowered it.

"This is inexcusable," Frank Drummond said.

"May we come in?" said Petra. "At this point, it's either that or the station."

Drummond pressed his fists together and grimaced. Isometric exercise; no gain without emotional pain. "What do you mean 'this point'?"

"We found evidence in Kevin's car of criminal intent."

"What kind of evidence?"

"Let's talk inside," said Petra.

Drummond didn't respond.

His wife said, "Enough, Frank. Let them in."

Drummond's nostrils flared. "Make it short," he said.

But all the fight had been taken out of him.

The living room spoke of financial success acquired through achievement rather than legacy. The coffered ceiling was several feet too high for the modestly proportioned space. A faux-marble finish glossed the walls. Prefab moldings were slathered like whipped cream. The furniture was heavy, machine-carved, blond, bleached by too many crystal light fixtures. Machined copies of Persian rugs were arranged haphazardly over a bed of thick, beige wall-to-wall.

Three paintings: a harlequin, a ballerina, a too-bright rendition of an imaginary arroyo under a salmon pink sky. In the landscape, flecks of silver paint passed as reflection. Dreadful. Kevin Drummond hadn't grown up with fine art.

And he'd escaped. The dingy Hollywood flat was less than an hour away, but for all intents, we were talking different planets.

His father dropped heavily into an overstuffed sofa. Terry settled herself a foot away, crossed long, dancer's legs encased in skintight capris, tossed her flame-colored hair, and displayed no self-consciousness as her unfettered breasts bobbled.

High heels, no bra. The smell of canned spaghetti wafted from the kitchen.

I wondered more about Kevin's childhood.

Frank Drummond exhaled, sat up straight. Terry Drummond's face was heavily made-up but cosmetics failed to mask her grief. Yet, her body posture remained languid—Cleopatra-on-a-Nile-barge.

A handsbreadth between them. No touching.

Petra said, "I know this is hard for you—"

"And you're making it a lot harder," said Frank Drummond.

His wife tilted her face toward him but kept silent.

"What would you have us do, sir?" said Petra.

No answer.

Milo said, "Looks like Kevin flew somewhere. Any guesses where?"

"You're the detectives," said Frank Drummond.

Milo smiled. "If I was in your situation, I'd like to know where my son was."

More silence. I scanned their faces for the slightest hint of deception. The errant eye blink, the facial twitch, the merest shift in body language.

All I saw was anguish. A pain I'd seen far too often.

Parents of seriously ill children. Parents of runaways. Parents living with adolescents whose behavior had long since stopped being predictable.

The agony of not knowing.

Terry Drummond's eyes caught mine. I smiled, and she smiled back. Her husband didn't notice, sitting stiffly, eyes dulled—off in some lonely place.

Milo said, "There is one good thing. For us, and maybe for you. Kevin never got a passport, so chances are he's still in the country."

Terry Drummond said, "This can't be happening."

"Honey," said Frank.

"This just can't be *happening—please*. What do you *want* from us?"

"Information about Kevin's whereabouts," said Milo.

"I don't *know* his whereabouts! That's why I'm going out of my mind!"

"*Terry,*" said Frank.

She ignored him, shifted her buttocks, and showed him her back. "Don't you people think if I knew where he was I'd tell you?"

"Would you?" said Petra.

Terry regarded Petra with contempt. "You're obviously not a mother."

Petra went white, then she smiled. "Because . . ."

"Mothers are protective, young lady. Do you actually believe I'd want Kevin to be hounded by you people? Maybe God forbid get *shot* because he *looked* at you the wrong way? I *know* how you people operate. Trigger-happy. If I knew where he was, I'd want him safe and beyond suspicion!"

Frank Drummond regarded his wife with what seemed like new respect.

No one spoke.

Terry said, "This is absolutely ridiculous—considering Kevin a suspect in anything. A mother knows. Are *any* of you parents?"

Silence.

"Ha. Thought so. Now you people listen to me: Kevin's a good boy, he's done nothing wrong. That's why I *would* tell you if I knew where he was. Because I *am* his mother." A glance at Frank said she considered that several ranks above father.

He said, "Okay?" in a soft voice. "Will you please go now?"

Milo said, "Why would Kevin leave town?"

Terry said, "You don't know that he did."

"His car was near the airport—"

"There could be any number of reasons for that," Frank broke in. Pugnacious inflection. Back to lawyer's mode.

His wife shot him a disgusted look, then turned to Petra. "If you were really interested in doing your job, young woman, you'd stop regarding my son as a criminal and look for him as if he were just a regular person."

"Meaning?" said Petra.

"Meaning—I don't know what I mean. That's your job—*your* world."

"Ma'am—"

Terry wrung her hands. "We're normal people, we don't know how to behave in this situation!"

"Answering our questions would be a good start," said Petra.

"What questions?" Terry shouted. Red-nailed fingers clawed the air. Trying to rip through an invisible barrier. "I haven't heard any intelligent questions! What? *What?*"

Milo and Petra let her calm down, then went through their routine. Twenty minutes later, they'd learned little more than the approximate date of Kevin's last call to his parents.

Nearly a month ago.

Frank's admission. Terry blanched as he said it.

A month between calls spoke volumes about the parent-child relationship.

"Kevin needed space," she said. "He was always my creative one."

Frank started to say something, stopped himself, began picking lint from the sofa.

Terry muttered, "Stop that, you'll ruin it."

Frank complied, closed his eyes, rested his neck on a throw pillow.

Terry said, "Kevin's twenty-four. He has a life of his own."

I said, "When's the last time you sent him money?"

The subject of cash rejuvenated Frank; his dark eyes snapped open. "Not for a long time. He wouldn't take any more."

"Kevin refused money?"

"Eventually," he said.

"Eventually," I repeated.

Terry said, "He was always independent. Never wanted to rely on us."

"But you did finance *GrooveRat*," I said.

Mention of the magazine made both of them wince.

Frank said, "I bankrolled it in the beginning."

"And after that?"

"Nothing," he told me. "You're wrong about our being involved in everything he did."

"His *life* we were *involved* in," countered his wife. "He's our son, we'll always be part of his life, but . . ." She trailed off.

I said, "Kevin needed to establish his own identity, and you respected that."

"Exactly," she said. "Kevin's always had his own identity."

Frank blinked, and I addressed him: "So you sent him money to start up the magazine, then stopped."

"I sent him money for whatever he needed," said Frank. "It wasn't specifically for the magazine."

"What did you think of the magazine?"

He shrugged. "Not my thing."

Terry said, "I thought it was cute. Very well written."

I said, "And after the first few months . . . ?"

Frank's eyes narrowed. "He stopped calling—"

"Don't say it like that," said Terry. "It wasn't like we had a fight. You and he—" To us: "My husband's a dominant man. The other boys can deal with it. Kevin needed to find his own way."

"Great," said Frank, "it's my fault."

"It's no one's *fault*, Frank, we're not talking about *fault*, no one's done anything that's a *fault*. We're trying to give them a clear picture of Kevin so they can see him as a *person*, not some . . . some *suspect*."

Frank folded thick arms across his chest.

Terry said, "This is not about you, Frank."

"Thank God."

She moved a few inches farther from him. Took hold of an accent pillow and held it on her lap like a pet.

He glanced toward the kitchen. Rolled his jaw. "You know something? I've had it with this. I've been in court all day, figure I deserve a goddamn home-cooked dinner. You people interrupted our dinner."

But Terry didn't back him up, and he didn't budge.

I asked her, "How did Kevin support himself after he stopped asking for money?"

"He never asked," said Terry. "Not even in the beginning. We *offered*, and Kevin *agreed* to take it."

"Did us a big favor," said Frank.

Terry said, "Kevin's not materialistic. When he graduated we offered to buy him a nice car. He went and got an old clunker." Her face clouded. Thinking of the Honda by the airport.

I thought: Wanting an unobtrusive crime car? Then: If so, why not choose a dark vehicle?

I said, "At some point Kevin actively refused money."

Terry said, "Yes."

Frank said, "There are different ways to ask." He unfolded his arms, cracked his knuckles. "I've been financing his hobbies for years."

"Which is what a father *does*, Frank."

"That's me," said Drummond. "A father."

Terry glared at him. Her fists were small and white. "Now you people have seen us at our worst. I do hope you're happy."

The shame in her voice made her husband flinch. He scooted closer to her. Placed a hand on her knee. She didn't budge.

Milo looked at Petra, then me. She gave a small nod. I didn't object.

He reached into his briefcase, produced a death shot of Erna Murphy and flashed it at the Drummonds.

"Oh my God," said Terry.

"Who the hell is that?" said Frank. Then: "So much for dinner."

Milo and Petra kept them there as the spaghetti smell faded. Asking the same questions several times. Rephrasing, alternating between sympathy and aloofness. Probing for details, pressing for a Murphy-Drummond link.

The Drummonds denied it—denied everything. No anxiety. I believed them. Believed they knew little about their son.

At some point, a certain looseness entered the conversation. Low voices all around.

Discouragement all around. We'd learned nothing vital, and they had a missing son.

Terry said, "That poor woman. You say she was homeless?"

"Yes, ma'am," said Milo.

"Why in the world would Kevin know anyone like that?"

"He lived in Hollywood, ma'am," said Petra. "You run into all kinds of people in Hollywood."

All kinds of people made Frank Drummond grimace. Thinking about Kevin's sexual orientation?

He said, "I never liked him living there."

Terry said, "He needed something *new*, Frank." To us: "Kevin wouldn't—I mean he might be kind to someone like that, give them money, but that's it. He's never been interested in mental illness or anything like that."

"Just the arts," I said.

"Yes, sir. Kevin loves the arts. He got that from me, I used to dance."

"Really?" said Petra. "Ballet?"

"I took ballet," said Terry, "but I specialized in modern. Rock 'n' roll, disco, jazzercize. I used to be on TV." She touched her hair. "*Hullabaloo, Hit List*, all the dance shows. Back in ancient times. I worked a lot back then."

Frank's eyes glazed over.

Her talking about her career made me think of something. I said, "Have you ever heard of Baby Boy Lee?"

She bit her lip. "He's a musician, right?"

"Ever meet him?"

"Let's see," she said. "No, I don't think he was on any of the dance shows. I did meet The Dave Clark Five and the Byrds, Little Richard—"

Frank's loud exhalation cut her off.

"Why did you ask about that?" she said.

My turn to get an okay. Milo and Petra both nodded.

"Baby Boy Lee was murdered," I said. "Kevin ran a profile on him in *GrooveRat,* and he called the police to ask for forensic details."

"*That's* what this is about?" said Frank. His laugh was coarse. "My God. What utter and complete horseshit." Another laugh. "A *phone* call? I don't *believe* you people!"

Milo said, "There's more to it, Mr. Drummond."

"Like what?"

Milo shook his head.

Drummond said, "Beautiful."

I broke in: "How much money did you give Kevin?"

"Why's that important?"

"Why's it a secret?"

"Because—"

Terry said, "Ten thousand dollars."

"Beautiful," Frank repeated.

"It *is* no secret, Frank."

I said, "One payment or in installments?"

"One payment," he said. "Graduation gift. I wanted to break it up, but she . . . I also pay his car insurance and his health coverage. I figured ten would cover a year's rent and expenses if he didn't overdo it."

"How did Kevin finance the magazine and the rest of his living expenses for two years?"

"Don't know," said Drummond. "I assumed he'd gotten some kind of job."

"Did he mention a job?"

"No, but he didn't ask me for anything."

Terry said, "Kevin's always been independent."

"What kind of jobs had he worked before?" I said.

"He didn't work as a college student," she said. "I advised against it. He concentrated on his studies."

"Good student?"

"Oh, yes."

Kevin's advisor—Shull—had seen it differently: *no honor student.*

I said, "So he worked before college."

"Oh, absolutely," she said. "He worked at a tropical fish store, sold magazine subscriptions, did yardwork for us." She licked her lips. "Several summers he helped Frank out at the office."

"Paralegal work?" I asked Drummond.

"He filed papers for me." His expression said it hadn't been a good match.

Terry picked up on it. "Kevin was always . . . he's always had his own ideas."

Frank said, "He doesn't like routine. My office, any law office, there's a lot of routine. My bet is he found himself something . . . unconventional."

"Such as?" said Petra.

"Writing, something like that."

"He's fine," said Terry. "I just know he is." Her voice shook. Frank reached over and tried to hold her hand, but she pulled away from him and burst into sobs.

He sat back, disgusted.

When she quieted, I said, "You're worried about Kevin."

"Of course I am—I know he hasn't done anything to anyone. But that—the picture you showed us."

More sobs.

"Stop," said Frank Drummond in a harsh tone. Then he forced his voice lower. "For your sake, Ter. You don't need to do that, honey."

"Why?" she said. "Because you *tell* me?"

"So what's the deal beyond basic dysfunction?" said Milo, as Petra drove us back to his unmarked.

"Kevin left home two years ago," I said, "but he was a stranger long before that. They have no idea what goes on in his head. If they're telling the truth about his turning down money, I'd like to know where he got the money to finance his publishing venture."

"Something illegal," said Milo. "Something on the street. That's how he met Erna."

"Not his cousin," said Petra.

"Doesn't look like it."

I raised the issue of a crime car. Kevin selecting a white Honda over something dark.

"He's unsophisticated," said Petra. "Over the phone, he sounded like a kid."

"Nasty kid," said Milo. "Mommy's worried he's a victim."

"Mommies think that way," said Petra. She sounded nearly as sad as Terry Drummond.

38 Petra and Milo wanted to talk more so we found an all-night coffee shop on Ventura near Sepulveda, ordered coffee and pie from a waitress who read our faces and kept her distance.

He told me, "You're right about the money. Ten grand might've covered Kevin's computer equipment—and maybe not all of it. That leaves printing expenses, marketing the magazine, rent and food."

Petra said, "Kevin's landlady said he'd paid six months in advance. The place goes for five hundred a month, so there's three grand. He also paid for six months of POB rental up front. Not a big deal, but he was obviously spending Daddy's cash up front. Daddy just said Kevin preferred 'unconventional' jobs."

She'd ordered Boston Cream, cut away the cream, picked at the chocolate.

Milo inhaled half of his apple *à la mode deluxe* (two scoops of vanilla), and I realized I was hungry and made inroads on a slab of pecan.

"The thing is," she said, "I've been out on the streets three days running, can't find anyone who even knows him, let alone a hint of criminal enterprise."

"What's your guess?" I said. "Drugs?"

"Rich kid with a bankroll. It fits."

Milo said, "Ten grand doesn't make him a cartel, but it's more than enough to finance an initial stash, mark it up, peddle it, use the profit for another stash."

Petra said, "The spot where he picked up Erna is a well-known illicit pill market. Maybe Kevin knew it from previous experience."

Milo finished his pie, began work on the ice cream. "Once upon a time, you worked at a hospital, Alex. Anything you want to toss in, here?"

"Never caught a hint of a black-market pill trade."

"Still in touch with anyone at Western Peds?"

"From time to time."

"What about the neighboring hospitals?"

"I've got a few contacts."

He looked at Petra. "What do you think of his showing Kevin's picture around to white coats?"

"Couldn't hurt," she said. "Maybe they'd be more open with a colleague. You mind, Alex?"

"No," I said, "but if someone's dealing pills, they're not going to 'fess up to it. Or admit they know any dealers."

"But you could study reactions," said Milo, "see if anyone comes across weird. We'd take it from there."

"Okay."

"Don't wear yourself out, give it one day. It's a long shot, but you never know."

"I'll do it tomorrow," I said. "But we should also consider other sources of income for Kevin. All that computer equipment, the printers, the scanners. And Kevin collected pornography."

Both of them stared at me.

Petra said, "I should've thought of that. When we visited Frank Drummond's office, his secretary asked if this had something to do with porn. Jeez, right under my nose—maybe she knew the kid had a history."

"Summers at Daddy's office," said Milo. "Didn't seem to be a happy memory for Daddy."

"Kevin being creative," said Petra. "Maybe in ways Daddy didn't like. The stuff Junior collects is hard-core S & M."

"Or it wasn't just Kevin in the biz, and they had creative differences," I said. "What if there's more than parental protectiveness to Frank's hostility?"

Both of them were silent. Petra played with her fork. "Family business . . . you know, Terry looks like she could've done dirty movies in her youth." She bounced the fork's tines on the tabletop. "I'll check it out with Vice."

I spent all day talking to friendly faces at Western Peds and other Sunset Boulevard hospitals. No one recognized Kevin. I tried a few less friendly faces, got blank stares, headshakes.

I drove by the spot where Erna Murphy had been picked up. During the day, the street was quiet, sunny, lined with old apartment buildings. Not a hint of what went on after dark.

I spotted a young Hispanic woman walking twin babies in a double stroller. Smiling. The infants dozed.

A few miles west, she'd be wearing a uniform and they'd be someone else's babies. Here, mothers took care of their own.

And locked them in at night.

Before heading home, I called Milo to let him know I'd come up empty. He said, "Comrades in arms, pal. No progress at the airlines, and I've been on the phone to Boston all morning, trying to find out if Kevin checked in anywhere near there—both now and during the period when Angelique Bernet got carved up. Nothing on the former, hard to be certain regarding the latter because most of the smaller hostelries claim not to hold on to their guest registers for more than a year. A few places did crack their computers, but if Kevin's staying at any of them, it's not under his own name. The bigger hotels report being booked the week of Bernet—lots of conventions—and they do keep records. Again, no Kevin."

"What kind of conventions?"

"Let's see . . . there were six good-sized affairs that week. Three at Harvard—rehabilitation medicine, media and public policy, and history of science—one on plasma physics at MIT, a law symposium at Tufts, something to do with the Middle East at Brandeis. Any of those sound like our boy's cup of tea?"

"No," I said, "and a student on a limited budget wouldn't have stayed at the Four Seasons or the Parker House."

"That's why I concentrated first on motels and budget places. I also checked car rental outfits and bugged Boston and Cambridge PDs to check their traffic files, on the chance that Kevin rented another under an assumed name and got a parking citation. It's how Son of Sam got nailed, why shouldn't I be lucky?" Long breath. "*Nada*. And Petra found out the Drummond pornography connection isn't Kevin, it's his daddy. Franklin D. has represented over a dozen adult filmmakers. The Valley is Porn Central, so an Encino mouthpiece makes sense."

"Constitutional issues?"

"Bread-and-butter civil issues: overdue bills, contract disputes, workman's comp. Frank comes across as your basic hardworking solo practitioner. Guess he doesn't blush easily. Given all the X-rated types in and out of the office, I can understand his secretary wondering about Kevin getting his feet wet. So to speak."

"But no evidence Kevin got involved?"

"Not so far. Vice knew about Frank but never heard of Kevin. They checked all the corporate doing-business-as registrations. *Nada redux.*"

"What about Terry?" I said.

"Nothing. But even assuming Mommy did make some dirty movies. Maybe that's even how she and Frankie met. So what, if Kevin didn't take up the family biz."

"The family biz could've contributed to Kevin's sexual confusion," I said. "By itself it means nothing, but toss it onto the pile and it helps define Kevin a bit more. I can see him wanting to distance himself. Becoming obsessed with art for art's sake. Getting enraged at people he views as selling out—prostituting themselves. But in the privacy of his apartment, he stockpiles dirty pictures."

"Sexual confusion," he said. "Nice euphemism. He's gay, Alex."

"It's not a euphemism to me. He could be straight and be confused."

"Guess so—don't mean to get touchy but like Ol' Bob D. said, too much of nothing. Okay: The Drummonds are highly screwed up. Now how the hell do I find Kevin before he channels his confusion into offing another poor, unsuspecting *artiste*?"

I had no answer for that.

He said, "We're still exploring the Erna Murphy angle. On the off chance that Frank and Terry lied to us about not knowing her, or maybe Erna's smart, artistic cousin really does exist. Stahl's been working the Internet, searching the family tree using the name of the battle-ax aunt—Trueblood. Turns out she really is in the money. Married an appliance king, lives in a big house in Pasadena."

"A neighbor of Everett Kipper," I said.

A couple of beats passed. "Didn't think of that . . . well, let's see what Stahl turns up. Meanwhile, Petra and I have adopted the showbiz approach: got no ideas, take a meeting. The next one's tonight, nine P.M., her turf: Gino's on the Boulevard. You're welcome to come, but I can't promise you any excitement."

"Shame on you," I said. "No rose garden, and now this."

39 Allison had a break between her last outpatient of the day and a man dying of Lou Gehrig's disease whom she was seeing at the hospice. I bought some takeout deli, picked her up on Montana Avenue in front of her office, and we drove to Ocean Park and ate while watching the sun sink. A few windsurfers lingered on the beach, incorrigibly optimistic. Pelicans flapped their wings and scanned the water for dinner.

She attacked her sandwich, wiped her mouth, and watched the birds. "I love them. Aren't they gorgeous?"

Pelicans have always been favorites of mine. Ungainly fliers but efficient feeders. No pretense, just do the job. I told her so, put my arm around her, and finished my beer. "My idea of gorgeous is more like you."

"Shameless flattery."

"Sometimes it works."

She put her head on my shoulder.

"Tough night ahead?" I said. She'd talked to me a few times about the ALS patient. A good man, a kind man, he'd never make it to fifty. She'd counseled him for four months. Now, as he faded, so had Allison's feelings of usefulness.

"This job we chose to do," she'd said, a few weeks ago. "We're supposed to be experts, but which god appointed us?"

"The Baal of Academia," I said.

"Exactly. Get good grades, pass the right exams. It's not exactly spiritual training."

Neither of us spoke for a very long time. I heard her sigh.

"What is it?"

"Have the stomach for another confession?"

I squeezed her shoulder.

"My little chromium friend," she said. "I've used it once."

"When?"

"Soon after I got it. Before I got my own place, when I leased space in Culver City. I used to work really late. Because I had nothing to come home to. One night, I was in the office doing paperwork until after midnight. I came out to the parking lot and some kids—punks— were hanging out, smoking dope, drinking beer. By the time I got to my car, they'd moved in on me. Four of them—fifteen, sixteen, they didn't seem hard-core, but they were clearly blasted. To this day, I can't be sure they meant to do anything other than hassle me. But when the leader stepped up to me—really got in my face—I gave him my best girlish smile, pulled the gun out of my purse, and stuck it in *his* face. He peed his pants, I could smell it. Then he backed away, ran, they all did. After they were gone, I just stood there, the smile still plastered to my face—it felt wrong, smiling, but for a moment I couldn't move my facial muscles. Then I began trembling, couldn't stop, the gun was flopping around. Catching moonlight—the reflection on the barrel was like shooting stars. When we were up in the canyon watching the sky, that image came back to me . . . I was gripping the gun so hard my fingers began to ache. When I finally calmed down, my hand still remained tight. I'd actually pushed the trigger down partially."

She lowered her head, black waves of hair fanning out.

"After that I thought of ditching the gun. But I decided that wasn't the answer. I needed to master it—master more of my life . . . and here's the real confession: part of what attracted me to you was the fact that you got involved in crime cases. Someone in the same field as me who *got* it. I felt we were kindred spirits. I thought about you a lot. When you finally called me, I was thrilled."

She touched my hand. Her nail tickled my palm. My erection was sudden, disembodied.

First with Robin, now this. Reacting to everything with the little head.

"Of course," she said, "that was only part of it. Your being handsome and smart didn't hurt."

She looked up at me.

"I'm not telling you this to lord it over Robin, because she had problems with your work and I want to be the big, brave kindred spirit. It's just the way it is."

She gripped my fingers. "Does all this sound twisted?"

"No."

"Does any of what I just said change things? I really don't want it to. I'm so happy about what we've got going—I'm taking a risk, here. Letting you know who I really am."

"Nothing's changed," I said. "I like what I know."

"You're sweet to say that."

"It's the truth."

"The truth," she said, rolling on her side and pressing herself against me. "That'll do, for now."

I dropped her at her office and was setting out for the meeting at Gino's when Milo called.

"Canceled. Another body turned up. Similar to ours but different, because it wasn't found near any artistic venue. Dumped outdoors, in the wetlands, near the Marina. Not buried but half-hidden by marsh plants. Some cyclists saw birds clustered, went to check. Significant decay, coroner estimates it's been lying there two, three days."

"Right after Erna got picked up," I said. "Right around the time Kevin's car was left near the airport. The Marina's not far from the airport."

"The dump site's right on the way. Looks like Kevin gave himself a going-away present. The victim's definitely an artistic type, sculptor named Armand Mehrabian. He's based in New York, came out to audition for a big corporate project downtown. Works in rocks and bronze and running water—kinetic sculpture they call it. He was staying at the Loews in Santa Monica, had gone missing. Young, gifted, just starting to get noticed by the art world. Good shot at winning the corporate gig. He was gutted just like Baby Boy and had his neck yanked by a corrugated ligature. I told the coroner's tech it was probably a low E guitar string. She was very impressed."

"Marina dump site makes it Pacific's case."

"Two Ds I don't know," he said. "Schlesinger and Small. Petra says Small used to work Wilshire, she collaborated with him, he's okay. We're rescheduling the meeting for later so they can show up. We're an equal opportunity organization, share the despair. Figure on tomorrow morning, so Schlesinger and Small have time to do a preliminary workup on Mehrabian. Not Gino's, the Westside for their sakes. My Indian pals', say 10 A.M. That work for you?"

"Like a charm."

40

The same small back room at Café Moghul, the same smells of hot oil and curry.

Two more people huddled around the table made the space feel like a cell.

The Pacific detectives were men in their forties. Dick Schlesinger was big, dark, rangy, long-faced, and thoughtful, with a mink-colored mustache that crossed his face like a freeway. Marvin Small was smaller, chubby and blond-gray, his ode to facial hair a silver brush, prickly as a straw bed, bursting from under a boxer's nose. He chuckled a lot, even when nothing was funny.

The woman in the sari brought *chai* and ice water and left, smiling at Milo.

Marvin Small said, "This joker, Drummond, anywhere else he could've rabbited other than Boston?"

Milo said, "Your guess is as good as ours."

Dick Schlesinger shook his head. "Another whodunit."

Petra said, "Had a few, lately?"

"Two others still on the burner. Little girl disappears from a supermarket where she's shopping with her mom. We're thinking one of the box boys, he's got a molestation record. But no body, no evidence, and for a stupid guy, he's being smart. We're also working a shooting on

Lincoln, one of the hookers who works the stretch between Rose and LAX. Whoever did it left her with a purse full of dope and cash, and this time we've got a pimp who actually seems to care. They had three kids together. A few city employees have been busted there recently, mostly Cal Trans losers and bus company folk heading home after the night shift, veering off for a quickie. We're hoping it's not the beginning of another serial. A municipal employee killer, at that."

Small said, "But don't weep for me, Argentina. Sounds like you guys have been plenty busy, yourselves."

Knock on the door. The smiling woman entered with a tray of free appetizers that she placed on the table. Milo thanked her and she left.

"That one has a crush on you," said Marvin Small.

"The old charm," said Milo.

Petra grinned.

Everyone trying to deal with the frustration with levity. Except Stahl, he just sat there.

Detective Small eyed the food with some anxiety. "Multicultural time. This is one culture I've never done, food-wise."

"It's not bad, Marve," said Schlesinger. "My wife's a vegetarian, we go to Indian restaurants a lot." He reached for a samosa, held it up, named it. Petra and Milo and Marvin Small took food. Stahl didn't.

The remnants of a pastrami sandwich had taken residence in my gut—Milo's call interrupting my digestion—so I stuck with the hot spiced tea.

Stahl seemed off in another world. He'd arrived with a large white envelope, placed it in front of him. Hadn't talked or budged since the meeting had started.

The rest of them munched as Small and Schlesinger summarized the Armand Mehrabian case. Passing around death photos to the sounds of chewing. I flipped through them quickly. The abdominal wound was a horrible gape. Shades of Baby Boy Lee and Vassily Levitch.

The outdoor dump matched Angelique Bernet and China Maranga.

Flexibility. Creativity.

I said so. They listened, made no comment. Ate some more. Went over old ground for twenty minutes. Then Milo said, "So what's up with the Murphy family tree, Eric?"

Stahl opened the white envelope and removed a computer-printed genealogy chart. "I got this from the Internet, but it seems reliable. Erna Murphy's father, Donald, had a brother and a sister. The brother, Edward, married a woman named Colette Branigan. Only cousin there is one daughter, Mary Margaret. Edward's dead, Colette lives in New York, Mary Margaret's a nun in Albuquerque."

"There's a hot lead for you," said Small. "Maniacal Sister Mary."

Stahl said, "Murphy's sister is named Alma Trueblood. I ran into her at the rest home where Murphy's dying. She's got two sons from a previous marriage, one's deceased. Her first husband's dead, but she divorced him before he died. I found a few distant cousins but none of them are local and none are Drummonds. No connection to Kevin I can find."

"The whole cousin thing was probably nut talk," said Small.

"A cousin who likes art," said Schlesinger. "So what?"

Milo reached for the chart, scanned it absently, gave a disgusted look. I took a look.

"Who's this?" I said, pointing.

Stahl leaned across the small table and read upside down. "Alma Trueblood's first husband. He was a real estate agent in Temple City."

"Alvard G. Shull," I said. "Kevin's faculty advisor at Charter College is a guy named A. Gordon Shull. The two sons you've got listed here are Bradley—deceased—and Alvard, Junior."

"A. Gordon," said Petra. "My first name was Alvard, I'd want to use the middle name."

"Damn," said Marvin Small. "This professor like art?"

"As a matter of fact," I said.

Dead silence in the room.

I said, "Shull told me he'd grown up 'grounded' in art and literature and theater. He's also got red hair."

"Big and strong enough?" said Milo.

"Easily," I said. "Six feet, close to two hundred. Outdoorsy. Outgoing. And not at all protective of Kevin, the way you might expect from a mentor. At first, he expressed surprise that Kevin was under suspicion of anything. But as we talked, he warmed to the subject of Kevin's eccentricities. I remember one phrase he used: 'Kevin wasn't the type of kid you'd want to have a beer with.' At the time, I didn't make much of it, but in retrospect, it's cruel. One of the last things he told me was Kevin was a lousy writer."

"Oh, boy," said Petra.

Milo rubbed his face.

"Something else," I said. "When I first talked to Shull's department head about Kevin, she put on a full-force stonewall. Cited academic freedom, confidentiality. Exactly what you'd expect from a department head. Then she found out Shull had been Kevin's advisor, and her attitude changed completely. All of a sudden she was more than willing for me to talk to Shull. I didn't think much of it, but maybe she had a reason. *Wanting* Shull to have problems."

"Shull's been a bad boy?" said Petra.

"For a professor," said Small, "being a bad boy could mean giving the wrong kid a bad grade. What do we really have on this guy except he likes art and had a nutty cousin?"

"A cousin who got strangled," said Petra. "And was spotted at the scene of one of our 187s."

Small tickled his own mustache. "So, what, we're thinking two bad guys, now? Teacher and student? Like Buono and Bianchi, Bittaker and Norris, pair of lowlife scumbag psychopaths pulling a duo?"

"We've got a *literal* teacher and student," said Petra. "Maybe they branched out of academia." To Stahl: "You said Shull's mommy has dough. That could explain Kevin's financing."

I said, "Shull's influence could also explain the shift in Kevin's writing style. Kevin started off simple, but Shull guided him toward greater complexity. I told Shull Kevin's style had gotten pretentious. He laughed, and said, 'Ouch.' But maybe he wasn't amused."

Milo said, "He show any signs of weirdness, Alex?"

"Not really. Very self-possessed. But right from the beginning I've thought our guy wouldn't come across strange. Someone who can move in and out of artistic venues without being conspicuous. Someone smart enough to plan."

"Someone older than Kevin," he said. "His age bugged you from the beginning."

"Shull's how old?" said Petra.

"Midthirties to forty."

"Right in the zone."

Schlesinger said, "Where's the family money from?"

Stahl said, "The second husband."

I said, "Some of it may have found its way to her sole living child. Any idea how Shull's father and brother died?"

Stahl shook his head.

Petra said, "Good work, Eric."

The merest flicker of emotion livened Stahl's eyes. Then they went flat, again.

"Life's like that," said Marvin Small. "All of a sudden things change."

"A philosopher," said Schlesinger, with the good humor of a long-suffering spouse. "I wouldn't mind some good change. *For* a change. You guys gonna learn more about this professor?"

Petra said, "Minute we're out of here, I'll run him through the data banks."

Stahl said, "I don't recommend interviewing his mommy."

"Not a nice lady?" said Milo.

"Not someone I'd like to have a beer with."

The first bit of humor I'd ever heard from him. But no comic inflection. Mechanical voice. The deadened tone of someone beaten down. Or maybe he just had a weird personality.

He placed the chart back in the white envelope and studied his empty plate.

Milo turned to me. "What's the name of that department head?"

41 Alvard Gordon Shull had been run through the law enforcement files. No criminal record, but Guadalupe Santos, Kevin Drummond's landlady, thought she recognized Shull from the DMV photo Petra showed her.

"Hmm . . . maybe."

"Maybe what, ma'am?"

"Once I saw Yuri on the street talking to a guy. Could've been him."

"Where on the street, Mrs. Santos?"

"Not far from here, like up on Melrose, couple of blocks that way." Pointing east. "I figured Yuri had gone shopping or something."

Petra shook her head as she recounted it to Milo and me. *She never thought to mention this?* "Ma'am, was he carrying a bag that indicated he'd been shopping?"

Santos thought. "It was a while ago—maybe."

"But you think this was the man he was with?"

"I'm not sure . . . like I said, it was a long time ago."

"How long ago?"

"I'd have to say . . . months. Only reason I noticed was I never saw Yuri with anyone. But it's not like they were hanging out or anything."

"What were they doing?"

"Just talking. Like maybe the guy asked Yuri directions or something. Then Yuri walked home alone."

"The man left on foot?"

"Um, I think so. But there's no way I could testify or anything. I couldn't honestly say I remember details, it's more like maybe. Who is he?"

"Maybe no one. Thank you, ma'am."

Santos closed her door, looking worried.

Shull lived in a house on Aspen Way, in the Hollywood Hills, and Stahl had been stationed down the block all night, with nothing to report.

"How far is Aspen," I asked Milo, "from the Hollywood sign?"

"Right down the hill and east. Not far from Kevin, either." He'd dropped by soon after the meeting, kept busy on the phone, finally sat down at my kitchen table to toss things around.

"Not far from the recording studio where China was recording," I said. "Or the Snakepit. I'd say Shull likes his Hollywood comfort zone, but we've also got three murders on the Westside, not to mention Boston. This guy's hard to pin down."

"How do you see the affiliation between Shull and Kevin? Teacher-student thing gone evil?"

"That's one possibility. I visit Shull, he gets nervous, tells Kevin to make himself scarce. Either or both of them pick up Erna and get rid of her, then Shull drives Kevin to the airport, ditches the car, takes a taxi back."

"I'll have my Ds check the cab companies." He made another call, put in the order. "What's the other possibility?"

"Terry Drummond's right and her boy's innocent."

"If he is, he's also probably dead." He went to the fridge, poured milk, brought it back. "If Kevin did rabbit, I doubt it was to Boston. Shull'd be smart enough not to want Kevin there."

I knew what he was thinking: How many other cities? How many other bodies?

His beeper went off. The coroner's office. He called in, and I went to my office and ran A. Gordon Shull through all the general search engines.

A reference to Shull's personal Web site connected to an inactive notice. Thirty-one additional hits, two-thirds of them duplications. Twelve of the original twenty were citations of Shull's name in Charter College publications. Presiding over Communications Department symposia, papers he'd delivered.

The Role of the Artist in Contemporary Society
Advocacy Journalism: Acceptable Tool for Change or Subterfuge?
Rock 'n' Roll Hoochy Coo: Sexuality As a Metaphor in Contemporary Music
Linguistics As Fate: Why Noam Chomsky Might Be God

One title grabbed me by the throat:

A Cold Heart: The Ultimate Fatalism of Artistic Endeavor

No text summary, no reference. Shull had delivered the paper at a coffeehouse in Venice. A late-night party honoring the memory of Ezra Pound.

I checked the venues of his other presentations. All were informal gatherings at cafés and the like. Padding the résumé. Was that why Dr. Martin disapproved of her faculty member? Or perhaps it went beyond that.

I recalled Shull's easy manner with the coed who'd waited outside his office. Cool prof? Too-friendly slickster? Like politics, academia posed all sorts of possibilities for an amoral guy.

Venice Coffee Shop. What relevance did the concept of comfort zone have in L.A.? Here, if you had a car you mastered your destiny.

Then I thought of something else . . .

Milo returned. "The wounds on Mehrabian match Baby Boy's. So do the ligament striations. And guess what: This time our bad boy left physical evidence. Couple of short facial hairs, red-gray. Mehrabian had a beard, too, but it was long and black. The killer got in his face. Literally."

"Shull sports one of those five-day beards. Ginger-gray."

"Hey, Sherlock, coroner estimates the hair was five, six days old."

"So now what?" I said. "You question him and get a warrant to pluck?"

"We're a ways off from that, yet."

"Even with the hair?"

"I phoned an ADA. They want more. Significantly more."

"Shull being a rich kid make a difference?"

He smiled. "ADA would shudder at the thought."

"This might help." I pointed to the "Cold Heart" reference on my screen.

He said, "Oh, my."

"Is Shull warrantable, now?"

"Probably not. Literary pretension doesn't qualify as probable cause."

"What about this, then: There were six conventions in Boston the week of Angelique Bernet's murder. You mentioned one had something to do with the media. That sounds like something Shull might be interested in."

He whipped out his notepad, flipped pages. "The media and public policy. Harvard."

"Who ran it?"

"This is all I've got," he said.

"Want me to look into it?"

"Yeah," he said. "Put that Ph.D. to good use. Please."

He left with a promise to return in an hour. It took nearly that long, but finally I had a copy of the mass-media convention's attendees in hand.

Confidentiality and all that slowed the process, but one of my grad school classmates taught at Harvard, and I called him, made connections, combined shameless name-dropping with my academic bona fides, and spun a yarn about planning a symposium on the media and violence. Wanting the list so I could "target the right people."

The final target of that lie was one of the symposium's cochairs, a fast-talking professor of journalism at the University of Washington named Lionel South.

"That was mine, all right. Harvard let us use the K School—the

Kennedy School—so we stuck one of their faculty members' names on it as a cochair. But Vera Mancuso and I—she's at Clark—really ran it. You say yours is going to be at the med school? What, a psychiatric slant?"

"Eclectic," I said. "Meanwhile, I'm running interference between the med school, the psych department, and the law school." Sometimes falsehood came so easy. In spare moments, I wondered about that.

"Media violence," said South. "Great funding for that."

"Not bad," I said.

"Couple more schoolyard shootings, and you'll really be set."

I forced a collegial laugh. "Anyway, about your roster."

"I'll e-mail it to you right now. Do me a favor and keep us posted. And if you need a cochair . . ."

I found it on the third page, halfway down the "S's":

Shull, A. Gordon, Prof. Comm., Charter College.

A bit of self-aggrandizement; Shull was a lecturer.

That fit.

Milo came back, and I pointed.

"Oh, yeah! Great work . . . did Shull deliver a paper?"

"No, he just attended. Or signed up to attend."

"Playing hooky?"

"It would've been easy. Once he registered, no one would've checked to see if he actually sat through the meetings. Shull had a free schedule."

"Plenty of time to take in the ballet."

"Ballet might very well be his thing," I said. "Growing up with culture, and all that."

"Cold heart . . . son of a bitch." He checked his notes, found the list of Boston hotels, began working the phone. Forty minutes later, he had confirmation. Shull had stayed at the Ritz-Carlton the week of Angelique Bernet's murder.

"Not far from the ballet hall," he said. "He picks her up in Boston, takes her to Cambridge where he does her and dumps her. Because it's away from his hotel and close to the symposium . . . carve up a girl, be back for another bullshit lecture." His eyes had heated.

"Time for a warrant," I said.

He cursed silently. "I picked the most agreeable judge I could find. She's sympathetic but wants physical evidence."

"Like the facial hairs found in Mehrabian's beard," I said. "But you can't verify the hair is Shull's until you have grounds to ask him for a sample."

"Viva Joseph Heller," he said. "At least we've got a target. Petra's retracing her steps armed with Shull's photo. I also talked to Small and Schlesinger about the hair. They said, thanks, keep them informed. My sense is they'd love to dump Mehrabian on us. My sense is also that's where Mehrabian's gonna end up."

He eyed my computer. "Anything else interesting out in cyberspace?"

"Shull had a Web site, but it's no longer operative."

"Covering his tracks?"

"Or technical problems," I said. "An ego like that, he'd want to be out there. I'd like to know what he's been up to, recently. Dr. Martin could help us there."

"Think she'll cooperate?"

"Like I said at the meeting, my sense is Shull's not her favorite employee, so maybe."

"Let's do it," he said. "At her house, not her office."

"Why?"

"Get her away from *her* professional comfort zone."

Elizabeth Gala Martin's office had been filled with antiques, but at home she preferred modern.

Her house was a wide, gray collection of cubes set on a large lot in a good part of Pasadena. The landscaping was low-profile, Japanese-inspired, glossed by strategic lighting. A sculptural gong stood off center in the broad, impeccable lawn. Two cars shared the double-wide driveway: a silver, late model BMW sedan and an identically colored Mercedes coupe of slightly older vintage.

Every blade of grass in place. As if the exterior was vacuumed regularly.

Half a mile from Everett Kipper's place, but that didn't seem relevant, now. It was 8 P.M. when Milo knocked on the front door.

Martin answered her own door, wearing a long, green silk caftan embroidered with golden dragons. On her feet were gold sandals. Her toenails were pink. Her hennaed hair appeared freshly set, and she wore huge gold hexagonal earrings. Behind her was a wide, white entry hall floored in travertine.

Her initial surprise was replaced by flinty scrutiny. "Professor Delaware."

"Thanks for remembering," I said.

"You made an . . . impression." She studied Milo. I introduced him.

"The police," she said, evenly. "More about Mr. Drummond?"

Milo said, "More about Mr. Shull."

Martin's hands flexed, and she let them fall to her side.

"Come in," she said.

The house was rambling, mood-lit, topped by skylights. A rear wall of windows looked out to a softly illuminated garden and a long, skinny lap pool that traced the curves of a high white wall. Large, abstract paintings hung on the walls. Brass cases were filled with contemporary glass.

Elizabeth Martin seated us on a low, black suede couch and took her place in a black leather sling-chair.

"All right," she said. "Tell me what this is all about."

Milo said, "Professor Martin, we're looking into possible criminal activity on the part of A. Gordon Shull. I'm sorry I can't tell you more."

Sounds filtered from across the dining room. Footsteps and rattles behind white double doors. Utensil clink, running water. Someone in the kitchen.

"You can't tell me more, but you'd like me to tell you whatever *you* want to know."

Milo smiled. "Exactly."

"Well, that seems fair." Green silk rippled as Martin's legs crossed. She was wearing perfume—something grassy—and it drifted toward us. Body-heat activated? She looked composed, but you never knew.

"Professor Martin," said Milo, "this is a very serious matter, and I can promise you that the information will come out eventually."

"What information is that?"

"Mr. Shull's problems."

"Oh," she said. "Gordon's got problems, does he?"

"You know he does," I said.

She turned to me. "Professor Delaware, when you came to me you said Kevin Drummond had something to do with a murder. That's not an everyday occurrence for a boring academic. That's why you made an impression." Back to Milo: "Are you now saying that Gordon Shull's suspected of being a murderer?"

"You don't seem surprised," he said.

"I try to avoid being surprised," she said. "But before we proceed, you must tell me this: Is something highly embarrassing to my department fulminating?"

"I'm afraid yes, ma'am."

"That's too bad," said Martin. "A murderer." Her smile was sudden, feral, unsettling. "Well, I suppose when too much garbage piles up, the best thing to do is to take it out. So let's talk about Gordon. Perhaps you'll be able to take him off my hands."

She recrossed her legs. Seemed amused. "A murderer . . . I must admit, I've never thought of Gordon in those terms."

"What terms have you thought of, ma'am?"

"Lack of substance," said Martin. "Gordon's a phony. All talk, no action."

The kitchen doors opened and a man stepped out, bearing a hefty sandwich on a plate. "Liz?"

The same gray-haired man I'd seen in Martin's office photos. He wore a white polo shirt, beige linen trousers, brown loafers. Tall and well built but running to paunch. Older than Martin by at least a decade.

"It's okay, honey," she said. "Just the police."

"The police?" He approached us. The sandwich was a triple-decker, full of green stuff and turkey.

"Something to do with Gordon Shull, dear."

"What, he stole something?" He positioned himself next to Martin's chair.

"This is my husband, Dr. Vernon Lewis. Vernon, this is Detective . . ."

"Sturgis," said Milo. To Lewis: "Are you a professor, as well, sir?"

"No," said Martin. "Vernon's a real doctor. Orthopedic surgeon."

"That comment about stealing, Doctor," said Milo. "Sounds like you know Gordon Shull, too."

"Mostly by reputation," said Vernon Lewis. "I've met him at faculty parties."

Elizabeth Martin said, "Honey, why don't you relax?"

Lewis shot her a quizzical glance. She smiled at him. His eyebrows rose, and he looked at his sandwich. "How long will this take, Liz?"

"Not too long."

"Okay," he said. "Nice meeting you fellows. Don't keep my sweetheart too long." He continued across the room, turned a corner, was gone.

Milo said, "What reputation was Dr. Lewis referring to?"

Martin said, "General amorality. Gordon's been a problem—my problem, since the beginning."

"Does amorality include theft?"

"If that were all of it." Martin frowned. "Lord only knows what I'm doing to myself by talking to you, but the truth is I've had my fill of nonsense with that man. I run a three-person department, should have control over who I bring on."

I said, "You were forced to hire Shull?"

" 'Forced' would be too . . . coarse a word." She looked as if she'd swallowed something spoiled. "I was strongly *advised* to hire Gordon."

"Because his family's got money."

"Oh, yes," she said. "It's always about money, isn't it? Six years ago, I was brought to Charter College to create a first-rate department of communications. Promises were made to me. I had several other offers—larger schools, better facilities. But all were in other cities, and I'd just met Vernon and his practice was established here. I chose romance over practicality." Small smile. "The right choice, but . . . there are consequences to any decision."

"Charter broke its promise," I said.

"Broken promises are a given in the academic world. The issue is the proportion of truth to nonsense. Don't get me wrong. For the most part, I'm not miserable. Charter's a good school. For what it is."

"Which is . . ."

"A small place. A very small place. That affords one the opportunity to interact with students closely, which was initially appealing and still is. All in all, the kids are a nice bunch. After five years at Berkeley, all the left-wing nonsense, Charter seemed positively quaint. But sometimes it's limiting."

"Which promises were broken?" I said.

She ticked her finger. "I was pledged a five-person faculty and got three; my budget was cut by thirty percent because several pledges dried up—the recession was in full force back then, donors' stock portfolios had tumbled, et cetera. My planned curriculum was severely attenuated, because I now had a smaller faculty."

"Which promises did they keep?"

"I got a nice desk." She smiled. "I could've walked. Vernon's practice is more than adequate in terms of financial support. But I didn't go to school for twenty-three years in order to play golf and have my nails done. So I resolved to make the best of the situation and set about enjoying the one thing they hadn't reneged on: 'wide latitude' in hiring faculty. I was fortunate to snag Susan Santorini because she, too, wanted to remain in Southern California, her partner's a film agent. Then I set about finding the third member of our tight little group and was informed by the dean that a strong candidate had come up and that I was highly advised to look favorably upon his application."

She touched a pearl earring. "Gordon Shull is a joke. However, his stepfather is one of our wealthiest alumni. Gordon's an alumnus, as well."

"A joke in terms of scholarship?" I said.

"A joke, period. When his application came across my desk and I noted that he'd graduated from Charter, I got hold of his undergrad transcripts."

"Suspicious?"

She smiled. "I was rather displeased to be *advised*. When I read the transcript, my displeasure turned to wrath. To say Gordon had been an undistinguished student would have been too kind. He was on academic probation several semesters, put together a C-minus average by taking Mickey Mouse courses, took five years to graduate. Somehow along the line, he managed to get himself a master's." Her lips curled. "I got my doctorate at Berkeley, did a postdoc at London University, and another at Columbia. Susan Santorini's doctorate is from Columbia, she taught in Florence, Italy, and at Cornell before I snagged her. The way the job market for academics is running, we could've had our pick of bright Ph.D.s from top places. Instead, we were forced to occupy the same intellectual space as that clown."

"Which helps the budget," I said.

"Oh, yes," she said. "Every year the department receives a check from The Trueblood Endowment—the stepfather's foundation. Just enough to keep us . . . motivated."

"Academic stranglehold," said Milo.

"Very well put, Detective. And, truth be told, your visit tonight may very well have crystallized things for me. If Gordon's transgressions have stretched beyond my wildest imagination, I may finally have to make some serious life choices. But before I tell you more, I need one thing: You must keep me informed, provide me enough lead time so I can take my leave well before the storm and thus avoid embroiling myself in criminal-legal matters."

"You're resigning, ma'am?"

"Why not, if the parachute's sufficiently golden?" said Martin. "Vernon's been talking about cutting back, the two of us have been itching to do more traveling. Perhaps this is providence. So if you want to know more about Gordon's character flaws, you *must* keep me in the loop."

"Fair enough," said Milo. "What problems have you had with Shull?"

"Pilferage, sloppy expense accounts, spotty attendance as a teacher, shoddy grading," said Martin. "His lectures—when he chooses to show up—are execrable. Low-level discourses on pop culture with cretinous reading lists. Everything centers on Gordon's insight of the moment, and Gordon's attention span is severely attenuated."

"A dilettante," I said. Shull had applied the term to Kevin Drummond.

"He'd have to *work at* being a dilettante," said Martin. "Gordon is everything I despise about what passes for scholarship in contemporary academia. He fancies himself an avatar of pop culture. Oracle on the mount passing judgment on the creative world. No doubt because he sees himself as an artist but has failed miserably."

Milo sat up. "How so?"

"Gordon fancies himself quite the Renaissance man. He paints horrid blotchy canvases—garden scenes purporting to be Impressionistic but at a level of competence most middle school children could surpass. Shortly after he came on, he brought several canvases to me, asked for a one-man show sponsored by the department." She snorted. "I put him off and he went to the dean. Even Gordon's connections couldn't help with that."

"Renaissance man," said Milo. "What else?"

"He plays drums and guitar very poorly. I know that because he's always talking about gigging or riffing, whatever. Last year he volunteered to play at a party Vernon and I threw for the honor students. This time, I was foolish enough to agree." Her eyes rolled. "As if all that self-delusion wasn't enough, he also claims to be working on a novel—some magnum opus in progress that he's been touting since I've known him. I've never seen a page of manuscript."

"Big talk, no walk," said Milo.

"A real *California* guy," said Martin. "Without family money, he'd be waiting tables and lying about his next big audition."

"You said his attendance was spotty," said Milo.

"He's always off on some jaunt, financed by his stepfather."

"What kind of jaunts?"

"Alleged research trips, symposia, conventions. In addition to his other pretensions, he sees himself as an adventurer, has been to Asia, Europe, you name it. It's all part of that macho thing he has going on—plaid shirts with ties, hiking boots, the Arafat beard. He always claims to be working up some profound paper, but, again, he's never produced." She jabbed a finger. "In a sense, the world's fortunate he never follows through. Because Gordon's a *horrid* writer. Incoherent, puffed up, pompous."

"Faithful Scrivener," I said.

Her eyes widened. "You know about that?"

"Know about what?"

"Gordon likes to refer to himself in third person. Graces himself with a slew of obnoxious nicknames. The Gordster, The Intrepid Mr. Shull, Faithful Scrivener." She bared her teeth. "He's always been a *joke*. Unfortunately, he's *my* personal *sick* joke. And now you're telling me he killed someone . . . and our offices are footsteps away . . . that is unsettling. Am I in danger?"

"Not that I see, Professor," said Milo.

"Who has he killed?"

"Artistic individuals."

Martin's eyes saucered. "More than one?"

"I'm afraid so, Professor."

She sighed. "I'm definitely going to take some time off."

"What can you tell us about Kevin Drummond?" said Milo.

"What I told Professor Delaware was true: I have no specific memory of the boy. After the visit, I took a closer look at his transcripts. Mediocre student, absolutely nothing out of the ordinary."

"You have no memory of his hanging out with Shull?"

"Sorry, no. Students come in and out of Gordon's office. To a certain type, he's appealing. I don't recall Mr. Drummond, specifically."

"What type of student finds him appealing?" said Milo.

"Gordon stays abreast of all the latest trends, and that impresses the easily impressed. I'm sure what he'd really like would be to host a show on MTV."

I said, "Has Shull acted out sexually with students?"

"Probably," she said.

"Probably?" said Milo. "Just like that?"

"There've been no complaints, but it certainly wouldn't surprise me. Most of the students who take advantage of Gordon's office hours seem to be female."

"But there've been no actual sexual harassment complaints."

"No," said Martin. "Faculty-student sex is a fixture of college life and complaints are very rare. For the most part, it's consensual. Isn't that so, Professor Delaware?"

I nodded.

"Kevin Drummond's gay," said Milo. "Should we be looking at that?"

"You're asking if Gordon's bisexual?" said Martin. "Well, I haven't picked up on that, but the truth is nothing you'd tell me about him would surprise me. He's what used to be referred to as a scoundrel. Nice word, that. Too bad it's fallen out of usage. He's your prototypical spoiled brat, he bounces along, doing exactly what he pleases. Have you met his mother?"

"Not yet."

Martin smiled. "You really should. Especially you, Professor Delaware. Right up your alley."

"A font of psychopathology?" said Milo.

Martin regarded him with a long, amused look. "The woman's *devoid* of basic courtesy and simple good sense. Every year at the endowment luncheon she corrals me and reminds me how much money her husband's doled out, then she proceeds to lecture me about the wondrous accomplishments of her baby boy. Gordon comes by his pretentiousness honestly. She presents herself as *so-ciety*, but from what I've gathered, her first husband—Gordon's real father—was a drunk. An unsuccessful real estate agent who spent time in prison for fraud. Both he and Gordon's brother died in a house fire when Gordon was young and a few years later, the mother found herself a sugar daddy."

Milo scrawled in his pad.

Martin said, "This has been educational, but I'm tired. If that's all—"

"If you've got a writing sample from Shull, that would be helpful."

"Back at my office," she said. "I've got his latest end-of-year self-assessment. Every faculty member's required to submit one—listing accomplishments, goals. Gordon's is a formality because we both know he's got life tenure."

"Maybe not," said Milo.

"What a lovely thought," said Martin. "I'll come in early tomorrow, messenger it to you first thing."

She saw us to the door, and Milo thanked her.

"My pleasure," she said. "Really . . . you know, now that I think about it, Gordon's being a murderer doesn't really surprise me all that much."

"Why's that, ma'am?"

"Someone that false, that shallow, could do *anything*."

42 Petra was having a decent night.

The air was cool, the sky was a velvety purple-black where Hollywood neon didn't bleach it gray, and A. Gordon Shull was well known at clubs and dives and alternative bookstores.

The recollections of a hungover barkeep at the Screw, a rancid thrash-metal cave on Vermont, were typical:

Yeah, I seen him. Wears black and tries to pick up young chicks.

Does he succeed?

Maybe, sometimes.

Any girl in particular?

They're all the same.

What else can you tell me about him?

Just an old guy trying to be cool—y'know.

I know what?

It's the way things go.

A whole different ball game than her futile attempts to find any links to Kevin Drummond. But something gave her pause: none of the sightings paired Shull with Kevin. Was the younger man even involved in the bad stuff?

*   *   *

Despite the IDs, her attempts to link Shull specifically to dope, violent tendencies, aberrant sex, or Erna Murphy were unsuccessful. By shift's end, she realized it added up to very little they could use in the short term, and she felt her mood sinking. Then she got a little gift from God: During her first pass down Fountain Avenue, the Snake Pit had been closed—NO SHOW TONIGHT—but when she passed by on the way to the station, she spotted cars parked in front and a door left slightly ajar.

She went in and encountered a fat, ponytailed bouncer nursing a gin and tonic. The place smelled like a toilet.

"Closed," the fat guy told her. "Maintenance."

That meant him standing around guzzling and a diminutive man who looked like a rain forest Indian sweeping the sticky floor. Music—some kind of harmonica-driven, bass-heavy Chicago blues—blared on the sound system. Bare, plywood tables were arranged haphazardly. A drum kit sat on the stage. A microphone stand with no mike looked decapitated. Nothing sadder than a dive without patrons.

Petra stepped in farther and looked around some more and smiled at the bouncer.

"Yeah?" He folded thigh-sized forearms over his sumo belly. His skin was the pink-gray of raw pork sausage. A brocade of tattoos turned the arms into kimono sleeves. Prison art and finer work. A swastika graced the back of his neck.

He hadn't been one of the interviewees on Baby Boy's murder. She showed him the badge and asked him about that.

"I was off that night."

She'd requested a full staff list from the management. So much for that. She showed him Shull's photo.

"Yeah, he comes here." Pork Sausage downed his drink, waddled behind the bar, and fixed himself another. He took a long time cutting a lime, squeezed it into the glass, then tossed the slice into his mouth, chewed, swallowed, rind and all.

"How often does he come here?" said Petra.

"Sometimes."

"What's your name?"

He didn't like the question, but he wasn't the least bit intimidated. "Ralf Kvellesenn."

She had him spell it for her, write it down. Ralf with an "F." Some Viking ancestor was rolling over in his grave. "Be more specific than 'sometimes,' Ralf."

Kvellesenn frowned, and his greasy forehead furrowed. "Dude comes in once in a while. He ain't a regular, I only know him because he comes on real *friendly*."

"With you?"

"With the acts. Dude's into talking to them. Between sets. He digs going backstage."

"Is he allowed to do that?"

Kvellesenn winked. "It ain't the Hollywood Bowl."

Meaning a few bucks opened doors.

Petra said, "So he's kind of like a groupie."

Kvellesenn emitted a wet laugh. "I never seen him giving head."

"I didn't mean literally, Ralf."

"Whatever."

"You don't seem curious about why I'm asking you about him."

"I ain't a curious person," said Kvellesenn. "Curious gets you fucked up."

She recorded Kvellesenn's address and phone number, sat down at a bare table as he stared, took her time rereading her notes and found the name of the bouncer who'd been on the night of Baby Boy's murder.

Val Bove.

She left the club, phoned Bove's home number, woke him up, described Shull.

"Yeah," he said.

"Yeah, what?"

"I know the dude you mean, but I don' remember if he was there when Baby got offed."

"Why not?"

"House was packed."

"But you definitely know who I'm talking about."

"Yeah, the professor dude."

"How do you know he's a professor?"

"He calls himself that," said Bove. "He told me he was a professor. Like trying to impress me. Like I give a shit."

"What else did he tell you?"

"Basically, he's like 'I'm cool.' 'I write books,' 'I play guitar, too.' Like I give a fuck."

"An artistic type," said Petra.

"Whatever." A loud yawn came over the phone, and Petra could swear she smelled the guy's rotten breath.

"What else can you tell me about the professor dude?"

"That's it, babe. Next time don' call so early."

She made careful, copious notes, was about to phone Milo, call it a day well spent, but drove to Dove House, instead. The assistant director, Diane Petrello, was at the downstairs desk. Petra had brought her a few people.

Diane smiled. Her eyes were pink-rimmed and raw. Her expression said, *What now?*

"Rough day?" said Petra.

"Terrible day. Two of our girls OD'd last night."

"Sorry to hear that, Diane. They were doping together?"

"Separate incidents, Detective. Which somehow makes it worse. One was right around the corner, she'd just left for a walk, promised to come back for evening prayers. The other was in that big parking lot behind the new Kodak Center. All those tourists . . . the only reason we found out so quickly is both girls had our card in their purses, and your officers were kind enough to let us know."

Petra showed her Shull's photo. Diane shook her head.

"Is he involved with Erna?"

"Don't know yet, Diane. Could I please show this to your current residents?"

"Of course."

They trudged upstairs together and Petra began with the males—six profoundly inebriated men, none of whom recognized Shull. On the women's floor, she found only three residents in one room, including Lynnette, the gaunt, black-haired junkie Milo had spoken to about Erna.

"Cute," she said. "Kind of like a Banana Republic ad."

"Have you seen him before, Lynnette?"

"I wish."

Behind smudged eyeglass lenses, Diane Petrello's eyes shut tight, then opened. "Lynnette," she said softly.

Before Lynnette could reply, Petra said, "You wish?"

"Like I said, cute," said Lynnette. "I could do him so good he'd buy me pretty things." She grinned, revealing ragged mossy teeth. Yellow eyes, hepatitis or something in that league. Petra felt like stepping away, but she didn't.

"Lynnette, have you ever seen this man with Erna?"

"Erna was a skank. He's way too cute for her."

One of the other women was elderly and whisker-chinned, stretched out on the bed, sleeping. The other was fortyish, tall, black, heavy-legged. Petra glanced at the black woman, and she drifted over, sliding worn bedroom slippers over threadbare carpeting and sounding like a snare drum.

"*I* seen him with Erna."

"Right," said Lynnette.

Petra said, "When did you see him, Ms.—?"

"Devana Moore. I seen him here and there—talking."

"To Erna."

"Uh-huh."

"Right," said Lynnette.

Devana Moore said, "I did."

"Here and there?" said Petra.

"Not here . . . like you know—*here,*" said Devana Moore. Talking slowly. Slurring. Forming sentences was an ordeal. "Here and . . . *there.*"

"Not in the building," said Petra, "but in the neighborhood."

"Right!"

"She's lyin'," said Lynnette.

"I ain't lyin'," said Devana Moore, without a trace of resentment. More like a kid protesting her innocence. Petra was no expert, but she was willing to bet this one's IQ made her a disastrous witness. Still, work with what you have . . .

Lynnette snickered.

Devana Moore said, "Girl, I be lyin', I be flyin'."

Petra said, "When's the last time you saw this man with Erna, Ms. Moore?"

"*Mizz* Moore," said Lynnette, cackling.

Diane Petrello said, "C'mon, Lynnette. Let's get some coffee."

Lynnette didn't budge. The old woman snored loudly. Devana Moore stared at Petra.

Petra repeated the question and Moore said, "Had to be . . . few days ago."

"How many days?"

Silence.

"About?" pressed Petra.

"Dunno—maybe . . . dunno."

Lynnette said, "They gonna bust you for lyin'. *Mizz* Moore." To Petra: "She's a retard."

Moore sagged and pouted, and Petra thought she'd break into tears. Instead, she lunged at Lynnette, and the two woman flailed their arms ineffectually until Petra got between them, and shouted, *"Stop it right now!"*

Silence. Downcast looks. Lynnette cackled again, and Diane Petrello ushered her out of the room. Devana Moore *was* crying. Petra said, "She's just being mean. I know you're telling me the truth."

Sniffle. Moore looked at the floor.

"You're really helping me, Ms. Moore. I appreciate it."

"Don't bust me," said Moore. "Please."

"Why would I bust you?"

Moore kicked her own ankle. "Sometimes I whore. It's a sin, and I don' want to, but sometimes I do it."

"That's your business, Ms. Moore," said Petra. "I'm Homicide, not Vice."

"Who got homicided?" said Devana.

"Erna."

"Yeah," said Devana. "That's true." Relaxing, as if confirmation upped Petra's credibility. She blinked, scratched her head, pointed at Shull's picture. "He do Erna?"

"Maybe. Where'd you see him and Erna?"

"Um . . . um . . . it was over on Highland."

"Highland and where?"

"Sunset."

"North or south of Sunset?"

"This way," Devana pressed her hand against her chest which Petra supposed meant south. Two more attempts to pin down the location failed.

Either way, Highland and Sunset made sense. Right near Erna's doctor's office—Hannah Gold. "What were they doing, Ms. Moore?"

"Talking."

"Talking angrily?"

"Uh-uh. Just talking—you aksing this because he did Erna?"

"Maybe," said Petra. "What else can you tell me about him, Ms. Moore?"

"That's it," said Devana. She crossed herself. "He did Erna, he's a *sinful* man."

Petra returned to the station at 4 A.M. Stahl's desk was unoccupied. Still surveilling Shull; he'd started just after dark. All those hours, sitting there. The guy had an attention span, that was for sure.

She checked her message box. Stahl hadn't called in. He never did. Meaning no progress. How did he stand the inactivity?

She supposed Stahl's willingness to play statue made him the perfect partner on this one. How cases that required more teamwork would work out was anyone's guess . . . no sense wondering about that, she needed to keep focused on the here and now.

Four in the morning was no time to bother a friend, so she phoned Milo's desk at West L.A. and left a message. Knowing he'd be likely to wake her when he returned but that was okay. She wanted to let him know Shull was an habitue of the Snake Pit. Liked to go backstage.

She was thirsty, got up, and poured herself terrible police coffee and drank it standing, alone, in the corner of the detective room. Thought about Shull.

Hollywood night-scene regular.

The professor.

Too bad neither bouncer could verify his presence the night of Baby Boy's murder. Maybe she'd go back over her witness list, do a major re-contact with the photo, see if anyone remembered.

Yeah, she'd have to do that. Big-time tedium. The core of detective work.

With Shull under surveillance, it could wait until tomorrow. She was exhausted, needed to shower and stretch out and catch a few hours of dreamless sleep. So why was she loading up on caffeine?

She tossed the muddy swill, returned to her desk, got her coat. Stood there some more. Visualizing how it had probably gone down between Shull and Baby Boy.

Shull pays his cover, orders enough drinks to hold on to a nice, dark seat at the back. He takes in the show, watches, listens.

Applauds.

Clapping for himself, more than Baby Boy.

Baby Boy finishes his first set and leaves. Shull's watched him before, knows his habit of heading back to the alley for a smoke.

He sits for a moment, sipping, planning, makes sure no one's watching as he slips out of the club.

Linus Brophy had said the killer was wearing a long, dark coat. Shull wore all black, habitually, when he night-crawled.

A big black coat would be perfect for concealing a big, sharp knife.

Ready for business, Shull makes his way to the alley, conceals himself in the shadows.

Waits.

Baby Boy shows up, lights a smoke. Shull studies him, taking his time. Savoring the moment.

Finally, he approaches Baby Boy. Unaware of Brophy, but the wino's presence turns out to be irrelevant.

Baby Boy, unsuspecting. A sweet guy, a warm guy. He's used to the adoration of fans, and here's another one. Shull's demeanor nurtures the subterfuge: big smile, tossing out the heartfelt praise of a true believer.

The professor. Ingratiating himself the way he'd done with lots of artists.

None of them knowing he considers *himself* the ultimate artist.

A loser in real life, a legend in his own mind. Like Alex had said, psychological cannibalism.

If you can't beat 'em, eat 'em.

Petra shuddered.

Baby Boy, a trusting man, a naïve man, smiles back.

Both of them smiling as Shull plunges the knife.

She put on her coat and left.

When she reached home, there was a message from Milo on her machine. "Call me, I'm up."

She reached him on his cell. "You're up late."

"The bad guys don't sleep, why should I. What's up?"

She gave him a progress report.

Milo said, "Good work, very good. We're closing in."

"Meaning?"

"Meaning you earned your shut-eye, and I'll be at the courthouse by nine tomorrow to see if Judge Davison is a little more open-minded."

"Let me know."

"You bet. Thanks, kid."

"You're welcome. Pop."

43

The first time Eric Stahl saw the house, he knew it wasn't an ideal situation.

All that was visible from the street were bleached wooden gates flanked by brick posts. Beyond the posts were six-foot-tall ivy-covered walls. Behind the walls, junipers and cypress towered, and some kind of vine sprawled.

Nice place. Shull had money.

It always came down to money.

Soon after he positioned himself down the hilly block, Stahl entertained a brief fantasy: scale the fence, B and E the house, find Shull doing something evil, and finish the bastard off the way bad guys deserved to be finished off.

Nice movie. Reality was that he sat and watched and waited.

Tonight, for some reason, his talent for inertia was being tested. By 9:30 P.M.—two hours after he'd arrived—the hero fantasy recurred.

He visualized how he'd do Shull. The neck snap, or if Shull resisted, a knife.

Eric Stahl, big hero, providing *closure.*

Ugliest word in the English language.

Justice was a close second. He wondered how long he could do this job.

Maybe forever. Maybe till tomorrow.

There were three positives to the layout: Shull's house was positioned at the end of a cul-de-sac, meaning one way in, one way out. Parking was permitted on the west side of the road, allowing Stahl to find himself a spot between two other vehicles and avoid conspicuousness.

The best thing: This was an out-of-the-way street, hard to find without a map, no sidewalks, no reason for a casual pedestrian to come up here.

Nice for a bad boy . . .

By nine-forty-five, he still wasn't sure if Shull was even home. Guy kept professor's hours and according to Sturgis, not much of that. For all he knew, Shull was bunking in all day, had yet to emerge. Or, the bastard hadn't come home at all, was somewhere below, in the flats of Hollywood, trolling city streets.

Digging *art.*

Since Stahl had arrived, only two cars had appeared within the first hour, each stopping well short of his surveillance spot. In both cases, the drivers were young women with terrific figures driving foreign compacts. Stahl watched them carry groceries to their cute little hill houses.

Poor choice of neighborhood for a woman alone. Too isolated, too far from help. Not that crowds kept you safe . . .

He wondered how the tight-bodied women would react when they found out they'd been neighbors to a very bad person. He imagined the usual, horrified newspaper quotes: *"I had no idea." "I can't believe it, he seemed like a nice person."*

Believe it, ladies. Anything's possible.

The night sky gelled and turned shiny—purplish black, like boysenberry jam. Black napalm. Stahl ate a ham sandwich and drank from his thermos of espresso and risked a couple of forays across the road so he could pee in the bushes. Then back to his car, where he kept his eyes out for either of the two vehicles registered to Shull: a one-year-old BMW and a two-year-old Ford Expedition.

The Beemer was probably Shull's show wheels. The four-wheeler was what he used for exploration. Not a van—guys like Shull loved vans because you could turn one into a prison-on-wheels easily enough. But a trendy guy like Shull, living up here in the hills, would view a van as déclassé and the oversized SUV provided some of the same benefits: big, unobtrusive.

Lots of storage space.

A hundred to one Shull had blackened the windows.

Headlights brightening Stahl's rear window made him slink down and turn his head.

Small vehicle.

A dark car—there it was, the BMW grille, zipping toward the end of the cul-de-sac. The BMW passed too quickly for Stahl to make out the driver in the darkness but when it stopped at the bleached gates, he sat higher and watched.

Electric gate. The car passed through. Exactly thirty seconds later, the gate closed—some sort of time-release mechanism.

Stahl waited until 11 P.M. before exiting his car. Figuring even a hip guy like Shull was probably buttoned down for the night. Had he arrived alone? No way to know.

Checking out the street and finding it dead, Stahl crossed the road again, peed, continued. Sticking close to the foliage; if anyone did appear, he could conceal himself in the brush.

He proceeded slowly, with rubber-soled silence, feeling loose, the old prowl-zen kicking in. Good trackers and snipers were born with it.

A neighborhood this remote should've been silent, but an insistent hum filtered up from the base of the foothills. The sounds of Hollywood, the real Hollywood, percolating a couple of miles below.

He got within yards of the bleached gate. Through the big trees fronting Shull's property, distant lights sparked and blinked. A few stars in the sky, too, struggling to be noticed through the smog.

Guy had a terrific view.

The good life.

Stahl made it to the gate, surveyed the street again, got his nose up close and was able to inspect the gate's construction without using his penlight. Two-by-fours, tongue-and-groove, arranged in a pretty chevron design and framed by heavier boards. The frame bottom was stout and steady, provided a nice toehold. He put his foot in place, lifted himself up high enough to peer over.

On the other side was a round brick courtyard surrounded by greenery. Plants in pots. Tiled fountain off to the left; no drip. Soft lighting revealed the house, a split-level Spanish design, tile-roofed, with nice arched windows.

Very good life.

No sign of the BMW or the Expedition, but the courtyard terminated in an attached three-car garage that sat under a wing of the house. A low-wattage bulb revealed a trio of bleached wood chevron doors that matched the gate. To the right, an iron-railed staircase led up to what Stahl assumed was the house's main entrance. Hard to say how big the place was, it looked good-sized.

He thought about the layout. The door up the stairs would be where you had your guests enter, if you wanted to make an impression. First thing they'd see would be a windowful of city lights.

With no one to impress, Shull would drive in through the garage, take an interior staircase into the house. No BMW in sight said that's what he'd done tonight. Meaning, he was alone.

Or with someone he didn't care to impress.

Stahl stood there, perched on the gate frame, figuring this would be another uneventful night. Then a rustle of leaves—several rustles— tightened the back of his neck, and he got down and pressed himself against the ivy-colored wall.

More noise. More than a rodent scurrying. Someone sniffing the air.

Stahl waited. Nothing happened.

Then the sound repeated itself, louder, and twenty feet down, the brush parted and a deer—a smallish doe—began prancing across the road.

The animal stopped in the middle, stood there twitching. Stahl's heartbeat was way slow—the way it always was after it had been tweaked. Quick recovery . . . from some things . . .

The deer considered her options, finally bounded off and ran down a driveway, disappearing between two houses.

A regular; she knew who was home and who wasn't. Now someone's garden would be a late-night snack. And, eventually, the doe would be some coyote's dinner. Or maybe a puma would get her. Stahl had heard that the mountain lions were making a big comeback—wildlife, in general, was inching its way toward the urban jungle. That had certainly been true near the base. All sorts of critters turning up in the strangest places—his favorite was the snake who chose a colonel's wife's bidet as a drinking fountain. She squats in the dark, gets a slithery surprise . . .

Stahl felt himself smiling.

Noise on the other side of Shull's gate wiped his face clean.

Ignition rumble.

He ran to the gate, regained his foothold, chanced a quick look. The center garage door slid open, and he jumped down, sprinted back to his car.

He barely made it back as the gate swung back.

Headlights, a new set, higher up than the BMW.

The Expedition nosed its way out, paused, sped away.

Black SUV. Blackened windows.

One-man tails were impractical, often impossible, but with an arrogant guy like Shull, the job was easier. Why would the bastard even imagine he was being followed?

Stahl drove with his lights off as Shull sped down the hill way too fast. The Expedition headed north on Cahuenga and over to a jazz club just south of the Valley. Not far from Baby Boy's apartment. Shull left the Expedition with a parking valet, stayed inside for forty minutes, and retrieved the SUV. Now it was nearly 1 A.M., and with the traffic thinned, Stahl had to keep his distance.

Shull didn't go far, just a quick jaunt into Studio City, where he had coffee and a burger at an all-night coffee shop on Ventura near Lankershim. No valet, here. Stahl parked in the half-empty lot, observed the window.

Four cups of coffee, black. Shull inhaled his burger.

Fueling up.

Shull paid in cash, got back in the SUV.

Back to the city on Laurel Canyon, a right turn on Sunset. A few blocks up, Shull pulled in front of a bar called Bambu. Neo tiki-hut décor, bored bouncer in front. Another valet situation.

Stahl drove a block, hung a quick U, watched from across Sunset as Shull got out of the SUV smoking a cigar.

Dressed in a black leather jacket, black jeans, black T-shirt. Swaggering, shmoozing with the parking attendant.

No nerves; obviously, Delaware's showing up at his office didn't worry him. Just the opposite: Shull had taken Delaware's questions about Drummond as proof he was safe.

If Drummond had been Shull's partner in crime—if Drummond had known anything—Delaware's asking about him had probably accomplished something else: Drummond was now a severe liability, bye bye, Kev.

Sturgis had opined as much at the last meeting. Drummond's car near the airport meant Shull had probably taken care of the kid, used the Honda to pick up Erna Murphy, then planted it to imply Drummond's long-distance rabbit. And it had worked. All those days wasted checking out airline rosters. All the time Stahl had spent watching Drummond's apartment.

Meanwhile, Drummond was probably moldering somewhere.

Even if Drummond hadn't been in on the bad stuff, he was a likely corpse. Because his disappearance provided distraction—terrific cover for Shull.

And because Shull liked killing people.

Modern art.

Bambu's fake-grass door swung open and Shull exited with a knockout blonde in tow. Late twenties, big golden hair, a real Barbie. She wore a red glittery crop top under a short, black jacket, shredded second-skin jeans, high-heeled boots. Breasts way too high and too large to be real, too much makeup; Stahl upped his age estimate: the wrong side of thirty.

Your basic Sunset Boulevard party girl past her prime. But not a pro, she looked too happy positioned on Shull's leather arm for this to be work.

Giggling. Staggering. Giddy.

Shull smiled back at her but he was composed.

Life is going so well for me.

Stahl sat in his car and watched the two of them flirt. Fixing on Shull's macho posturing, just about feeling the heft of the sniper rifle on his shoulder.

The Expedition arrived and Shull was careful to hold the passenger door open for Barbie. Taking her hand as he did it. She kissed him in appreciation.

Once the blonde was inside, Shull and the parking valet exchanged conspiratorial glances.

Someone's getting lucky tonight, bro.

Not the girl.

Shull stayed on Sunset and continued west, through the Strip and into Beverly Hills, speeding into even ritzier Bel Air. At Hilgard, he turned south, drove through Westwood Village, got on Wilshire and resumed a westerly route.

Making Stahl's job easy, because even at this hour—2 A.M.—the brightly lit boulevard had its share of traffic. He hung three car lengths behind the Expedition, accompanied Shull and the blonde all the way through Brentwood and Santa Monica.

Down to Pacific Coast Highway. The beach. Here, the traffic was sparse, and the job became trickier. Stahl hung back, fixed his eyes on the SUV's taillights. Shull picked up speed, traveling nearly seventy—twenty miles over the limit—as he crossed the coastal boundaries of Pacific Palisades and continued into the city of Malibu.

Going seventy-five per, eighty, eighty-five. Big hurry. No concern about being stopped on a traffic violation because he thought of himself as the kind of guy bad things didn't happen to.

Or because a speeding ticket was just money, and he had plenty of that.

Did it also mean anything of forensic value been expunged from the SUV? A perfect cleaning was hard to pull off; one errant hair, a speck of body fluid could tell a tale. Shull didn't transport his victims, he left them in place but, still, his own garments, the seat of the car—anything could've picked up some transfer.

Yet, here he was playing Daytona 500. Was the guy that arrogant?

Stahl's mental meanderings were cut short when the Expedition made an abrupt right turn off the highway, into the parking lot of a white-board, blue-shuttered motel. The Sea Arms.

Caught off guard, Stahl continued another quarter mile, pulled over to the shoulder, turned around, and drove back.

Parking on the beach side of PCH, he studied the Sea Arms.

Two-storied, Cape Coddish building, behind an open parking lot. No rear property, the motel was nestled against the mountains. The usual AAA endorsement, a pink neon VACANCY sign on a tall pole.

Six units on each floor, the manager's office down below to the right.

Thirteen cars in the lot, including the Expedition. Twelve occupants, plus the manager.

A. Gordon Shull, lucky boy that he was, had snagged the last empty room.

Stahl lost it.

Falling asleep in his car. Rudely awakened by a rap on the window. Blinding light in his eyes.

He opened the window and a voice barked, "Let's see some ID."

Stahl's hand had moved instinctively toward the holstered 9 mm. concealed under his car coat, but fortunately his brain kicked in once he saw the robocop countenance of a highway patrolman.

Eventually everything was cleared up, and the CHP guy sped away in his cruiser.

Stahl sat there, humiliated. How long had he been out? Three-forty A.M. meant nearly half an hour.

The ocean roared in his head. The beach sky was full of stars; the sea was ash gray speckled with pinpoints of gold.

Eleven vehicles in the lot. Shull's Expedition, one of them.

Stahl got out, took in a headful of salt air, stretched, cursed his stupidity, got back in the car, resumed watching.

At 4:20 A.M., A. Gordon Shull stepped out of a downstairs unit. Alone, no blonde. Carrying his black leather jacket over his shoulder, rubbing his eyes. He got in the Expedition, swung out of the lot, and made a quick, illegal left turn across the highway, crossing a set of double-yellows. Speeding off back to the city. Where was CHP when you needed them?

Quick decision time: follow the bastard or check on the blonde?

Did the blonde fit Shull's pattern? Some kind of artistic type? A would-be actress? Did that qualify? Or maybe she was a dancer. Those legs.

Shull had already done a dancer. Would he repeat himself?

The one in Boston had been a ballerina. This one looked more like the lap-dance type. Enough kill variety?

He goes in with her, comes out without her. Meaning the room could be a pretty sight.

Stahl drove across the highway, straight into the Sea Arms lot. Parked at the far end, wanting to examine the spot where the Expedition had stood.

Nothing but a grease stain. Stahl walked up to Unit Five, knocked on the sea blue door, got no answer, tried the knob. Locked.

A louder knock—thunderous in the early-morning calm—brought no response, and Stahl glanced at the manager's office. Lights out. Should he wake the manager up and get a key, or pull off a do-it-yourself? The lock was a mediocre dead bolt, and his kit was back in the car. He could always say he'd found the door open.

He assessed his options, talking to himself in the stilted self-justification of courtroom cop-speak.

A serial murder suspect entered with a female companion and remained at the site for . . . an hour and fifty-two minutes before departing alone. I initially attempted to gain entry by knocking, and when I received no answer after a significant lapse in time, I felt the situation demanded . . .

The sea blue door opened.

The blonde stood there in her red crop top and ragged, tight jeans. Zipper half-up, the faintest swell of belly above pink lace panties. Low-slung thong panties; several platinum pubic hairs strayed above the elastic.

She blinked, staggered, looked at the spot where the Expedition had stood, then at Stahl.

Several beats of the rolling tide caressed the morning. The air was cold and wet and smelled of driftwood.

Stahl said, "Miss—"

The blonde wore no makeup, was bleary-eyed, her hair stiff as a bird's nest, the way sprayed hair got when you slept on it.

Tear streaks striped her perfect cheekbones.

Not as hard a face as Stahl had thought—cleansed of greasepaint, she looked younger. Vulnerable.

"Who the hell are you?" she demanded in a voice that could've dissolved rust from a rain gutter.

So much for vulnerability.

Stahl showed her his badge and pushed his way in.

Despite the beach location, the Sea Arms was just another tacky motel and the room was just another moldy, by-the-day cell. Cottage-cheese ceiling, rumpled double bed with a U-pay vibrator hookup, woodite end tables, plastic lamps bolted down. A small-screen TV bolted to the wall was topped by a chart of movies by the hour, at least half of them X-rated. A mud brown carpet was marred by indelible stains.

Stahl spotted white grains on the nightstand. A folded piece of stiff paper—the coke chute. A crumpled Kleenex stiffened by snot.

Kyra Montego knew Stahl had seen the dope leavings, but she pretended to be oblivious.

"I don't understand," she said, tight butt perched on the edge of the bed. Zipper all the way up, now. Her bra was slung over a chair, and her nipples pushed through the red top.

She fooled with her hair, had little success organizing the wild yellow thatch.

Stahl said, "The man you were with—"

"It wasn't like that," said Montego.

Kyra Montego. No way that was on her birth certificate.

Stahl asked her for ID and she said, "What gives you the right? You're implying I'm a hooker or something, and that's bullshit—you have no right."

"I need to know your real name, ma'am."

"You need a warrant!"

Everyone watched too much TV.

Stahl took her purse off the dresser, found three joints in a plastic baggie and placed them on the bed next to her. A long blond hair curled atop a crushed pillow.

"Hey," she said.

He removed her wallet, found her license.

Katherine Jean Magary, address in Van Nuys, a three-digit apartment number that said she lived in a huge complex.

"Katherine Magary's a fine name," he said.

"You think?" she said. "My agent said it's too clumsy."

"Film agent?"

"I wish. I'm a dancer—yeah, the kind you think, but I've also done legit theater, so don't go assuming anything about my morals."

"I don't think it's too clumsy," said Stahl.

She stared at him and her eyes softened—big, moist irises, deep brown, almost black. Somehow they went okay with the white-blond hair.

"You really think?"

"I do." Stahl replaced the wallet in the purse. Put the joints back, too.

Magary/Montego arched her back and flipped her hair and said, "You're cool."

He talked to her for twenty minutes, but after five, he believed her.

She'd never seen Shull before, had drunk too much (wink, wink), Shull had seemed cute. Masculine. Funny. Kinda smart. From his clothes, she thought he had money.

"His clothes?" said Stahl.

"His jacket was Gucci." Magary/Montego smiled. "I managed a peek at the label."

Stahl smiled back in a way that told her that had been clever and kept her talking.

Shull had spun her a good yarn, telling her he was a professor of art and a landscape painter, had exhibited all over the world, was represented by galleries in New York and Santa Fe.

"Landscapes." Stahl remembered Sturgis's description of the Kipper woman's paintings. Sturgis had gone into detail, more than was necessary. He'd clearly liked the pictures.

"That's what he said."

"Did he name the gallery?" said Stahl.

"Uh . . . I don't think so." Katherine Magary—he'd decided to think of her by her birth name—licked her lips and smiled and placed her hand on his knee. He let it sit there. No reason to alienate a witness.

"Was it all b.s.?" she said. "What he told me?"

"He's not a good guy," said Stahl.

"Oh, boy." Katherine sighed, knocked a fist against her blond bangs. "I've gotta stop doing this—getting wasted, getting picked up. Even when they're cute."

"It is dangerous," said Stahl.

"I'll bet you know all about that. Being a detective. You could tell me stories."

"Unfortunately."

"Yeah," said Katherine. "It must be fascinating. Your work."

Stahl didn't answer.

"Was I in serious danger?" she said. "Being with him?"

"I wouldn't go with him again," said Stahl.

"Jesus . . . I'm sorry."

Apologizing to *him*? He said, "Living by yourself, you need to keep yourself safe."

"Yeah, I do . . . I've been stressed-out. Haven't worked for a while."

"Must be tough," said Stahl.

"Oh boy. You learn to dance when you're a kid, let me tell you it's hard, it's really hard work. An Olympic athlete wouldn't work any harder. And then all they want is . . . you know."

Stahl nodded. Grimy drapes pocked with cigarette burns blocked the motel room's sole window. Through the glass and the fabric, he could barely make out the rush of the tide.

Slow rhythm; easy come, easy go.

He said, "Did he treat you okay?"

Katherine Magary didn't answer. Stahl turned to her. She was blushing.

"Was he weird to you, Katherine?"

"No. That's the point. He couldn't . . . you know . . . he came on like a big stud and then he couldn't . . . so instead, we—he . . . I really don't want to incriminate myself."

"You won't," said Stahl.

She remained silent.

He said, "He was impotent so he concentrated on packing his nose."

"Like a pig. He wanted me to use, too, but I didn't. Honest. At that point, all I wanted to do was get some sleep, but I was nervous. Because when he couldn't, he got real jumpy—restless, pacing around. And the coke just made it worse. I finally calmed him down by giving him a massage. That's my other skill, I'm a certified massage therapist—real massage, not you-know-what. I rubbed him down real good, and he relaxed. But something about him—even when he slept he was uptight. Grinding his teeth, he had this real . . . unpleasant look on his face."

She squinted, jutted her lower jaw, strained.

"Uptight," said Stahl.

"When I met him, he was totally mellow, loose. Real easygoing. That's what I liked about him. I've had enough stress in my life, who needs bad vibes." She shrugged. "I thought his vibes were good. Guess I'm stupid."

Stahl's thigh, where her hand rested, had grown hot. He patted her fingers lightly. Removed her hand and got up.

She said, "Where are you going?"

Alarm in her voice. Stahl said, "Stretching."

He moved closer to the bed, stood by her.

She said, "When I woke up—when you woke me up—I was

freaked out to learn he was gone. How am I supposed to get back to my place?"

Stahl said, "I'll take you."

She said, "You're really cool." Reached for his zipper, pulled it down very slowly.

"Nice," she said. "Nice man."

Stahl let her.

44

I put the photocopies down. "It's pretty obvious."

It was 10 P.M. and Milo had dropped by to show me the end-of-year summaries Elizabeth Martin had pulled from Shull's faculty file. When I scanned the material, bloated paragraphs jumped out at me. Phrases bunched together like Tokyo commuters. Disorganization, pomposity, lack of grace. Shull could plot and carry out murder with cleverness and decisiveness, but when faced with the written word, his mind lost traction.

He'd proposed a course he wanted to develop. *"The Cartography of Dissonance and Upheaval: Art As Paleo-Bioenergetic Paradox."*

I reached into my file box, found what I was looking for: the *Seldom-Scene* review of Julie Kipper's show penned by "FS." There were the words: *paradoxical, cartograph,* and *dissonance.* I searched further. When FS had picked Angelique Bernet out of *"la compagnie"* he'd raved, *"This is DANCE as in paleo-instinctuo-bioenergetic, so right, so real, so unashamedly erotic."*

I pointed it out to Milo. "He recycles. Limited creativity. It's got to be frustrating."

"So he's a hack," he said. "So why couldn't he just write for the movies instead of killing people?" Muttering, he circled the matching phrases with red pen.

"Now that we know it's him," I said, "I'm getting a new slant on his victim selection. Until now, I'd been thinking along purely psychological lines: capturing stars on the ascent, swallowing their identities before they became corrupted."

"Psychic cannibalism," he said. "I was starting to like that. You don't, anymore?"

"I do. But another factor is the disconnect between Shull's inflated sense of self and his accomplishments. The grand artiste who's failed at music and art. He hasn't killed any writers, so he probably still thinks of himself as a viable writer."

"The novel he talks about."

"Maybe there is a manuscript in a drawer," I said. "The bottom line is, Shull's a good bet for bitterness and pathological jealousy, but that's only part of it. I think he's being practical: Murder someone really famous, and you bring down big-time publicity and persistent scrutiny. Pulling off something that grandiose would be tempting for Shull, but at this point he's smart enough to be deterred by the risk. So he lowers his sights, targets not-quite-celebrities like Baby Boy and Julie Kipper and Vassily Levitch. Their stories don't make the papers."

"You're saying he'll eventually go for the big time?"

"If he keeps succeeding. Murder's the only thing he's ever been good at."

"You're right. With a famous victim, I'da gotten a warrant a long time ago."

"Still no luck?"

"I tried the three most permissive judges I know. Went to the D.A. for backup, no dice. Everyone says the same thing: The totality is suggestive but insufficient foundation."

"What do they want?"

"Short of an eyewitness, body fluids, anything physical. Detective Stahl may have helped things along. Early this morning, he watched Shull pick up a girl at a bar on Sunset, take her to a motel in Malibu, and leave the place without her. Stahl assumed the worst and abandoned the tail to check the room, but it was just a case of Shull leaving early. But while he was interviewing the girl, ol' Eric got consent from her to look around. She was the resident, so it's full consent. What he took with him was a cardboard coke chute, a tissue caked with snot and what're probably blood flecks, a drinking glass the girl said Shull used, and the bedsheet. Any of that matches the little red hairs in Armand Mehrabian's beard, we're in business."

"When will you know?"

"We put a rush on, but we're still talking days. Still, it's progress."

"Good for Stahl."

"Weird guy," said Milo. "But maybe our hero."

"Speaking of Mehrabian's beard," I said, "you phrased it as Shull getting in his victim's face. I'm wondering if he actually kissed Mehrabian."

"Kiss of death?"

"The image might've appealed to Shull—seeing himself as a mafioso or the Angel of Death. The sexual ambiguity might also be relevant. That would tie in with his relationship with Kevin."

"Think Kevin's alive?"

"I wouldn't take odds on it," I said. "Whether or not he was Shull's confederate, once I started asking about him, Shull would've seen him as a liability."

"Petra says no one can confirm seeing the two of them together, so whatever they collaborated on, it was private."

"One thing I'd wager: Shull financed Kevin's magazine and got himself an outlet for his writing. Ten to one he's been trying for years to get in print at real magazines, piled up the rejection slips."

"Kevin was his vanity press," he said.

"Shull used Kevin as a front because Kevin was young, edgy, and impressionable, and if anything went wrong with *GrooveRat*—as it did—Shull would be spared public embarrassment. Right after Baby Boy's murder, Kevin called Petra, trying to get gory details. Either Shull put him up to it—aiming for psychic souvenirs—or Kevin suspected something about his teacher and was checking it out. Either way, he'd be in trouble."

He frowned.

I said, "What's next?"

"More of the same. This is Stahl's second day on surveillance. He called in an hour ago, and all Shull's done so far is spend a few hours on campus, run errands, come home. He's still there, but Stahl figures he'll likely get going soon. He usually begins night-crawling around now."

"Where does he crawl?"

"All over town. Clubs, bars, restaurants. He drives a lot, moves around constantly—which fits, these guys are always mileage freaks. Tonight, Stahl switched cars to a rental SUV, just in case. Petra's run out of things to do, so she may join in. A two-person surveillance is always better. I showed Shull's photo to the gallery people and Szabo and Loh. No one recognized him, why would they? He wears the uniform, black-on-black, your prototypical L.A. Guy. His name doesn't show up on Szabo's invite list, either, but I'll keep looking."

"What kind of girl did Shull pick up?" I said.

"Stahl didn't say. The main thing is, he didn't kill her. Stahl describes Shull's general demeanor during the pickup as relaxed. He's certain Shull's unaware we're looking at him. So maybe he'll slip up, actually make a move on someone."

"Caught in the act," I said.

"Yeah, yeah," he said. "A boy can dream."

The next morning Milo phoned, and said, "Boring night. Shull just drove around. Up in the hills, then out to the beach all the way into Ventura County. He turned off on Las Posas, got on the 101 north, went another ten miles, returned, stopped at an all-night coffee shop in Tarzana—he likes cheapie-eats places, probably thinks of himself as slumming. Then he drove home alone, went to bed."

"Restless," I said. "The tension could be building up."

"Well," he said, "let's see if he blows."

Just as I was leaving for a jog, Allison phoned to say she'd had to add three appointments to her patient schedule, wouldn't be through until 9:30 P.M.

"Crises?" I said.

"When it rains it pours. Are you up for a later reservation?"

We'd arranged an eight o'clock dinner date at the Hotel Bel Air.

Fabulous food, impeccable service, and when the weather was kind, which was often in L.A., you could dine outside and watch swans glide on lagoons. Years ago, I'd seen Bette Davis glide across the patio. That night I'd been with Robin. She and I used to hit the Bel Air on special occasions. I thought the fact that I was ready to take Allison was a healthy sign.

"How about ten?" I said. "Will you have the energy?"

"If I don't, I'll fake it," she said.

I laughed. "You're sure? We can do it another time."

" 'Another time' isn't a concept I admire," she said. "Sorry for the shuffle."

"A crisis is a crisis."

"Finally," she said. "Someone who gets it."

45 Night three of the surveillance found Petra stationed up the road from A. Gordon Shull's house. Not nearly as close as Stahl had gotten because fewer vehicles were parked on the street, and she had to blend in. But she still had a nice clear view of the gates.

Stahl had suggested she take the hillside position while he stayed down in the city in the rental SUV. Just about the only thing he'd said to her all of yesterday. He seemed more distant than ever, if that was possible.

He was down on Franklin, in a Bronco. A cute, shiny, black thing Petra had admired in the station parking lot.

"Nice, Eric."

Stahl's response was to produce an oily rag, bend down and rub the cloth on the greasy asphalt, flick off flecks of grit and begin dirtying the Bronco's side panels and windows. Soon the poor thing looked as if it had been driven all day from Arizona.

"Schoelkopf must've been in a good mood," said Petra. "Okaying cool wheels."

Stahl picked up more parking lot dirt, continued to filthy the Bronco. "I didn't ask him."

"You paid for this with your own money?"

"Yup."

"You might still be able to collect," she said. "If you put in the voucher soon."

Stahl did something with his head that might've been a nod. If you were looking for a nod. He opened the Bronco's driver door, said, "Let me know when you're all set." Got in. Drove off.

They maintained contact every hour, using a tactical band on the radio.

Four calls tonight, so far, each the same:

"Nothing."

"Okay."

It was a quarter to eleven and Shull, whom they assumed was home, hadn't emerged.

Staying in, just as he had last night?

That had been a downer. Sitting, waiting, fighting drowsiness. The crushing boredom Petra detested. At least Shull wasn't out killing anyone.

Then she flashed an evil grin. Too *bad* Shull wasn't out for the kill. This case had been nothing but false starts and dead ends and way too much of nothing and Lord forgive her, she craved some *action*, was willing to trade public safety for a little adrenaline fix.

What's a little attempted murder between friends?

A voice in her head said, *Naughty girl.*

She said, "Up yours," just to hear the sound of her own voice.

At 11 P.M. she shared another two-word communication with Eric the Dead. Sat back and stared at the black sky above the gates.

She'd avoided fluids well before the surveillance but by now, her bladder was cramping.

Not easy for a girl.

Not that she'd ever complain to anyone.

She was considering her urinary options when Shull's gate swung open and headlights stared out at the night. The BMW or the Expedition?

She was down in her seat when it passed.

Neither. A Cadillac—dark gray, shiny.

Despite her surprise, she was able catch to the license number. Whispered it out loud in order to commit it to memory.

Stahl had said only two vehicles were registered to Shull. Interesting. She got back on the tac band, told Stahl what to look for. He'd be the primary tail, now, because she was going to call in the plates.

Soon she had it: Five-year-old Sedan DeVille registered to William F. Trueblood, Pasadena address.

Shull's rich stepfather.

She put Trueblood's name into the system, got two more DMV hits: a one-year-old Eldorado and a 1952 Jaguar.

Stepdaddy gets a new Caddy, donates the old one to Junior. William F. Trueblood hadn't bothered to change the registration. Meaning he was probably still paying the license fees and the insurance.

Nice gift for Gordie, free and clear. The Cadillac offered Shull the use of a completely legal, unregistered set of wheels.

Spoiled brat.

Petra started up her Honda, turned around, headed down to the city. The first clean, safe rest room she spotted was at a French-type café on Franklin, seven blocks west of Beachwood. She left her car with the valet, tipped him, and told him to keep it there. The restaurant had a bar and a few tables, was jammed and noisy and rich with the smell of ratatouille and shellfish. She elbowed her way through a crush of laughing, flirting pretty people, picking up bits of stale pickup dialogue and smiling, despite herself. Then resenting the fact that some people had lives and she didn't.

On the way to the ladies' room, someone pinched her butt. Normally, she'd have dealt with it. Tonight, she found the attention welcome.

By the time she was back in her car and calling in, she expected Stahl and Shull to be miles away. But Stahl said, "I'm on Fountain near Vermont."

"He stopped somewhere?"

"He drove straight to Fountain, has cruised up and down three times. Past the Snake Pit."

"Revisiting the scene," she said. "Memory trophy. Has he gone into the alley where he did Baby Boy?"

"Not yet," said Stahl. "He just drives by, does a three-point, heads up the block, drives by again. The street's dead, I can't get that close."

"Where are you?"

Stahl pinpointed his location.

Petra said, "I'll come in from the west end, cruise through at a moderate speed. If he leaves before I get there, let me know."

She drove to Western, turned left on Fountain. The street was empty, dark, eerie. When she was three blocks from the Snake Pit, Stahl called. "He's finished. Heading your way."

Petra spotted two sets of headlights. Not Stahl, no way would he be following that obviously. She maintained her speed as her windshield whitened.

A pickup truck, then the Cadillac.

In her rearview, she watched Shull continue to Western, catch an amber light, and sail through the intersection.

Moments later, the rental Bronco sped by.

Petra hung a U, followed at a safe distance.

They picked up the Cadillac on Wilton heading south. Moderate traffic made their life easier, and they alternated positions: first the Bronco would lag three or four cars behind, then Stahl would slow and Petra's Accord would fill in.

We're dancing, she thought. This was as intimate as she ever wanted to get with Stahl.

Shull drove to Wilshire, turned right, continued west. Maintaining a nice steady pace within ten miles of the speed limit.

Driving as recreation.

When Petra was the primary tag, she got close enough to notice that the Cadillac's windows had been tinted nearly black. She couldn't see an old guy from Pasadena doing that. Shull had customized the car.

The Sedan DeVille drove through Beverly Hills and veered right at the junction of Wilshire and Santa Monica. Staying on Wilshire, Shull continued into Westwood, then headed north on San Vicente, hugging the western perimeter of the Veterans Administration grounds. Passing the cemetery studded with white crosses and Stars of David. Then: the boutique/latte jungle that made up lower Brentwood.

Shull took another northern turn on Bundy, followed by a left on Sunset. Too few cars for cover, now. Stahl was in front, and he took his time before following. Took so long Petra was certain they'd lost sight of the Caddy.

She called in. "Any idea where he is?"

"Nope."

Great.

"But I can guess," said Stahl.

He sped ahead of her, drove a while, turned right.

Onto Bristol. The site of the Levitch murder.

Petra entered the lush street very slowly. Looked for the Bronco and spotted it parked a half block up, lights off. She killed her beams, rolled several yards up, pulled to the curb.

Stahl said, "Don't know if he's here."

So what, we just wait? Petra kept her mouth shut. Looked around, admired the mansions, the massive deodar cedars, the grassy, tree-shrouded turnarounds that slowed traffic and gave the neighborhood character. Your perfect upper-crust suburban scene. If you had a seven-figure income.

Lights glimmered in some of the big houses. She caught glimpses of crystal chandeliers, rich paintings, crown moldings. Outside: Herds of sleek cars luxuriated in commodious driveways.

Then: lights in the distance. Moving, enlarging. Maybe two blocks up. Could be anyone.

It was Shull. Heading their way, pausing at the turnaround. Making an easy slow circle and retracing northward.

Back and forth, back and forth. Drinking in the scenes of his crimes. There was a sexual nature to it, and she wondered if the fool was playing with himself.

"Should we get closer?" said Petra. Annoyed with herself for consulting Stahl. She was the senior partner.

But Stahl had been the one who'd figured out Shull's intentions.

"It's a risk," he said.

"Still, if he doesn't return within five, I'm going to have a look."

"Okay."

Four minutes later, the Cadillac reappeared, passed the turnaround, continued to Sunset and made a quick right turn.

Stahl's lights switched on. She followed him, and they both put on speed and spotted the Cadillac as it continued into the Palisades.

Back to the beach? Shull had taken a girl to a motel in Malibu, but as far as they knew he'd never killed anyone there.

As far as they knew.

At Pacific Coast Highway, Shull reversed direction again, turning left—south—away from Malibu and toward the lights of the Santa Monica pier.

Zig and zag, up and down.

They followed him up the drive to Ocean Avenue. When Shull got to Colorado, he drove east, past the noise and activity of the Promenade and over to Lincoln, where he headed south again.

Toward the airport. The route he'd taken when he stashed Kevin Drummond's car.

If he'd stashed Kevin, too, maybe this would tell them where.

At Rose, Shull surprised her, yet again. Turning back toward the ocean and driving all the way to the Venice Walkway, where he pulled toward the right side of the street but didn't park.

Idling. Lights on.

She hung back at Pacific, maintained her distance. Stahl dimmed his lights and got within a block of the Cadillac.

The Caddy made a ponderous three-point turn, sped back toward them. By the time they were in gear, all three vehicles were back on Lincoln.

For this guy, driving was something way beyond getting from one place to another.

Shull drove past the Marina and Playa del Rey, not far from where he'd dumped Armand Mehrabian, then into the bleak, industrial wasteland on the outskirts of El Segundo.

Great dump ground, and the isolation made it terrible for a tail. Both detectives had switched their lights off a half mile back.

Shull lowered his speed as he glided past empty fields, oil derricks, marshland.

Kevin's final resting spot? Nope, here Shull was, again, speeding. Continuing another mile, then east to Sepulveda. Another right turn.

Driving rapidly into Inglewood. Definitely LAX.

But, as if thumbing his nose at Petra's theories, Shull slowed three blocks short of the airport and jerked the Caddy suddenly onto a side street.

This was walking distance from where Kevin Drummond's car had been found.

The Caddy chewed up four more blocks before pulling over. On both sides of the street were warehouses and small factories. Poor lighting. And Petra knew what else.

A hooker strip.

She settled a hundred feet behind Stahl. He called in: "I've got binocs on him. He's out of the car, now . . . walking. Talking to a woman."

"What's she look like?" said Petra, remembering what Small and Schlesinger had said about working an unsolved streetwalker murder in this neighborhood.

"She's wearing hot pants," said Stahl.

She said, "I'm getting closer."

A. Gordon Shull talked to the prostitute—a chubby woman, the hot pants were red and so was her top. Nothing but talk; he got back in the Cadillac.

Petra radioed Stahl: "I'm going to stay behind and check her out. You continue."

46

At 9 P.M., as I left to pick up Allison at her office, the phone rang. I decided to let the service pick up but as I drove, my cell phone beeped.

Milo said, "I'm on my way to Pasadena, got a panic call from Kipper's girlfriend, Stephanie Cranner. Kipper knocked her around pretty badly, then took some pills. I 911'd Pasadena PD, but I wanna go over there, myself. She seemed like a nice kid . . . here we go, good, freeway's nice and clear. Here's the latest on the main stuff: my baby Ds came through. I had them go over every single name on the Levitch invitation list, call each invitee, make sure they were actually there. Turns out one couple—old folks from San Gabriel—couldn't make it and gave their tickets away. Guess what? They're on the board of Charter College and pals of Mr. and Mrs. William Trueblood."

"Shull got the tickets. Who'd he go with?"

"No one, only one ticket was used. It's not proof positive Shull was actually there, he could always claim he gave the ticket away, too. But it was enough—along with my assurances that we're highly likely to pull a DNA match to the hairs on Mehrabian to nudge Judge Foreman into granting me a limited warrant for Shull's house. After I'm through in Pasadena, I'm driving out to Foreman's house. After that, we converge on Faithful Scrivener. Foreman lives out in Porter Ranch, so I'm figuring at least three, four hours before everything's in place."

"Where's Shull, now?"

"Last time I talked to Petra he was still home, but that was hours ago. The plan's for an early-morning surprise, say 2 A.M. If he night crawls, Stahl and Petra tail and we take the house. If he's home, we all party."

"How limited is the warrant?"

"I've requested permission to confiscate all written materials as well as personal belongings of victims, low E guitar strings, and weapons. Reason I'm calling is I want to know if you've got any other suggestions before I complete the application."

"Audio- and videotapes," I said. "Sketch pads, drawings, paintings. Any medium in which Shull might express himself."

"You're saying he re-creates the killings."

"There's a good chance he does."

"Okay," he said. "Thanks . . . this is good, I'm up for it. Time to give him a bad review."

As I neared Montana Street, the cell beeped again. This time I ignored it.

Thinking what a beautiful night it was. Wondering what Allison would be wearing.

47

Slow night; a couple of drive-by trawlers, no takers, and some of the women were lounging in the shadows, smoking.

Petra left her Accord two blocks down, continued on foot, found a vantage point near some garbage bins outside a toy warehouse and watched for a while. The air stank of vinyl and fuel. Every so often jumbo jets roared overhead, assaulting the sky.

She took her 9 mm. out of her purse and transferred it to the lightweight mesh holster that rode her hip, concealed by a loose, black jacket. Richard Tyler markdown, a real bargain. Way too nice for this kind of thing but the way her life had been going a bit of couture was her sole link to civilization.

What would Tyler think, seeing his duds on Prostie Avenue?

She decided to make her move, walked toward the hookers, aiming for nonchalance but feeling the chill of anxiety. As she passed the first two women, both black, they dangled their cigarettes and stared. One said, "Hey, sister, you like to munch?"

Giggles.

"Cause I ready for anything."

Petra continued walking. One of the women called out: "You ain't even thinking of setting up here, Skinnylegs, cause this is private property and you dressed for Beverly Hills."

More laughter, but an edge to it.

Someone with a high, nasal voice said, "*Privates* property."

Receptive audience for the wisecrack. Petra looked for the comedian. A big smirk said it was her quarry: the stocky brunette white girl in the red vinyl ensemble.

Smiling at Petra. Petra smiled back and the woman cocked a hip. The hot pants were tight, ruby sausage casing for flaccid pale flesh. The woman's face was broad, coarse, appeared well beyond middle age, though Petra guessed her age as late twenties.

"Hey," she said.

Red Vinyl said, "What can I do for you?"

Petra smiled again, and the woman's hands balled. "What *you* lookin' at?"

Petra stepped close, flashed the badge.

The woman said, "So?"

"I want to talk to you."

"Talk's by the hour."

"Here or at the office," said Petra. "Your choice."

"For *whut*?"

"For your safety." Checking to see that none of the other hookers had inched closer and keeping her eye on the brunette, Petra produced a business card and her penlight and directed a beam on the small print.

The prostitute turned her head, refused to read.

Petra said, "Take a look."

Red Vinyl finally complied, lips moving laboriously. *Home—hom—icide.*

"Someone got killed?"

A jet killed the silence. Then: staccato clatter as the other hookers hurried over. They crowded around Petra, but she felt safe—they were scared.

"Whusup?" said someone.

Petra said, "That guy who was just here, in the gray Cadillac."

"Oh, him," said Red Vinyl.

"You know him?"

"He bad? He never been bad to me."

"I never liked him," said one of the black women.

"He don't go for *you*," said Red Vinyl, shaking her bosoms. Prostie-pride, but forced.

Petra said, "What's his thing?"

"What'd he do?" insisted Red Vinyl.

Petra smiled.

Red Vinyl said, "You don't need to do that."

"Do what?" said Petra.

"Smile like that. It's freaky."

She drew the woman aside, wrote down the undoubtedly phony name, printed on an impressively state-sealed, bogus California ID.

Alexis Gallant. Alleged address in Westchester.

All Gallant could—or would tell her was that A. Gordon Shull was a somewhat-regular customer with mundane sexual tastes.

One to three times a month, oral sex, no kinky demands, no complications.

"He takes a little long, but big deal. If they were all like him, my life would be easy."

Petra shook her head.

"What?" Gallant protested. "You ain't tellin' me nothin', and what I know is he likes to be blowed."

"What about the girl who was murdered around here a while back?"

"Shaneen? That was a pimp thing."

"My colleagues say she and her pimp got along."

"Your colleagues got they heads up they asses. And that's all I'm sayin'."

"Suit yourself, Alexis. But Mr. Caddy's bad news."

"You say."

"Why you being stubborn, Alexis?"

The woman mumbled something.

"What's that?"

"It ain't easy makin' a livin'."

"Ain't that the truth," said Petra.

48 Stahl followed the Cadillac to the street where Kevin Drummond's car had been abandoned. A. Gordon Shull parked but kept his engine idling, got out of his car, raised his arms to the sky, and stretched.

Stahl heard something sickening.

Shull howling at the moon.

Waving a fist as he did it. Starring in his own private movie. Stahl's hands were cool on the steering wheel. Just the two of them, so easy . . .

He sat there, and Shull shook his head like a wet dog, returned to the Cadillac, continued another five blocks west to a self-storage unit.

The sign said twenty-four-hour access, but Shull just slowed down, didn't stop. Stahl made a note of the address as the Cadillac put on speed, zipped another half mile, then took a side-street route that forced Stahl to cut his lights again.

They emerged on Howard Hughes Boulevard, where Shull switched direction, yet again. North, back toward the city.

Back to Venice, where Shull, once again, drove west on Rose.

Asshole was on a memory-jog. What memories were here?

Back to the walkway, again? Had Shull done someone here?

But this time, instead of continuing to the end of the road, the Cadillac swung a right onto a side street—Rennie.

Dark block of one-story bungalows and tiny houses.

Shull cruised up, down, up, down.

Stahl wanted to follow but the narrow quiet street made it way too risky. He remained on Rose, close enough to the corner to follow Shull's headlights. Taillights.

Back and forth.

The memory of the howl reverbed in Stahl's head.

Bastard saw himself as a big bad predator.

49 Allison was waiting for me outside her office.

Black suit, orange scarf. Her hair was tied up in a chignon.

She got into the car before I could come around and open the door. Before the dome light switched off I saw that the suit was actually dark green. "Great color."

"Black emerald. Glad you like it, I bought it for tonight." She pecked my cheek. "You hungry? I'm famished."

The Bel Air dining room's one of those places that can be nearly full, but still quiet. Irish coffee for her, gin and tonic for me. The complimentary ramekins of soup, then salad, rack of lamb, Dover sole, a bottle of Pinot Grigio. A real waiter, not a pretty-face biding time till the next big break. A man I recognized—one of the Salvadoran busboys who'd earned his way up doing the job well.

We'd made it to dessert when he approached the table looking pained. "Sorry, Doctor, there's a call for you."

"Who?"

"Your answering service. They insist."

I used the phone in the bar. The operator said, "This is June, I'm sorry to bother you, Dr. Delaware, but this guy keeps on calling, claims it's urgent. He sounds pretty agitated, so I figured . . ."

The phone ring I'd ignored in the car. "Detective Sturgis?"

"No, a Mr. Tim Plachette. Did I do right?"

"Sure," I said, wondering. "Put him through."

Tim said, "Where is she?"

"Robin?"

"Who else?" He was talking loud, nearly shouting, and his gorgeous voice had lost its silk.

"I have no idea, Tim."

"Don't screw with me, Alex—"

"Last I heard she was in San Francisco with you."

Pause. "You'd better be leveling with me."

"I'm out to dinner, Tim. I'm going to hang up, now—"

"No!" he shouted. "Please."

I took a deep breath.

He said, "I'm sorry, I assumed . . . it was logical."

"What was?"

"Robin being with you. She left this morning . . . we had a fight. I figured she'd run back to you. I'm sorry . . . where is she?"

"If I knew, I'd tell you, Tim."

"If you asked me what the fight was about, I couldn't tell you. One minute we were getting along and the next . . . my fault, I was too damn busy, didn't pay her enough attention, this lousy show—"

"I'm sure you'll work it out, Tim."

"You didn't."

I let that ride.

"Sorry," he said. "I'm being a total asshole, I'm really sorry. It's just that she was so angry with me, I assumed she went back because . . . the truth is, she still feels for you, Alex. It's something I've been dealing with. It's not easy—"

"You have nothing to worry about," I said. "I'm having dinner with another woman. Someone I've been seeing for a while—"

"The psychologist. Robin told me. She talks about you more than she realizes. Tries be casual about it . . . I'm willing to put up with it if it's just a matter of time . . . I really love her, Alex."

"She's a great woman."

"She is, she is . . . goddamn, if she's not with you, where the hell *is* she? Her flight got in at five, I gave her an hour and a half to get home, called, got no answer. Called again, kept calling—"

"Try her friend Debby, in San Diego."

"I did. She hasn't heard from Robin, either."

"She probably just needs time by herself," I said, feeling my stomach knot.

"I know, I know . . . okay, I'll keep trying. Listen, thanks, Alex. Sorry for being such a moron. I shouldn't have presumed—"

"Don't worry about it," I said.

Easier said than done.

When I got back to the table, Allison said, "You look like *you* just handled a crisis."

"I suppose I did."

"Anything you'd care to talk about?"

My mind was racing and shutting her out seemed wrong. I recounted Tim's call.

"Nice of you to calm him down," she said.

"That's me, Father Teresa."

She sidled over, showed me the dessert menu.

"Whatever you're in the mood for," I said.

Allison said, "Too full for dessert?"

"No, I'm just not picky."

"Okay, then . . . chocolate or nonchocolate?"

"Whatever."

"You know," she said, "*I'm* pretty full."

"No, let's go for it."

She shook her head. "I changed my mind, it's getting late."

"I've spoiled it."

"Not at all, baby."

"Chocolate," I said.

She patted her tummy. "I really am full, please call for the check. And then let's drive to Venice."

"What?"

"You're worried," she said. "I'm sure it's nothing—she probably doesn't want to take his call. But let's make sure and set your mind at ease."

I stared at her.

"It's okay," she said.

"Some date."

"It's been more than dating for a while."

We left the hotel. Allison was smart and perceptive enough to know I'd been concerned, but I hadn't told her the extent of it. The nagging, sickening, chain of thought set off by Tim's call.

China and Baby Boy; two victims Robin had worked for.

The break-in; only cheapie electrics stolen. Except for Baby Boy's acoustic.

Shull fancied himself a guitarist, the instruments were ideal trophies.

And Robin had just gotten some nice publicity: The *Guitar Player* profile. *GP* was a specialty magazine, but just the kind of thing Shull, with his self-image as a musician, an insider—an arbiter of art—might be likely to read.

I sped to Venice.

Allison switched on the radio, tuned the music low, pretended to listen. Leaving me to my thoughts.

Something Shull had said, when I'd interviewed him in his office came back to me: *For some reason your name's familiar.*

Soon after, I'd asked Shull if he'd noticed any change in Kevin Drummond's writing style.

How so?

He seems to have gone from simple and direct to wordy and pretentious.

I'd had no idea at the time, but that had been a direct assault upon Shull's massive ego. And Shull didn't respond well to deflation.

How had he taken it . . . calm, smiling, an aw-shucks smile—*"Ouch.*

On the contrary, the little I saw of Kevin's development seemed to indicate improvement."

Then he'd dismissed me.

A pathologically jealous psychopath, and I'd slapped him across the face.

For some reason your name's familiar.

From time to time I made the papers. Not in any big way, just a bit player in crime stories. Some psychopaths followed crime pieces. Had Shull? Was his memory good enough to pounce upon my name?

Then I got it: Baby Boy's CD. A record Shull was likely to own—researching his quarry.

I pictured him listening to the disc repeatedly. Poring over the liner notes. Drinking in the details.

Milo, a casual listener, had come across Robin's name—and mine—in the small-print credits. Shull would've been sure to see it.

Baby Boy thanking *"the beautiful guitar lady"* for keeping his instruments in fine shape.

Thanking *"Dr. Alex Delaware for keeping the guitar lady happy."*

All those pictures of Robin in the magazine, the adulation.

Rising star.

I told it all to Allison. "Overactive imagination, huh?"

"It's a spooky case, you're entitled. Let's call her now, maybe she's in, and that'll be that."

I used the cell. No answer. Tried Milo's desk. Away; a machine answered *his* cell number.

Then I remembered: He was out in Porter Ranch with the judge, angling for a signature on a warrant application.

I phoned the Hollywood station. Petra was out, too. I didn't have her cell.

Allison said, "You can put on some speed."

Robin's street was quiet, dark. Little houses tucked in and put to bed, lots of parked cars, the brine of the ocean.

"There," I said. "Her truck's in the driveway. You were right, she's not taking calls. Her lights are on, everything looks fine."

"If you want to check on her, it's okay," said Allison.

"What is this, the bond of sisterhood?"

"Hardly. I don't know her. Don't even know if I'd like her. This is for you, my dear. If anything's going to keep you up tonight, I want it to be me."

"You're okay waiting?"

"Sure," she said. Big grin. "Or I can get out and flaunt my Jimmy Choo's and my black-emerald hoo-hah."

As I looked for a parking space, she said, "I'll bet she's beautiful."

"I'd rather talk about you."

"That means she's beautiful. Oh well."

"Allison—"

"Yeah, yeah." She laughed. "There's a space—right behind that Cadillac."

I started to tell her something—to this day I don't remember what.

A scream cut me short.

50 I left the Seville in the middle of the road, double-parked, blocking the Cadillac. Jumping out, I ran to Robin's house. Up the pathway. The screams continued.

Louder, when I reached the door.

"No, no—stop! Who are you, whoareyou—stop, stop!"

I shouldered the door but it swung open and I lost my balance, tumbled, caught myself on my palms, shot up, continued running.

Dark house, but for a triangle of light up the hall to the left.

The studio.

The screams . . . I rushed in, nearly tripped over a man on the floor. Black clothes, facedown, blood pooling beneath him.

Robin was crouched at the far end, up against the wall, holding her hands out protectively.

She saw me. Pointed to the left.

A man in black came from around the door, advanced on her, wielding a knife. Big kitchen knife. One of Robin's. I recognized it. I'd bought the set.

She screamed, he kept coming. Ski mask over a black sweatshirt and nylon pants.

Benetton logo on the shirt, the things you notice.

Something in Robin's eyes made him whirl. He took a half-second to decide, charged me, slashing.

I jumped back as Robin lunged for her worktable, picked something up, wrapped both hands around it, and lunged for him. A chisel. She missed, lost her grip, the tool clattered out of reach.

He glanced at it but not long enough to give me an advantage. Returned his attention to me. Played with the knife. I danced away from the blade's tiny arcs. Robin got hold of something else.

I looked for a weapon. Too far from the bench. A few feet away, a couple of guitars in disrepair were propped in stands ... Robin screamed again, and his head moved back involuntarily. He saw the hammer in her grip. Moved on her, changed his mind and returned back to me. Then her. Me. Her.

Predator 101: pick off the small ones.

He charged her. Running full force, the knife arm extended.

Robin threw the hammer at him, missed, dropped to the ground, rolled under the workbench. He bent his knees, reached under, got hold of her hand, slashed, missed, lost his grip.

She scooted toward the center of the bench.

I got hold of his free arm. He tried to shake me off, couldn't, wheeled and faced me and drew me close.

Face-to-face.

The embrace.

I broke free, made a grab for one of the guitars, Mexican-made Strat, a cheap one. Solid ash body. I swung it like a bat and hit him full face.

His knees gave way. He went down on his back. The knife flew through the air right at me. I dodged it, and it hit the floor, skittered away.

He stayed down, lying still, one leg curled beneath his body.

White filled the eyeholes of the ski mask. His breathing was rapid and steady.

I peeled back the mask, felt the fabric snag on whiskers. Gordon Shull's rugged face looked as if he'd kissed a lawn mower.

A small voice behind me said, "Who is he?"

Robin, shaking, teeth chattering. I wanted to hold her but couldn't. Shull had begun to stir and moan. He bore my full attention.

I searched for the knife, found it. Purpling of the steel blade snapped my attention at the wounded man I'd jumped over when I came in.

Kevin Drummond? A two-man game?

How had Robin gotten the best of him?

His chest was inert. The blood pool had widened.

"Oh my God, we have to help him," said Robin.

I thought that was curious, said, "Call 911." She ran out and I went to examine Drummond. Dark hair, no mask. Faint pulse in his neck. I rolled his head carefully.

Not Drummond. Eric Stahl.

The blood beneath him was copious, rich red, syrupy. His skin was taking on that green-gray cast. I ripped off my coat and set it gently beneath the wound. I saw no signs of respiration, but his pulse was still going.

I said, "Keep going, Eric, you're doing great." Because you never know what they hear.

Several feet away, Shull stirred again. His bent leg quivered.

I jumped to my feet just as Allison appeared in the doorway.

"He's the bad guy," I said. "This one's a cop. Robin's calling 911, make sure she's okay."

"She's on the phone with them right now. She's doing fine." She walked in carefully. Stepping around the blood on her deep green Jimmy Choo's.

Little chrome friend in her hand. Cool, unwavering appraisal in her blue eyes.

Not afraid. Annoyed.

Shull groaned and flexed his right hand. His eyes opened. Allison was at his side in a flash.

Shull tried to punch her but his fingers refused to clench. Hers didn't. She hit his arm hard, pressed the barrel of the gun against his temple.

"You need to be quiet or I'll shoot you," she said, in the calm voice of a therapist.

51 Petra hung out in the ICU observation area, doing nothing. The closest she'd gotten to Eric was looking at him through the glass wall.

No new information since an hour ago when the trauma surgeon, a good-looking guy named LaVigne who looked like a TV doctor, had told her, "He'll probably make it."

"Probably?"

"He's not in imminent danger right now, but with abdominal wounds, you never know. The key is preventing infection. There's also the blood loss. He's almost been totally replaced. He was in shock, out, could go in again."

"Thanks," she said.

Something in her tone made LaVigne frown. "I'm being honest."

"Only way to be." She turned her back on him.

Shortly after that, Milo came by with Rick, and he used his MD credentials to read the chart, confer with the staff behind closed doors.

He came out, looking doctorly, and said, "No promises, but my instinct is he'll pull through."

"Great," said Petra, drained, weak, useless, guilty. Thinking: Hope your instincts are worth a damn.

When she stepped out into the waiting room, the only other person there was a blond woman in her midthirties, sitting in a corner with a copy of *Elle*, wearing a tight, black, ribbed turtleneck, equally snug white jeans, high-heeled sandals, pink toenails. This one had it all: the hair, the chest, a once-flawless face now only terrific.

Dress for distress.

She and Petra exchanged glances then Petra sat down and the woman said, "Excuse me are you a . . . police person?"

"Yes, ma'am."

The woman stood and walked over. Petra recognized her fragrance. Bal a Versailles. Lots of it. Pink nails, too. A lighter pearlescent shade. She wrung her hands nonstop.

"Can I help you?"

"I'm a . . . I know Eri—Detective Stahl. The hospital called me because he had my number on a piece of paper in his pocket, and they . . ."

The woman trailed off.

Petra stood and extended her hand. "Petra Connor."

"Kathy Magary. Is he all right?"

"He's doing better, Kathy."

Magary let out a long whiff of spearmint breath. "Thank goodness."

"You and Eric are friends?"

"More like acquaintances." Magary was blushing. "I mean we just met. That's why he had my number. You know."

Stahl, you Don Juan. May you live long enough to keep surprising me.

Petra said, "Sure."

Magary said, "I mean I didn't know if I should come over. But they called me. I felt kind of . . . an obligation?"

"Eric needs friends," said Petra.

The woman seemed confused. Given the circumstances, that seemed the appropriate state of mind.

"I do hope he gets okay. He's a nice guy."

"He is."

"What . . . exactly happened?"

"Eric was involved in a police incident," said Petra. "Apprehending a suspect. He got stabbed in the abdomen."

Magary's hand flew to her perfect mouth. "Omigod! All they told me is he was hurt. And then, when I got here, they said I couldn't go inside." Pointing to the ICU door. "I guess you got in because you're a police person."

"I'm his partner," said Petra.

"Oh." Magary's eyes got wet. "I'm so, so sorry."

"He's going to be all right," said Petra with phony confidence. Magary relaxed and smiled.

"That's great!"

Maybe, thought Petra, I picked the wrong career. There's always telemarketing.

Magary said, "I guess I'll go now. Think it's okay if I come back tomorrow? Maybe he'll be better, and I can go in there?"

"It's more than okay, Kathy. Like I said, he needs all the support he can get."

Something about that knocked Magary down a notch. "It's still real bad, isn't it? Even though he's going to make it."

"He incurred a serious injury. He's getting really good care."

"Good," said Magary. "The only doctor I know is my orthopedist. I'm a dancer."

"Ah," said Petra.

"Well," said Magary. "I'll be going. I'll come back tomorrow. If Eric wakes up, tell him I was here." She kissed her fingertips, waved them at the ICU door. Smiled at Petra and sashayed down the hall.

Shortly after that, Petra spotted Dr. LaVigne exit an elevator, talking to two gray-haired people. The three of them stopped and continued their conversation out of her earshot.

The man was in his sixties, short, slight, wore a brown sport coat, a white shirt under a tan sweater, and pressed beige slacks. Gray crew cut, steel-rimmed glasses. The woman was tiny—maybe five feet tall, also slender. Blue sweater, gray slacks.

LaVigne said something that made both of them nod. They followed him past Petra, into the ICU. LaVigne emerged a half hour later, ignoring Petra as he hurried by. A quarter hour after that, the gray-haired couple came out.

Petra had been slumped in a horrid orange Naughahyde chair that squeaked every time she exhaled. Trying to chase away her thoughts by reading a magazine. The words might as well have been Swahili.

The woman said, "Detective Connor?"

Petra stood.

"We're Eric's parents. This is the Reverend Stahl, and I'm Mary."

"Bob," said her husband.

Petra reached for Mary Stahl's hand, covered it with both of hers. "I'm so sorry, ma'am."

"They say he'll be all right."

Reverend Bob Stahl said, "We'll be praying."

"We sure will," said Petra.

"How did it happen?" Mary Stahl asked her. "If you know."

"What I know," said Petra, "is that your son's a hero."

What she thought was: *It didn't need to happen.*

Stahl had stopped calling in an hour before the confrontation with Shull. She'd tried reaching him twice on the tac band but couldn't get through. Meaning he'd ignored her. Or switched off his radio.

Why?

She sat with Bob and Mary Stahl for over an hour before the answer took shape.

Learning they lived in Camarillo, where Eric had grown up, a short drive from the beach. Eric had been a good student, lettered in baseball and track, loved junk food, played the trumpet. Surfed on weekends—so her initial guess hadn't been that off, after all. She suppressed a smile. Suppressing wasn't hard, thinking of Eric lying there, his abdomen stitched from sternum to navel. Shull's blade had ravaged his intestines, missed the diaphragm by millimeters . . .

Mary Stahl said, "Eric's always been a good boy. Never a lick of trouble."

"Never," Bob agreed. "Almost too good, if you know what I mean."

Petra urged them on with a smile.

Mary Stahl said, "I wouldn't say that, dear."

"You're right," said Reverend Bob. "But you know what I mean." To Petra: "The P.K. syndrome. Preacher's kids. It's hard for them—keeping up the image. Or thinking they need to. We never pressured Eric. We're Presbyterian."

As if that explained it.

Petra nodded.

Reverend Bob said, "Still, some kids feel the pressure. My other son did. Put himself under serious pressure and sowed some wild oats. He's a lawyer, now."

"Steve lives on Long Island," said Mary Stahl. "Works at a big firm in Manhattan. He'll be flying in tomorrow. He and Eric used to surf together."

"Eric never seemed to be bothered by the pressure," said her husband. "Really easygoing. I used to joke that he'd better get upset about something, or he wouldn't have any blood pressure."

Mary Stahl burst into tears. Petra sat there as Reverend Bob comforted her.

"Pardon me," she said, when she recovered her composure.

"Nothing to pardon, dear."

"Eric needs me to be strong. I don't like making a scene."

Petra smiled. Smiling seemed the only damn thing she could do. She hoped it came across real because it sure didn't feel real.

Mary Stahl smiled back. Cried some more. Said, "A few years ago, Eric's life changed."

"Mary," said Bob.

"She's his partner, dear. She should know."

Bob's eyes flickered behind his trifocals. "Yes, you're right."

Mary sighed, touched her hair. Sat back. Became rigid, again. "Eric used to have a family, Detective Connor. Back when he was in the Army—in Special Forces. A wife and two children. Heather, Danny, and Dawn. Danny was five and Dawn was two and a half. They were all living in Riyadh. Saudi Arabia. Eric was assigned to the American embassy, he never really told us for what—it's like that, in Special Forces. You can't talk about what you do."

"Of course not."

"They killed his family," said Mary. "One of the royal family cousins in a fast car—a Ferrari. Heather was walking the children in a stroller on a main street near a big shopping mall. This person came speeding through and hit them, and they were all killed."

"My God," said Petra.

"Our grandchildren," said Mary.

Reverend Bob said, "On top of the trauma, what bothered Eric was the way the government—our government treated him. The killer was never punished. The Saudis claimed Heather had been jaywalking, it was her fault. The Saudis offered Eric a cash payment—one hundred fifty thousand dollars."

"Fifty thousand for each life," said Mary.

Bob said, "Eric turned to the Army and the embassy for support. He wanted prosecution. The Army and the State Department told him to accept the money. In the national interest."

"Eric resigned," said Mary. "He was different after that."

"I can understand that," said Petra.

"I wish he'd talked about it," said Mary. "To me, his father, anyone. Before that, he could always talk. We had an open family. Or at least I thought so."

She shook her head.

Bob said, "We did, darling. Something of that magnitude, you can't prepare for."

"You've been working with him how long?" Mary asked Petra.

"A few months."

"I'll bet he doesn't talk much, does he?"

"No, ma'am." Petra flashed on something: The stricken look in Eric's eyes after the interview with Uncle Randolph Drummond. Eric had taken an instant dislike to the man. A drunk who'd crashed and killed his family.

Mary Stahl said, "Now, this. I don't know what this is going to do to him."

"He'll heal up," said Bob. "Who knows, maybe this will get him to open up."

"Maybe," said Mary, doubtfully.

"The main thing, right now, is that he heals up, dear."

"He gets so depressed," said Mary. "We've got to do something." To Petra: "Are you a mother?"

"No, ma'am."

"Maybe one day," said Mary. "Maybe one day you'll know."

She stayed with the Stahls for another three hours. Day broke, and the parents left for an hour to make personal calls.

Petra entered the ICU.

A nurse said, "He's doing a lot better, Detective. Amazingly better, actually. Vitals are good, temperature's just slightly elevated. He must've been in really great shape."

"Yup," said Petra.

"Cops," said the nurse. "We love you guys, hate when this happens."

Petra said, "Thanks—can I go in?"

The nurse glanced through the glass. "Sure, but gown up, and I'll show you how to wash your hands."

Clad in a yellow paper gown, she approached Eric's bed. He was draped from neck to toe tip, connected to multiple IV lines and catheters, backed by a bank of high-tech gizmos.

Eyes closed, mouth slightly parted. Oxygen tubes running up his nose.

So vulnerable. Young.

With the gut wound obscured, he looked okay. If you blanked out the apparatus, he could be sleeping peacefully.

She placed a gloved hand on his fingers.

His color was better. Still pale—pale was his normal state—but none of that creepy green around the edges.

"You had an adventure," she whispered.

Eric kept breathing evenly. His vitals remained steady. No dramatic movie-of-the-week response to the sound of her voice. He couldn't hear her. Which was fine.

Not a bad-looking guy, when you got past his personality.

She'd thought him weird, now she knew him as another victim.

Life was like a prism; what you saw depended on how you turned the glass.

His mother described him as depressed. Sometimes depressed people duked it out with the police, wanting to end it all but lacking the courage and hoping to force the police's hand.

Suicide by cop, they called it.

Had Eric chosen suicide by perp?

Experienced guy like that—all that Special Forces experience—how had he ended up getting shanked by a ninny like Shull?

It made you wonder.

She looked down at him.

Not a bad-looking guy at all. Kind of handsome, really. She tried to picture him younger, tan, easygoing as he rode the waves.

"Eric," she said, "you're going to pull out of this."

No response. Just like when they rode together.

Petra stroked his fingers, feeling warmth through the latex of her gloves.

"You are *definitely* going to pull though, Detective Stahl. And then you and I are going to *talk*."

52 Allison and I were naked on her bed. My left hand rested on the nape of her neck. Her nails grazed my arm.

She released a long exhalation, freed herself, slipped under the covers. Lifting her hair above her head, she knotted it loosely. "How's Robin doing?"

"Better."

"Good. Could you hand me that water, please?"

"Sure."

"Thank you."

Moments ago we'd been lost in each other. Now we were having a civilized conversation.

I said, "Robin's on your mind?"

"I'm not preoccupied with her. I feel for her."

She drank water. Placed the glass down carefully. "Darling, eventually you're going to have to deal with it."

"With what?"

"Saving her. What it means to her."

"Tim's with her. She's getting support."

I'd stopped by the house in Venice two days ago. Tim had met me at the door, wanting to say something. The words had frozen in his throat—vocal guru struck mute. He clasped my hand, shook it hard, walked out. Leaving Robin and me alone in the living room. Strange to see her, just sitting there. As long as I'd known her, she'd had trouble doing nothing.

She accepted a hug, thanked me, told me she was okay.

I agreed that she was.

Both of us, getting through the moment. I stayed for a while, then left.

Allison said, "I'm not talking about support, darling."

I said, "The way I see it, I didn't save her. Far from it. Tim's the hero, his call got the ball rolling. I didn't even answer the first time he tried to reach me. And if it wasn't for you, who knows if I'd have followed through."

"If not for me, you'd have been there sooner." She smiled.

"What?"

"A group effort," she said. "That's how you see it."

I got up on my elbow. "Is this the best time to have this discussion?"

"What better time?"

"Tonight," I said, "I was thinking more of a romantic evening."

"To my mind, honesty's part of romance," she said. "At least a bit of it." She rolled toward me, took my face in her hands, kissed my lips.

"I'd better not argue," I said. "Woman with a gun and all that."

She smiled again. Lay back down.

Got up on her elbows. Kissed me in a new way.

53 "An ironic tale for when they write my biography," said Milo, finishing his sandwich. "I get my warrant, am feeling like an ace, and the show goes on without me."

"Shull's mommy hired a good lawyer," I said. "It ain't over till it's over."

"True," he said, wiping his face. The sandwich was a do-it-yourself project. Turkey and steak and cold meatballs and whatever vegetables he'd found in my fridge, stuffed between slabs of hand-cut rye. Big enough to require a building permit.

"Still," he said, "I confess to optimism."

"There's a switch."

"You see, Alex: I *am* open to change."

"You are, indeed."

He folded his napkin. "It kills me that I missed it. Nothing like catching one in the act. In twenty years, I can count the times."

The act had been Robin. I said nothing.

"Stahl's doing better," he said. "Rick says he'll definitely live. Guy's lucky. And stupid. Going one-on-one with Shull, no call for backup. Petra says his explanation is everything happened too fast."

"Thank God he was there to slow Shull down."

"Thank God you were there."

"I owe that to Allison." Thinking: *Robin owes Tim and Allison.*
Thinking: *Life is complicated.*

"How's Robin doing?" he said.

"She's coping."

He played with his napkin. "I went by to see her, right after. She looked pretty numb."

I got up and poured myself a cup of coffee.

"Anyway," said Milo, "this morning Stahl talked a bit more to Petra. Not a word about getting stabbed, and she didn't want to stress him. What he was anxious to tell her was that before Shull drove to Robin's, he headed for a vacant lot in Inglewood, not far from where Kevin's car was found. We found the place, dispatched a couple of cadaver dogs, and they went nuts. Couple of hours ago, we dug up some bones. Techies are headed over to Encino right now, to get dental records on Kevin."

"Sad," I said.

"Yeah." He worked on his sandwich. Took a breath. "We went through Shull's place with the proverbial teeny little comb. Great big house for one guy. All this old expensive furniture he got from Mommy. But he lived liked a pig, didn't take care of anything. He had a camera hooked up to remote, took photos of himself and hung them all over the place. All dudded up, posed like some Ralph Lauren sophisticate, but there was rotten food and roaches on the floor. We found all the good stuff in a basement storage room–combo–wine cellar. Shull kept a nice collection of vintage reds, there. From the empties all over the floor, looks like he sampled frequently. Along with copious amounts of happy powder." He tapped the side of his nose. "Pills, too. Pharmaceuticals, some still with hospital tags, so you were right about that. He knew the area where he picked up Erna because he bought medical dope."

"What was Erna's role?" I said.

"I thought *you'd* tell *me*."

"I'm not sure we'll ever know. My best guess is he thought of her as his crazy cousin who he could use. Exploited her instability, her love of art. We know he expropriated her name for bylines. That allowed him to cover his tracks in case the articles were connected to the victims. He probably figured Erna would be too incoherent to do any damage if she was ever linked to the byline. Eventually he changed his mind and killed her."

"I think he also used her as a red herring," he said. "Sending her over to the gallery and maybe to other sites, too. Figuring people would notice her, get sidetracked, and he could skulk around, check out the scene. Which is exactly what happened. Except that it back-fired because looking into Erna's death is what finally connected us to him. Best-laid plans of psychopaths and all that."

He unfolded the napkin, patted it flat, put it aside. "You're proba-bly right. His main motivation was fooling with Erna's head. For the fun of it. Like he did with Kevin Drummond. Pretending to mentor the kid, helping to finance *GrooveRat* so he could keep Kevin delusional about his chances as a publisher. Meanwhile, Shull had an outlet for his own crappy articles—again, with his tracks covered. This making sense to you?"

"Perfect sense," I said. "And once again, he got too cute. Having Kevin call Petra for details on Baby Boy. He probably told Kevin it would be great material for a follow-up piece. Unless Kevin was in on the killings and the call was for his pleasure, too."

"So far we haven't turned up a shred indicating Kevin was anything but a dupe. Unless we do, he remains a victim—give his parents at least a little comfort."

He got up, paced the kitchen. "Shull saw himself as a cut above, but he's nothing but a cookie-cutter power freak. Before he made his move on Robin he spent hours driving around. Revisited the Snake Pit, Szabo and Loh's place, the Marina where he dumped Mehrabian. Snacking on memories, working up the arousal. One thing does puzzle me, though. He changed his technique. Up until Robin, he did the smooth bit. Walking up friendly, slipping the knife in. Doing it in pub-lic places—taking risks. With Robin, it's like he regressed. Covert break-in, blitz attack. Which is probably what he did to Angelique Ber-net. Any idea why?"

"He would've preferred the smooth bit," I said. "Being subtle and dramatic meshed with his sense of theater. He probably decided to be cautious because of my questions about Kevin. He didn't feel threatened enough to stop, but he knew we were getting closer."

"Guess so," he said. "Still, the idiot never lost his arrogance. Drove all over town without thinking to check for a tail."

"In the end, an amateur," I said.

"Once a loser, always a loser." He stretched, paced some more, sat back down. Stared past me. Crust in the corner of his eyes. Hit-or-miss shave.

All those days with no sleep.

I said, "What's the good stuff you found in his basement?"

"Baby Boy's guitars, seven sets of low E guitar strings, a black trench coat that had been dry-cleaned recently, a box of surgical gloves, and newspaper clippings about all the victims. Not organized, tossed together in one big box file. He clipped reviews, interviews— like the one Robin gave to that guitar magazine—and newspaper accounts of the killings."

His jaw tightened. "Here's the bad thing, Alex. In addition to Baby Boy, Julie, Vassily, China, the Bernet girl, and Mehrabian, there were four others. All within the last five years, filling the time period we wondered about. A potter snuffed in Albuquerque, another dancer— male theatrical dancer—killed in San Francisco and dumped in the Bay, a glass artist from Minneapolis, and Wilfred Reedy, the old jazz guy killed four a half years ago down on Main Street. Everyone assumed that was a dope thing, because like I told you, Reedy's kid was an addict and Main Street can get mean, but looks like he was Shull's first."

"Shull have all of Reedy's LPs?"

He stared at me. "Yeah. In terms of the out-of-town cases, we're looking for conventions Shull might've attended."

I tried to feel relieved that it was over. Tried to get past the image of all those bodies.

"You were right about something else, Alex. Shull didn't go for writers because he considers himself an active writer. On top of the box file, was an envelope marked *T.G.A.N.* Took me a while to figure that out. The Great American Novel. Inside was a title sheet. I xeroxed it for you."

He drew a folded piece of paper from an inside pocket, opened it, spread it on the table.

Blank, except for three lines typed in the center:

The Artist
A Novel by
A. Gordon Shull

"That's it?" I said. "Just the title?"

"That's all he wrote. Literally. Guy must've blocked."